Praise for *Out of the Ashes*

"It is one of those books you can't put down. This is a delightfully fresh and entertaining yet poignant tale." — *Readers Favorite*

"It was completely different from the other books I have read in the past." — *Book Obsessed Chicks*

"This was a fantastic story. Fans of historical romance should definitely pick this up. I thoroughly enjoyed this read." — *Paperbacks and Frosting*

"One of the best I've read this year. By the last page I didn't want it to end." — *Two Indie Ladies*

"I thought it would be a fun romantic read but I had no clue that I would fall in love with this book from the very beginning." — *Goodreads*

"The book I waited years to read." — Jennette Marie Powell, author of *Time's Enemy*

"*Out of the Ashes* is a book that will capture your imagination. It is crafted with deliberate precision, and will appeal broadly to readers who love romance set in exotic times and places." — *Night Owl Reviews*

"It is just one of those stories that makes you wish you didn't read it, so you can read it over." — *Pen Met Paper*

"I can honestly tell you that I cried while I read this book! I highly recommend it, and give it the highest score possible." — *Critique de Book*

"I recommend this book to anyone who enjoys paranormal romance, who has interest in Pompeii or archeology, and who wants a good, well-told story." — *Paranormal Romance Guild*

FIRE

OF THE

DRAGON

Lori Dillon

Amari Press

Amari Press

ISBN: 0615801218

ISBN-13: 978-0615801216

DEDICATION

For my daughter, Rachel, who once loved dragons more than dolls.
Thanks for giving me the inspiration for DRAGON.

And for my dad, Bob "not the singer" Dillon.
You were the first hero in my life. I love you and miss you so much.

ACKNOWLEDGMENTS

I'd like to thank my critique partners, Donna, Liz, and Mary Ann, who told me to stop sitting on DRAGON and publish the thing already.

I'd also like to thank Aemelia and Alyssa at The Authors Red Room for their editorial expertise in catching all my grammar goofs.

In addition, I'd like to acknowledge the encouraging and innovative authors at IndieRomanceInk who have held my hand as I waded into the deep end of the indie publishing pool. The wise and knowledgeable authors at Hearts Through History, who helped me research all those pesky medieval details—any historical screw-ups are all mine. And to Virginia Romance Writers, my home RWA chapter and an amazingly supportive group of writers. Thank you all.

ChAPTER ONE

Carytown
Richmond, Virginia

Desperation has a way of gripping most people in an ice-cold fist.

In Jill Donahue's case, it threatened to wrap around her ankles, tie itself into a hangman's knot, and trip her on her face as she half-jogged down the uneven sidewalk of Carytown.

Overhead, red, white, and blue banners waved on the street posts, remnants left over from the Fourth of July celebration. With a national holiday five days before her niece's birthday, she should've been able to recall the special occasion was coming up. But as she dodged around a wrought iron table parked outside a cozy sidewalk café, she conceded America's birthday hadn't helped her remember Zoe's impending sixth birthday one bit.

In the grand scheme of things, speed shopping was not one of Jill's greatest life skills. Yet here she was, peering in every shop window she passed, hoping for inspiration. But all she encountered were chic clothing boutiques catering to the country club elite, and antique shops full of heirloom furnishings from area estate sales. She even glanced in a jeweler's display window offering custom designed settings, but they were more wearable art than everyday adornments. Plenty of diverse stores selling everything imaginable, but nothing appropriate for a soon-to-be six-year-old girl.

Where the hell is that damn toy store? She could've sworn there was one stuck in among all the eclectic shops. Jill tried to squash the niggling sense of panic creeping its way into her brain. Why hadn't she gone to Toys R Us like any sane person would've done? Why had she waited until the last minute to look for a gift?

Because 'procrastination' is your middle name, that's why.

Glancing at her watch, she groaned. She was so screwed. There was no time to drive to the mall across the river. If she didn't find something soon, she was going to have to write Zoe an IOU or give her cash in an envelope. But if she did that, her whole family would hold the gift faux pas over her head for years to come.

She could hear her mother now. *For heaven's sake, Jill. You're twenty-nine years old. Why can't you be more responsible? How can you expect to accomplish anything important in your life if you can't even manage to get a simple birthday present for a little girl?*

And her sister Ann certainly wouldn't be far behind in the not-so-subtle reprimand department. *Messed up again, eh sis? It figures. You only have one niece and her birthday comes the same day every year. How could you screw that up?*

Apparently, she could. Royally.

Distracted by the imaginary Jill-bashing party going on in her head, she was caught off guard when she was suddenly shoved from behind. Stumbling forward, she slammed into the plate glass window of a storefront, hitting the pane so hard she was surprised it didn't shatter into a thousand tiny pieces and rain down on her in jagged, pain-inflicting shards.

Stunned, she massaged her throbbing forehead as she scowled at the moving horde. Not even an apology or murmured 'excuse me' from the human ramrod who continued blindly on his or her way.

Strong hands grabbed her from behind and yanked her off the busy sidewalk and into a small covered alcove.

"Oh, my dear. Are you all right?"

She turned to find a tiny woman who could've been an extra in the "Wizard of Oz" staring at her through thick-lensed glasses. Still dazed from the impact, she couldn't quite grasp the munchkin lady's presence as the woman took Jill by the arm and ushered her into the shop.

"Come in here and let's get you out of harm's way."

The cheerful tinkling of a bell over the door announced their entrance and she motioned for Jill to sit in an old Victorian-style chair near the front window, the red velvet cushion crushed to a glossy sheen from years of use.

"Thank you," she said to the lady before turning to acknowledge the other person seated across the tiny, lace-covered table. "Hel—whoa!"

The woman had no nose.

Jill wondered briefly if she'd hit her head harder than she thought. Then she realized it was an old mannequin, garbed in a fringed flapper's dress and feathered hat, serving non-existent tea in dainty china cups, their yellowed glaze crackled with age.

"Oh, don't mind Fannie. She has that effect on people all the time. But she's pleasant enough company. A real good listener, but not much of a talker." The shopkeeper giggled at her own joke, her kind face creased with a web of wrinkles. "I'm Clo, by the way. Owner, operator and sole employee of Clotho's Bygone Treasures."

"Nice to meet you," Jill replied as she glanced around, trying to get her bearings. The cramped shop was filled with vintage clothing, some modeled by equally vintage mannequins like her current tea party companion. Scented candles did little to mask the pungent smell of mothballs, decades-old dust, and musty wool emanating from the aging garments.

Odd, but she passed this way every day on her way to work and had never noticed this tiny shop wedged between The Yarn Lounge and Le Visage Makeup Boutique. How had she not seen it? By the look of the worn floorboards and sagging shelves, it had been here for quite a while, probably as long as the 1920s Byrd Theatre down the street.

She moved to stand, but Clo kept her in place with a firm hand to her shoulder. "You should probably sit here for a bit to make certain you're okay."

"I'm fine. Really."

"No, you're not." Clo *tsked.* "From the sound of that crash, I'd say you're going to have a rather large knot on your forehead in a few minutes."

Jill cupped her palm over the throbbing spot, feeling a tender lump already forming. "Great. That's all I need. A concussion on top of everything else."

Clo patted her shoulder, concern evident on her weathered face. "Oh, you poor dear. You look so upset. Is there anything I can do?"

Jill snorted. "Unless you have a birthday present for a six-year-old girl hidden among all these old clothes, I doubt it."

She regretted the words as soon as they left her mouth. The lady's small stature perked up and her eyes gleamed with dollar signs.

"Oh, I'm certain I have something."

Caught, Jill groped for an excuse, any flimsy reason to beat a hasty retreat. But the woman's wistful eyes—enlarged twice their normal size behind the thick lenses—froze Jill in her tracks. She glanced back at the face of her battered drinking partner, thinking they could both use something stronger than make-believe tea.

"Thanks anyway, but somehow I doubt it."

"Does she like to play dress up? We have children's clothing in the back—pinafores, crinolines, tiny gowns perfect for little girls to play princess in."

Jill snorted. "Oh, I don't think so. Her idea of dress up is to put on a fake fur pelt and pretend to be a Siberian snow leopard. I doubt Zoe's ever played at being a princess in her life."

"Really?" Clo remarked, her voice tinged with disbelief. "That seems a bit unusual."

Now that was an understatement. "My niece isn't like most little girls, which makes it a pain in the as—makes it difficult to shop for her. She adamantly refuses to play with dolls and boycotts any and all tea parties. If anyone gets her a Barbie, it ends up in the bottom of the toy box faster than the wrapping paper can hit the floor."

Jill watched the woman's pencil-thin eyebrows inch higher with each word.

"It's true. Sweet little Zoe would rather play with rubber alligators, fake snakes and plastic dinosaurs than anything that comes in pink." She tossed in a heavy dramatic sigh for effect, certain Clo was ready to admit defeat and boot her out the door. "She's not a girly-girl, so I can't get her prissy stuff. There probably isn't anything she'd like here." Jill smiled, standing to make good her escape. "I'm sorry I've wasted your time."

Rather than the confused expression most people acquired when she described her niece, the tiny shopkeeper grinned. "On the contrary, I think she sounds like a delightful and unique young lady." Then an odd twinkle glinted in the woman's eye. "So you say she likes alligators and dinosaurs?"

"Yes, but—"

"What about dragons?"

"Dragons?" Jill hadn't really thought about it before. "I guess so. They're sort of similar, aren't they?"

"Wonderful! I have the perfect thing," Clo said, grabbing her by the arm.

Her initial shock at the lady's pushiness was offset by her surprising strength. Before Jill knew it, Clo had towed her into the dark recesses in the rear of the shop.

Finally letting go, the shopkeeper shoved an old wooden ladder along the shelves reaching up to the twelve-foot ceiling. The wheels screeched in the metal rails overhead, further aggravating the pounding in Jill's skull.

"It's right up here somewhere," the woman said as she started up the rickety rungs.

Jill reached out to stop her. "Wait. I don't want you to go to so much trouble. All I really need is directions to the toy shop around here."

Clo paused in her search. "Oh, it's no trouble. I'm certain the thing I have in mind will be perfect." Then she winked at her. "Trust me, dearie."

Great. This was one shrewd saleswoman, already halfway to guilting her into buying something whether she wanted it or not. Jill may as well be wearing an "I'm a sap" sign around her neck.

Attempting to steady the ladder, Jill worried the woman might come tumbling down on top of her at any minute, along with every kitschy knickknack and vintage whatnot crammed on the towering shelves. After shifting several items out of the way, Clo pulled a rolled bundle off the top shelf. Clutching it under one arm, she began her wobbly decent, heaving a big sigh as she hopped off the bottom rung with the spryness of a woodland elf.

"Here we go," she said as she led Jill back to the front of the shop

5

where she placed the rolled piece of old fabric on the glass display case. "Go ahead. Open it."

The woman looked rather pleased with herself. Not quite sure if Clo was playing with a full deck, Jill decided it might be best to humor the woman for the moment, and she tried to untie the leather cord from around the rolled bundle. Hard and brittle, the thin strap refused to give up its tight knot.

"I can't seem to get—"

"Here, let me try," Clo offered, and with more dexterity than those stubby little fingers should be capable of, she had the tie unknotted within seconds.

What was this place? Part magic shop? Jill would've sworn the knot was not going to come undone unless she took scissors or a blowtorch to it. At Clo's nod, she unrolled a section of the fabric, expecting to see a dancing purple dinosaur or the cartoon characters from "Dragon Tales" on it. Instead, she gasped in surprise.

"Is that needlepoint?"

"Actually, it's a tapestry. Amazing detail for something so small, isn't it?"

Jill had to agree. The piece before her was only about the size of a place mat, but the intricate weaving revealed a tiny work of art.

"Look closely and you can see it tells a story."

The woman was right. The threads whispered a tale of long ago, depicting a quaint medieval town set in a fairy tale land of majestic mountains and rolling green hills. Whoever the weaver was, they did beautiful work. She could almost smell the smoke curling up from the villagers' huts and hear the rustle of the leaves as the trees swayed in a crisp spring breeze. In the foreground, a knight sat astride his big white horse, looking strong and brave. His helm obscured his face, but in her little girl's heart, Jill imagined him to be handsome and dashing, as only a knight in shining armor should be.

There was a girl standing nearby, wearing a flowing white gown with long blonde hair down to her knees. Jill shook her head, a lock of mousy brown hair falling into her line of vision. Why were the girls in fairy tales always blonde? Granted, there was Snow White with her black hair, but for the most part they were all medieval Barbie dolls with long, flaxen locks and perfect size two figures. Couldn't she once be a brunette with a bad case of the frizzies and cellulite on her thighs? She laughed to herself as she tucked the errant curl behind her ear. Guess it wouldn't be a fantasy then, would it?

The girl's face in the picture was indiscernible, the area where her head should've been lost off the ragged edge. But Jill knew without a doubt she'd once been beautiful and that the brave knight had rescued her in the nick of time from some horrible fate worse than death. Of course, they'd fallen instantly in love and were living happily ever after in a castle somewhere. Wasn't that how those stories always ended?

Jill stroked the colorful threads. "It's beautiful."

Clo clasped her stumpy hands over her round belly. "Yes, it is."

"It looks very old."

"Over a thousand years, I'd say."

"What?" Jill stared at the woman, surprised the thing hadn't crumbled to dust in her hands. "Doesn't that make it rare? Shouldn't it be in a museum?"

"Maybe, if it were complete and in better shape."

She noted the tattered edges where the tapestry was unraveling, whatever story the rest of it told now lost in a snarl of threads. "It looks like it used to be part of a bigger piece."

"Perhaps." Clo shrugged. "Or maybe it just isn't finished...yet."

The lady wasn't making sense. "You mean it wasn't finished, right?"

"Yes, of course," she corrected herself. "I'm sure there used to be more to it, but through neglect and time, this is all that's left."

"That's a shame." Jill experienced an odd stabbing twinge in her chest, as if she shared the tapestry's physical pain at having parts of it slowly stripped away, one thread at a time.

"Some people don't have respect for old treasures. Now, it's only worth something to those who can appreciate the magic it holds."

Jill couldn't tear her eyes away from the beautiful design. Gold swirled with brilliant reds and blues on a dazzling field of green, the colors so vibrant it looked like it was stitched only yesterday. The lady had to be pulling her leg, trying to make a raggedy tapestry seem more valuable than it actually was. It must be a reproduction. There was no way it could really be a thousand years old, but damn if it didn't look like it was.

She pushed it back toward the saleslady. "It's nice, but not quite what I had in mind."

"Wait! You need to see this before you go." Clo uncurled the last section until the entire remnant lay flat on the display case. Just as she did so, the morning light filtered into the shop through the front window, chasing away the shadows and illuminating the tapestry in all its brilliant glory.

"I really don't think…" And then Jill couldn't think at all. She couldn't even speak a coherent word as the diminutive shop lady shoved the tapestry back in front of her.

A magnificent woven dragon stared back at her.

Crafted in complex detail and radiant threads, the beast seemed to come to life on the cloth before her. The creature was breathtaking, from the fine rendering of its scale-covered body to its glowing, golden eyes. Spellbound, Jill held her breath, half expecting the monster to spread its wings and fly off the tapestry at any moment.

"It's g-gorgeous," she gasped, her voice barely above a whisper.

Feeling the texture of the weave against her fingers, she peered closer. The dragon's rust-colored scales shimmered, giving the illusion of its massive chest moving, expanding then contracting. As impossible as it seemed, it looked like the dragon was breathing.

Clo smiled and nodded her head with its tight little bun. "The moment I saw you, I knew. It's been sitting on that shelf all these years, waiting just for you, Jill."

Strange, Jill didn't recall mentioning her name. But before she could comment on it, a whistle blew from somewhere in the back of the shop, startling her from her stupor.

"Oh, the kettle is ready. I'll be right back. Would you like some tea?" Clo asked, leaving her without a backward glance.

Before she could tell her no, Jill felt a tug on her blouse. She looked down, horrified to find a thread snagged on a button, unraveling the tapestry, row by row. She slammed her hands on the zigzagging strand to prevent any more damage from being done.

"Shit! Shit! Shit!"

"Do you take lemon and sugar in your tea?" Clo called from the back room.

"No. Yes. Fine."

Jill tried to shove the threads back into place with desperate fingers, but the weaving was so tight and compact she couldn't get them between the remaining strands. Maybe she should pull out the traveling sewing kit in her purse and try to stitch the thing back together?

Yeah, right. Like you can even sew a button on straight. How can you possibly think you could restore an ancient tapestry?

Jill risked a panicked glance toward the back of the shop. *I sure hope you have to go all the way to China for that tea, lady.*

She attempted to repair the weaving as best as she could. But as soon as she shoved one thread back into place, other parts of it unraveled before her eyes.

"Damn it!"

She started to hyperventilate. *Why do these kinds of things always seem to happen to me?*

"Because it was meant to, Jill."

Clo stepped behind the glass case, startling Jill. She didn't realize she'd spoken aloud. Or had she?

"What did you say?" Jill asked as she tried to hide the unraveling threads with her hands like a guilty child. Heat radiated under her palms, dizziness flooded her, and the room tilted. The only thing remaining in focus was the dragon, golden-eyed and brilliant as it stared at her from the tapestry. She tried to draw away, but something pulled at her, tugging her in, refusing to let her go. She fought the sensation of toppling forward and falling... falling...

Her gaze locked with Clo's. Through a blurry haze, the munchkin lady smiled at her.

"Say hello to the dragon for me."

CHAPTER TWO

Jill opened her eyes to find a drab, gray sky overhead.

Why was she outside staring at clouds?

A head popped into view, peering down at her with wide, wary eyes—a head with matted, unwashed hair and a mouth missing several teeth. It was followed by another and then another, until her vision filled with dirty, weathered strangers.

A cold shiver rippled through her. She wasn't lying on the wooden planks of the shop, or on the rough cobblestone of the sidewalk, or even on the black pavement of the street, but on hard, damp, earthen ground.

"She's awake," one woman stated in an accent so heavy Jill barely understood her.

"Aye, that she is," said another as the group leaned closer.

"Where did she come from?" one of them asked.

"From the Devil, I'd say. Out o' nowhere, she came. You saw it happen."

"Aye. In the blink of an eye, she were here."

They were definitely speaking English. Of course, it was a form of the language she'd never heard before. That part did have her a bit worried. Had she been in an accident and wrecked her car into a busload of elderly European tourists?

"Look at her clothes." A man with a long, drooping hat pointed at her. "Dressed like a man, she is."

"And her hair," a woman exclaimed. "'Tis shorn. What do ye reckon happened her?"

Jill fingered her shoulder-length hair. She'd never thought of it as short. Sure, it didn't hang down to her waist, but it wasn't a buzz cut either.

"Mayhap she had the fever?" Several people in the crowd nodded in agreement.

Fever? What did that have to do with the length of her hair?

The people talked around her, all the while gawking at her as if she were a piece of roadkill they couldn't identify.

"Umm, excuse me." Jill pushed up on her elbows, interrupting their guessing game. "Can someone tell me what happened?"

The mob glanced from one to another, mumbling incoherent words.

"Let's try this again. Can anyone tell me how I ended up on the ground?"

"Ye fell," a tall, lanky man offered.

Jill gritted her teeth. "Thank you for pointing out the obvious."

"No, that's not right," a woman corrected him. "I'd say she more like dropped."

"I dropped?"

"Aye." She smiled a toothless grin. "Toppled from the sky like a bird felled by the huntsman's arrow."

The others murmured in agreement.

Jill rubbed the back of her head, not at all surprised to find a knot the size of a goose egg. Wonderful. First, the run-in with the plate-glass window and now this. She was definitely going to need some extra-strength Tylenol before the day was through. She struggled to her feet. She needed to find out where she was, how she got here, and most importantly, how she was going to get away from these odd people as fast as she could. After all, she still had to get to Zoe's birthday par-ty...didn't she?

Jill glanced at the crowd surrounding her. They looked like reenactors from some cheesy medieval theme park or a Ren Faire. She peered over the disheveled horde to find equally disheveled houses. Smoke wafted down from thatched roofs to cloak the ground where pigs and chickens wandered loose in a muddy street. While Carytown had its share of characters, it didn't have pigs, or peasants, or lopsided hovels.

Had she somehow stumbled onto a historical movie set filming in the area?

"Would somebody mind telling me where I am?"

"This be the village o' Gosforth."

"Yeah, that doesn't help me much. Where exactly is Gosforth?"

The 'peasants' traded wary looks before one man spoke up. "Why in England, of course."

"England? Yeah, right. Look, I know I'm lost, but I'm not that lost." She shook her head in an effort to clear the muddled conversation and make sense of what was going on. "Anybody happen to know how I got here?"

"We told ye, lass, ye fell—"

"Right. From the sky. I know." She huffed out a sigh. "Fine. Does anybody have a cell phone? Since I can't remember where my car is, I need to call somebody to come get me, if I can figure out where the heck I am."

This brought more puzzled expressions and a few shrugs.

Jill held one hand to her ear and made a dialing motion with the other. "You know—a telephone? Téléphone? ¿Teléfono?" At their continued perplexed stares, she dropped her hands, ending her ridiculous miming act. "Haven't any of you ever heard of a phone?"

One of the men pushed closer, shoving his whiskered face mere inches from her own. The raw stench of sweat and filth made her gag.

"Whoa! Guess not." She took an involuntary step back and muttered under her breath, "since apparently 'soap' doesn't seem to be in your vocabulary either."

Turning to leave, she noticed a young woman dressed in a flowing white gown. She stood in the bed of a wooden cart, a crown of colorful flowers in her long blonde hair. An eerie recollection pricked Jill's memory.

The girl looked exactly like the one in the tapestry.

She shook herself. It had to be a coincidence. She scrutinized the girl again and reason kicked her brain into gear. These people must be participating in a medieval-themed wedding. That would explain a lot. She blew out a cleansing breath, relieved she'd finally figured out one part of the puzzle. Of course, one would think the rest of the guests would have dressed better for the occasion. At the very least, showered and put on some deodorant. The bride definitely stood out from the mangy crowd, the crisp whiteness of her gown nearly glowing compared to the drab hues of the villager's rags.

"Obviously you're in the middle of something here." She started backing away. "I didn't mean to interrupt. I'll just be on my way and you can continue with your little ceremony."

Behind her, the group parted and she nearly made good her escape—until a man standing on the platform next to the young blonde pointed at her. "Are ye wed, girl?"

The odd question stopped Jill in her tracks. "Pardon me?"

Someone in the crowd laughed. "Are ye interested in taking a new wife, Hob?"

"Nay." The man shook his head, his expression serious. "But mayhap a better sacrifice."

A collective gasp rose around her. As one, they turned from the man to stare at her, looking for all the world like eager children given an unexpected gift.

"Offer her up in Aldet's stead," the man went on. "Why sacrifice one of our own when we have a stranger in our midst who can take her place? Give her to the beast."

Sacrifice? Beast? What in heaven's name were these people talking about?

"She's a bit old for a maid, don't you think?" someone pointed out. "The offering has to be a maiden."

Jill scowled at the man, temporarily forgetting that she'd rather not be picked to be whatever this 'offering' was. "Who are you calling old? I'm only twenty-nine."

Horrified looks turned her way. You'd think she'd just told them she was a hundred years old.

"A score and nine?" gasped the toothless woman.

"And ye're not wed?" exclaimed another.

"No." They talked about her single status as if it were some great offense. Up until now, it'd only been a crime in her mother's eyes.

"Well, there ye have it. A fine sacrifice."

But there still seemed to be some question as to whether she was good enough or not, and people started arguing amongst themselves.

"We cannot sacrifice her. The lot has been drawn."

"Aye, Aldet is the chosen one."

Ignored, at least for the moment, Jill began to edge away.

"Besides," another voice shouted, "the offering has to be a maiden from the village."

"This one's here in the village now, isn't she?"

"Aye, but she's not from here. Could be a bad omen if we switch the sacrifice."

"She fell from the bloody sky and landed at our feet on the day of offering. I don't think ye can get a clearer sign than that."

"We don't know her. She's no blood kin to any of us."

Jill had almost inched out of the circle of preoccupied peasants when one voice out-shouted the others, bringing her to a halt. "What if the dragon can tell and rejects her?"

The dragon?

Oh, for Pete's sake. These people are taking this reenactment stuff a little too—

Two men grabbed her from behind.

Jill's mouth went dry. Dear God, what if they weren't reenactors after all? What if this was some kind of weird cult? A cult that makes human sacrifices. Wasn't the National Enquirer full of crazy stories like that? Figures some of it would turn out to be true and here she was, smack dab in the middle of one.

"Now hold on a second," she managed to choke out. "I don't know what's going on here, but nobody's sacrificing me to anything." She struggled to extract her arms from the grip of the two burly men re-straining her, with little effect. "Just let me go and I promise I won't say a word about any of this and you can get back to whatever it is you're doing."

No one paid her any attention. She locked her knees against the men as they tugged her toward the platform, her heels carving twin ruts in the dirt. Her panicked brain grappled for any possible way out of this rapidly deteriorating situation. Suddenly, a tiny detail popped into her head, a minor technicality from some long ago childhood tale, but perhaps enough to save her.

"Wait! Don't you have to be a virgin to be sacrificed to a dragon?"

Silence fell over the crowd and they stood still as statues.

"You know, if I'm not mistaken, virginity is definitely one of the criteria for being a sacrificial offering."

The men ceased dragging her forward as several of the villagers gasped.

Hurray for loopholes! Not that her sex life was something to brag about, but she figured just one instance was enough to get her disqualified. She tried not to act too smug in response to their slack-jawed stares. Fine, if they were going to continue with this twisted version of a fairy tale, then she'd make them play by the rules.

"Ye're not a maid?" someone asked.

"That's right."

"So you be a widow, then?" another questioned.

"Nope. Never been married."

"And yet ye say ye're not a virgin?"

"Right again." Jill nodded, quite pleased with herself for that bit of quick thinking.

"She's lying," a woman shouted from the back of the crowd.

"Now why would I lie about something like that?" she asked, then immediately wished she'd kept her big mouth shut.

"To save yer hide, o' course. To spare yerself from being sacrificed to the dragon."

"Fornication be a dreadful sin, don't ye know," said the massive oaf clamped onto Jill's left arm. He glared at her through narrowed eyes. "We brand whores."

Jill tried to swallow the lump in her throat. Branding? As in, like a cow?

"Which is it, lass?" said his companion on her right. "Are you a virgin or a whore?"

As shocked expressions turned into condemning glares, she began to have second thoughts about the brilliance of her little out-clause. At the moment, the idea of being offered to some non-existent dragon didn't sound quite so bad.

"Call the midwife," Hob shouted.

Jill gaped at the man. What would they need a midwife for? Weren't they used by the earth-mother types for having babies?

"Aye," someone concurred. "Nona will be able to tell if she's been bedded or not."

Bedded? A sick panic churned in her stomach. She felt like Alice in Wonderland watching the white rabbit go hopping by.

A little crone of a woman approached Jill and eyed her up and down.

"Will ye be able to tell if she be speaking the truth?" Hob asked the old hag.

The hag in question, cheeks smudged with soot but with a gaze as sharp and clear as a crisp autumn sky, nodded. "Aye, I'll be able to tell if she's ever lain with a man or not. Won't take a blink to poke about to see if her maidenhead's been breached."

She gaped in horror at the old woman. "Now wait just a gosh darn minute. Nobody's poking anything inside any part of me."

Those turned out to be Jill's famous last words.

The men dragged her to the nearest hut and shoved her inside. She tried to dart back out, but several of the village women jerked her into the dim interior as the door slammed shut in her face.

Jill struggled as the burlier ones pinned her down on a rough-hewn table. She kicked and clawed, but it was no use. There were too many of them. She screamed as they swiftly stripped her of her shoes, slacks and panties. What followed was the most humiliating gynecological exam of her entire life.

With help from two other women, the midwife pried Jill's legs apart. The crone didn't even wash her filthy hands before she shoved her gnarled fingers inside her. The shock of the brutal intrusion was almost worse than the horrifying reality that this was actually happening to her. Bile rose sharp and bitter in Jill's throat. She'd never been so mortified, nor so scared.

"She's still a maid." The midwife nodded in satisfaction as she wiped her fingers on the front of her dirty apron.

Momentarily forgetting the humiliation of the crude examination, anger and shock set in.

"What? Now who's lying, you old bat?"

The old woman grinned, revealing blackened, broken teeth. She leaned in close, her gaze telling more than the whispered words she spoke. "Aye, dearie, ye're the one."

Straightening, the hag barked a single order to the others as she left the hut.

"Prepare the dragon's bride."

Her back pressed against the rough wooden stake, Jill jerked at the ropes binding her hands, hoping she could wiggle them free. But as the tender skin of her wrists burned in protest, she conceded escape that way was not going to be possible. Not if she wanted to keep her hands attached to her arms, that is.

How could this be happening to her?

"I'm not the crazy one around here!" she shouted. "This is the twenty-first century, people, not the Middle Ages. It's against the law to make human sacrifices and there are *No. Such. Things. As. Dragons!*"

Why was she yelling? No one was around to hear her.

Those people were delusional. But at least for now Jill felt a little safer. Apparently, they weren't going to cut her heart out on an altar, or burn her at the stake, or do something as equally unappealing and life ending. At least she hoped not.

She breathed deeply, trying to calm herself. She'd just have to play along with their crazy game for now. Eventually they'd come back and let her go. After all, what harm could come from standing out in a field for a few hours? A few bug bites? Maybe a little sunburn? Nothing she couldn't survive. Right?

Or maybe not.

Deciding it probably wouldn't be in her best interests to still be here when or if they returned, Jill glanced overhead and wondered if she could shimmy up and flip her bound arms over the top of the stake. It was worth a try. She squeezed the post with her arms, braced her feet against the stake in an awkward *plié* and pushed with her legs. She made it all of six inches before her feet slipped, the rough wood snagging at the white gown they'd made her wear as she skidded back down the post.

Great. Now on top of everything else, she was going to have splinters in both butt cheeks. What had she been thinking? *Sure, Jill, climb a twelve-foot pole with your hands tied behind you. And do it backwards, no less. Like you could do it frontwards with booster rockets tied to your ass. It's not as if you're a prime candidate for Cirque de Soleil.*

Okay, so scaling the pole like a monkey wasn't an option. What else could she do? One thing was certain, she was not about to sit and wait for…what? More crazy villagers? Or whatever those fanatical loons thought was coming to get her? No, thank you.

Think, Jill, think. What would MacGyver do in a situation like this? Of course, he'd have a stick of gum stuck up his sleeve and a paperclip in his shoe. She was strapped to a giant fence post wearing little more than a nightgown and a wilting crown of flowers. A lot of good they would do her.

Damn. Where was Lassie when you needed her?

Her only hope was either someone would come along and set her free—slim chance there—or she could untie herself.

Relax. Just breathe and relax. If she concentrated, she might be able to untie the knots by feel. She closed her eyes, visualizing the rope binding her wrists, and wiggled her fingers until they touched a knot. Her arms and shoulders burned from that little bit of effort. How was she ever going to manage to get the knot loose?

Calm down, Jill. One thing at a time. Think positive. You can do this.

She managed to wedge one fingertip under the knot, feeling her nail tear to the quick as she attempted to pry it loose. She concentrated harder, ignoring the pain in her arms and back. Yes! She felt some give in the rope. She was making progress. It was slow, but it was still progress. Unfortunately, at this rate it would be the middle of next week before she got herself loose.

Deep in concentration, at first she didn't notice the drumming sound in the distance.

The wind. It had to be the wind.

Still, her heart rate sped up as her fingers began a frantic dance with the stubborn knot.

Concentrate on the rope. Don't think about anything else but getting yourself untied.

Struggling with the bindings, she tried to shut out the *whoosh-whoosh* drawing closer.

Don't look up. Whatever you do, do not look up.

But she did, and the sight that met her eyes would have dropped her to her knees if she wasn't still firmly tied to the stake.

Calm down. It's just a bird. Some enormous bird making an awful lot of noise.

But as it drew nearer, she realized it was too big to be any kind of bird she'd ever seen.

Maybe it's a plane. Yeah, that's it. A plane...with big, flapping, bat-like wings.

Jill's stomach plummeted as the thing soared closer, any hopes it might be Superman coming to her rescue dashed when she saw the long, reptilian tail trailing behind it.

She couldn't believe what she was seeing. A giant, flying lizard swooped down through the clouds, heading straight for her.

Her mind screamed in silent denial as reality crashed in with a gut-churning jolt.

Holy shit! She really was being sacrificed to a dragon.

ChAPTER ThREE

Jill squeezed her eyes shut, desperate to block out the inconceivable sight of the creature soaring in the sky above her.

It's because of the tapestry. Yeah, that's it. This is a concussion-induced delusion triggered by hitting your head, then seeing the dragon tapestry. Please, please, let traumatic brain injury be the only problem I have to deal with right now.

A fierce wind kicked up around her. Startled, she opened her eyes. Fear kept them open.

The dragon circled above her like a mutant seagull, then coasted down, landing with more grace than she thought a giant flying lizard would have. It tucked its enormous wings close to its body and cocked its head to look at her.

Jill froze. She didn't dare twitch or breathe. A childish notion reasoned that if she stayed perfectly still, maybe the thing wouldn't see her.

The dragon crept forward on clawed feet and leaned in until its snout halted mere inches from her face. Its breath huffed hot and moist on her skin, the stench of burnt sulfur suffocating, and any hopes that she might go unnoticed plummeted to the ground with a nearly audible splat.

Giving up on the playing possum routine, Jill tugged in renewed desperation at the ropes.

A deep growl rumbled from the creature's throat and she ceased struggling.

All right, no need to make the thing angry.

The dragon shifted its head from side to side, as if at this close range it couldn't quite see her with both eyes at the same time. Scales of brown and rust shimmered in the sunlight, undulating across the muscles under its hide, while paler plates curved down its underbelly. Its golden eyes held her spellbound, the dark slit of its pupil reminding her of a cat's as it studied a cornered mouse, trying to decide not whether, but when, it would pounce.

Then the dragon blinked and shifted closer, jarring Jill out of her temporary enchantment. A whimper escaped her throat as the beast's snout began a slow descent down the length of her body, its nostrils flaring and puffing foul, gusty snorts.

Oh, my God. It's sniffing me!

When its nose reached her bare feet, it reversed direction, inching its way upward again, its warm breath fluttering the material of her gauzy gown against her thighs. As it rose higher, its muzzle bumped against her left breast before it stopped to look her in the eye once again. For an insane moment, she thought the thing grinned at her. Then it opened its massive jaws, revealing its teeth. Lots of long, sharp, pointy teeth.

Raw, pulse-stopping fear consumed her. Even if she weren't tied immobile to the stake, the sheer terror of what was happening held her paralyzed. She now knew exactly what the fly caught in the spider's web felt like. Desperate. Terrified. Helpless.

A long, forked tongue slithered out of its mouth. It stroked her neck, just below her ear, eerily reminiscent of a lover's kiss.

Oh God, now the thing is tasting me!

She wanted to scream, but no sound would come. She wanted to close her eyes against its penetrating stare, but she couldn't will them to shut.

Faint. Please, for the first time in my life, let me faint. Now.

She didn't want the last thing she saw on this earth to be the inside of a dragon's mouth.

The beast pulled back and she drew in a ragged breath, much to the appreciation of her air-starved lungs. Then its large body lumbered to the side, easing around behind her.

Panic gripped her chest, squeezing tight. She couldn't see it, had no idea what it was doing. Was it leaving? Or was it going to eat her from behind? Somehow, facing the monster head-on seemed better than not knowing what was coming.

Jill tried to stifle the hysteria threatening to make her thundering heart explode. She might not be able to see the dragon, but she could hear it, could feel its heated breath on her back.

She stiffened against the stake as she felt a tug on the ropes. What was it doing?

Something long and smooth slid between her wrists. Was it a claw? A tooth? Oh God, was it going to bite her hands off first and then eat the rest of her?

The rope around her wrists fell away.

She stood motionless, her hands hanging limp as pins and needles shot up her arms, her fear-addled mind having difficulty grasping what just happened.

The dragon had cut her loose.

Then the creature's bulbous snout eased around the side and her sense of self-preservation kicked into high gear. Jill bolted.

She hiked the long skirt to her knees and ran for the woods. Her gasping breaths and the drumming of blood in her ears drowned out all other sound until the telltale whoosh-whoosh of the dragon's wings overrode all else. Without turning, Jill knew it was airborne again—and coming after her.

The trees. Just get into the woods and you can hide. It was too big to fly in after her, wasn't it?

She'd almost made it to the timberline when the creature crashed to the ground in front of her. Without breaking stride, Jill skidded and reversed direction, running as if the hounds of hell nipped at her heels. Hounds in the form of a twenty-foot dragon.

She dared a swift glance behind her. The creature took flight again, its scaled belly gliding bare inches from the ground. Her legs ached and her lungs threatened to burst from her chest. Oh, why hadn't she taken up jogging? She was in no condition for this. There was no way she could outrun the thing.

The beat of wings grew louder and the dragon's breath singed the back of her neck. She didn't need to look to know it was almost upon her. Was it even now taking aim to spit a bolt of fire at her and burn her to a crisp? Jill didn't want to find out.

She dodged to the left, then to the right, hoping its large size would hinder its ability to make quick maneuvers. Sure enough, the dragon whizzed past her, nearly knocking her down with the downdraft from its wings.

Jill continued to duck and sidestep in an effort to evade the beast. Running up one hill and down another, she dashed barefoot across the grassy terrain like a manic gazelle. Tiring, she knew her only hope was to make it to the woods. She changed direction again, praying her legs would hold out long enough to get her there.

An enraged roar ripped through the air and she braved a glance over her shoulder. She didn't have to be an animal psychologist to know the thing was pissed and its game of cat and mouse was over.

She focused on the trees. A few more yards and she would make it. Just a bit more—

Her feet slid out from under her.

Nooo! her mind screamed as she fell, sprawling in something wet and gooey. She couldn't tell what it was, but it was thick, dark and oozed between her fingers as she tried to push herself up. With her luck, she'd just fallen in a big pile of dragon shit.

A gust of wind whipped at her gunk-caked hair, slapping the slimy locks in her face. She rolled over to find the beast hovering above her, its broad wings flapping back and forth to keep its massive body airborne. One of its front claws, the sharp talons spread wide, reached for her. She tried to crab-crawl backwards, but her hands and feet found no purchase in the muck.

It was hopeless. She couldn't get away.

This is it. This is how I'm going to die.

The scream Jill had been holding inside ripped from her throat as the dragon grabbed her around the waist and took off into the sky.

She gripped a claw as she watched the ground slip further and further away, not sure if plummeting to her death would be preferable to whatever fate awaited her when the thing decided to land.

It tucked its wings, turning them into a stomach-rolling dive as it sliced through the clouds. She clutched the talon tighter and groaned. Then with one mighty sweep of its powerful wings, the beast soared up once again, leaving Jill's churning stomach somewhere in the vicinity of her feet before it leveled out, soaring on the breeze like a giant Chinese kite.

She shut her eyes against the icy wind battering her face until the dragon plummeted once again. Startled, her eyes shot open to discover they were heading straight for a rocky mountainside.

The dragon flapped its wings in a backward motion, coasting in toward a large, dark crack in the sheer rock face. Realization dawned on her frazzled mind. A cave.

It must be taking me to its—Oh, what did they call it?—lair. Yeah, that was it.

This was probably not a good thing.

The creature landed on the ledge, depositing her on the ground with a gentle touch at odds with the brute strength in its grip. The minute the dragon released her, she was on her feet and backing away, looking for any possible avenue of escape.

Stone walls surrounded her on both sides, the jagged, gray rock soaring high above her head. A brief glimpse behind her revealed the vast bowels of a cavern, too dark to see beyond what the fading sunlight could illuminate. Then there was Godzilla in the flesh crouched in front of her, blocking the mouth of the cave.

A low growl rumbled from the dragon as it lumbered toward her. Instinct for self-preservation backed her deeper into the dark inner recesses. This was so not good.

Please, please let there be a back door to this place.

The dragon continued to advance, its large body blocking out what little light there was. Reaching blindly around her, she groped for a hiding place. Could dragons see in the dark? Lord, she hoped not.

She bumped into something heavy, yet not quite solid. It shifted before slithering to the ground beside her. She shrieked and jumped away.

Oh, please don't let it be another dragon.

The beast in front of her roared, its deafening bellow reverberating off the stone walls. Then a bright light flared as fire shot out from its jaws, blinding her. Jill dropped to her knees in a protective crouch, covering her head with her hands as the flame shot over her, instantly heating the cool, damp air.

Long seconds ticked by. When she didn't feel her skin blister and peel from her body or smell the stench of singed hair, Jill raised her head. And her jaw dropped.

Dozens of torches embedded high in the stone walls illuminated the cave's interior with dancing light and shadows. She peeked at the dragon. It still crouched at the entrance, its scales shimmering in the torchlight, watching her. Waiting.

Okay. Why would a dragon need light?

Why, the better to see you so I can eat you, my dear.

Sure, dinner and candlelight—with her as the main course.

The burning torches hissed and somewhere deeper within the cave she heard the sound of trickling water. When the beast made no move to come after her, she rose on unsteady legs.

No quick moves, Jill. Slow and easy.

She'd taken only one step before the beast bolted up and snarled. Startled, Jill stumbled back, falling on her backside amid a mound of cold, shifting metal. Her heart settled in her throat as the dragon lunged at her. She scrambled to her feet and glanced around desperately for a weapon.

She didn't have far to look.

Swords, shields and lances littered the cave. A pile of small, linked metal rings lay in a jumbled heap at her feet. Was that a suit of mail armor she'd just tripped over? Leftovers, no doubt, from some poor, brave knight who tried to slay the dragon and got barbecued instead.

Grabbing the weapon closest at hand, Jill pointed a long sword at the dragon. It stopped, its eyes flaring bright, then frowned at her—or it would have, if it had eyebrows. She managed to hold the sword at chest level for all of five seconds before the weight forced her to lower the point to the ground.

"Damn, that's heavy."

The dragon advanced, a low rumbling growl issuing a dire warning if she ever heard one. Refusing to go down without a fight, Jill gripped the sword with both hands and aimed it at the creature's chest, determined to use it to keep from being lizard lunch if it killed her.

"Stay back or I swear I'll gut you like a biology class frog."

The dragon stopped and tilted its head, then huffed, snorting a tiny puff of smoke out of one nostril. Narrowing its golden eyes at her, the creature eased to its belly. With the sword firmly in her grip, Jill dared to take her eyes off it just long enough to glance around and get her bearings. She was amazed at what she found.

What in the world was this place? The cave was full of…stuff. Besides the medieval weapons, there were hides and tapestries, chests and trunks, bits of furniture piled with plates and goblets, and who knew what else. In the center of the chamber, branches lay stacked in a fire pit, waiting to be lit. Near it, a mound of furs formed an inviting bed to cushion some weary sleeper from the cold stone floor.

Why did a dragon have all these things? Unless…

Someone lived here. Someone human.

Taking a deep breath, Jill called out, "Hello. Anyone here?"

Her voice echoed, sounding pitiful and distant as it faded away into the darkness beyond the torchlight. No one answered. Guess nobody was home in the bat cave. Well, except for her and the mutant salamander with Ginsu knives for teeth.

Deciding to put some much needed space between them, she crept further into the cave.

A small chest caught her eye and she lifted the lid—and almost dropped the sword. A treasure of ancient gold coins and ornate jewels glittered up at her. Running her fingers through the riches, she whistled softly. A tiny fortune at her fingertips.

A quick glance at the dragon reassured her it hadn't moved. Feeling braver, she decided to move on in the hopes there was another way out. Removing a torch from the wall, Jill ventured deeper into the cave, dragging the heavy sword after her and hopefully leaving the Puff-the-very-real-dragon far, far behind.

The first chamber opened up into a large cavern, the flickering light revealing damp slate walls from the lightest gray to deep shades of green, blue-black and rust. Slabs of shattered rock covered the cave floor while jagged stones jutted high overhead, waiting to fall. The dangling shards looked like giant serpent's teeth and she couldn't shake the feeling she'd escaped the jaws of one monster only to be thrust into the gapping mouth of another.

She glanced over her shoulder, reassuring herself that the flesh-and-blood one was still where she left it. The plink-plink of dripping water once again beckoned to her from the back of the cave. Her tongue suddenly felt twice its size and her parched throat constricted, reminding her she'd had nothing to drink since this nightmare started this morning.

Her bare feet screamed in agony as she stumbled over the jagged rocks. Following the call of trickling water, Jill made her way to the back of the cave to find the polished black surface of a subterranean pool, the meager light of her torch failing to illuminate the fathomless bottom. She wedged the torch into a fissure and knelt at the water's edge, the trusty sword at her side. Rinsing as much dirt off her hands as she could, she cupped the cold water to her mouth.

With her thirst quenched, she tried to peer into the shadows beyond the pool. If water could get in, maybe there was an opening large enough for her to get out. But first, she had to get past the mammoth rock formations surrounding the water on each side.

With no flat area to stand on, she edged her way around a large boulder, wedging her fingers into narrow cracks while her feet sought purchase on the slippery rock. A soft, rustling sound unnerved her. *Oh, there'd better not be bats in here. One large, demented dragon is about all I can handle right now.*

Reaching for another precarious handhold, her toes slid through the slime growing on the surface and she lost her balance. Wavering by one hand, she grappled desperately for anything to hold onto, crying out as she fell backwards and plunged into the icy water.

Jill came up gasping for air, the frigid dunking a sudden, disorienting shock. Finally, her feet located the murky bottom and she stood, surprised to find the pool was only thigh deep. She sloshed her way back to the flat rock she'd started from. Hair dripping and the soaked gown clinging to her chilled body, she wrapped her arms around herself and glared at the water lapping the rock near her toes.

"Damn, that was cold!"

A low growl rumbled behind her and she spun around, nearly tumbling back into the icy pool. How had the dragon snuck up on her without making a sound?

She scrambled for the sword and held it before her. It shook its horned head, advancing as if she wielded nothing more threatening than

27

a toothpick. Jill retreated until the jagged stones of the cave wall poked at her back. Just when she feared it was going to open its massive jaws and finally eat her, sword and all, the dragon turned its attention to the water.

Opening its maw wide, fire erupted from the dragon's mouth, shooting out over the pool like a military flamethrower. Jill watched as it moved the flame back and forth over the surface, the intense heat kicking up tiny waves to lap against the rocky walls. As the sound reached a deafening roar, the dragon snapped its mouth closed, swallowing the fire. It looked at her once, then the creature retreated, leaving her alone at the water's edge.

Bewildered, she turned her attention back to the pool. The once glassy surface now rippled and swirled with small currents, while fingers of whisper-thin steam drifted up from the heated water. Had the dragon understood her remark about the water being cold?

That's ridiculous. It probably saw you shiver.

Jill closed her eyes and mentally berated herself. *Yeah, like that makes sense.*

Quaking, the soaked gown dripping a puddle at her feet, she eyed the pool of steaming water and couldn't help imagining it was a giant pot and she was about to become dragon stew.

Ignoring that train of thought, she took advantage of the opportunity and slid back into the water, wading over to the far side. She searched every crack and crevice, even groping along the ledge under the water's surface, but found no rear opening to the cave. It was a dead end. Apparently the only way in or out was blocked by a twenty-foot, fire-breathing dragon.

Her upper body chilled, she crouched down in the middle of the pool where the heated current wrapped around her like a warm blanket. Loose silt from the bottom oozed through her toes but she didn't care. As long as the Creature from the Black Lagoon didn't rise up from the depths, she wasn't going to whine about the little things.

She needed to calm down and think. She had to come up with a plan to get out of here before gator breath got hungry and came looking for its dinner. But how did anybody escape a dragon? They didn't teach this kind of stuff in her Self-Defense 101 class.

But as the water cooled and her chattering teeth resonated through the chamber, she gave up the struggle and pulled herself out onto the rocks. Wondering what to do next, she stood at the water's edge as the wet dress clung to her body, sucking all residual warmth from her limbs. Getting warm and dry was on the top of her list of things to do.

She peeled off the sodden gown, the white material stained beyond repair but at least now free of the thick globs of mud weighing it down. It wasn't until she tossed it on a flat rock that she realized she didn't have anything to wear while it dried.

Well, that's just great. What are you going to do, walk around the cave naked, freezing your butt off? At least now you don't have to worry about the dragon. You'll die of hypothermia before it gets around to eating you...unless it has a sudden craving for a human freezer pop.

A low, strangled noise rumbled through the cavern. Jill glanced at the dragon and froze as her gaze locked with the creature's, unnerved to find it staring at her. Hot flames burned within its golden eyes, its stare was so intense a shiver raced through her body that had nothing to do with the chilly subterranean temperature.

You're being silly, she chided herself. *It's an animal. Granted, one that shouldn't exist, but an animal all the same. It could care less if you're naked or not.* But convincing herself it was only her imagination was hard to do when its eyes seemed to glow with a barely concealed heat, burning with a needy, aching...hunger.

If she could, Jill would've laughed at herself. A dragon lusting after her? Hardly. It was probably thinking what a nice, fat ass she had to eat.

Grabbing her trusty sword, she staggered toward the pile of furs. Dragon or no dragon, it was a risk she had to take. She had to get warm.

She wrapped herself in one of the skins and curled into a tight ball. The dragon blinked, as if coming out of a trance. It gave her one last, lingering look before lowering its lids and turning away, concealing whatever thoughts a creature like that could have and taking the illusion of their heat with it.

Jill tried to relax. So far, the thing hadn't hurt her, if she didn't count the half a dozen times it had scared her to death. Making sure the sword was close at hand, she glanced once again at the cave entrance. Sitting on its haunches with its back to her, the dragon resembled a big, winged guard dog.

She snuggled deeper into the warm fur, wondering vaguely if it was trying to keep her in or something else out.

Jill awoke with a start.

What time was it? Had she missed Zoe's party? Shaking off the last vestiges of the crazy dragon dream she'd had, she sat up.

And nearly lit herself on fire.

A small blaze crackled next to her, the flames casting everything around her in shadow. As the wood popped and sparks danced like drunken fireflies in the gray smoke, she struggled to make sense of it. Why was she sleeping by a campfire wearing nothing more than a bearskin rug? Slowly, her eyes adjusted and she recognized the jagged walls of her stone prison. So much for it all having been a dream.

A strange noise drew her attention to the mouth of the cave, raising chills along her naked skin. She hugged the fur tighter. There, silhouetted against the vivid orange and magenta of a brilliant sunset, sat the dragon. It gazed off into the distance, its wings spread wide as if trying to catch the last warm rays of the sun. A low, keening moan began and she watched in fascinated horror as its body twisted and contorted on the ledge.

The creature was…changing.

Jill rubbed her eyes. She had to be seeing things. In profile, the long snout receded and the spikes running down the creature's spine disappeared. The dragon no longer looked as large as before, its dark scales now more tan than brown and smoothing out, taking on the texture of…skin.

But that wasn't what alarmed Jill the most. It was the sound the creature was making. What started out as a soft groan evolved into a nearly human cry of suffering.

Was the dragon in pain?

With an earth-shattering roar, fire burst from the dragon's jaws, shooting a fireball into the sky like a comet. Jill covered her eyes against the brilliant blast. An eerie silence surrounded her, with only the soft crackle of the campfire filling the stillness. She peeked through her fingers at the cave entrance.

The dragon was gone.

Then a movement on the ledge caught her eye, a slight shift of the shadows. A form unfolded and rose, until it was clear a man stood at the entrance with his back to her.

A back that bore a pair of dragon wings.

The man turned and looked at her, the firelight illuminating his smooth skin and shining off a strange, starburst-shaped scar in the center of his chest.

Jill couldn't believe what she was seeing. The dragon had just turned into a man.

A very handsome, very naked man.

For the longest time he seemed content to stare at her. The feeling was mutual—she couldn't tear her eyes away from him either. Caramel-brown hair fell in soft waves to his broad shoulders and heavy brows slashed over dark, intense eyes. His ripped body conveyed strength and power, while his full lips whispered of hot, knee-melting kisses.

Then he moved and broke her trance, walking toward her with measured precision. Alarmed, Jill scrambled to her feet, clutching the fur around her like a shield. She glanced at the sword. Instinct told her to pick it up, that she needed to protect herself until she could figure out what was going on. But to do that, she'd have to let go of the fur and then she'd be just as naked as he was.

Her inhibitions won out. Besides, he was so big he could probably yank the sword away and snap it like a twig before she could even scratch him with it.

He stopped on the other side of the fire. When he made no further movement toward her, she let out the breath she'd been holding. It didn't take long for shock to set in.

"You...you were a dragon. And now, you...you're a man."

Jill's addled mind tried to wrap itself around what she'd seen happen. She couldn't do it. It was all too unreal. So her frazzled brain grabbed onto the nearest thought it could, inappropriate and irrational though it was.

"You perverted flying lizard. You saw me naked!"

ChAPTER FOUR

In all his 216 years as a dragon, Baelin of Gosforth had never been so surprised by someone's reaction to him.

Most of the maidens trembled in fear when they witnessed his change. Many screamed, some ran to hide in the back of the cave, several swooned, and one had—

Baelin stopped himself. There were some things he preferred not to remember.

But this one...

He did not frighten this one at all. Instead, she was angry he'd seen her unclothed while in his dragon form.

"If I'd known you were a man—"

"But I am not a man," he corrected her, interrupting her tirade. "Not anymore."

Her mouth snapped shut and her eyes traveled his body from head to toe before settling near his hips. Unaccustomed to such bold scrutiny, Baelin battled for control under her intense stare. He did not have to look down to know he failed miserably.

It could not be helped. First, the woman disrobed before him, torturing the man inside the beast beyond bearing, and now she eyed his rod like a camp follower. She did not blush or turn away in maidenly modesty. Instead, she arched a finely curved brow and continued to ogle him.

"I beg to differ. There are parts of you that are every inch a man."

Her comment shocked him at first, and Baelin couldn't help but return her brazen remark. "Now 'tis my lady who looks aplenty."

Her head snapped up and her face flamed a becoming shade of pink. He couldn't resist giving her a slow, cocky grin.

She took an instant step back, clutching the fur tightly around her bare shoulders. Like a snuffed candle, the humor of the moment vanished. As brave as she pretended to be, the maid still found him repulsive. Just like all the others. The ever-familiar sense of disappointment returned. Did he truly believe after all this time, this one might be different?

"Fear not. I will not touch you."

"Yeah, well, you just be sure to keep that," she managed to wiggle one finger between a gap in the fur and point it at the offending part in question, "far away from me."

Baelin bowed his head. "As my lady wishes."

He strode around the fire and made his way to the trunk containing his clothing, dressing with his back to her. After donning tan breeches, he slipped on a white linen tunic, the material slit in the back to accommodate the loathsome wings that still remained from his transformation. As he fastened the ties, his senses stayed alert to the woman in the cave with him. She had yet to move from where she stood by the fire. He could hear the soft pant of her breath, could smell her freshly washed skin with a scent uniquely her own. But more than anything, he could feel her eyes on him, burning into his human flesh as no dragon's fire ever could.

As he turned to face her again, she quickly looked away. Was that a flash of disappointment he saw flicker across her face? A trick of the light, no doubt. But then he watched her gaze dart about the cave, in every direction but at him, before a telltale blush crept up the ivory skin of her throat. It took great effort to keep from smiling. So, he'd been correct—she had watched him dress. Had it been out of curiosity, or something else, he wondered?

He strode to another trunk and lifted the lid. "These are for you."

The girl glanced from him to the chest and back. Then she squared her shoulders and walked toward him. Stopping a few safe steps away, she craned her neck and peered inside. The trunk contained smocks and embroidered kirtles in a rainbow of colors, from the softest wools and linens to the finest silks. There were hose and soft leather shoes, warm cloaks and delicate veils. Everything a lady could want.

"I hope they please you."

Her stiff posture relaxed somewhat in her obvious surprise. "These are for me?"

"Aye, unless my lady prefers to remain draped in fur for the remainder of her stay."

Holding the pelt tightly in one fist, she stepped closer and reached out with the other hand to run her palm over the gowns.

"They're beautiful, but to be honest, I'm more of a t-shirt and jeans kind of girl."

What did she mean? Did she not approve of the gowns? Truth be told, they may be a bit out of date. It was a tiring effort to keep up with the changes in woman's fashions from year to year, especially when he had but a month as a human to acquire them.

"I am sorry if these are not to your liking. If you will but tell me what it is you require, I shall obtain it for you on the morrow."

"On the *morrow*?" She laughed softly, the sound strange in a place that had known no happiness in all the time he'd been forced to live here. "Somehow, I get the feeling you're not going to find a Target around here. These are fine."

Baelin bowed to her, not quite certain he understood her meaning. The maid's manner of speech was strange, like none he'd ever heard before.

"Then I shall leave you to it," he said as he turned away.

"You're giving me privacy?" She made an unladylike snort. "Why start now?"

He stiffened, aware he deserved the censure. "On my word as a knight, you shall have it now, my lady."

"So I guess it didn't count when you were a dragon, huh?"

Duly chastised, Baelin left her and busied himself by filling two silver goblets with wine from one of the many barrels stacked in the cave. He tasted the heady drink, thankful it survived the year without souring. Returning to the fire, he sat down to wait. But not in silence.

Behind him, his acute hearing perceived the soft rustle of clothing.

Determined to honor his promise, he kept his eyes averted, only to have them land on a large shield propped against the cave wall. The shiny metal reflected a wavy vision of the girl as she stepped into the gown, her pale skin glowing like pearls in the firelight. Though the hammered metal distorted her image, he could easily picture her as she'd been while he watched her move about the cave in blissful ignorance, streams of water trickling down her naked body, her dusky nipples constricted to tight peaks he ached to suckle. His groin tightened at the memory.

But she was aware of his presence now and he'd given her his word. He closed his eyes, but the image of her burned behind his closed lids, taunting him with every rustle of linen, every whisper of silk.

The slam of the trunk lid signaled the end of his torment, but he did not look up. Not until he heard her approach. Baelin set down the goblets and stood. She'd chosen a gown of dark green wool, simple in cut but lovely nonetheless. The color brought out emerald flecks mixed in the brown of her eyes. She wore no veil to cover her hair, even though he knew there were many to choose from.

"Could you, um," she cleared her throat, "help me out?"

"Certainly. You have but to ask."

"I didn't see anything with buttons or a zipper, so..." She turned, offering her back to him. "I can't seem to tie this thing."

The back of the kirtle was a web of laces from neck to the small of her back, designed to secure the garment tightly to her upper body.

He closed his eyes and stifled a groan. Sweet Mary, the woman wore nothing underneath.

Baelin approached her slowly, half fearing she would change her mind and perform the task herself. The other part of him prayed she would. So soon after the change, it was difficult controlling his dragon impulses without this added temptation.

His hands shook as he began drawing the laces closed and he cursed the weakness of the man in him. Through the gaping slit, he could see the white of her flesh, the graceful curve of her back. He longed to run his hand down her spine, to feel that which only his eyes were able to touch. Without meaning to, his knuckles skimmed the warm softness of her skin and he jerked as if the slight contact burned him.

Wary, Baelin waited for the repulsed reaction certain to come. But the girl continued to stand there patiently, as if she hadn't noticed his transgression.

Now it was he who felt ill at ease. None of the other maids had ever requested this of him. Somehow, they'd been able to manage. Then again, they'd always maintained a safe distance, ever watchful he did not venture too near. None of them had ever allowed him this close, much less permitted his foul hands upon their bodies.

And yet, she did not seem to mind. She even pulled her hair up as he drew near the end of his task, revealing the smooth arch of her neck and the wispy curls at her nape.

What would it be like to brush his lips where her pulse beat just below her ear? He could still taste her from when he'd dared to stroke her with his dragon's tongue while she stood bound to the stake. Would she taste different now that he was human?

Tearing himself away from his lustful thoughts, Baelin tied the knot tighter than it needed to be. He cursed his actions. Now he would probably end up having to cut the gown off her later. As soon as the thought invaded his mind, the vivid image of doing just that nearly brought him to his knees.

He took a much-needed step away from her.

"'Tis done." The words came out as a growl, but he couldn't take them back. Nor could he allow her to see how much her presence affected him.

Letting her hair fall, she turned to face him. "Thank you."

Trying to regain his calm through courtesy, he offered her one of the goblets. Suspicion narrowed her eyes and she kept her hands at her sides.

"What is it?"

"Wine."

She looked from him to the goblet and back. Her lack of trust held a bitter taste, but he reminded himself it was always this way in the beginning.

"Fear not. 'Tis only wine. I wish you no harm."

"I'm not so sure of that yet." But she accepted the goblet anyway. As she reached for it, her sleeve slipped, revealing her wrist and angry red welts marking her flesh, the skin raw and torn.

"God's teeth!" He grabbed her arm, startling her. Her cup clattered to the ground, the spilled wine spreading a crimson river on the stones at their feet. "Why do they always struggle so, when it only brings them harm?"

"Why don't you try standing still as a huge flying lizard comes swooping down at you and see if you don't get a sudden urge to run like hell?"

His gaze shot from her chafed wrist to her challenging eyes.

"Believe me, my lady, I have. 'Tis no easy feat." Realizing he was scaring her yet again, he released her. "I am sorry if I frightened you."

"Frightened is an understatement. I thought I was going to have a heart attack when you dive-bombed out of the sky at me."

While he may not understand all her strange words, he could discern the implication behind most of them. "It could not be helped. There was no other way."

He left her standing by the fire to gather what he would need to tend her wounds.

A long silence stretched between them before she spoke again. "You said 'they' always struggle. Do you make it a habit of snatching defenseless women tied to stakes?"

"I endeavor not to be greedy." A faint smile tugged at his lips, helping to temper his fierce mood. "I try to limit myself to but one maiden a year."

"How considerate of you."

Continuing his search, he attempted to explain. "Alas, 'tis necessary. My curse can only be broken by a maiden from the village."

"Of course. There's a curse. Why wouldn't there be one in this Camelot Gone Wild?" The girl paused before continuing. "So that's why you take the sacrifices?"

Her biting tone confused him. Frowning, he returned to the fireside. "Aye, why else would I take them?"

She cocked a finely arched brow at him. "Let me see. You're a man with dragon wings sticking out of your back, living alone in a cave with only yourself for entertainment and…other things. Several possibilities instantly come to mind and none of them are very good."

The stinging insult couched in her strange words was not lost on him. "No harm will come to you while you are under my protection."

"Your protection?" she huffed. "This is kidnapping and where I come from, that's considered a federal offense. For all I know, I need protection from you."

Crossing her arms, her stance mocked him as surely as her sharp tongue. What kind of woman was this, who entered the dragon's lair and dared challenge the beast with little more than the stiff tilt of her chin?

Uncertain how to best proceed with this odd girl, Baelin attempted to put her at ease. "Upon the rise of the next full moon, if the curse is not broken, you shall be released—unharmed, untouched, and with wealth enough that you will never go wanting."

Her brow puckered, but she appeared to relax a bit. "That's good to know...I think."

Gesturing to a flat rock near the fire, he offered her what comfort he could. "Please, sit."

She eyed him, her expression guarded, before complying.

He refilled her goblet and she took it from him with obvious caution, sniffing the wine before taking a tiny sip. She nodded her head, offering silent approval of its quality. He let out the breath he'd been holding, not realizing until then that her opinion of the wine—and by relation, himself—mattered.

He knelt on the ground and reached for her free hand. She leaned back, her entire body retreating from him until he feared she might fall backwards off the rock.

"I only wish to tend your wounds so they do not fester."

"Oh." She seemed to ponder this, then finally put her hand in his.

Relieved at this small act of trust, he examined the raw red welts marking the tender flesh of her wrists. Her hands were delicate and soft, no calluses marring the palms from long days of grueling work. Who was she that she did not have to labor like the other villagers, women and children alike?

"What's that?" she asked as he scooped green paste out of a jar.

"'Tis a salve. It will help the cuts to heal."

The girl wrinkled her nose at the foul-smelling ointment, but she did not flinch when he smoothed it over the angry scrapes. "So it's some kind of antibiotic cream?"

"Forgive me. I do not know what this *antre bæðweg* is you speak of."

"You don't know what an antibiotic is?" She gaped at him as if he were daft. "What rock have you been living under?"

He gritted his teeth, sensing the insult behind her strange words. "I call this cave my home, if that is what you consider living under a rock."

"Oh. Sorry. No offense."

He bent to his task in an effort to regain control over the umbrage she instilled in him. Once both wrists were coated with the salve, he tore a piece of linen into strips, all the while aware of the maid watching his every movement. She took another sip, this one longer than the first, then broke the uneasy silence closing in around them.

"This is some potent wine. I'll be drunk after one mug on an empty stomach."

"Then you should not partake overmuch, for I have no food to offer you."

"Right." She lifted the goblet in a mockery of a toast. "After the day I've had, I'm ready to drink myself into oblivion. I may wake up with a killer hangover, but hopefully I will be back in my own bed and all this will be nothing more than the hazy leftovers of a very bad dream."

"This is not a dream."

She made an unladylike snort. "Tell that to the rational part of my brain. Where I come from, people don't live in caves, planes are the preferred mode of airborne transportation and there are no such things as dragons."

Her words pierced through him, as though she denounced his very existence. Baelin gripped her arm with more force than he intended, causing her to wince.

"Then what am I?"

The girl shivered under his scrutiny and tried to pull away, but he refused to release his hold. He wanted her to experience the warmth of his skin, to know the solid grasp of his hand on her flesh, to feel that he was a living, breathing creature.

Her hand fisted, her jaw tense. She ceased straining and countered his grip with a challenging glare. "Good question. What exactly are you?"

He released her instantly.

"I am what you see. Half man, half beast."

The girl swallowed hard, then sat without uttering a word while he wrapped her wrist with a linen strip. He felt her eyes on him, watching him as he tended her. He didn't dare look up. He didn't want to see what she was thinking.

When he turned his attention to the other wrist, his gaze was drawn to where his hand had circled the tiny limb. Already bruises were forming to join the vicious welts marring her pale skin. He cursed his lack of control and the beast within that urged him to lose it. He bit back an oath, angry with himself for causing injury to her not once, but twice, and she'd been in his possession for less than a day.

"So, what's your name?" the maid asked, her voice soft, gentle.

After tying off the last bandage, Baelin stood and stepped away from her, lest he be tempted to lay his hands on her again.

"I was once called Baelin of Gosforth." The dancing flames held his attention as memories of the life he once had drifted out of reach as surely as the rising smoke disappeared into the darkness high overhead. "Now I am only called Dragon. Beast. Devil."

"How about if I just call you Baelin?"

"That would please me greatly."

Setting her wine aside, she rose and held her hand out to him. "It's a pleasure to meet you, Baelin of Gosforth. I'm Jill of Richmond."

He stared at her outstretched hand, surprised she would offer it to him when it was no longer necessary to suffer his touch. He took her delicate fingers in his and bowed over them.

"I am honored, Lady Jill."

She smiled as he straightened. "Wow, you don't see that much any-more."

"See what, my lady?"

"Never mind." She resumed her seat and picked up her wine. "So, how about telling me exactly what the heck is going on around here?"

Baelin tensed. How much to tell her? For the moment, she seemed calm. Dare he risk upsetting her again? The truth was more than most of the maids could grasp.

"Perhaps you should rest and I will explain all to you in the morn."

"No." She sent a stern look his way. "I think I'd like to hear it now. As you can tell, I have nothing better to do at the moment."

"Very well." Baelin went to sit on the opposite side of the fire before beginning his tale. "When I was a young knight, I was cursed by the Dark Witch."

Lady Jill blinked twice, then shook her head. "Wait. A witch? As in the spell-casting, broomstick-riding variety?"

"She has servants to sweep her hall, but aye, she is a sorceress, with the gift of spells."

"O-kaayyy."

"Her warriors captured me in battle and when I refused to serve her, she placed a curse upon me, turning me into the very creature I hunted."

"And I'm guessing that would be dragons?"

Baelin nodded. "The Dark Witch holds sway over them, using the winged beasts against mortal men."

Lady Jill looked uneasy. "And are you under this witch's 'sway' now?"

"Nay, she only has power over the dragon within me when I am within her realm."

Her gaze darted to the wings folded against his back. "But you're still part dragon."

"'Tis true in human form I retain some of the dragon's power, but she has no control over me here."

"Uh huh." She fingered the hammered design on the side of her goblet. Baelin sat silent, waiting for the questions he knew would come. "So how long have you been this way?"

"Two hundred and sixteen years."

"Amazing." She made a clucking sound with her tongue. "You don't look a day over thirty-five."

"I only appear that way. In truth, I was born in the year of our Lord, 978."

She held up her hand. "Hold it. Stop the video and hit rewind. Did you say you were born in 978?"

"Aye."

She stared at him for the longest time before speaking. "You're serious. You believe this. Everything you just said, you actually believe it's true." She shook herself as if a sudden chill had swept into the cave. "And I can't believe I'm even having this conversation. It's gotta be the wine going to my head."

She set her half-empty goblet down and stood. "Look, you seem like a nice guy and I'm sure when they get you back on your medication, everything will be fine." She rubbed her forehead. "Maybe I need to be put on heavy meds. This is a warning sign of an impending mental breakdown if I ever saw one."

She began to pace. "There has to be a reasonable, sane explanation for all this. I just have to figure it out."

Lady Jill continued to prattle on, talking, he believed, more to herself than to him. "You know, I've seen some weird stuff in my life. People do strange things to their bodies all the time—full body tattoos, piercings to parts of the human anatomy that should never be pierced. Heck, I saw a guy once who had metal balls implanted under his skin." She waved her hand in his direction. "So I wouldn't put it past someone to have bat wings surgically attached to their back."

She tapped a finger to her chin. "The medieval village...well, I've heard those reenactors can take their parts a little too seriously some-times. That's easily explained." She paused, frowned at him, then began walking again. "I'll admit, the dragon part, that's not so easy to reason away."

Lady Jill stopped abruptly, staring at a shield propped against the cave wall before turning away, her eyes round as goose eggs.

"I know! This is some role-playing theme park where sicko geeks get their kicks living out their Dungeon and Dragon fantasies."

Baelin watched in stunned silence as she covered her mouth with her hand as if to hold back words too incredible to utter.

"Oh my God. What if that crazy saleslady was some kind of white slave trader? I knew it smelled weird in that place. I bet she drugged me and sold me into a warped, medieval sexcapade game." Spinning in a circle, her wild gaze darted from object to object in the cave. "Yes, that has to be it. And the drugs would explain the flying dragon hallucina-tion. It all makes perfect sense in a freaky, twisted sort of way."

Lady Jill finally stopped her frantic movements and fisted her hands on her hips, eyeing him with suspicion. "You're not going to dress up in a chain mail diaper and have me spank you while you call me 'mommy', are you?"

He'd never been so confused in his life. The woman chattered so fast, it was almost as if she spoke a foreign tongue. All he could do was shake his head and pray it was the response she wanted.

"Thank God." She sighed, her shoulders sagging in relief. Then the walking started again. "I wish I could just go back to before all this insanity happened. I wish I'd never stepped foot in that strange vintage clothing store and I wish I'd never met that kooky munchkin lady with her stupid dragon tapestry."

Baelin stiffened, instantly alert to the one sensible thing in all her ramblings. "What is this dragon tapestry you speak of?"

"What?" She stopped, as if surprised he was still listening to her. "Oh, it was some ratty piece of cloth with woven pictures all over it. The saleslady said it was a thousand years old, but I didn't believe her for a minute. It was probably booby-trapped with chloroform or something. Now that I think about it, it was right after she unrolled it to the dragon part that I started feeling strange…"

Baelin left the odd woman to mutter to herself. He walked to the far wall and reached into a dark crevice in the rock formation. When his fingers brushed the treasure hidden within, the familiar emotions of anger and bitterness, sorrow and hope resurfaced as they always did.

Returning to the fireside, he unwrapped the object he'd spent the last 216 years guarding with his life.

Lady Jill stopped talking and stood stone still, all color draining from her face.

"Oh, my God. That's it! That's the tapestry!"

Surprised at her claim, Baelin clutched the edges of the tapestry, threatening to rip the woven cloth in his white-knuckled grip.

"Are you certain?"

"Oh, I've never been more sure of anything in my life." She eyed the object that had controlled his fate for over two centuries, her breathing rapid and shallow.

"That's the damn thing that brought me here."

CHAPTER FIVE

Jill's world tunneled in on the tapestry cradled in Baelin's hands.

She watched him grip it tighter, as if he feared she might try to take it from him.

"You must be mistaken."

"Oh, no. I'd know that damn thing anywhere. It's permanently imprinted on my brain." A sickening feeling churned in the pit of her belly, then crept its way up her throat until it threatened to choke her. "Where did you get it?"

"The tapestry has always been in my possession. I have guarded it every day of my life as a dragon, for it holds the beginning and the end of my curse."

Jill searched her memory, trying to recall the details of the incredible story he'd told her only moments ago. Chills prickled her skin and her breath came in short, desperate gasps. She dreaded asking the question *rat-a-tat-tatting* in her mind like the drum roll before an execution, but she had to know.

"What year is it?"

"'Tis the year of our Lord, 1214."

"Twelve...?" She swayed as she shook her head in denial. "No. No. *Noooo.*"

The walls of the cave closed in on her. She stumbled in a circle, desperate to find anything that would snap her back to reality. But everything she saw—a shield, a sword, even the gown she wore—

confirmed exactly *where* and *when* she was. She covered her face with her hands, trying to block the objects from her vision, but they remained in her mind's eye, irrefutable evidence of an inconceivable truth.

"This isn't real. This cannot be happening." She staggered toward the mouth of the cave, desperate for fresh air before she passed out. But before she could gain the entrance, a strong arm wrapped around her waist, jerking her back against a rock-hard chest.

"You cannot leave."

Jill struggled against his powerful grip as the acidic taste of bile rose in the back of her throat. "I can't breathe and if you don't let me go, I might heave what little I have in my stomach all over you."

A long moment passed, then the grip on her waist eased. "I will take you."

With his arm still around her, Jill stumbled out onto the ledge and managed to sit before her legs buckled from under her. She dropped her head between her knees and drew in large gulps of air. When she was reasonably sure she wasn't going to faint or vomit or both, she raised her head and looked out over the valley illuminated by the full moon far below.

No city lights glowed in the distance. No headlights passed by on a road below. No beacon blinked atop a cell tower warning planes not to fly too close. Just the unending darkness of an empty, desolate landscape, devoid of even a twinkle of electric-powered light from the twenty-first century.

Somehow—though logic and common sense dictated otherwise—she had traveled back in time. To the freakin' Middle Ages of all places! How was that even possible?

She glanced to where Baelin's steely fingers still circled her arm. "You can let go now. I'm not going anywhere."

"'Tis dangerous." His grip relaxed, but he did not release her. "I do not wish you to…fall."

"I'm fine. Obviously, there's nowhere for me to go." She stared into his dark eyes as he squatted beside her, his shadowed face only inches from her own and way too close for her peace of mind. "What do you think I'm going to do? Jump?"

"It has happened before."

"*What?*" She wasn't sure she'd heard him correctly.

"One of the maids…" He glanced away, a muscle twitching in his jaw. "She preferred death to remaining here with me."

Jill peered over the ledge into the dark nothingness far below. Her stomach flipped just imagining such a fall. "You mean she…?"

"Aye. I was not swift enough to stop her." He turned his attention back to her. "Since then I have become much more vigilant in guarding my…guests."

She tried to swallow past the lump in her throat. There was more than concern for her safety in his eyes. They revealed a hurt that ran soul deep at having someone kill themselves rather than stay with him.

"Well, you don't have to worry about me. I kind of like the idea of staying alive."

Those dark eyes bored into hers, searching for something. Pity? Compassion? Understanding? Long moments passed and then finally, with obvious reluctance, he released her and stood. But he did not move far from her side.

Able to breathe once again, Jill hugged her knees tight to her chest. She couldn't let herself feel sorry for the guy. He might be just as demented as those crazy villagers were. For all she knew, he'd tossed the girl off the ledge himself.

But somehow, she knew he was telling the truth. Jill groaned, confused and upset by the conflicting thoughts ping-ponging back and forth in her mind.

"Are you still unwell?" Baelin asked softly behind her.

"Oh, I'm just peachy. When I woke up this morning, it was the twenty-first century and my biggest problem was finding a birthday present for my niece. In the past twenty-four hours, I've somehow been teleported back to the Dark Ages, experienced the strip search from hell, been hog-tied to a stake, and sacrificed to a fire breathing dragon. Can it get any better?"

Jill dropped her head on her raised knees, wanting desperately to cry but not having the energy to do so. None of this was making any sense and yet how else could she explain everything that had happened.

"Forgive me, my lady, but did you say you are from the twenty-first century?"

She sighed heavily, trapping her warm, moist air breath in the folds of her gown. "I was this morning."

"'Tis not possible. To say you are from the future...'tis madness you speak of."

Her head snapped up and she gaped at his disbelieving face. *He* thought *she* was the crazy one?

Jill stood, not liking the way he looked down at her, as if she was some loony mental patient. Now that she was starting to accept the possibility of what happened to her, she was mad. Angry mad. Someone was responsible for this mess and since the lizard king was the only one nearby, he got the bulk of the blame.

"*You* don't believe *me?* This from a man who tells me the queen of bitchy witches put a curse on him? The same person who flew me around in the air as a dragon belching fire though his nose and then morphed into a naked man in front me? Please, tell me exactly what makes my story any more unbelievable than yours, hmmm?"

She tapped her foot, waiting for his answer. He didn't say a word in his defense but uncertainty clouded his eyes.

"Let me see that." She reached for the tapestry, but Baelin pulled back, shielding it as if it were his child instead of a frayed piece of fabric. "Take it easy, I'm not going to hurt it. I just want to look at it."

"I never allow others to touch it."

"Oh, for Heaven's sake, I'll give it right back." When he continued to hesitate, Jill huffed and held up her little finger. "Pinky swear."

Well, that certainly brought a confused look to his handsome face. Guess that wasn't a common saying in the thirteenth century. "Please?"

Baelin finally handed the tapestry to her, though the rigid set of his body told her he'd rather do otherwise.

She carried it back near the firelight so she could examine it more closely. She studied the intricate detail of the weaving, so very familiar to her even though she'd only had a few moments to examine it in the shop. She didn't know how, but deep down in her soul she knew that somehow this tapestry had brought her here.

Jill closed her eyes and hugged the cloth to her chest, wishing with all her heart it would send her back where she came from. She even clicked her heels together three times and chanted "There's no place like home" for good measure. But when she opened her eyes, she was still in the cave with the king of the dragon people staring back at her as if she'd sprouted horns.

She plopped down on the pile of furs, feeling so lost and alone, terrified she was losing her mind. Baelin sat near her, his intense gaze locked on her face.

"You have seen this tapestry, in your time?"

She cocked a brow at him. Did he believe her now? Maybe. Or maybe he was humoring the crazy lady who sees fire-breathing dragons and babbles about time-travel. At this point, she didn't care what he thought of her. She just wanted to go home.

"When did you last see it?" he persisted.

"Today."

"'Tis not possible. It was with me, here in the cave, as it has been for 216 years."

"Stop telling me what is possible or not. I know without a doubt that I saw this in a vintage clothing shop in Carytown this morning. And judging by the ratty look of it, it'd been there for quite a while."

She watched as Baelin turned his attention to the fire, confusion creasing his brow. "But how can that be?"

"I don't know. None of this makes sense. All I can tell you is that, um, twelve, carry the one..." Damn, she sucked at math in her head. "Eight hundred and some years from now, this tapestry is for sale in a shop in Richmond, Virginia."

"You are certain it was the same one?"

"Positive. I mean, it wasn't in as good a condition as it is now, but it had the same dragon, the same knight, the same girl with long, blonde hair."

Baelin shook his head. "But you are mistaken. The maiden in the tapestry does not have yellow hair. She never has."

"What are you talking about? Of course she does." She held the tapestry up to the firelight to show him. "Look right here..."

Jill felt as if someone had thrown a bucket of cold water on her.

There was a girl in the weaving, just like there'd been in the little shop. Only the image had changed. Her hair was now shorter, wavy and light brown in color.

"I don't understand. That's not right." Jill shook her head and examined the tapestry again, trying to recall the details. "Everything's the same except the girl. She had blonde hair. I remember it fell from her shoulders all the way down to her knees. Of course, the last time I saw this thing, it was unraveling along the edges. The girl even has a face now, which she didn't have before."

Baelin snatched the tapestry back and his tan skin paled in the glow of the firelight.

"'Tis not possible. I have guarded this tapestry for over two centuries and in all that time the weave of the maid has never been complete, never shown her likeness." He paused, his voice raspy and low. "Until now. Now, the maiden has a face."

He turned his full attention on her. "And she looks like you."

As the first rays of dawn broke outside the cave, Baelin watched the woman sleep, curled deep in the furs. At least he thought she slept now. She'd fainted when faced with her own image in the tapestry and not woken since. He could hardly fault her for it. He'd nearly swooned himself when he saw how the weaving had changed.

He rubbed his thumb over the woven face of the maid and tried to calm the racing of his dragon heart. In over two centuries, the image of the maiden had never been complete and now it was. Was it a sign? Could this strange woman lying near him possibly be the one to break the curse? After so long, he was afraid to hope.

And her story of how she came from the future still confounded him. How was it possible? She said that where she came from, people did not believe in dragons and yet he himself was proof they existed.

Perhaps in her world without dragons, people could travel through time.

Lady Jill stirred and mumbled something about a mannequin and not wanting any tea. She jolted up, glancing around the cave with wild, startled eyes before they came to rest on him.

"Damn. I'm still here."

Baelin winced at her disappointment. "Good morn, my lady."

"If you say so." She dragged a hand through her tousled locks. "It would be a better one if I was waking up in my own bed. In my own apartment. In my own time."

She stood and stretched, the movement pulling the gown tight across her full breasts. Baelin's own breeches grew uncomfortably snug and he quickly looked away.

This maid the villagers had chosen for him was a bit…healthier than the ones who had come before. The gowns he kept for them fit her tighter, outlining every curve of her body—a body he recalled seeing all too much of as she'd stood wet and naked in the firelight.

She rubbed her arms to chase away the constant chill he had grown accustomed to over the years. He almost laughed. At the moment, icicles could be hanging from the cavern's ceiling and he would still think it too hot with her so near.

As she walked to the mouth of the cave, he had to restrain himself from jumping up to snatch her back as he'd done the night before. If they were going to get on together until the next full moon, he must learn to trust her. After all, she wasn't like the one who chose to take her own life rather than suffer his presence. Come to think of it, Lady Jill wasn't like any of the others with her strange manner of speech and odd ways.

His tension eased when she stopped at the opening and made no move to venture further out onto the ledge. Instead, she leaned her shoulder against the rock wall with a heavy sigh.

"Looks like there's nothing out there in the light of day either."

"What is it you search for?"

"Oh, I don't know. A car. A plane. A twenty-story skyscraper. Any hint the modern world might still be out there somewhere."

Baelin went to retrieve some food, hoping it would make her feel more at ease in her newfound surroundings. "Are you hungry? I obtained fresh supplies from the village in the valley while you slept. There is bread, and—"

"There's a village nearby?" She craned her head to peer once more out the entrance. "Where?"

"'Tis not far." He stood still, the knife in his hand poised over the wedge of cheese he was about to slice. "Do you wish to go there?"

His back to her, he stared at the platter before him, waiting for the inevitable plea sure to come. Instead, he heard her snort or chuckle—he wasn't sure which.

"Not if it's anything like the last village I ended up in. After the rude welcome wagon greeting I received there, it would suit me just fine to avoid a place like that again."

Surprised and a bit confused by her easy acquiescence after her tirade the night before, he resumed the preparation of her meal. All the maids before were always eager to return to their homes. They begged, pleaded, and cried for days for him to release them. This one seemed content, at least for the moment, to stay.

Baelin heard her shift at the cave's entrance and glanced over to find her scrutinizing him with narrowed eyes.

"Wait a minute. When I got here, the people treated me like I was an alien from another planet and offered me up to the local dragon on a silver platter. How did you manage to walk around a village unnoticed with giant bat wings sticking out of your back?"

He relaxed. This was a question he could answer. "'Tis simple. Allow me to show you."

He retrieved the cloak he'd tossed aside earlier. Folding his wings, he swept the heavy garment over his shoulders and clasped it in place at his throat.

Astonishment registered on her face, but his own shock surpassed it when she walked up to him and ran her hand down the dark wool from shoulder to hip. He held himself perfectly still, straining to feel the slight touch through thick folds of cloak and layers of clothing. Perhaps he felt it. Perhaps he only imagined it. Either way, it was bliss to know another's touch after all this time. As he watched her expressive face, he realized she had no idea of her effect on him.

"Wow. They fold flat against your back, just like a bird's. And with your cape dyed the same color as your wings, they practically disappear underneath it. I can hardly tell they're there. Great illusion. David Copperfield would definitely be impressed."

Baelin knew a moment's pride that she—and whoever this David of Copperfield might be—approved. All too soon, her attention was drawn away from him and to the food he'd arranged on the platter nearby.

"Oh, thank God. I'm so hungry, it feels like my stomach is touching my spine."

"Then by all means, my lady, break your fast."

She snatched a small loaf of dark bread and took a bite, closing her eyes as she moaned. His gaze caressed the delicate line of her throat as she chewed, following the curve of her neckline to where the tempting swell of her breasts threatened to spill out of the snug gown. Baelin stifled a groan, his mouth watering from an all too different type of hunger.

Her eyes flew open, startling him. "Oh, I'm sorry. Did you want some?" She held out the bread to him.

"Nay. I broke my fast earlier while you slept." He coughed into his fist and backed away, lest the dragon in him grab her and attempt to sample more than she what offered. "I am pleased the bread is to your liking."

"It's a little grainy, but good. Of course, as hungry as I am, it could be made of sawdust and I'd still think it tasted like a buttery croissant."

She picked up the platter of food and walked over to sit by the dying fire. She broke off a piece of the cheese and was about to pop it into her mouth when she stopped and turned those large, inquisitive eyes on him again.

"So, are you going to clue me in on the specifics of this curse thing and exactly what it has to do with me or not?"

Chapter Six

How much do I tell her?

Baelin didn't want to make the mistake of frightening her, as he had done with the others. If he'd learned one thing in all his years of taking the sacrificial maidens, it was that women's sensibilities were delicate. It was probably best not to overwhelm her with too much at first.

He walked over and joined her by the dwindling fire. "As a young knight, I was cursed by the Dark Witch to live as a dragon eleven months out of each year."

"Right. I remember that much."

"The curse also requires that each year, on the day of the first full moon of summer, a maiden from the village be offered as a sacrifice to the dragon."

Lady Jill held up her thumb and forefinger, leaving a tiny gap in between them. "Um, we might already have a teensy, weensy problem there."

"What is it?"

"I'm not actually from the village."

"What?" Baelin stood as he felt the first flames of anger churn in his belly.

"Yep. Sorry, but it looks like they pulled the old bait-and-switch with you, buddy."

"I do not understand."

"Like I told you last night, I'm not from around here. I'm not even from this century." Lady Jill sighed. "I don't know how it happened or why, but somehow I traveled through time and landed in the village. Those people were all set to give you another girl but—lucky me—when I fell in their laps they decided to use yours truly instead."

"How dare they?" He stiffened as rage and betrayal tore through him at their deceit. "For over two hundred years, they have offered up a maiden with the understanding that the dragon would leave them in peace. In return, I have kept them safe, allowing no harm to befall their people from outside attack or oppression. It is the way it has always been. They know this!"

He stalked to the mouth of the cave, his fists clenched and his fury rising to dangerous levels—levels he might soon be unable to control.

"Did they not think I would find out?" he growled, the sound more animal than human. "Do they not realize with one breath I can burn all their huts to the ground and set their fields ablaze before they have even risen from their beds?" He spread his wings, the dragon blood in his veins demanding he take to the sky.

Lady Jill came up behind him and stopped him with little more than a hand on his arm.

"Easy there, dragon dude. Calm down and let's talk about this. Don't go and do something you might regret later."

He looked at her pale face and saw her fear, of him and of the beast he kept barely contained. And yet here she stood, prepared to defend the very people who'd shown her no mercy and thought nothing of offering her as a sacrifice to the dragon.

His anger subsided at her gentle persuasion, if only a little. "To break the curse requires a maiden from the village of my birth. If you are not from Gosforth, then it will not work."

"Maybe. Then again, maybe not. While—technically—I'm not from the village, I was, well, there for a little while. Plus who knows, maybe some great, great, great, grandmother of mine was born in the village. It's entirely possible, if you trace my family tree back far enough. So if we go by the Kevin Bacon six degrees of separation theory, I might qualify."

Baelin tried to follow her odd reasoning. If he understood her rambling words, then there might still be hope. After all, the tapestry had changed after she came and that had never happened with any of the others. It had to be a sign.

He willed the tension in his body to ease and stepped back into the cave. Behind him, he heard Lady Jill's heavy sigh of relief. He cursed himself, knowing he needed to maintain better control over his dragon impulses or he would fail them both.

She walked past him and resumed her seat by the fire, eating in silence until he joined her. She considered him as she took a sip of wine from her cup.

"Okay, so let's figure this thing out. You said a girl from the village is required to break this curse of yours."

"Aye."

"So, since I happen to be the maiden by default, what exactly do I have to do to break the curse and return you to Normal-ville?"

"You must pass three challenges before the rise of the next full moon to free me."

"I see. And these challenges are?"

"That I do not know."

She raised her brow at him. "You don't know what they are? That makes it a little difficult, doesn't it?"

"I only know they involve the knightly virtues."

"What are the knightly virtues?"

"Honor, courage, bravery, just—"

"Whoa." Lady Jill held up her hand. "You mean the maid—I—have to do something knight-worthy to break the curse?"

"Aye."

She shook her head and chuckled. "Well, I certainly hope I'm not expected to go out and win a joust or rescue a damsel in distress because then we're going to be in big trouble. I don't think I have the job skills for something like that."

"I pray it will not require anything so trying on your part."

Jill took a bite of bread and chewed thoughtfully as she gazed into the dying fire. She was silent for so long, it startled him when she spoke again.

"So I take it since you're still the lizard king, none of the others have succeeded in breaking this curse of yours."

"Nay."

She frowned. "Did any of them ever try?"

"Only one or two. Most hid in fear in the back of the cave, not venturing out until their time with me was over."

"And the ones who did?"

"Obviously they failed."

He watched her visibly swallow. "Did they ever come close?"

For a brief instant, Baelin considered not telling her the truth. What if, in doing so, she changed her mind? But his honor would not allow him to deceive her.

"Nay. None have ever been able to pass even one of the tests."

"Well, that doesn't bode well for my chances, now does it?" she sighed. "So what happens if the challenges are not met?"

"If the curse is not broken, I return to my dragon form with the rise of the next full moon."

"I see. And what happens to the girls?"

"I release them."

She picked up a bowl of pottage and sniffed it. She made an odd face and set it back on the platter. "At least it's good to know you don't gobble them up for dinner when they fail your tests."

Baelin flinched as if she'd struck him. Did she actually think he would eat the maidens? If the possibility crossed her mind, then she must truly believe him more beast than man.

"I allow no harm to befall the maidens while they are under my protection," he replied through gritted teeth. "The challenges are not of my making. If it were within my power, I would not involve another to break the curse."

"But you do involve them. You kidnap innocent women and force them to come here against their will. Not very chivalrous, if you ask me."

He looked away, shamed by the truth in her words. "They are rewarded well for their time spent with me. When I release them, I give them enough gold to live without want for the rest of their days."

"Gee, thirty days in a damp cave with komodo man in exchange for a lifetime of luxury. That actually doesn't sound like such a bad deal." Lady Jill cast a pitying glance his way. "Well, for the girls, anyway."

"Perhaps." He sighed, knowing he had to tell her the whole truth. "But for some, the wealth they receive is not enough for all that they lose."

"What do you mean?"

"Once the maidens are sacrificed to me, they can never return to the village. To do so would be their death."

Her brow puckered. "Why?"

"After living in the company of the beast, they are deemed soiled." He poked the hot embers with a stick before tossing it into the flames. "The maiden would be burned at the stake for bringing back the evil of the dragon with them."

Her wide eyes followed the dancing sparks as they rose above the fire, only to extinguish and fade. "Oh, my God. That's horrible."

"'Twas a mistake made only once. Since then, the maidens have heeded my advice, taken their coin and fled, never to return."

"Can't say I blame them."

Lady Jill wrapped her arms around her knees and stared into the fire. What thoughts occupied her mind, he could not tell. He waited in silence, anticipating the moment she would refuse him as all the others had before her.

She stood abruptly and rubbed her hands together. "Okay, so let's get started."

He spoke softly, not quite certain he'd heard her correctly. "You intend to aid me?"

"I don't seem to have much choice, do I?"

"There are always choices, at least for most."

"Well, that doesn't seem to be true for me at the moment. No offense, but if I had a choice, I'd rather be surrounded by a dozen sugared-up, shrieking six-year-old girls at a Chuck E Cheese birthday party instead of where I am right now. But since I appear to be an unwilling star in this real live Excalibur, I figure I'm going to have to play my part out to the end."

He watched her glance around the cave, as if seeing it for the first time. When she shook her head and sighed, he wondered if she'd changed her mind. Yet, when her gaze returned to him, it was one of resolved determination.

"I don't understand the hows or whys of it, but for some reason, my fate seems to be tied to this curse just as much as yours is, otherwise I wouldn't be standing here right now. And if I'm guessing right, breaking the curse is somehow the key to getting me back to my time. So that means until we figure this thing out, consider me your new best friend."

Friend.

Something strange turned in the dragon heart beating within his chest. It had been so long since someone had called themselves such. All friends he'd known from his mortal life before were long dead. Dare he hope she might grow to care for him enough to consider him a true friend? Or perhaps, in time, something even more?

"Okay, so what's the plan?"

Her simple question caught him off guard. "The plan?"

"Yes, the plan."

Baelin didn't know what to say. None of the maids had ever wanted to help him. The two who tried had been reluctant at best. With the others, he never progressed much farther than alleviating their fears enough to allow them to speak a word or two to him from the shadows.

"Well?" Lady Jill prodded, indicating with a wave of her hand for him to continue. "You've had over two hundred years to think about this. How do we find out what the challenges are?"

"We wait and when the challenges present themselves, I will aid you to overcome them."

She stared at him in silence before she clucked her tongue and walked to the chest containing the maiden's clothing. "Right. How's this for Plan B? Let's get packed up and go."

"Go?"

"As in get out of this cave and go find these challenges." The hinges on the chest creaked as she lifted the lid. "The sooner we get this over with, the sooner I can get back home. And since you've chosen to live in a hole a mile up a sheer cliff, I don't think whatever tests I'm supposed to face are going to come knocking at your door. Logic tells me we're going to have to go out there and find them and that means leaving the cave."

"Leave the cave?"

She stopped pulling gowns from the chest and rested her hands on her hips as she glanced about the cavern. "There seems to be an echo in here." She ended her inspection of the cave ceiling and focused her gaze back on him. "Yes, we leave. Is there a problem?"

Baelin glanced to the mouth of the cave and the dawning horizon beyond it, his pulse quickening. He'd never left except for quick excursions to replenish supplies or to retrieve the maidens. This was his home—his lair—and every dragon impulse in him demanded he stay to protect it.

Taking his silence for acquiescence, Lady Jill resumed her search through the chest. "So, seeing as we'll probably be gone for a while, we need to pack some supplies. Warm clothes, food. Oh, and some of that gold you have stashed away wouldn't be a bad idea to take along, either."

His gold? Baelin had to restrain the urge to snatch up his treasure and hide it from her. He cursed the greedy nature of the dragon that made him hoard his riches.

She turned from her task of sorting the gowns into piles at her feet. Her expression was one of innocent expectation, not that of greedy desire to steal his gold.

"Do you have any backpacks around here?"

"Backpacks?"

"Here we go with the echoing again," she muttered. "Yeah, you know, something to carry this stuff in. If it takes us the whole month to find these challenges, we're going to need to take along a lot of supplies." Glancing behind the chest, she spotted a large sack. "Aha! This should do."

She dragged it out and upended it, dumping pewter plates and silver goblets on the cave floor. Baelin cringed as the clanging cacophony rang against the stone walls, adding to the pounding in his head. Oblivious to his discomfort and apparently having no regard for his treasures, she began stuffing the clothing she deemed acceptable into the now empty sack.

"I do not believe 'tis wise to leave the cave. What if the challenges are meant to happen here?"

Lady Jill snorted. "I don't think it works that way. Usually people have to take a hand in their own fate."

"What if you are wrong?"

She stopped packing and looked at him. "What if I'm right? Do you really want to waste the thirty days you have to be human hiding in this dark, dreary cave?"

"I do not hide."

"Then what's the problem?"

He felt the blood pound in his ears. How could he explain it to her when he didn't truly understand it himself? Each year, the pull of the dragon became more powerful than the last. As century blurred into century, the beast's urges became harder to resist, sometimes to the point where he felt more dragon than man, even in his human form.

Lady Jill straightened, her brow creased in question. "Baelin, why are you so against the idea of leaving?"

"I have never left the cave for long periods of time. It has never seemed necessary." When she continued to stare at him, he found himself unable to hold her gaze. "This is my home," he added, his voice barely above a whisper. "This is all I have left."

"Are you worried someone might steal your things?" Her words were spoken with understanding, not the condemnation he expected.

Guilt for giving into the dragon—for not having the strength to deny the beast's nature, if even for one moment—nearly choked him. Shame kept him from answering her.

"Look, I may have only gotten a brief glimpse when we first landed here, but to my recollection, this cave is three thousand feet up a sheer, rock wall. Correct me if I'm wrong, but I don't believe rappelling is a big pastime in the Middle Ages. The only people who are insane enough to even consider scaling a vertical cliff like this one won't be born for centuries. I think your treasure will be safe here until you get back."

He knew she was right, but that didn't make leaving any easier. He looked at her standing there, this strange maid determined to go out and face a world unknown to her, ready to fight for herself and for him. If she could do it, then so could he. He beat down the beast within, refusing to allow the dragon to rule over him any longer.

"Very well. Pack only what is necessary. You will want your satchel to be no heaver than need be."

She laughed. "Oh, don't worry. Without the usual necessities of makeup and a blow dryer, my bag will be light as a feather."

Less than an hour later, two satchels sat ready at the cave entrance. Baelin stood dressed in his best mail with his sword strapped to his side and his shield slung over his back, secured between his dragon wings. He glanced back once more into the darkened cave, the only home he'd know for over two hundred years.

Lady Jill touched his shoulder. "Don't worry. With any luck, you'll be back before you know it, hopefully as a full-blooded man instead of a dragon." Her hand brushed down the long cloak covering his folded dragon wings before she stepped away. "Of course, without your wings, you may have a harder time getting back up here."

She picked up her satchel and peered over the ledge. "Speaking of which, how the heck do we get down?"

For the first time since she suggested they leave the cave, excitement and anticipation pumped through his veins instead of gut-churning apprehension. Baelin grinned wickedly at her, and then swept her up in his arms.

"We fly."

ChAPTER SEVEN

"Ow!"

Jill sat down and pulled yet another rock out of what was supposed to pass for shoes in this godforsaken place. For Pete's sake, they didn't even come in a left and a right. And forget about arch support. She was going to be paying for it big time later on.

"It would be much easier to fly."

"No! I'll keep my feet safely planted on terra firma, thank you very much. If people were meant to fly, they'd have wings."

Baelin cleared his throat and she glanced at the barely discernible twin lumps under his cloak. "Okay, so most normal people. You fly. I'll catch up to you later."

"That would be unwise. 'Tis unsafe for a woman to travel alone."

"I'm a big girl. I can take care of myself." She stood and dusted off the back of her gown. "Besides, you can't carry me and all the stuff we're lugging along at the same time."

In addition to the over-stuffed satchels of clothing and food they each carried, Baelin had deemed it necessary to bring along a small arsenal of various-sized swords and daggers, a crossbow and arrows, plus a shield the size of a satellite dish. It had taken him three air-borne trips back and forth to the cave to cart it all down after he'd deposited her safely on the ground—shaken, but not stirred—and now she was forced to carry half of it like a pack mule.

"Don't you have a horse we could be riding to make this trip a little easier?"

He stared out over the field to some point far in the distance. "Nay."

"You're kidding. I thought all knights were supposed to have a big, white charger to go galloping around the countryside on, saving damsels in distress."

He began walking again, leaving her to follow, but not before she saw a dark shadow pass over his face.

"What? What did I say? I may be a little rusty on my history lessons, but isn't riding a horse the preferred mode of transportation in this century?"

"A horse is not possible. If you refuse to fly, we must walk."

"Why? If it's because you think I can't ride one, you're wrong. I spent two weeks every summer at horse camp when I was a kid."

"We cannot ride."

Jill had to do double-time to keep up with his long strides. When she caught up to him again, she chuckled. "Don't tell me the big, brave knight is afraid of horses?"

"I do not fear horses." His voice was muffled, as if he spoke the words through clenched teeth.

She made a mental note not to joke with him anymore. Apparently, he'd left his sense of humor back at the bat cave. That is, if he had one to begin with, which she was seriously beginning to doubt.

"Then what is it?"

"Horses fear me."

"Oh, come on. Horses are afraid of you? Get real. You must be imagining it."

Baelin stopped so suddenly, she nearly ran into him. He turned and glared at her. "Horses fear me because as a dragon I eat them."

"You do?"

Was he the one trying to be funny now? Was this some strange kind of medieval humor?

"I do. I have also been known to consume deer, cattle, sheep, and the occasional stray dog or two when I was particularly hungry."

Nope, he wasn't joking. His expression was as serious as they come.

"Even in my human form, animals can sense the predator in me. All creatures can. And they fear me for it."

She shivered at the golden blaze that flared in his eyes. She was surprised she hadn't noticed it before, but this close his eyes resembled those of a snake or crocodile, the pupil a dark slit against an amber iris. Just as quickly, the glow faded and his eyes returned to a normal shade of brown, the pupil a perfect black circle within them. Shaking herself mentally, she told herself it must've been a trick of the light.

"Oh. Well, I guess that explains it." She tried to swallow around the lump wedged in her throat. "So we'll walk. Walking is good."

The tension left his face, and then he surprised her with a cocky smirk. "Flying would be faster."

"No!"

He nodded to her in that annoyingly patronizing way of his. "As my lady wishes."

Jill was the one to walk ahead this time, but he was soon by her side, the thump of his booted feet drumming out a steady rhythm.

"Look, I'm sorry, but I don't like flying in the twenty-first century either, and compared to the dragon method, that's relatively safe considering you're strapped inside a metal tube with explosive fuel tanks hurtling you through the sky. With you, it's like hanging onto the wing of a barnstormer with no parachute as a backup if you drop me. You'll have to humor me—I've never been the daredevil type."

"Dare devil? What sort of demon is that?"

Jill shook her head. It never ceased to amaze her how words so common to her could have such a different meaning to Baelin. She felt like she was becoming a walking dictionary.

"It's not a real demon. It means someone who's adventurous, willing to take dangerous, death-defying risks with their life on a daily basis, which definitely doesn't describe me."

"You are brave enough to walk with a dragon."

She glanced at his profile. In another time and place, she might consider him hot if she weren't constantly aware of the dragon part of him hidden beneath his cloak. "You're not so bad, in a warped fairy tale kind of way."

He turned a raised brow at her. "Was that intended to be a compliment?"

"It was." She grinned.

When he smiled back, her stomach did an odd flip.

Whoa. Definitely hot.

Jill turned her attention to the vast, open hills ahead. She needed to get her mind off handsome dragon men and onto something safer. But with his tall, broad form walking so close to her, it was nearly impossible. His presence surrounded her, the girlish fantasy of a real-life knight in shining armor filling her senses.

"So, that dragon-to-man metamorphosis was pretty impressive last night. Can you shift back and forth whenever you want to?"

"Nay, I can only become human one month out of each year."

"Yeah, you told me. But when you're human, can you turn back into a dragon?"

He looked at her as if she was insane. "Why would I wish to?"

"I don't know." She shrugged. "Maybe just because you can?"

"If you were forced to live eleven months out of every year as a flying lizard, would you wish to waste your time in human form being that which you despise?"

Jill grimaced. Had she really called him that? "When you put it like that, I guess not."

He was silent for a long time before he spoke again. "To answer your question, I cannot take dragon form while I am human any more than I can shift into human form while I am a dragon. I have no choice in the matter."

"I understand." Not really, but she was trying hard to wrap her mind around the reality of the dragon-man walking at her side. "So, since you've been a dragon for over two centuries, how old does that make you?"

Baelin shrugged. "I am not certain. I was cursed when I was in my twentieth year and have lived most of that time since as a dragon."

"You don't look like you're still twenty." Jill studied the lines beginning to form around his eyes, the kind that usually only came with age or smiling a lot. Somehow, she didn't think he smiled very often. "You look like you're more in your mid-thirties or so."

"It only appears that way. Because of the curse, I am only human for one moon's cycle and as such, I age but one month each year."

"Oh, kinda like the dog years thing."

"I do not understand."

"Well, they say a dog ages seven years for every human one. It sounds as if you age one month for every dragon year."

"'Tis possible. I never thought on it over much. The seasons come and go very much the same. After the first century, I stopped counting them."

He said the words so casually and yet it tore her apart to think of him living in that cave, year after year, decade after decade, all alone.

"When you're a dragon, do you still think and feel like a human?"

He looked at her and the toll his isolation had taken on his soul nearly broke her heart.

"Aye."

Jill's throat tightened and she had to look away. She knew then that he hadn't been completely honest with her.

He had counted those years. Each and every one of them.

"We will camp here for the night."

Jill plopped down where she stood and proceeded to tear off her shoes and massage her aching feet. She'd been ready to stop an hour earlier when they first entered the forest, but she'd bit her tongue and didn't complain. She knew if she had, Baelin would only suggest flying again, and she would endure blisters the size of watermelons over medieval hang gliding any day.

Glancing around at the small clearing within a stand of tall birch trees and thick holly bushes, she noted there were more leaves than grass on the ground and not a bed in sight. That didn't matter. She was so tired from walking, she could sleep on a pile of rocks and not notice the difference.

Baelin dropped his satchel and shield beside her, and then he swung the crossbow and quiver of arrows from his back. He drew back the bowstring and cocked it. Looking down the sight, he released the trigger, firing an imaginary arrow at an invisible target.

"What are you doing?"

"I shall attempt to find us fresh game. The supplies from the village will only last so long, and we do not know when or if we shall pass another to procure more. It would be wise to make what food we have last."

Jill halted her foot rub and glanced up at him. "You're going hunting now?"

"Aye, before the light fades."

"What about me?"

"Would you care to accompany me?"

At the mere thought of taking another step, her feet screamed in protest. "Not really."

Baelin nodded, as if he'd anticipated her answer.

"Wait a minute. After all your dire warnings about how dangerous it is for a woman to be traveling alone, you're going to go off and leave me here by myself?"

"You should be safe enough as long as you do not wander off into the forest. I shall not be gone long."

He pulled a wicked-looking dagger from his belt and tossed it to the ground beside her, its sharp blade embedding itself deep in the dirt, while the jewelled hilt glinted in the sunlight filtering through the trees.

"What's that for?"

"In case I am wrong." Baelin looked down at her, his humor fading as wariness narrowed his eyes. "I trust you to remain here until I return."

"Where would I go?"

"You might try escape."

Jill huffed. "Now why would I do that? I told you I would help you."

"Once I am out of sight, you may have a change of heart. I advise you not to attempt it." With that, he turned and walked away.

Stunned by his lack of trust, she watched his broad back blend into the trees until he disappeared.

"Fine," she shouted. "Go off and hunt, Daniel Boone. Leave me alone here to...what? What the heck am I supposed to do while you're out stalking some poor, defenseless animal?"

"A fire would be beneficial," his disembodied voice answered from the forest. "Unless you prefer sitting in the dark and eating your meat raw."

"Ha, ha. Very funny."

The tall trees offered no further comment and suddenly she felt terribly alone in the clearing. The forest probably hid all manner of creatures hunting their own dinner. She'd already met a dragon. There was no telling what else roamed this strange land with an appetite for human flesh.

She jumped, startled by the call of a bird, then took a calming breath as she tried to get a grip on her overactive imagination. Vulnerable was not a feeling that sat well with her. She glanced at the knife sticking out of the dirt. She was more apt to cut herself and bleed to death than be able to use it in self-defense. Mace or pepper spray was definitely more up her alley.

Stop thinking that way, she chided herself. After all, they hadn't seen another human being all day as they traipsed across the countryside. What were the chances someone would come jumping out of the bushes now?

A twig snapped somewhere behind her. Apparently, the chances were high. Jill reached for the dagger. She may not know how to use it but whatever was lurking in the woods didn't know that.

When a snarling wild beast or sex-crazed maniac didn't immediately pounce on her, she let out her breath and tried to relax. *There you go again,* she thought. *Psyching yourself out over nothing. It was probably just a squirrel chewing on a nut.*

Steeling herself, she rose to her feet. She needed to gain control of this situation before she completely lost her mind. So, first things first. She did not want to be sitting here in the dark all night long if, for some reason, Baelin didn't come back.

A fire. She could build a fire, couldn't she?

After gathering several armloads of downed branches without venturing too far into the dark woods, Jill stacked them high and eyed the pile of wood as if staring at it would be enough to catch it on fire. It didn't work.

Okay, so what did people use to start fires these days? Spying Baelin's satchel, Jill knelt to rummage through it. Knowing she wouldn't find a cigarette lighter of any kind, she hoped he had something that could be used to create a spark. Had matches been invented yet? She hoped so.

As she searched around in his belongings, her fingers brushed across the rolled form of the tapestry. She unfurled it in her lap and once again, her image stared back at her. It was hard to believe one piece of embroidered fabric controlled her fate.

Two people's fates, she corrected herself. Baelin needed the answers hidden within the threads as much as she did. But if what he said was true, then that meant he was probably also right about her having to pass those darn challenges. Wonderful. She'd had a hard enough time passing high school algebra. Damn remnant table reject. Jill rolled it up and retied the string around it before shoving it back into the satchel.

Blowing a wayward lock of hair out of her face, she turned her attention to the stacked firewood that should already be giving off heat. Instead, the branches lay on the ground where she dropped them, mocking her with her inability to do something so simple as light a fire.

Gritting her teeth in determination and still fuming in the face of Baelin's distrust, Jill stomped over and knelt by the wood pile.

"Oh, I'll light a fire all right. When Baelin gets his alligator ass back here, I'll have a freakin' bonfire going."

CHAPTER EIGHT

Baelin stepped out of the forest to spy Lady Jill bent over a pile of wood, rubbing two sticks together with furious effort.

"My lady. What, pray tell, are you doing?"

She glared at him, a fine sheen of sweat wetting her brow. "What does it look like? I'm giving myself a pedicure."

She tossed the sticks on the woodpile in disgust and arched her back with a groan, thrusting her breasts against the neckline of her gown. Baelin was forced to bite back his own groan. Would that he could cup those plump mounds in his hands, test their weight in his palms, taste their dusky peaks with his tongue.

To combat his errant thoughts, he tried to turn his attention elsewhere. "Are you having trouble with the fire?"

"You caught me. I flunked out of the Girl Scouts and never got my fire-starter badge."

Ignoring a response he did not even attempt to understand, he stepped up beside her. "If you will stand back, I shall light it for you."

She rose and dusted off the front of her gown. "By all means, knock yourself out."

When he was certain she stood a safe distance away, Baelin drew in a deep breath and spat a ball of fire, instantly igniting the dry kindling.

Lady Jill jumped back, nearly falling over the satchels behind her.

"Holy cow! Remind me not to kiss you. I don't think my tonsils could handle the heat."

Baelin stiffened, any thought of wanting her vanishing in an instant. He needed no further reminder he was no more than a monster to her, though the beast now wore a man's face.

"I shall make every effort to keep my distance."

A betraying flush reddened her cheeks and he knew in that instant she realized the insult of her careless words.

"I'm sorry. I didn't mean—"

"Aye, you did," he cut her off. "You just did not intend to voice the thought aloud. Fear not. You will not suffer unwanted attentions from me for the duration of our journey together."

An awkward silence stood between them, broken only by the crackle of the fire.

Finally, she cleared her throat. "So, did you have any luck hunting?"

Baelin tossed a fat, gray hare on the ground at her feet.

Lady Jill paled and covered her mouth with her hand, her face stricken. "You killed the Easter Bunny."

"You do not care for rabbit?"

"Not when it comes with the fluffy bunny fur and cute wiggly nose still attached." She visibly shivered. "You have just succeeded in murdering one of my childhood illusions."

He clenched his teeth as emotions waged battle inside him. Incredible as it seemed, the woman had managed to both wound and insult him in almost the same breath.

"It appears there is no pleasing my lady this eve."

An unladylike curse escaped her lips as she focused her big, green-flecked eyes on him. "I'm sorry if I offended you about the horse, and the rabbit, and...the other thing." She waved her hands around, unable to utter the last word. But he knew what she meant. Was the idea of kissing him so abhorrent she could not even say it aloud?

He read the sincerity in her face, could hear the contrition in her voice, but it did little to soothe his wounded pride. When he offered no response, she continued on.

"You'll have to bear with me. I'm new to this world of yours. And since we're going to be spending a lot of time together, you'd better get used to the fact that I'm going to make mistakes. Apparently a lot of them where you're concerned."

"Then I consider myself forewarned."

Baelin scooped up the hare and stalked off before he did something he would regret—like strangle the maid with his bare hands.

Jill swatted at the pesky bugs swarming around her face. As the sun went down, they had multiplied by the hundreds. Hearing another high-pitched whine as one made a dive bomb for her neck, she waved her hands in a fruitless effort to keep them at bay.

"Why are these mosquitoes eating me alive and they don't seem to be bothering you one bit?"

"Mosquitoes?"

Baelin glanced up from where he was busy driving two branches into the ground on either side of the fire to serve as a makeshift rotisserie for the recently deceased rabbit. It was the first time they'd spoken in over an hour and Jill was acutely aware she was treading on shaky ground with him. She figured mosquitoes were a safe enough topic to talk about.

"Ah, those are midges."

"I don't care what they're called, they're driving me crazy. What kind of medieval bug repellent are you using?"

He frowned a moment until understanding eased the creases on his brow. "I am not doing anything. They naturally avoid me."

"Let me guess. They can *sense* the predator in you." Jill said it as a joke, trying to lighten the mood between them, but Baelin surprised her by confirming her words.

"Aye, there may be some truth in that."

"What do you mean?"

"Dragon's blood flows through my veins. If I were to bleed, it would burn anything it touched. I can only assume they sense to drink of it would mean their death."

"Really? You mean your blood is like some kind of acid?"

"Aye, if this acid you speak of burns like fire."

"That doesn't sound very healthy for your arteries, but the built-in bug-be-gone is a nifty side affect."

Baelin stilled. "My lady, I would gladly suffer the bite of a thousand vermin every day of my life than to live one more day as a dragon."

Jill could've kicked herself. There she went, saying the wrong thing again. "Right. I guess when you put it like that, the small benefit isn't worth it. Sorry."

She scratched at the dirt with a stick, feeling awkward and irritated with herself. Every time she opened her mouth, she managed to offend him. The difference in their times could explain a lot, but she knew if she stopped to think before she spoke, it would go a long way toward easing some of the tension between them.

She sat quietly as he prepared the rabbit for roasting. Finally, curiosity got the better of her. "So, how did you end up being cursed to be a dragon anyway?"

Baelin nearly dropped the rabbit in the fire as he attempted to balance the skewered carcass between the two stakes.

"I see forthrightness is also one of your...virtues."

Jill snorted. "If that's what you call it. Most people say it's being nosy." When he didn't answer her, she prodded again. "So, dish. Give me the gory details. Inquiring minds want to know."

"'Tis not something I talk about."

Something in his voice caught her attention—a bitterness tinged with regret.

"Is it because you don't like to talk about it or because none of the other girls ever bothered to ask?"

He sat on the opposite side of the fire. She could tell he was thinking, probably remembering, and she was all too aware she'd touched on a painful subject for him.

"They never asked."

"Well, I'm asking." She spoke without demand, offering without saying the words to listen to his story and perhaps, in the telling of it, relieve some of his lonely burden.

He looked away. "I prefer not to remember that time. It was long ago, when I was too young, too proud." He paused for the span of a heartbeat. "Still human."

She was surprised when he returned his gaze to her, those warm, brown eyes filled with an intense pain he didn't bother to hide.

"What does it matter now? I am what I am."

His softly spoken words recalled the hurt in those same eyes when she made the comment about not wanting to kiss him. How could she have been so insensitive? The poor guy had been alone in a cave for two centuries. It's not as if he'd had a lot of opportunities to get any action, and she had to go and say something stupid.

She chose her words carefully, aware this was her chance to bridge the gap between them, to mend the hurt she'd already caused. "It might help me understand you better."

He straightened, his haunted expression transforming to one of puzzlement. "Truly?"

"Yeah." Jill shrugged, trying to give the impression the conversation they were having was as casual as talking about the weather. "Sort of like 'you show me your scars and I'll show you mine'."

She watched him swallow, as if the words fought to come out but he wanted desperately to hold them back. "'Tis not a pretty tale."

"Somehow, I didn't think it would be."

He sat there staring into the fire so long, Jill wondered if he was going to say anymore. Finally, he sighed and rested his arms on his raised knees.

"When I was a lad of about seven years, my father sent me to foster with Amdarch the Black."

"The Black?" The nickname gave Jill visions of a swarthy barbarian overlord who would think nothing of beating a young boy into obedience. "Was he called that because he was mean?"

"Nay." Baelin smiled as some fond memory eased the tension in his face. "He was called The Black because in his youth his hair was dark as night. But by the time I went to foster with him, it had turned more gray than not. He was a good man, wise yet firm, and he taught me well."

"You were so young. Did you miss your family?"

"Aye. 'Twas but four days walk betwixt our lands, so I was able to return home once or twice a year. Besides, his son Osmund was of a like age and we became as brothers."

He paused in his tale to turn the rabbit over the fire so it wouldn't burn.

"When I reached my seventeenth year, we set out on a journey to Egremont to fetch Osmund's intended bride. He and I rode with his father and half of The Black's knights. 'Twas a dark time for England, when the barbarians of the north plagued the land far and wide. We stayed ever vigilant, always on guard against attack. Little did we know there was another danger lurking near. Something more evil and deadly than the Vikings." A dark shadow passed over his face, like a cloud covering the sun. "Something hunting us."

"What?" she asked, although she already suspected the answer.

"Dragons. Three of them. They flew out of the sky like demons from hell. We had heard tales of winged creatures that breathed fire, but 'twas the first time any of us had ever seen them. They swooped down, burning grass, horses and men alike. I watched as half of the Black's men were either consumed by flames or mortally wounded by fang and claw. They attacked while we stood out in the open, defenseless against their power. We did not know how to fight them."

He shifted his gaze back to the fire, staring at it, almost hypnotized by it. Did it remind him of the dragon's fire? she wondered.

"They caught Osmund first. I watched him burn to death before my eyes and I could do naught to save him."

Jill covered her mouth with her hand to stop a sob from escaping. Her throat ached from the effort of holding it inside. She couldn't imagine watching someone she loved die such a horrible, painful death.

"Certain I would be next, I turned to see the beast almost upon me. Determined to fight to the very end, my last thought was to die with honor, with my sword in my hand."

His words recalled the all too recent terror she'd felt when Baelin had chased after her in his dragon form. She couldn't imagine the horror he must have gone through, a boy who was not yet a man, witnessing so much death and then trying to be brave facing his own.

"Somehow as the beast fell upon me, my sword found its mark and ran the creature through its black heart." His voice softened, the words broken. "I was knighted that very day, out there on a charred, bloody moor, by a man who had just lost his only son."

Jill jumped when his golden dragon eyes suddenly turned her way. It was the second time she'd seen them take on that eerie, unnatural glow. Did high emotions trigger the transformation, or was it the dragon inside him rising to the surface?

"I was knighted for slaying a dragon. It was the first of many."

His body tensed and she knew his tale was not over. The worst was yet to come.

"From that day on, we knew how to fight them. How to kill them. The Black and I dedicated our honor, our very lives, to destroying the beasts. Others soon joined us in our fight to rid the land of this winged plague. We called ourselves dragonslayers."

Baelin looked away, shielding his own dragon eyes from her.

"We learned that for centuries upon centuries, the creatures had lived peacefully high in the mountains, only venturing out of their dens to feed. The loss of a cow here or a few sheep there generally went unnoticed. But then the Dark Witch discovered a way to control them, to harness their power, and she began to use them against mortal man."

"So, this Dark Witch, she's not human?"

"Nay. She looks human enough, but she is not. As far as anyone knows, she has existed as long as the dragons have."

He shifted where he sat, but still refused to look at her as he continued his tale. "Our battle was no longer against the dragons alone, but with the Dark Witch as she used them against us. Three years passed. Three long years of hunting these creatures with every waking hour. Then the day came when we faced her army, a thousand warriors strong, with countless dragons under her power in the air. By the end, we were defeated, our entire force destroyed."

She watched as Baelin tensed, could tell by the way he clenched his fist that he was remembering holding his sword, reliving the battle.

"That day, I held Amdarch the Black in my arms as he breathed his last."

He glanced down at his hands, uncurling stiff fingers until the palms lay open. What did he see as he looked at them? Was it his sword, his only defense against the dragons? Or was it the blood of the man he loved like a father, slipping through his fingers as his life ebbed away?

"To this day, I can still smell the stench of charred flesh and boiled blood as it poured in rivers from the lifeless bodies of the men around me. I can still hear the screams of agony from those who had yet to embrace the blessed relief of death. I can still feel the bloody battlefield beneath my feet as I stood surrounded by those dying men, awaiting my own."

Jill shivered, held spellbound like a child listening to ghost stories around the campfire. But she had to remind herself this was no made-up tale meant to frighten small children. It was something he'd lived through. It was what made him who—or rather, what—he was.

"But you didn't die."

"Would that I had. Instead, the warriors captured me and took me before their queen, as a spoil of battle."

"A spoil of battle?"

"A token of their victory. A prize. And once inside her realm, instead of allowing me to die with honor, the Dark Witch offered to spare my life if I would serve her."

"Serve her? How?"

"Since I had managed to defeat so many of her dragons, she wanted me to fight for her, to use my sword in battle against my own people." His nostrils flared and his jaws clenched as he ground his back teeth. "And when I was not fighting, she wanted to use me…for other things."

Jill sucked in a breath. She didn't have to be a rocket scientist to figure out what he meant. Baelin was a handsome man now. She could only imagine what a golden boy he must have been in his youth and what *other things* the witch might want from him.

"What did you do?"

"I refused. But she kept me there, deep in her mountain kingdom. Day and night, she tried to break me to her will until all I longed for was death. But she would not grant me that small mercy and I would not beg for it. Finally, she took the choice away from me. She turned me into the very creature I had hunted. I have been this way ever since."

"But you were human. How could she turn you into a dragon?"

"With her dark magic, she tore my human heart from my breast and replaced it with a dragon's."

"You mean like some kind of medieval heart transplant?"

He gave her a questioning look.

"Never mind. After everything I've seen in the last twenty-four hours, I don't think there's much that can surprise me anymore." Jill paused as an image tickled her memory, of him naked in the firelight of the cave. "Is that how you got that wicked scar on your chest?"

Baelin placed his hand over the spot. She wondered if he could feel through the layers of padding and mail to the dragon heart within, beating against his palm.

"Aye."

"So if the dragon's heart is inside of you, what did she do with yours?"

"She put it in the dragon's breast, where it still beats to this day. Only by breaking the curse can I get it back and return to the man I once was."

The silence of the night surrounded them, broken only by the occasional hiss of the fire as juice from the hare dripped into the flames. Finally, he looked at her. The glowing serpent eyes filled with anger and rage were gone. In their place were deep, soft pools of brown.

A man's eyes.

But they were no less powerful, searing her with their raw pain.

"There you have it, Lady Jill," he spoke softly, his voice barely above a whisper. "I have shown you my scars. What of yours?"

What could she say? Her heart broke for this poor man who had been through so much. His face blurred as her eyes filled with tears. She sat frozen, unable to stop their fall.

"Now that I've seen yours, mine don't seem to run nearly so deep."

ChAPTER NINE

Jill groaned from under her blanket. Her nose felt like an ice cube had frozen on her face and her entire right side was numb from sleeping on the cold, hard ground.

The day before had been fine—warmer than she expected England to be. But once the sun had set, it got downright chilly. Never an outdoorsy type of girl, she wasn't prepared for roughing it like this.

She peeked over at the lump snoozing peacefully on the other side of the dwindling fire, wrapped up in his cloak like a caterpillar in a cocoon. He hadn't budged all night while she froze her butt off. Why didn't the cold to bother him?

Probably because he's a walking furnace.

Jill finally gave up the battle. It was just after dawn and she couldn't go back to sleep. Her back ached and at any moment her bladder was going to explode. She tossed her blankets aside and walked to the edge of the trees, venturing into the woods only far enough for privacy's sake and not far enough to get hopelessly lost.

Without a port-a-john or outhouse in sight, Jill found a suitable spot and went pioneer. After heeding the call of nature, she glanced around for something to use for toilet paper—one of the many modern conveniences she was discovering it was very hard to live without. She eyed various plants with suspicion. It would be just her luck to wipe her butt with some strange variety of medieval poison ivy.

She was almost done when a mail-clad bear came crashing through the underbrush. She screamed before she realized it was Baelin, sword raised and teeth bared.

He came to a skidding halt and slowly lowered the sword, his mouth hanging open like a gaping fish. It was only when his eyes traveled down to where she squatted that Jill realized her gown was still hiked up to her waist, her rear end displayed for all the creatures of the forest to see, included one ogling dragon-knight.

She bolted to her feet and batted her skirt down in a futile attempt to retain what little modesty she had left. Baelin looked away, his gaze darting from tree to tree. Anywhere but at her. He spun around and headed back to camp, only taking a few steps before he turned and retraced them.

"My apologies, Lady Jill. I did not intend to dishonor you in any way. When I awoke and found you gone…"

She cleared her throat in an effort to suppress the chuckle threatening to erupt. If it were possible, Baelin appeared more mortified about catching her in the embarrassing position than she did. He refused to look at her as he sheathed his sword.

"That's okay. No harm, no foul. My *honor* is still intact. After all, it's not like you haven't seen me buck naked before."

She heard him suck in a quick breath and a betraying flush crept up Baelin's neck. *My God, he's blushing!*

"Were your father to find us like this, after spending the night alone together, we would be forced to marry…if he did not geld me first."

"Well, since my father hasn't even been born yet, I think you're safe from a shotgun wedding any time soon," she said as she walked past him and headed back to the clearing.

"I am surprised you are not already wed."

"You and my mother both," she grumbled as they reached the camp and he began packing up their supplies.

Baelin nodded in agreement. "I can understand her unease."

"Excuse me?" Jill stopped in the middle of rolling up her blanket.

He looked as if he wanted to say something but was having a difficult time finding the right words. "You are a bit old to be a maid, are you not?"

"Why you—I'm not—Why does everyone keep saying that?" she

sputtered. "I'm only twenty-nine and where I'm from, that's considered in the prime of life."

Baelin shook his head. "I did not say you were old. I am just surprised you have remained this long without a man."

"Well, now I never said anything about not being with a man."

"What?"

Jill couldn't help but roll her eyes. *Here we go again.* "Like I told them in the village. I'm not a virgin. I haven't been since I was seventeen and lost it to Tommy Henderson in the back of his dad's Lincoln Continental on prom night."

"What do you mean you are not a virgin?" Baelin growled and his eyes did that shifting thing again, turning to a glowing gold. "The sacrifice is supposed to be pure."

Not one to sleep around, Jill's pitiful little black book contained more blank pages than not. But to see Baelin's appalled look, you would think she was the biggest slut in the world.

"Whoa, don't get snippy with me, buddy. It's not my fault. I tried to tell those crazy villagers I wasn't good sacrifice material but the old bat of a midwife lied and told them I was still a virgin—which, by the way, is not nearly as overrated in my time as it seems to be in yours. But, like it or not, you're stuck with me now."

"Then there is no hope. It will not work."

Jill watched his broad shoulders slump. At his desolate expression, she felt some of her pique ease. She had to remind herself this was not the twenty-first century, and people's values were light-years away from her own.

"Look, I don't know what won't work or not, but if it takes breaking this voodoo curse of yours to get the time machine working again, let's get on with it."

"But what is the use? If you are not pure, then you cannot be the one."

Jill couldn't believe she needed to continually defend herself to the man. "Says who? Is it written in the tapestry that the girl has to be a virgin? Is there some rule in the dragon sacrifice handbook against it?"

"I...nay. 'Tis just the way it has always been."

"Then let's review the facts, shall we? When I saw the tapestry in my time, the girl had blonde hair, and now she has brown, like mine." She tugged at a chunk of her own hair for added emphasis. "You said in all the time you've had the tapestry, the girl had no face and now she does—mine. It seems to me some rules are meant to be broken here, or at least revised as we go along. So since I'm the one who won the door prize this time around, apparently my virginity or lack thereof doesn't have much bearing on this curse of yours."

He looked unsure of her argument but she had to give him credit. The big dragon dude didn't completely discount her theory either.

"Baelin, for better or worse, we're in this thing together. Let's just play along and see what happens. After all, what have we got to lose?"

He shook his head as he tossed his satchel over his shoulder and began walking.

"Everything."

Jill felt like they'd been walking for a month. In reality, it'd been a little more than twenty-four hours since they started on this strange journey. Twenty-four long, foot-numbing, blister-inducing hours of walking without laying eyes on another single human being.

She glanced at the man trudging his way through the forest beside her. Considering the fact he could spit fireballs at will and his shoulder blades sported dragon wings under his heavy cloak, she couldn't technically count him as a full-blooded human either.

But there were moments, like last night by the fire, when he seemed all too human. For a brief time, she'd forgotten that he was part dragon and instead thought him a flesh and blood man, full of pain and heartache. A man who needed a friend more than anyone she'd ever known.

But was she ready to be that to him? The little girl who constantly brought home stray animals begged to reach out and hold him until all the bad memories were chased away. But her alter ego, the woman who rationalized that she wasn't going to be here any longer than she had to be warned her against getting too attached. That road would only lead to heartache—probably for both of them.

The rumble of Jill's empty stomach redirected her thoughts off the current path and onto something more basic. She swung her satchel off her shoulder and rummaged around inside. She pulled out a slightly bruised apple and prepared to take a bite.

Baelin snagged her wrist and halted the apple before it reached her mouth, causing her teeth to gnash together with a hard click.

"What are you doing?" he asked.

"What does it look like? I'm going to eat an apple."

He continued to hold onto her wrist, denying her her breakfast.

"Listen, I figure there's not a snowball's chance of getting a cup of coffee around here but if I don't get something to eat, I'm going to start getting grumpy and believe me, you don't want to be around me when that happens."

He let go of her arm, but his expression remained doubtful. "You should not eat it uncooked. 'Tis unhealthy."

"Says who? I'll have you know this apple is probably a lot healthier now than the ones are in my time with all the pesticides and hybridization that goes on. Besides, do you realize you lose half the vitamins and minerals when you cook fruits and vegetables? They are much better for you this way." She proceeded to take a big, healthy bite to prove it to him.

He watched her closely, probably worried she might drop dead right in front of him, as if eating an apple was the most deadly thing a person could do. Okay, so it hadn't turned out so well for Snow White, but in the end she got a prince out of the deal, didn't she?

"See. I'm fine and it tastes delicious." She groped around in her satchel and pulled out another apple, offering it to him. "Want one?"

He looked horrified, as if she were offering him *The* apple. She had half a mind to check around for a big snake whispering, *Go ahead. Take a bite. What harm can it do?* The wily old serpent must've been somewhere close by, because the devil in her had her smiling her sweetest, most innocent smile and holding the apple out to him.

"I dare you."

Baelin's eyes narrowed, recognizing the challenge for what it was. He snatched the apple from her and took a bite, the crunch loud in the silence of the forest. He chewed slowly and swallowed with great care.

Satisfied when he didn't immediately suffer death by fresh produce, he began walking again. Casting a sideways glance at his profile, Jill watched him take another bite. Not one to rub in a small victory, she took satisfaction in the look of pleasure on his face and found herself captivated by the way the tendons in his jaw worked as he chewed. Heavens to Betsy, even his face had muscles.

He took another bite and juice squirted down his chin. When he licked it off, her fascination turned to shock.

"What the heck was that?"

Baelin stopped in mid-chew and glanced at her, his expression cautious. "What?"

"That thing that just came out of your mouth. What is the deal with your tongue?"

"'Tis naught." He turned his attention to the path ahead of them, refusing to look at her as he picked up the pace. She had to hurtle over a fallen tree before she caught up with him.

"Nothing my Aunt Fanny. That looked suspiciously like a forked snake's tongue."

He sighed and stopped walking. "You already know I retain some of my dragon traits in my human form. That my tongue is forked should not shock you so."

"Wings on your back, fireballs in your lungs, acid in your blood, and now a dragon's tongue in your mouth. What else on you failed to make the transformation?"

Her gaze raked him from head to toe, before coming to a screeching halt at his crotch. Her memory recalled in intimate detail the first night when he'd stood before her naked in the firelight. There was no doubt just how nicely his male anatomy had made the transformation. No sirree Bob, definitely no dragon remnants left there. Baelin's impressive package had made the shift just fine—every red-blooded, glorious, male inch of him.

When she realized what she was doing, her eyes shot back to his face to find him watching her intently. She felt herself blush, embarrassed to be caught ogling him once again.

This time she was the one who started them walking again, but she was so distracted she had difficulty maneuvering around several bushes and nearly ran into a small tree. Try as she might, she was unable to get the image of his nude body or his tongue out of her mind.

His forked tongue.

What would it feel like if he kissed her with it? How would it feel in her mouth?

On her body?

In her body?

A burst of fire shot down between her legs. Jill groaned. Well, if this just wasn't the most warped thing she could imagine. Her, lusting after dragon-man. What in the world was wrong with her? She'd never been into kink and yet here she was, all hot and bothered over a walking, talking human iguana.

Baelin's hand on her shoulder startled her and brought her face to face with the object of her raging libido.

"Are you unwell?" he asked. Concern filled his eyes—eyes like pools of rich, creamy chocolate she could easily drown in.

"I'm fine. Just having a momentary lapse of sanity, that's all."

He nodded in understanding. "'Tis probably the apple. I warned you it was unwise to eat it uncooked." To prove his point, he tossed his half-eaten fruit into the forest.

"Oh, believe me. It has nothing to do with the apple," she mumbled.

But he wasn't paying attention to her. Instead, he stared into the woods in the direction where his apple had disappeared. She craned her neck to see what he was looking at, but all she saw were trees, trees, and more trees.

Finally, he urged her to resume walking with a gentle push on her shoulder. "Come, we had best keep moving."

A twinge raced down her arm from where his fingers brushed her, making the tips of her breasts tighten. It amazed her how a slight touch could carry such a spark.

"Good idea."

And it was probably a good idea to get her mind off hunky dragon men with wicked sex toys for tongues.

As they trudged through the forest, she could feel the tension radiating off him. Why? Was it because she'd glimpsed the briefest hint of desire in his eyes and he was feeling as awkward as she was? Or had it been nothing more than her twisted imagination? Probably best not to examine that bizarre train of thought.

But then he jerked her to his side, sending a thrill rippling through her body. Was he going to kiss her now? Did she want him to?

"Baelin…"

"Silence!" He hissed.

"Wha—"

He slapped his hand over her mouth so fast, she nearly choked on the air forced down her throat.

"Silence, woman. We are being followed."

Any desire she felt died in an instant. All she could do was make a garbled sound until he finally removed his hand.

"How do you know?" she whispered as her gaze darted around the forest, checking each tree and bush for someone lurking in the shadows.

"I can smell them."

"Smell them? What are you, part bloodhound now?"

Ignoring her comment, he scrutinized the area around them from beneath hooded eyes. "They have been following us for quite some time, mayhap since we broke camp this morn."

She didn't know whether to be scared or angry. "But that was hours ago. Why didn't you say something before?"

"I had hoped I was wrong, but I fear I am not."

The little hairs on the back of her neck prickled. "I take it this is not a good thing?"

"I have no desire to find out."

Baelin gripped her by her upper arm, guiding her between trees and underbrush. His other hand rested on the hilt of his sword, ready to draw it at any moment.

Her mouth went dry at the thought he might actually have to. The idea of a knight in shining armor ready to defend her was a heady thing, but the imminent reality of it—that if he drew his sword, it would not be for show—was something entirely different.

She attempted to move as quickly and quietly as possible, but every step she took snapped a twig or crunched dry leaves beneath her feet. Her breathing came in rasps and pants, sounding louder the more she tried to silence it.

From behind a tree, a man stepped in front of them, blocking their way. Savage and half wild, his beard was matted and his clothing stained and worn.

Baelin stopped, tensing at her side. She wondered why. After all, there was only one of him and two of them. Then one by one, more rough-looking men surrounded them, dark specters stepping out of the forest shadows. She counted five, but was afraid to turn around to see if there were more. Five was too many already.

No words were uttered, no demands made. The malicious intent of this scraggly band was evident in their cold, hard stares.

Shoving her behind him, Baelin's blade hissed from the scabbard. Two of the men charged him at once and the clang of metal against metal rang through the forest.

Jill used a tree to shield herself as he fought them, taking on each man as they attacked. Even to her inexperienced eye, she could tell these were not skilled swordsmen or practiced knights. By contrast, Baelin was fluid motion, his movements graceful, his blade glinting in the stray beams of sunlight filtering through the trees.

Two of men shifted behind Baelin while he fended off the other three. Jill panicked, wanting to help him, but she knew she would just get in the way. Her throat constricted, the urge to call out a warning to him nearly choking her, but she was afraid it would only distract him.

There was no need. Baelin seemed to sense their every movement before they made it. He whirled and with a sickening thud, chopped off one man's arm above the elbow. Blood spurted and pulsed from the severed limb, spraying the dry leaves on the ground as the man screamed, clutching at what was left of his arm.

Baelin did not pause. His blade sliced again, slitting open the stomach of another. Jill gagged as the man's intestines spilled from the gaping wound like ground beef from a butcher's meat grinder. Paralyzed, she stood transfixed, her mind frozen to the sight. It was like watching a B-horror movie, only these weren't bad actors playing parts. They were real flesh and blood men, dying in front of her eyes at the hand of the man sworn to protect her.

Two of them engaged Baelin as one shouted, "Get the woman!"

The third remaining man turned his attention to her with wild, crazed eyes.

Run, she commanded her shaking legs. *Run now or you will die here.*

Jill bolted into the trees, hoping against hope the man would not follow. The crash of his body through the underbrush told her that hope was in vain. As she raced through the trees, low hanging branches and thorny bushes snatched at her gown, as if deliberately trying to slow her down and prevent her escape.

"No!" she screamed as she was grabbed by the hair and jerked back against the man's hard body, a sharp blade pressed at her throat. "Please, don't hurt me."

"Ye're going to pay dearly for what yer man has done to mine." His foul breath hissed against the side of her face. "Ye'll wish ye were dead long afore we let ye breathe yer last."

He forced her back toward the others, dragging her through the trees by her hair.

"Unhand her!" Baelin shouted as the other two bandits abandoned the fight and joined the man who'd captured her.

The man twisted Jill around, holding her as a shield before him. "Not bloody likely. Drop yer sword or I'll slit her throat right afore yer eyes."

Baelin stood motionless, the rapid rise and fall of his mail-covered chest the only movement in his rigid frame. Growling low in his throat, he tossed his sword aside.

The man chuckled as he and the others backed away, dragging her with them into the woods. "Don't worry. We'll let her go—after we're done with her. But don't ye be thinkin' to follow us. If we catch sight of ye, the woman is as good as dead."

Baelin's eyes blazed, the golden fire within flaring with his rage. He reached up slowly and released the clasp on his cloak, letting the voluminous garment fall to the forest floor in a puddle at his feet. The dragon wings on his back unfolded and he made an inhuman sound, the warning hiss of a predatory animal about to strike.

The man holding her trembled. "Blessed Mother Mary."

Baelin advanced, his wings spread wide, his white surcoat splattered with blood, his fingers curved into claws at his side.

In his panic, the man stumbled and lost his grip on her. Jill shoved herself away from him. She tried to run as he made a desperate lunge for her. She fell with a thud, then clawed at the leaf-covered ground, kicking with her feet to escape him.

"Devil's whore!" he shrieked as he crawled up her body.

She turned just as the man raised his arm, a dagger clutched in his hand.

Baelin roared. A blinding flash of light flared as a fireball shot out of his mouth, blasting the man off his knees and slamming him into a tree. The bandit's cry of agony rose up into the forest canopy and the stench of burning flesh filled the air.

He spun as flames consumed his ragged clothing, igniting dry brush as he passed. Stumbling, he reached out blindly with flaming fingers before collapsing to the ground.

Unlike his two companions who'd fled into the forest, Jill couldn't move. She couldn't make a sound. All she could do was stare in detached horror at the body as it burned at her feet, a smoking, blackened husk that no longer looked human.

At the sound of crunching leaves, she tore her gaze away and watched as Baelin walked slowly toward her, his blood-covered hand outstretched.

Only then did she scream.

CHAPTER TEN

He ran as fast as he could, but gained no ground.

The blood-soaked earth sucked at his feet and the weight of his mail pressed down on him. His sword arm ached, not that he'd had a chance to use it. The weapon was useless against a dragon.

The trees. There would be protection in the trees. But the forest was so far away. He was never going to reach it in time. Even now, he could feel the heat of the beast at his back, coming for him.

Osmund raced ahead.

Run! he shouted. One of us must survive.

Hot. So hot. No air left to breathe. Smoke and heat choking him, smothering him. The steady beat of death on the wind drummed in his ears, coming closer, ever closer. A brave knight would turn and face death with honor and bravery. But he was not that brave. He had yet to see his first battle, had yet to kill another.

Blistering heat passed by his head and he smelled his burning hair as it crackled at the side of his face. He watched as a fireball shot by him like a flaming stone from the catapult and sailed through the sky.

Osmund!

The burst of fire blinded him, the heat of the explosion scorching his face. When his vision cleared, Osmund was nowhere to be seen. In his place stood a burning pillar, the dark outline of a figure barely visible within the center of the flames.

Then the figure turned. What had once been a face peered through the flames, the eyes dark, sightless holes and the skin blackened leather. The stench of burning flesh filled the air, drifting to him, the smoke enveloping him in a ghostly embrace. Through the roar of the fire and the screams on the battlefield, he heard Osmund's voice.

"Help me."

Baelin jerked awake, roused by the sound of his own rapid breathing, expecting to see the fallen bodies of his fellow knights frozen in charred agony on the scorched moor. But all that surrounded him were the tall trees standing silent while they slept. He looked at the girl across the dwindling fire, relieved to see her sleeping face instead of the blackened ones that haunted his dreams.

He rubbed his temples, trying to drive the images from his mind. It was futile. The dreams still tormented him, even after all these years. But this time, it was more vivid than ever before. Why? Was it because Lady Jill had made him remember? Or because he'd been forced to kill a man using the dragon's weapon?

He struggled to calm the rapid beating of the beast's heart as it sent its heated blood racing through his human body. If he did not gain control, the creature's rage might rise and turn on Lady Jill. He had to get away from her before that happened.

He rose and walked into the forest. Not far. Just enough to give him space to tame the beast raging within.

Coming upon a tall beech tree, he drew his sword. He hacked and chopped and sliced at the trunk, bits of bark and chunks of pulp flying in all directions. He attacked the tree viciously, all the while seeing the bandits' dirty faces, their filthy hands grabbing at Lady Jill. Threatening her. Frightening her. Touching her.

Bile rose in his throat. He'd felt so helpless, just as he had the day Osmund died.

When the man had raised his blade at Lady Jill, rage like none he'd ever known had gripped him. He couldn't risk losing her. Not if she was *the one*. Too far away to stop the man, Baelin had saved her the only way he could.

Dear God, the horror on her face. He couldn't blame her. He repulsed himself. He hadn't wanted to kill the man the way Osmund had been slain. No one should have to die that way. But he'd had no choice. In that one terrifying moment, desperation had melded with instinct.

The dragon's instinct. When the knight could not save the maiden, the dragon had.

Baelin ceased his attack on the helpless tree and leaned his forehead against the trunk. He cursed himself. All those years living in that damn cave, his skills had gone beyond useless.

Sparring with trees and imaginary foes was a poor substitute for real combat and because of that, he'd been ill-prepared for the attack. He looked down at the sword in his grip, all but snarling at it. Shame threatened to choke him. He was no longer the skilled knight he'd once been, but a man dressed in mail pretending to be one. Worse yet, forced to use his dragon's powers to save Lady Jill, now he couldn't even claim to be a man.

Shoving away from the tree, he resumed his practice, not wishing to be caught off guard ever again. Over and over, he swung his sword, until he and the blade became one. When exhaustion threatened to overtake him, he stopped, panting as sweat trickled down his neck into his *aketon.* His tension easing, he welcomed the calm and breathed deep of the moist forest air.

Examining his blade, Baelin checked for nicks and chinks in the metal. The tree had not been forgiving. He would have to sharpen it at first chance. He sheathed his sword, feeling once again in control.

The feeling didn't last long. Unease whispered on the air before he came in sight of the camp. In their brief time together, he'd become accustomed to Lady Jill's scent, aware of her every movement. At this moment, he was intensely aware of none of them.

She was gone.

Panic placed its icy grip on him as he started running. Had he been unwise to leave her alone, even for such a brief time? Had the remaining bandits returned and taken her?

Reaching the camp, he observed no signs of a struggle, no indication she had been taken against her will. Then he noticed her blanket and satchel were missing, and he knew the ugly truth.

She'd left on her own.

Baelin stared at the empty spot by the dying fire, the remaining embers little more than smoking ash. His dragon heart constricted painfully within his human chest. How could she run away from him? How could she break her word?

For a brief moment by the fire the other night, he thought she might be near to, if not liking him, at least understanding him. But he knew now any hope of that had vanished with the attack. The terror and revulsion in her eyes had been evident. Now, she no doubt saw him as all the others did—as a monster, something to be feared and despised. He should be accustomed to it by now, but somehow knowing she felt that way about him cut deeper than the rejection of all the other maids who had come before her.

As the reality settled in, he glanced around the campsite. Only one of the supply satchels was missing. Either she had a care and left him with something, or she'd taken only what she could carry.

Then a horrifying thought gripped him. He dropped to his knees and rummaged in the remaining satchel.

Gone. The tapestry was gone.

The edges of his vision darkened, tunneling to where his hands gripped the opening of the leather satchel. How could she take the tapestry? His only hope of returning to the man he once was, gone. The calm he'd tried so hard to regain in the forest vanished in an instant, replaced by the dragon's possessive rage.

Damn the wench. She had no idea what misfortune could befall her, traveling alone. She likely thought to sell the tapestry in the first village or township she came upon. She had no idea of its true worth.

Anger at her betrayal consumed the shock of her leaving. He would find her. In the short time they'd been together, he'd learned her scent. He knew her. There was no place she could run, no place she could hide, that he would not find her.

And woe beware the maid when he did.

Jill kept up a brisk pace along a rutted path cutting a jagged brown scar across the green grass of the rolling hillside, the tapestry tucked securely in her satchel. She refused to feel guilty about taking it. She'd only done what she had to. After all, it was her only way home.

She didn't want to think about the fact that the tapestry was also Baelin's only hope of breaking the curse. He'd had it for over two hundred years. He'd had his chance with it. Now it was her turn. She wasn't going to be stuck in this godforsaken place one more minute than she had to be, especially not with a half-crazed dragon-man.

But with each step she took, her conscience proved to be an irritating companion, whispering in her ear that what she was doing was wrong. That she should turn around and go back to Baelin.

No. She was not about to be swayed by her go-ahead-and-walk-all-over-me heart or his I'm-too-good-looking-to-be-a-bad-person face. She'd met her share of handsome guys, and more often than not, the gorgeous face concealed a snake beneath.

Or in Baelin's case, a dragon.

But she wasn't going to argue semantics. A reptile was a reptile. And although his sob story had sucked her in at first, he obviously had the cold-blooded heart of one.

He'd killed someone by setting them on fire, for Pete's sake!

She stumbled as her body convulsed in a head-to-toe shiver. What if he turned that violence on her? With the way she constantly insulted and irritated him, it was probably only a matter of time. She wasn't about to stick around and be turned into a human candlestick.

Jill straightened her shoulders and concentrated on navigating the winding path ahead of her. She had to stop worrying about Baelin's feelings. He wasn't her problem. Not anymore.

She needed to focus on getting herself back home and she figured the best way to do that was to find the person who created this jinxed tapestry in the first place. If lizard lips wouldn't confront the Dark Witch, then she would. Men always went about these things the hard way. All she had to do was reason with the sorceress woman to woman…she hoped. And if she could manage to break the curse for Baelin in the process, all the better. But she would do it without him because staying with him was definitely not good for her health.

She glanced over her shoulder, expecting to see an enraged dragon hot on her trail. There was no doubt he would be coming after her. Her gaze rose to the clouds where a few hours ago, the sun had chased away a blood-red sunrise. Red skies at morning, sailors take warning.

Would he swoop down from those clouds as he'd done when he was a dragon?

She quickened her pace.

Or would he follow on foot, his long strides eating up the ground, closing in on her step by step? Was he even now almost upon her?

She whipped her head around and scanned the footpath in front of her.

Or would he sneak around and get ahead of her? Was he even now just over that ridge, waiting for her?

Paranoia ate away at Jill. Every step she took had her wondering if she'd made a terrible mistake. Her stomach clenched, imagining how angry he would be. She knew it was not a matter of *if* he found her, but *when*—and what he would do to her when he did.

As she topped a hill, she spied a small village in the valley below, smoke curling from fires and animals dotting the surrounding fields. Thatched huts never looked so good. Surely someone there would know how to find this Dark Witch. Tucking the tapestry into her satchel along with any remnants of guilt, Jill set off to make her own destiny.

But as she neared the village, that destiny took on an ugly face. Gone was the quaint hamlet she'd viewed from a distance. A weathered gallows stood by the side of the road, a body swinging back and forth in the breeze like some life-size marionette, the man's skin pecked to the bone by birds. Missing eyes stared at her from hollow sockets, his mouth hanging open in a final scream, voicelessly warning her to leave this horrible place.

She fought back the bile rising in her throat. What kind of people did something like this? They'd hanged this poor man and left his body outside to rot. Maybe seeking help from these people wasn't such a good idea.

Turning to go in search of a friendlier place, Jill froze when she spotted a dark figure standing on the crest of the hill she'd just descended.

Baelin.

From where she stood, his expression was unreadable, but the murderous rage emanating from his body reached across the long distance to wrap its deadly fingers around her throat. If it were possible, his presence terrified her more than the dead body swinging behind her. She had no doubt he would kill her if he got his hands on her.

Daring to take her chances, Jill fled into the town, hoping to lose herself among the thatched huts and wooden sheds. But where could she hide where he wouldn't find her?

She searched desperately, not daring to ask for help. They'd hanged one of their own. They'd have no qualms about throwing a stranger to the dragon lurking outside their gates.

She spied one lone building constructed of stone standing tall among the wattle and daub huts, a simple cross etched over the doorway. Would a church offer her a safe haven? Would a priest help her? Could a creature such as Baelin even enter holy ground? Wait, maybe that only applied to vampires and not dragons. Regardless, it was her best option.

Jill dashed up the cobbled steps and shoved one of the massive wooden doors open with her shoulder. Slipping inside, she eased it shut as the sound of her rapid breathing echoed throughout the vaulted stone interior. Once her eyes adjusted to the dim light filtering in through glassless windows, she discovered the single, cavernous room was empty. Nobody home.

It was also completely devoid of furniture. There wasn't a pew, bench or chair to be found. What did the people do, stand through the entire service? Unfortunately, the lack of furniture didn't bode well for her finding a good hiding place should Baelin look for her in here.

She peered through the crack in the door, scanning the muddy street outside to see if he'd followed her into the village. Would he dare? Or would he lurk outside the town, waiting for her to emerge rather than risk the people seeing him and discovering what he was?

Long moments stretched by as she watched the villagers go about their daily routines. Farmers sold produce out of carts while children chased a pig through the rutted street. Two women gossiped across a rickety wooden fence separating their cottages as a boy drove a small flock of sheep through the center of the town.

Transfixed by this tiny slice of medieval life, Jill jumped when first one, and then another dog began to howl, until a chorus of baying hounds filled the entire village. Moments later, Baelin's large, cloaked form stepped into her view, his purposeful strides sloshing through the muck and refuse in what passed for a street.

She held her breath. *Don't look this way.*

A lone mutt ran out, growling and snarling, nipping at his heels while chickens and geese scurried out of his way. She remembered what he told her about why he didn't have a horse, because animals could sense the dragon in him. Is that why the dogs howled at him now? Did they know what he was?

Baelin stopped in the middle of the street and glared down at the dog. The poor animal skidded to a halt, whined and scurried away. He watched the dog's hasty retreat and then suddenly his entire body tensed, instantly alert.

Jill's did, too. *Please, please, don't look this way.*

His gaze shot to the church, those glowing yellow eyes of his burning two holes out of the shadow created by the hood covering his head, searing her where she stood.

She sucked in a sharp breath. She hadn't made a sound, hadn't moved an inch, didn't think he could really see her through the tiny crack in the church door, and yet somehow, he knew exactly where she was.

She struggled to lift the thick wooden beam to bar the doors but it was too heavy. Cursing the wisdom of coming in here in the first place, she ran to the back of the church, praying there was another way out.

Jill darted through an archway and rounded a simple altar draped with a white cloth. A lone iron cross stood at its center while two unlit candles flanked either side. The smell of burned tallow hovered heavy in the alcove, indicating they'd only recently been blown out.

She spied a door off to the side. Grasping the iron handle, she pushed and pulled, but it wouldn't open. Locked. There were be no escape that way.

Desperate for a place to hide, she glanced around the small chamber. Could she hide under the altar? She lifted the cloth. No such luck. The table was made of solid stone.

A door slammed, startling her and she ducked behind the altar. Oh God, it must be Baelin. He was coming after her. Was there any chance he wouldn't think to look for her up here? Jill didn't think she would be that fortunate.

She scurried to the side, trying to conceal herself in the shadows of the alcove, not that it would do her any good if he came to this end of the church. She bumped into something and caught a small statue just in time as it toppled from its pedestal. She held her breath, thankful it didn't go crashing to the ground and give her hiding spot away.

Footfalls echoed on the stone floor as he approached the altar. She clutched the statue to her chest like a child with a doll, praying by some miracle Baelin would not see her. If her prayers were ever going to be answered, this was the place it would happen.

Relief washed over her as a man dressed in cleric's robes stepped into the alcove. He grasped at the cross dangling around his waist, as startled to see her as she was to see him. But his surprise turned to suspicion as his gaze fixed on the statue she held in her hands.

"What do you here?"

"I...I..." What could she say? *I'm hiding from a dragon.* Somehow, she didn't think that would go over too well. Then a single word popped into her head. "Sanctuary?"

The priest either didn't hear her or it didn't mean what she hoped it would.

"What are you doing with the statue of Saint Kentigern?" His eyes narrowed. "What evil deeds are you about, girl?"

"Nothing. I bumped into it and it fell. I was getting ready to put it back."

"'Tis forbidden for a woman to enter the chancel," he sneered. "You have committed sacrilege by your very presence here."

It was quite obvious the good Father didn't have a very high opinion of women. Ignoring the insult, she figured playing the ignorant woman he thought her to be would be a good role to assume at the moment. "Oh. I didn't know that."

"Everyone knows 'tis forbidden. Now I ask you again, what are you doing here?"

"It's a church. Isn't it open to everybody?"

"Not to those who think to steal from the house of God."

Jill felt any hope of aid from the priest fade. How could a man of God turn her away in her hour of need? Wasn't that part of his job description?

"I wasn't trying to steal it. I bumped into the statue and it fell."

"Lies! What business have you here, if not to take something of value?"

The priest snatched the statue from her and grabbed her by the arm with his other hand, dragging her through the church toward the door.

"No! No! No!" Jill panicked and tried to break loose as her feet skidded across the smooth stone floor. "I can't go out there. You don't understand."

"I understand that which I plainly see—you where you do not belong, with Saint Kentgern's statue in your hands."

"But I wasn't trying to steal it. You have to believe me!"

"That is for the court to decide."

The priest hauled her outside into the glaring light of day. She glanced around, relieved when a certain flying T-Rex didn't dive from the sky and burn her to a crisp on the spot.

But Baelin was nowhere to be seen. She could've sworn he'd spotted her in the church doorway. Where was he now?

"Hark!" the priest shouted. "Let it be known that I, Father Gerald, have witnessed with my own eyes this woman attempting to steal from the house of God."

Jill cringed as he shouted at the top of his lungs to anyone within earshot. The villagers stopped what they were doing and looked their way as she stood on the church steps, the priest's pudgy hand a shackle around her wrist.

"What kind of priest are you? You're supposed to help people."

"I help those who are in need. Those who steal from the Lord are the lowest of thieves and deserve to go straight to hell."

It wasn't long before a mob of curious onlookers surrounded them, each one eyeing her with contempt. This was not looking good. The not-so-distant experience of the first village she landed in and the resulting circumstances taunted her memory. That time she ended up trussed up like a Thanksgiving Day turkey and sacrificed to a fire-breathing dragon. She didn't want to imagine the possibilities of what they would do to her this time.

"What's this all about?" someone in the growing crowd asked.

"I caught this woman trying to steal from the church. I found her only moments ago with the statue of Saint Kentigern in her hands." For added emphasis, the priest held the figurine above his head as if it might speak and condemn her, too.

A collective gasp arose from the people surrounding her.

"No. No." Jill glanced around at the faces in the crowd, willing them to believe her. "Like I told him, I bumped into the statue. I caught it when it fell and I was going to put it back. I swear!"

"She is not to be believed," the priest interjected. "Look at her. She entered the house of God with no covering on her head. Only a woman full of sin would dare to do such."

She thought back to the trunk in Baelin's cave filled with beautiful veils. Veils he urged her to take but she'd refused. Now she was regretting that fashion decision.

"And further," the priest continued, "she was in the chancel, where all here know women are forbidden to enter. Her actions show her clear contempt for God and the sanctity of the Church."

"I didn't know I wasn't allowed to be there."

Jill's hopes plummeted. She was so out of her element here. It was as if she was playing a game and everyone knew the rules but her. How could she keep from making mistakes if she didn't know what they were?

"Enough!" A man with a dark, bushy beard stepped forward and held up his hands, effectively quieting the crowd that had gathered. Then he turned his attention to her. "Are we to believe the word of a stranger against a man of God? I think not." Jill opened her mouth to defend herself, but he stopped her with a raised palm. "Say no more. Yer guilt or innocence will be put before Lord Hugh's court."

"Am I being arrested?"

"Aye, that ye are." Bush-beard pointed his finger at her. "'Tis off to *gaol* for ye until the gathering of the *hallmote*."

The sheriff of Nottingham or whoever he was grabbed her by the arm and tugged her down the steps. The priest stepped back, patting the statue on its marble head and looking smug in his righteousness.

Jill glanced around desperately, knowing there might be only one familiar face in the crowd, only one person who might to come to her aid. But he wasn't there.

Despair swelled in her throat, threatening to choke her. Why would he help her after she ran from him, taking his hope with her?

The people's accusing stares blurred before her tear-filled eyes.

Strangers, every one. She would get no help from any of them. She was alone and at their mercy.

Somehow, as the man led her away, guilt at what she'd done to Baelin made her feel that this time, she just might deserve whatever she had coming.

Chapter Eleven

The slide of the bolt in the door jarred Jill and her heart skipped a beat.

Dire scenarios of what might happen to her at the hands of the village court had kept her overactive imagination in hyper-drive for two days straight. With no one but herself for company in the dark confines of her prison, those scenarios had taken on a life of their own, leaving her a nervous wreck.

It didn't help that Baelin was nowhere to be found. She hadn't seen him since he'd stood in the street, staring at the church doors she'd hidden behind, fury and betrayal radiating in every fiber of his being.

Had he managed to get the tapestry back and left her to rot in this dank, dark cell? She wouldn't blame him if he did.

The door creaked open and a man stepped into the room. "On yer feet." With a nod of his head, he beckoned her to follow him. Outside the door, bush-beard waited for her.

"Yer fortunate," he said as they escorted her outside. "Lord Hugh's steward arrived this morn and is holding the *hallmote* today. Did ye know there've been people what have rotted a year in *gaol*, waiting for the manor court to come 'round?"

Lucky me, she thought. Next, he'll be saying she should be grateful they were only going to hang her because beheading was too much of a mess.

A large ash tree grew in the center of the village commons and a table was set up beneath it, its scarred wooden surface speckled with light and shadow from the leaves above. Several men stood on one side of the table talking to an official-looking man dressed in fine clothing seated on the other side. She assumed he was the steward bush-beard told her about, the man who would be acting as her judge.

There was another man sitting next to him, busy writing on a long scroll of parchment, his quill flicking back and forth from ink pot to paper with jerky movements. She figured he must be the equivalent of a medieval court stenographer. Not a speedy writer with pen and paper herself, she wondered if he could scribble fast enough with that bird's feather of his to get all the details of the proceedings written down.

Bush-beard led her to a holding area of sorts. "Wait here 'til yer called for."

He left her to stand with others who had court business today. Glancing about at her fellow defendants, there appeared to be more people who'd broken the law than spectators milling about, watching the proceedings. Morning crept into mid-afternoon as she waited through disputes that sounded downright absurd. One woman argued someone's dog had killed her prize chicken. Another claimed his neighbor's goat had jumped the fence between their properties and eaten half his wife's vegetable garden. Several men stepped forward to complain that the alewife was watering down her brew.

And people thought America was a litigious society.

The steward listened patiently to the arguments brought before him, but Jill soon realized it was the group of twelve men sitting off to the side—the equivalent of a modern jury—who decided the judgments and fines of each case.

Jill's tension began to ease. So far, nothing seemed to be too harsh. Most of the people found guilty of their ridiculously silly crimes received what amounted to a slap on the wrist and had to pay a fine of six pence.

Of course, she didn't know how much six pence was. If the jury demanded a fine from her, she wasn't sure where she would get the money. She hadn't found any to take with her when she'd made her pre-dawn escape from Baelin.

"Father Gerald and my lady Donahue, please step forward," the clerk announced.

Jill's pulsed quickened and she took several deep, slow breaths. Show time.

She attempted to tame her wild hair as she approached the steward's table, knowing she probably looked like she'd been hit by a bus. Considering her bed had been a pile of moldy straw last night, she wasn't surprised to find several stray stalks tangled in the back. She did the best she could and stood before her judge and jury with as much dignity as she could muster.

The clerk stood and addressed the steward.

"Master William, Father Gerald of Crosthwaite, who is here," he pointed to the priest, "complains of my lady Donahue..." The clerk paused while he glanced at the parchment in his hands. "...of Richmond, who is here," he pointed to her, "that yester eve he came upon her in the parish church trying to steal the sacred statue of Saint Kentigern."

The young clerk sat and then the steward turned his attention to Father Gerald. "Is this true, Father?"

"Aye, my lord. I found this woman concealing herself in the shadows of the chancel with the statue of our patron saint all but hidden within her cloak. If I had not happened upon her at that very moment, she would have surely made off with one of the church's greatest treasures."

"I see." The steward looked at Jill. "My lady, what have you to say in your defense?"

"Umm, not guilty?" She hoped that was the correct response.

The steward and clerk exchanged perplexed glances.

"Have you nothing more to say?" Master William asked.

So, this was her opportunity to tell her version of what happened. She prayed she didn't screw it up.

"Like I tried to explain to the good Father here, it was all an accident. I'd been walking for a very long time and stopped to rest in the church. I was saying my prayers..." She threw that tidbit in for good measure, but didn't elaborate that the prayers involved a certain fire-breathing human lizard not finding her. "...when a sound startled me and I accidentally bumped into the statue, causing it to wobble and fall. I caught it just before it hit the ground and that was when the priest found me."

Master William nodded. "I see. What have you to say to that, Father Gerald?"

"As all present can attest, the statue is kept in the back of the chancel.

One would have to leap like the hart over the altar to bump into it. For a woman to enter the chancel room is transgression enough, but to touch the statue with her sinner's hands is pure desecration. Even worse, she was trying to sneak out of the church with the statue hidden beneath her cloak, clearly breaking the Lord's commandment, thou shalt not steal."

Jill gasped at the priest's twisting of the circumstances.

"Is this true, my lady Donahue?" Master William asked.

"Of course not! I was not hiding it and I most certainly was not trying to steal it. If anything, you should be thankful I have quick reflexes or that precious statue of yours would be in a million pieces right now."

The clerk and the steward sat behind their table, their jaws slack at her outburst. The men in the jury shook their heads and mumbled to themselves. Jill mentally kicked herself. Her habit of speaking first, thinking second, was definitely not helping her case right now.

The steward straightened in his seat and turned to the priest. "Do you have the statue in your possession now?"

"Aye, my lord." Father Gerald retrieved the statue from a boy standing nearby. "But 'tis ruined, fouled beyond redemption by her sinner's hands."

Fouled? Jill thought. *I'll bet my hands are the cleanest ones in this whole damn village.*

"Look here," the priest pointed to a spot on the statue's arm. "There is now a crack where none had been before." He pointed an accusing finger at her. "This evil woman has committed a grave sin within the sacred House of God. Surely 'tis a sign of His displeasure."

"Now wait a minute," she interrupted, determined to stand up for herself. "There's no proof I cracked the statue when I caught it. How do we know it hasn't been that way for years? In fact, how do we know you didn't do it yourself and are trying to blame me for it now?"

"Lies! All lies!" The priest's face grew mottled and spittle formed in the corner of his lips. "Look at her. This wanton woman comes before the court in brazen disrespect with no veil covering her head, just as I found her in the church yester eve. Having defiled God's House with her actions, the harlot now stands here before you all, spewing forth untruths in an attempt to cast dispersions upon the Lord's servant with her devil's tongue."

Tumult erupted around her, men waving angry fists and women trying to shield their children as if she'd suddenly sprouted horns and a tail. This did not look good. If the priest continued getting them riled up like this, they'd string her up for certain.

"I am not a bad person!" she shouted over the uproar. "I made a mistake. An innocent mistake." She focused her plea toward the steward. "Please, you have to believe me."

Master William raised his hands, attempting to gain control over the proceedings. When the crowd quieted, he turned to Jill. "Have you any oath helpers to attain to your innocence?"

"Oath what?"

"Oath helpers. Those who can speak for your character."

Jill glanced around, her hopes plummeting. There would be no friendly face in the crowd to come to her defense. "I'm not from here. I don't know anyone in this village."

"She knows me," a deep voice cut through the murmurs of the crowd.

The people parted behind her and Baelin's tall form stepped forward to stand before the steward's table. Jill's legs trembled at the sight of him. In relief or fear, she wasn't sure which.

"And who might you be, sir?" the clerk asked.

"Sir Baelin of Gosforth."

She watched as the clerk scribbled his name on the parchment, the feather quill waving back and forth under his pointy nose.

The steward straightened, his brow creased in confusion. "Gosforth? Why, there has not been anyone of rank from there in…"

"Nearly two hundred years," Baelin finished for him.

Master William glanced at his young clerk, who did little more than shrug. The steward turned back to Baelin. "Gosforth? Truly?"

Baelin straightened, stretching out all of his six foot two height. "While 'tis true I have not been in residence for too many years to count, Gosforth is my ancestral home and I bear the family crest to prove it."

"And how is it you know this woman?"

For the first time, Baelin turned to look at her. She cringed at the anger in his eyes. What would he say? Was he going to defend her or toss her to the wolves?

He turned back to address the steward. "She is my ward. I was escorting her to her home when we were…separated."

"Your *ward?*" Master William spoke the word as if he believed she was something entirely different to Baelin. The crowd snickered, indicated many of them thought so, too. "I see. And are you aware of the charges against her?"

"I am, and I stand before you to swear to her innocence. As you can tell by her speech and manner, she was raised…abroad and is unaccustomed to many of our ways. Though her actions were wrong, her motives were innocent. This I swear before God and on my honor as a knight."

Jill couldn't tear her gaze away from him. She knew his sense of honor did not allow him to lie easily. The truth, as he was forced to stretch it for her sake, would be another strike against her. He appeared in complete control now, but heaven help her when he got her alone.

"With the court's blessing, I offer to pay for a new statue of Saint Kentigern, plus I will add threefold to its coffers, in recompense for any damage done to the good Father's name."

Master William hesitated, the mention of money producing dollar signs in his eyes. Jill thought he was about to accept Baelin's offer when the priest butted in.

"Think you your earthly coin will appease God? Nay, a crime against our Lord has been committed within the Holy Church. Tainted gold earned by the blood of a sword cannot buy away this woman's sin."

The steward acknowledged Father Gerald with a nod of his head, and then turned his attention back to Baelin.

"Your argument is strong, and as a knight of the realm, your oath has great weight. However you are but one and not known to this court. As to my lady Donahue's actions, we are all in agreement, even unto the lady herself, that she did enter the church and remove the statue from its rightful place. However, as to her ignorance of the consequences of the act, I do not believe there is enough proof." Father Gerald opened his mouth to speak but the steward held up his hand, effectively putting an end to any further religious tirades from the man. "Therefore, I leave the question of the lady's intent to the jury to decide."

As the men of the jury argued amongst themselves, Jill felt every eye in the village on her. The one person who did not look at her was Baelin.

He had not glanced her way but for that one, glaring moment. Instead, he stared at some point beyond the steward's table, his profile hard, his jaw tense.

Finally, one of the men spoke. "The jury is torn, my lord. If what Sir Baelin says is true, then my lady Donahue is innocent by fault of her weak woman's mind."

Jill opened her mouth to protest but a quick, almost indecipherable slashing motion of Baelin's hand stopped her. She snapped her mouth shut. Better to save the argument on women's intelligence for another day. Or another century, for that matter.

"We are in accord," the man continued, "that since her crime is against God and took place within the Holy Church, her innocence must be also decided by God."

A hush fell over the crowd. What did that mean? Jill looked to Baelin. The stiffening of his body did not bode well.

The steward turned to Father Gerald. "What method of proof does the Church require?"

"The rod," the priest replied, smirking triumphant in his small victory while the villagers cheered in agreement.

"Very well," Master William sighed. "Following three days of due prayer and fasting, my lady Donahue shall be brought forth to the parish church and submit herself to a trial by iron."

Baelin stepped forward as he reached for his sword.

Jill's heart leaped into her throat. Dear God, was it so bad he would kill to get her out of this mess? She moved in front of him, barring his way, and covered his hand with hers, forcing the sword to stay safely tucked in the scabbard.

"No, Baelin!" She kept her voice low so only he could hear her. "I can't let you hurt anyone because of me. Whatever this trial by iron is, I'll do it."

He glanced from their joined hands on his sword hilt to her face.

"Lady Jill, you do not comprehend what it is you will be required to do."

He brushed her hand away and sidestepped her to face the steward.

"I beg the indulgence of the *hallmote*. Since the lady is my ward, I ask that I be allowed to stand in her stead for the ordeal."

Gasps erupted from the crowd. What was Baelin doing? Was he offering to take her place for the trial? Could he do that? More to the point, why would he, after what she'd done to him? Every time Baelin looked at her, she saw the fresh wound of her betrayal in his eyes. And yet here he was, willing to take a punishment meant for her.

Well, she couldn't let him do it. She's the one who got herself into this mess, she'd be to one to face the consequences. A trial by iron. How hard could that be? She probably had to iron the entire village's laundry for a week.

She moved around him and put herself between his big intimidating body and the table. Much more of this little dance of theirs and they'd soon be sitting in the steward's lap.

"I won't let him take my place." She lifted her head in determination. "I am innocent and I will be the one to prove it."

Baelin hissed behind her. "Lady Jill, you know not what you do."

"Oh, yes I do," she said without turning to face him. "You're doing that chivalry thing again and I won't let you. This is my fault and I'm going to fix it."

Baelin made to speak again but Master William stopped him. "Enough. Three days hence, Lady Donahue will herself prove her guilt or innocence."

Jill turned to face Baelin, knowing he would be angry but hoping, for some odd reason, that he might also be a little proud of her, too.

He stared at her, a kaleidoscope of emotions crossing his face—anger, concern, betrayal, possession, and something akin to fear. For her?

"You have no idea what you have done in refusing my protection."

"Oh, I've seen the lengths you're willing to go to to protect me. I won't let one of these innocent people get hurt because of me."

He closed his eyes. "My lady, 'tis you who will be the one who is harmed."

"Oh, it can't be any worse than what I've already been through."

His eyes flew open and the resigned despair she read in them chilled her.

"That is where you are wrong, my lady. You have not yet begun to see what horrors one person can do to another."

ChAPTER TWELVE

"I'm going to have to do *what?*"

"Hold a metal rod fired in hot coals for nine paces. 'Tis what a trial by iron is."

"But that's barbaric!" Jill gasped, her mind reeling at the thought.

"'Tis to prove whether or not you are innocent of the crime."

"How does burning my hands with a red hot poker prove anything?"

She stared at Baelin through the lone, barred window. Or rather at his feet, since he stood outside and she was once again imprisoned below ground in the dank cellar the villagers used for a jail cell.

"'Tis in the healing your guilt or innocence is proven. If your hands do not fester after three days, you shall be judged innocent. If the wounds do not heal…"

She glanced around at the filthy room. Rotting straw covered the damp dirt floor, while something rustled in the shadows of one corner—probably a huge, flea-ridden rat waiting to gnaw on her ankles. She turned back to the window to find Baelin kneeling by it, his face framed in the narrow opening.

"How can a burn not get infected in a place like this? It's a case of gangrene just waiting to happen."

"You will be proven innocent. You *must* be." His clipped words revealed the anger he still harbored against her for leaving him. But his fury seemed to have cooled a degree or two, giving way to concern for her, which relieved and frightened her at the same time.

"But what if I'm not? We both know I'm innocent, but what if the burns get infected anyway?"

"Then they will hang you."

"Oh, God." The image of the dead man outside the village flashed before her eyes. Only now, her own body swung slowly in the breeze as crows pecked at her lifeless corpse. She took in deep gulps of air to prevent herself from vomiting.

"Fear not, my lady. Should the ordeal go poorly for you and your guilt comes to pass, I shall not let that happen."

Shock and disbelief gave way to fear of the atrocity to come. "My guilt won't come to pass because I probably won't make it that far. Baelin, I don't handle pain well. I nearly passed out when I had my ears pierced. How am supposed to get through something like this?"

"'Tis a circumstance you brought upon yourself. For every wrong committed, there is always a consequence to pay."

Jill heard the censure in his voice. He wasn't just talking about trespassing in the church or taking the statue. He was talking about the tapestry, too. A long, strained silence hung between them, any trust that had once been there stretched tight on a thread close to breaking.

"Baelin?"

"Aye, my lady?"

"I'm sorry. I was wrong to run away with the tapestry. But after what happened to the men in the forest, I freaked. I was scared. But I'm really, really sorry. Even though the tapestry may be my ticket out of here, it was yours and I had no right to take it."

His face softened a fraction and he nodded. "Do not fret, my lady. 'Tis already forgiven. Think on it no more."

Then another horrifying thought struck her. "The tapestry! It was in my satchel. They took everything from me when they arrested me."

"Fear not. Since I claimed you as my ward, they entrusted me with your belongings. 'Tis safely in my possession once again."

"That's good. At least that's one problem solved."

Baelin handed her a length of cloth through the bars. "Take this."

"What's this for?"

"'Tis a veil. The trial requires you to fast for three days. During that time, you will spend your waking hours in prayer to prepare your soul for the ordeal to come. You must wear a covering on your head whenever you enter the church."

"Right. That was another strike against me today." Jill crushed the delicate material in her hands, panic making her pulse race. "Please, Baelin, can't you do anything? I don't think I can go through with this."

"I offered to stand in your place, but you refused."

In an instant, the tension between them returned. He may have forgiven her, but bruised pride hardened his voice. She'd insulted him more than she realized by throwing his chivalry back in his face in front of the entire village.

"That was before I knew their idea of a trial was for me to walk around with a red hot poker in my hands!" Jill dropped the veil, wrapped her hands around the bars, and pulled. "Isn't there anything you can do? Can't you rip these bars off the window?"

"Nay, I have not the dragon's strength as a man. I am no match for iron and stone."

She glanced behind her to the bolted door. "What about the door? It's made of wood. Can't you hock up a fireball and burn it down?"

"And what of the guard who stands on the other side? Would you have me set him aflame to free you?"

"Of course not!" She paused and stared off into nothingness, various possibilities of escape churning in her head. "What about when they come to take me to the church? Couldn't you do something then? Create a distraction? Come charging in on a white stallion? Swoop down and grab me and we both fly away off into the sunset?"

"Nay."

"Why not?" She couldn't believe he was refusing to help her. "Is it because you're still angry I ran away? You want me to go through this gruesome trial of medieval torture because I hurt you? Is this your way of getting back at me? I said I was sorry. What more do you want from me?"

"'Tis not that, my lady. Not that at all."

"Then what is it?" She was trying desperately to understand.

Baelin sighed, regret weighing heavy in the lines of his face. "What would you have me do? You saw yourself the small garrison of armed knights accompanying the manorial court. Were I to reveal my dragon form, they, along with all the villagers, would attack me in their fear and hatred. Would you have me slay the entire village to spare you from that which you brought upon yourself? Would you have me slaughter them down to the last woman and child?" His expression changed, the caring man turning into the hardened knight before her eyes. "Because 'tis what it would take to free you now."

They came for her just after dawn.

Footsteps thudded on the wooden floor of the room above her and headed for the ladder leading down to the cellar, coming closer, ever closer.

Jill huddled in the corner, knowing it was useless to try to hide in the small, cramped room, but she did it anyway. If only the witch who'd cursed Baelin could turn her into a mouse, she could scurry under the straw. She wouldn't even mind being transformed into a disgusting cockroach for a while if it enabled her to slip through a crack in the wall and get away. But as the footfalls drew nearer, she knew there would be no escape for her.

She stood and went to the window. "Baelin? Are you still out there?"

"Aye, my lady."

Of course he was. For the past three days and nights, he'd stood vigil outside her window, always there, a calming constant in this terrible nightmare.

"They're coming."

"I know."

"I'm scared."

"I know that, too. You must be brave. Remember, I will never be far from your side."

Jill tried to choke back the sob stuck in her throat, but she couldn't. She wasn't that brave, not by a long shot. Instantly, Baelin was on his knees by the window. He reached through the bars and clasped her hand in his.

"Do not weep, my lady," he said, his voice tinged with frustration. "If only I could take your place. The fire will not harm me."

She squeezed his hand tight, already feeling the intense heat searing the tender flesh of her palm. "But you can't. There's nothing you can do to keep the iron from burning me."

Baelin's gaze flew to their joined hands, and then he straightened, hope lighting his features. "Perhaps there is."

He tossed his cloak over his shoulder and spread his wing, prying off first one and then another scale from the underside. The muscles in his jaw clenched and, though he did not make a sound, she knew it hurt him to do it. It probably felt like having your fingernails ripped off one by one.

"What are you doing?"

Baelin handed her the two dragon scales. "Hide these within the folds of your gown. You must find a way to place them in your palms before you grasp the iron. They may shield you from the worst of it, but take care no one sees you do this. It would mean your death if it is known you possess them."

Jill held the iridescent scales in her hands, a precious gift from the man she'd so recently betrayed. "Or it could mean your death if they find out they came from you."

"'Tis a chance I am willing to take."

The footsteps halted outside the door. She shoved the scales up her sleeves as the bolt was thrown back and light from the men's torches flooded the dark chamber. Her back stiff, she straightened her veil and turned to face them.

Be brave. Easy for Baelin to say when he was safe on the other side of the wall.

As the men ushered her out of the room, she cast one final glance over her shoulder to the tiny window, but he was no longer there.

They led her up a wooden ladder and outside into the crisp morning air. After crossing the common area, they ushered her up the stone steps leading into the church. She'd traveled the same path back and forth for the past three days.

She was shocked to find the church already filled with villagers. Apparently, there wasn't much in the form of entertainment for these people. They'd all come to watch her go through the trial. Jill touched the inner sleeve of her gown, taking small comfort in the concave shape of the dragon scale hidden underneath. She sent a silent prayer heavenward that she wasn't strip-searched before the ordeal began.

Brought forward, she was forced to kneel on the cold stone floor. Her knees screamed in agony, bruised to the bone from kneeling hour upon hour in the same position, forced to pray for forgiveness of her multitude of sins and to prepare her soul for what was to come. After the first day, she hadn't seen the point in repeating the experience. She figured God got it the first time.

Father Gerald walked to the altar and picked up a metal rod lying there. He turned back to the congregation and held it for all to see as the steward came to stand beside him.

"My lady Donahue," Master William began, "you are hereby charged with the act of sacrilege against the Church. Have you prepared your soul for trial?"

"Yes," she croaked. Her soul was prepared, but she didn't know if her body was.

The steward nodded and stepped back as the priest carried the rod to a brazier set off to the side and held it over the fire.

"Bless, O Lord God, this place that there may be for us in it sanctity, chastity, virtue, and victory, and holiness, humility, goodness, gentleness, and plenitude of law and obedience to God the Father and the Son and the Holy Ghost."

He dropped the rod into the glowing coals, sending red sparks dancing in the air above the brazier. Then the priest sprinkled the fire with holy water and the coals hissed like a snake about to strike. Jill felt her stomach roll and she would have collapsed in a puddle on the floor if she weren't already kneeling.

The priest spoke again, saying a prayer over her for her doomed soul. "O God, the Just Judge, we humbly pray You to deign to bless and sanctify this fiery iron, which is used in the just examination of doubtful issues. If this woman is innocent of the charge from which she seeks to clear herself, she will take this fiery iron in her hands and appear unharmed. If she is guilty, let your most just power declare that truth in her, so that wickedness may not conquer justice but falsehood always be overcome by the truth. Through Christ, our Lord. Amen."

Bring it on, Father. I can use all the help I can get.

Then Father Gerald began giving a sermon about the three children who were tossed into the fiery furnace and survived. Jill looked from the man droning on before her to the glowing coals and back again.

Please stop talking.

But he didn't. He continued to lecture about the wages of sin, eternal damnation and the torments of hell. She looked at the brazier again.

It's hot enough, she wanted to scream.

He extolled the saving grace of God and the blessings of living a virtuous life, but she wasn't paying attention. She couldn't take her eyes off the rod shoved in the hot coals.

Stop talking.

But he kept rambling on and on. Was he going to let the rod roast through the whole sermon?

Shut up, already!

Finally, the priest ended his long-winded speech and to the altar to perform the Lord's Supper. Jill was surprised when he came to stand before her, offering her Communion. After three days of forced fasting, her stomach growled at the thought of one morsel of stale bread and the muffled rumble echoed off the stone walls. A few snickers erupted from the congregation, quickly shushed by others. She opened her mouth to receive the Sacrament, hoping she didn't drool on the man's hand.

Father Gerald then offered Jill the cup of wine. She was tempted to grab it and chug the whole thing if it would numb her to what was to come. She prayed the whole congregation wasn't going to take Communion. At this rate, the rod would be a glob of molten metal before they got around to the ordeal.

The priest returned the cup to the altar, then paced off the floor, putting a mark on the stones indicating the nine steps she was to walk holding the rod.

He pulled Jill to her feet and brought her to stand by the glowing brazier. The heat was intense just standing beside the coals. She whimpered, imagining how hot the metal bar would be.

She looked around at the people in the church, their faces eagerly awaiting the moment of truth. She wanted desperately to find Baelin in the crowd. She needed his support if she was going to make it through this. She scanned each and every face until her eyes locked with his.

He was there, off to the side in the front row, just as he said he would be. He stood tall among the others, his face tense, his eyes willing his strength to her. She tried to smile, to let him know she wasn't afraid, but the effort was too much.

Father Gerald retrieved the rod from the coals with a pair of metal tongs and held it out.

"My lady Donahue, if you are innocent of this charge, you may confidently receive this iron into your hands and the Lord, the Just Judge, will free you, just as he snatched the three children from the burning fire."

Jill stared at the glowing metal rod.

No! her mind screamed, every instinct within her balking at the insanity of what she was about to do. Jill let her arms drop to her sides and the curved scales hidden in her sleeves slipped into her palms. The simple sleight of hand would not have made Houdini proud, but she hoped it was enough to fool the people watching her. When no one cried foul, she breathed a sigh of relief. So far, so good.

She prayed it would work, that Baelin was right and the scales would keep her hands from receiving the third degree burns she was sure the metal would inflict without wearing NASA-grade asbestos-lined oven mitts.

She kept her hands palm side down so the scales couldn't be seen. She cast one more look at Baelin, and then grabbed the red-hot iron the priest held out to her before she lost her nerve.

Fire shot up her arm instantly and she bit back a scream.

Nine paces.

She could do this. Just put one foot in front of the other and go nine paces.

The pad near her thumb and the ends of her fingers were burning where the scales didn't cover them. She gritted her teeth and kept going.

Eight paces.

Seven.

She tried to keep herself from running. But the closer she got to the finish line, the hotter the rod got in her hands.

Six.

Five.

Oh God, it hurt. It was as if she were holding a hot cast iron skillet with a worn out pot holder, the heat seeping in gradually until it felt as if she was grasping it with her bare hand.

Four more steps.

Three.

The pain was shooting up her shoulder now, setting the nerve endings at the back of her head on fire. She didn't know if she could make it to the mark. The distance was so short but seemed like a mile away.

Two.

One.

She dropped the rod and it clattered on the stone pavers, the metal already fading from pink to grey as it cooled. The charred scales fluttered to the ground, but she was too delirious from the pain to care anymore.

Her legs gave out from under her and she collapsed, barely noticing the two strong arms that caught her before she could crumple on the cold, hard stones of the church floor.

CHApCER ChiRCEEN

Baelin tried to suppress the sneeze coming on.

He managed to succeed only to have his ears feel as if they exploded from the inside out. If someone passed by, they'd no doubt see smoke seeping out of them.

He never hated the rain more than he did now. Since the trial, he'd stood outside in the elements, never daring to leave the place of Lady Jill's confinement should she awaken and call for him. But would she, even if she could? He'd sworn to protect her and he'd failed. Why would she rely on him now?

As he sat by the small window, his ears strained for any sound from the woman within. She seemed to be resting peacefully now. But even if she were not sleeping, she would probably not speak to him. No doubt she hated him now, angry he'd not tried harder to save her from this fate.

Perhaps she'd been right. Enraged at her deceit, perhaps there had been a small part of him that wished to see her punished for it. But no longer. After the trial, her cries of pain as she tossed and turned in her cell had nearly torn his dragon heart from his breast.

But three days had passed. Three days with just as few words from Lady Jill.

Baelin leaned his back head against the hard daub of the house and cursed himself. He'd risked both of their lives in giving her the scales, and for what? She had still suffered. Would that he could have spared her all of the pain. His only solace was that he'd been able to catch her as

119

she fell, blessed oblivion stealing away the worst of her suffering. No one witnessed him retrieve the charred scales and hide them in his cloak as he cradled her unconscious form to his chest.

The sext bells rang. Baelin tensed, knowing Lady Jill's guilt or innocence would be determined within the hour. If the outcome went poorly for her, he mentally prepared himself for what he must do. As much as he hated the thought of shedding innocent blood, he would do it if he must. If need be, he was prepared to slay every man in the village to save Lady Jill's life.

He would not—could not—let her hang.

Baelin sneezed again, this time unable to contain the force of it. A small fireball shot out, slamming into the side of the cottage across the way. For once, he was thankful for the rain—it kept the thatched roof too wet to catch fire.

"*Gesundheit.*"

The softly spoken word drifting through the window startled him. "My lady?"

"It means God bless you, for the sneezing."

Crouching in the mud by the window, Baelin peered into the darkness of the room, but he couldn't see her. "How do you fare?"

"As well as can be expected after being branded like a longhorn steer."

He wasn't sure what a long-horned steer was, but she was speaking to him and that's all that mattered.

"I am sorry you had to endure so much pain." He hesitated, searching for the right words, not quite certain what she would accept from him. "You were very brave. Braver than many a man I have seen put to the iron."

"Thanks." She made a humorless chuckle. "You know, the really scary thing is this is a common enough occurrence that you've seen it happen before." There was a long silence from the within the room and Baelin wondered if she'd succumbed to sleep once more. "Baelin?"

"Aye, my lady?"

"Thank you...for staying with me, even after what I did to you."

"I could do no less. I only wish I could have spared you all of it."

An unladylike snort punched the darkness of her cell. "Well, you can't stop me from being stupid. As you said, I brought this on myself. It's the story of my life. I'm a walking mistake waiting to happen." He heard her heavy sigh. "Although it usually doesn't hurt this much."

Mumbled voices came from within the house, followed by the thud of footsteps down the ladder to the cellar level. Baelin shifted out of sight as the door opened and two men entered. Lady Jill groaned and he imagined them jerking her to her feet with little, if any, gentleness.

Baelin soon joined the other villagers in the church to watch as Lady Jill was ushered inside, looking pale and drawn. He willed her to glance his way so she might know he was there for her. She raised her head and looked about the church, her eyes finally locking with his. Gone was the fiery spirit and teasing laughter he'd come to know in them. Now they were hollow, the light in them perhaps forever dimmed.

Be strong, my lady. 'Tis nearly over.

She knelt before the priest. With the steward and his clerk standing to the side to oversee the verdict, Father Gerald grasped Lady Jill's arms by the wrists and held them up so all could see the stained bandages on her hands.

He hardly heard the sound of the priest's droning voice as the man recited the beginning prayer. Baelin's entire focus was on his lady.

His salvation.

When the prayer was completed, one of the village women stepped forward to unwrap the bandages from Lady Jill's hands. As the last strip of cloth dropped to the stone floor, the woman gasped. "'Tis a miracle."

Both men approached to see what the woman was talking about.

"This cannot be," the priest sputtered. "Why, I saw her stealing the statue with my own eyes. She must be guilty."

The steward frowned at Father Gerald. "Then your eyes have deceived you, for the evidence proves otherwise."

Pulling Lady Jill to her feet, Master William turned her to face the congregation. Standing behind her, he held her hands so the people could see them. Her palms were red, the fingers terribly blistered. But thanks to the scales, her hands were not nearly as burned as they might have been.

"Let it be known to all that the accused's hands show no sign of festering, but are healing. By the laws of England and the divine judgment of our Lord God, it is the judgment of this court that my lady Donahue is proven innocent."

Lady Jill closed her eyes and a single tear trailed down her dirty cheek.

Baelin released the breath he wasn't aware he'd been holding, relief cooling the sticky sweat trickling down his neck. His hand eased off the hilt of his sword and he offered up a silent prayer of thanks that he had not been forced to harm the innocent to save her this day.

They walked for what seemed like hours before Baelin deemed it safe to stop for the night by the shore of a pristine lake. In reality, the sun wasn't even close to setting—if the sun could be seen behind the dark clouds overhead.

Jill knew he was stopping for her benefit. She didn't care. Her pride was in shreds. She'd take pity now, any way she could get it.

As he set up camp, the sound of lapping waves drew her to the lake's rocky bank. The thought of crisp, clean water beckoned to her. For days, she'd had nothing but murky sludge in a wooden bucket that looked as if it'd been used to clean stalls before they'd given it to her.

She sat on a large, flat rock by the water's edge, wanting nothing more than to jump in and wash away the filth and grime covering her body. But she couldn't. She couldn't even scoop up water to quench her thirst. Her bandaged hands made that simple task impossible.

Frustration welled within her. She felt so helpless, at a loss as how to survive in this godforsaken place, her very survival dependent on a man who wasn't even completely human.

Wrapping her arms around her legs, Jill rested her chin on her knees, her vision mesmerized by the reflection of the impending storm clouds passing overhead. She leaned closer, afraid of what she would see in her own reflection.

The truth staring back at her was hard to face. Her hair was a matted mess, as if some small woodland creature was using it for a nest. Her eyes showed dark circles, her cheeks hollowed. She didn't need a modern scale to tell her she'd lost weight. Dropping a few pounds was usually a welcome bonus in any given situation, but she wouldn't recommend the medieval diet plan to anyone.

Jill glanced back to find Baelin standing a few feet away, watching her with guarded eyes. Did he think she would try to leave him again? Probably.

"Don't worry. Even if I wanted to, I don't have the strength to run away now."

"I know." He approached her slowly, as if unsure how to deal with her. "I pray you will not attempt to do so again. You have as much to lose as I do if we fail to break the curse."

The sheer hopelessness of the situation caused despair to form a tight knot in the back of her throat. As each day passed, the chances of that happening seemed further and further away.

"Maybe we're wrong. Maybe I'm not the one to break this stupid curse." She held up her bandaged hands. "For Pete's sake, how can I do that when I can't even get myself a drink of water?"

Baelin's gaze turned soft and gentle. He knelt beside her and scooped water up with his hands. He didn't say a word. He just sat there, waiting for her to drink as water trickled between his fingers.

Jill almost cried. He couldn't have been more chivalrous if he'd taken off his cloak so she could walk across the mud on it. She bent her head and drank the coolest, clearest water she'd ever tasted from the hands of a dragon.

"Thank you." She swiped at the water dripping off her chin with her sleeve.

"My lady, know that you are not alone in this. You have only but to ask and I will help you through it."

Baelin stood and walked away, leaving her alone to finish feeling sorry for herself.

She sat by the lake and watched him as he prepared the camp for the night. She noticed he laid out several blankets they hadn't brought with them from the cave. Had he purchased them while they were in the village? Did he do it because he remembered how cold she'd been that first night?

She tried to reconcile the man with her now—the one who put her needs before his own. The man who sat outside her prison cell window for over a week, in the rain and damp, giving her what comfort he could when he could've easily sought shelter for himself. The man who risked his life when he came before the village court to stand in her defense.

But he was also the same man who'd killed several people before her very eyes. A man who'd set another on fire with a gust of his breath.

As she watched him move about their little camp, she wondered where the gentle knight ended and the fierce dragon began.

Jill stood and walked over to sit beside him. He looked at her, a wealth of questions in his brown eyes. Thankfully, he chose a safe topic.

"Are you hungry? I replenished our supplies while you were...detained."

"Famished. They starved me for the first three days and then after the trial, I had no appetite for the poor excuse for food they brought me."

"I know."

Of course he did. He'd shared every moment of her imprisonment as if it were his own.

He handed her a hunk of bread topped with a wedge of cheese.

"Thank you." She cradled the food in her bandaged hands, not sure how to go about eating it. He'd already let her sip water from his hands, she wasn't about to ask him to feed her, too. The thought of him doing that was way too personal. Jill managed to bite off a piece of the hard cheese. She chewed and swallowed without really tasting it.

"Actually, I was thanking you for everything."

He arched a dark brow, surprised. "My lady?"

"For standing by me. For saving my life—not once, but probably twice. If you hadn't been there at the trial, I probably would have ended up burned at the stake or worse."

"Aye, 'twas a near certainty."

Jill cocked her head at him. "Why Sir Knight, did you just make a joke?"

Baelin shrugged, but she couldn't miss the smile tugging at the corners of his full lips. As he reached into the satchel for something else, his smile vanished.

"What is it?" she asked.

"The tapestry."

She could tell something was wrong. Her skin grew clammy, her pulse erratic. "Is it gone?"

"Nay. But 'twas rolled and tied the last time I checked it."

"So?" She didn't understand what the problem was.

"Now 'tis not." He pulled the tapestry out and placed it on his lap, dangling tie from his fingers.

"Maybe the knot worked itself loose while we walked."

"I do not think that is the case."

Jill looked closer. The knot was still tied tight, but the leather cord was broken. "Was it cut?"

"Nay. The ends are frayed, as if it was pulled apart."

"How could that happen?" Then she glanced at the rolled tapestry in his lap. It appeared more rounded, thicker. "Um, Baelin? Is it my imagination or is the tapestry bigger than it was before?"

He dropped the broken strap and unrolled the tapestry with unsteady hands.

"Oh my God!" she gasped.

Somehow, a new section had been woven into the tapestry.

A section depicting the maid going through a trial by iron.

"What...? That is just... How could the tapestry change like that?" Jill sputtered.

"I do not know."

"Someone must have altered it while we were in the village."

"Nay. 'Tis not possible. The tapestry has not been out of my possession since..."

Jill couldn't miss the censure halting his words. "Since I took it," she finished for him. "So how and when did this happen?"

"The only time the tapestry changed was after you came, when the face of the maid became your own. Now it shows the image of that same maiden with a rod in her hands."

Jill was afraid to ask. "What do you think it means?"

He turned hope-filled eyes to her. "You have passed the first challenge."

Instead of feeling elated, panic gripped her, tightening like a vise around her chest until she thought she might suffocate. "You've got to be kidding me."

He frowned. "I do not jest. I believe this with all my heart."

Jill bolted to her feet and strode toward the lake. She stopped and took several deep, calming breaths before turning back to face him. "Baelin, if that trial by iron is any indication of what the other challenges are going to be like, I can't do this. I can't go through something like that again."

"But you must."

"*Nooo.*" She shook her head at him. "You've definitely got the wrong girl for this job."

He looked down at the tapestry in his lap and ran his finger over the woven face of the maid holding the iron rod. Then he turned his dragon gaze on her.

"But you are the one. You cannot deny your fate any longer."

"Stop looking at me like that. I can't do it, Baelin. I'm not cut out for this. There's no way I'll be able to survive two more challenges like that."

"Who is to say the others will be like the first?"

Jill sputtered. "Who's to say they won't be? Or maybe the tests get worse." She shook her head again. "No, I can't do it. I just can't."

"Then how will you get back to your time? If it is as you believe, breaking the curse is the only way you can return."

"Well, we'll just have to find another way to break the curse."

"There is no other way."

"Fine," Jill huffed. "Then it looks like we're both stuck here because I'm not going to go through something as grisly and painful as that trial by iron again."

"What do you intend to do, my lady?"

She glanced around at the rolling hills surrounding the lake. "It's not so bad here. I'll find a job. Maybe get a small place on the outskirts of a quaint little village somewhere. I can survive in this place. It's not so bad once you figure out how to blend in. I can do that. Before long, they won't even be able to tell I'm not from around here."

Baelin cocked a brow at her. "As they could not tell in the village we just left, or the one before that?"

The truth of his words burst her bravado-filled balloon. "Oh, God, you're right. We're both screwed."

She walked back and flopped down by his side. Neither of them spoke as he rolled the tapestry up and put it away, but tension governed his movements, his silence berating her with every unspoken word.

He was upset, frustrated at her refusal. But he did not argue, did not try to push her to do what she didn't want to do.

Thunder clapped in the dark clouds overhead and rain pelted down on them in big, fat plops.

"I don't believe this. Somebody up there must really hate me."

Miserable and still in pain—with more pain certain to follow if she agreed to go through with the remaining challenges—Jill was not a happy camper. As the cold rain fell, drenching her hair and clothes and with no shelter in sight, she crossed her arms over her raised knees, laid her forehead on them, and gave over to the overwhelming despair threatening to drown her.

Then, just as suddenly as it came, the rain stopped. Or at least it stopped falling on her. She could still hear the patter of rain around her, like a summer shower on a canvas tent.

She opened her eyes to find Baelin had tossed back his cloak and was shielding her with his wing. She watched as a raindrop trickled down his nose to drop off the end.

"I am sorry I cannot provide you better shelter, my lady. 'Tis the best I can offer."

Jill nodded and snuggled under his protective wing, guilt weighing heavy on her conscience. Here she was, telling him she couldn't help him in his quest to regain a normal life and yet he was still taking care of her, shielding her, protecting her.

She knew he was right, that she had to see the other challenges through, but that didn't make it any easier to face.

"What are we going to do, Baelin? Even if I try, I'll never be able to pass the rest of these tests. In two weeks, you'll turn back into a dragon and since I can't even last five minutes in a village without receiving a death sentence, I'll end up living in that dark cave with you for the rest of my life."

He reached out as if to comfort her. His fingers hovered over her arm a moment before he curled his hand into a fist and returned it to rest on his thigh, never allowing himself to touch her.

"Then, Lady Jill, for your future and mine, there is no choice. You must see the rest of the challenges through."

Chapter Fourteen

"Do not dare find your pleasure before mine."

Isylte rose and lowered herself again, driving her body down on the man beneath her. Her long hair spilled over her shoulders, silky silver waves brushing full breasts she would not allow him to touch. Not unless she wanted him to. She observed the man's torment through hooded eyes—so close to his release, but knowing it could mean his death if he allowed it to come before her own.

"If you spend before I am done with you, I shall turn you to stone so you shall never go soft again."

She smiled as the horror of the possibility drove Lorcan to please her even more. It was a game she played with any man she allowed into her bed—how long could they last before their bodies betrayed them? After countless centuries, she had the stamina to outlast all but the strongest if she chose to do so.

But tonight she was restless. She ground herself on the man's shaft, riding him like a prize stallion over the fields. Impatient to find her release and be rid of him, she maneuvered her long fingers to where they joined, rubbing the aching nub hidden there. Her climax came, as always, not because of the man straining and pumping beneath her, but because of another whose handsome face took the place of whatever lover currently occupied her fancy.

Spent, Isylte removed herself from Lorcan and slipped from the bed, leaving him lying there painfully stiff and panting.

"My poor pet," she crooned as she drew on a white silk robe. "You may find your own release now. But do not do it in my bed. It tends to leave such a mess on the sheets."

She sat at her dressing table and drew a silver brush through her hair with gentle strokes as only moments ago she'd stroked Lorcan's body to painful erectness. She watched in the mirror's reflection as he left the bed and strode silently from her chamber, his handsome body covered in glistening sweat, making the starburst scar on his chest stand out against his tanned skin. She sighed. Such a fine specimen of a man.

Too bad he wasn't the one she wanted.

As the door closed softly behind him, her eyes strayed to the tapestry hanging on the wall near the bed. There, woven in the magical threads, was the face of the one she truly desired. The one she wanted above all others.

The one she'd not been able to hold.

Thousands of strands of gold and silver twined with threads of burgundy and emerald silk, capturing in perfect detail the handsome face of her brave young knight. He looked as she had first seen him, that day so long ago, standing alone on the battlefield prepared to fight her dragons to the death. She'd laughed at him then. He'd been full of righteous might, certain his sword and his God would stand against her power.

Too proud.

But rather than crush him, as she'd done to so many before, she'd decided to keep him.

At every turn, he fought her. Even chained in her dungeon, stripped naked, exposed, he'd still denied her, refusing to submit and serve her. Or to warm her bed. And the more he resisted, the more she wanted him.

But her patience had its limits and in a pique of anger, she'd cursed him. Cursed him to be the very thing he hated.

She shook her head at the woven image of him. Baelin of Gosforth, the only man who'd ever had the courage to refuse her.

A weaker man would've been driven mad by the dragon inside him. But not Baelin. He was still out there, biding his time in the futile hope he could break the curse without submitting to her. The fool. It was only a matter of time before he came back to her.

He had to. He must.

Damn his pride. In over two centuries, he'd never set foot in her realm again. If he had, she would've known. If he had, her power over him would've been stronger, the call too great to resist.

She never thought he would last this long.

She stood and walked to the tapestry, running her fingers over his handsome woven face. "You will come back to me, Baelin. You cannot resist forever."

It was then that something caught her eye. Something small, waving in the draft of the chamber, delicate as a spider's web.

"No. It cannot be."

There, hanging from the bottom of the tapestry, dangled several threads. She stood still, fearing any sudden movement would set the tapestry unraveling further. It did no good. Before her eyes, row after row worked itself loose, the threads coiling on the floor at her feet.

"Nay!" the Dark Witch raged.

Somehow, after all this time, Baelin of Gosforth had found a way to break the curse.

Jill sat on a driftwood log and plucked at the last bit of cloth on her right hand.

Unfortunately, when it came off, so did a good deal of the scab that'd been stuck to it.

She winced as fresh blood oozed from a half-healed blister. She could really use a fresh bandage for it, but she had precious few left and they needed to be rationed. Baelin had torn one of the extra smocks she'd packed into strips for dressings, one of which now served as the make-shift maxi-pad she wore thanks to the untimely appearance of her period. And since underwear hadn't apparently been invented yet, she'd been forced to use more of the strips to hold it in place. She wasn't about to sacrifice the last few clean ones she had left for an oozing blister.

Jill shifted uncomfortably, feeling as if she was wearing a diaper instead of a feminine hygiene product. What did the women use before maxi-pads came along? She'd been too embarrassed to ask Baelin, but she figured he wouldn't know anyway. The very idea of menstruation gave even modern guys the heebie jeebies.

Reminded yet again of the inconveniences of the Middle Ages, she cursed whatever fate had landed her in this godforsaken place.

"My kingdom for a tampon!"

"Did you say something, my lady?"

She felt her cheeks flush. She hadn't realized she'd voiced her thoughts aloud. "Nothing. I'm just talking to myself again."

Baelin nodded but made no further comment. He went back to sharpening the blade of his sword. Evidently, he was getting used to her odd behavior.

She glanced out over the lake to the steep hillside jutting up on the far shore. After that first rainy night, they'd made their way down the shoreline to their present campsite, a pristine spot where a thick forest of oak and pine met the rocky beach, offering them both shelter and firewood, and a place for Jill to regain her strength and to heal.

She scratched at her neck. If she had a knife, she was sure she could scrape off several layers of dirt and dust covering every inch of her skin. She didn't even want to think about what might be crawling around in her hair.

Rummaging through her satchel, she pulled out her last clean gown and a small pot containing a soft soap concoction she'd snagged from the cave. Stuffing all her dirty clothes back in the satchel, she made a beeline for heaven in a lake, the twinkle of the sun on the water drawing her like a magpie to a shiny bauble.

As she passed by Baelin, his sharpening stone stopped in mid stroke. "Where go you?"

"I go to take a bath."

He stood and placed his broad mail-clad body between her and a much needed head to toe scrubbing.

"Is there a problem?"

His gaze shifted to her satchel and then back at her. "You bathed not long ago. 'Tis unhealthy to wash so often."

She snorted. "Are you kidding? It's unhealthy to be in my skin right now. I'm filthy, I smell, and I have an inch of God knows what under my nails. The last time I had more than a sponge bath was back in the bat cave when I fell in the pool."

Baelin glanced up at a sky blazing red and orange with the setting sun. "'Tis almost nightfall. 'Twould not be safe for you to venture far in the fading light. You may lose your way."

She pointed over his shoulder to a spot not more than fifty yards away. "I'm not going far. I'll just be right over there, around that bend."

"'Tis too far for my liking. There are dangers for a woman alone."

Jill's eyes darted to the dark shadows looming in the trees. "You don't think there are more medieval mountain men around here, do you?"

"Nay, but there is always the risk."

"Well, since you don't think there are any bad guys hiding in the bushes," she made to go around him, "I'm willing to take my chanc—"

Baelin grabbed her by the arm, stopping her. She glanced from where his large hand encircled her arm to his face and cocked a brow at him.

"I cannot allow it."

"You cannot *allow* it?" She couldn't believe was she was hearing. "Excuse me, but who died and made you king of the bathtub?"

His brow creased and he looked confused. "To my knowledge, King John still lives. Then again, a great deal could have happened during my past year as a dragon I am not aware of…" Baelin shook his head. "Who currently sits on the throne of England matters not. What matters is that I must protect you."

"So, you're protecting me from being clean?"

"I cannot keep you safe if I cannot see you."

"Oh." That made sense, sort of. "Well, it makes you feel better, I'll be sure to splash around and make plenty of noise so you'll know I'm all right."

He groaned, as if the idea caused him physical pain. Whatever his problem was right now, she wasn't in the mood to deal with it. She tried to pull her arm away, but he held her tight, just short of hurting her. This was unreal. He was acting more like a Neanderthal than a knight in shining armor.

"Do you mind?"

The muscles in his jaw bunched. "God's teeth, woman. Must you gainsay everything I say?"

"I will *gainsay* you or anybody else who thinks they can bully me around. I'm not your prisoner and I don't need your permission to do anything, including take a bath."

"A prisoner you are not, but as long as you are with me, you are under my protection. Have you so easily forgotten the trouble you encountered when you ventured off on your own the last time?"

Jill huffed. "Oh, fine. Throw that up in my face. I said I was sorry."

"I still cannot allow you to go." He continued to stand there, a human chain-link fence blocking her way.

"Why?"

"Because I cannot protect you if I cannot see you."

"Because you can't see—" Then the truth hit her. "Oh, my God. This isn't about protection. It's about trust, isn't it? You don't trust me out of your sight. You think I'm going to try to run away again, don't you?"

Baelin didn't answer. He didn't have to. His rigid stance, the constant glances to the satchel she carried, told her she was right.

"How many times do I have to apologize? I made a mistake. I learned my lesson, the hard way. I promise I won't do it again."

"A knight's word is his honor. Trust, once broken, is hard to regain."

Jill's stomach tightened into a knot. She understood what honor meant to him and the high value he placed upon it, and now he was questioning hers.

"You said you forgave me." Her words came out in a soft, timid voice, like a contrite child's.

"Forgiveness and trust are two different things. While I bear you no malice for what is in the past, I would be a fool to trust you again so soon."

His words sliced through her, reopening an all too familiar wound. Here she was, in another place and another time, and she was still screwing up. Always falling short. Always disappointing. She should be used to it by now. But somehow, seeing her failure reflected in Baelin's eyes—a man whose honor meant more to him than his life—cut deeper than it ever had before.

"Gee, Baelin. I'm sorry I'm not brave and honorable like you. I'm sorry I've disappointed you. You'll have to excuse me for being a little grumpy, but in the past two weeks I've been catapulted eight hundred years into the past, hog-tied to a stake by crazed villagers, chased down by a fire-breathing dragon, attacked by Robin Hood and his Not-So-

Merry-Men, witnessed one of those men get Kentucky fried before my eyes, locked in a dungeon, and nearly executed by molten metal. And all the while, you're hovering around me, expecting me to be this paragon of maidenly virtue and Xena the Warrior Princess all rolled into one. But I'm not. I never said I was and I probably never will be."

He stood silent, listening to her rant and rave without so much as a single retort in return. His dark eyes bored into her and she couldn't help but feel she was being tried and judged all over again. Only this time, the pain hurt more than any hot iron could, because she brought it on herself.

She fought back the tears that threatened to choke her. She would not cry. Not this time.

"Fine. If you don't trust me out of your sight then you'll have to come with me, because like it or not, I'm taking a bath."

Baelin reared back, shocked at the suggestion. "I would never dishonor you so."

"Oh really? That precious honor you cling to so tightly didn't stop you from playing the peeping tom—or should I say peeping dragon—when I walked around the cave naked, did it?"

The shared memory flashed between them and the flare in his eyes told her he recalled it too—in every intimate, bare-skinned, glistening-wet detail.

"You didn't think I'd remember that, did you? Seems like we both have a little work to do on the trust issues."

Baelin flinched as if she'd slapped him. He let go of her arm, a mixture of anger, shame and frustration in his eyes.

Her conscience smacked Jill in the back of the head. What was she doing? In her foul mood, she'd struck out and hit him where it hurt most, his honor. She glanced at the ground between them, unable to face him. How could she be so self-centered? This man needed her. He was counting on her to help break this damn curse of his. He was not the type of person to rely on anyone but himself and yet here he was, forced to depend on her of all people. Boy, did he get the short straw on that one.

Okay, so maybe she was being a little unreasonable.

All right, a lot unreasonable.

But could anyone blame her? After everything she'd been through, it would make even Mother Teresa a bit snarky. Throw in PMSing big time and being unable to stand the smell of herself, and she was behaving like a major bitch with a capital B.

But no matter how crappy she felt, it didn't give her the right to be nasty to the man who'd saved her life. Finally, she gathered the courage to look him in the eye again.

"I'm sorry, Baelin. That was completely uncalled for. You've been nothing but patient and kind to me since I've been here. You've taken care of me and put up with more than anyone should have to. I didn't mean what I said. I'm just tired and dirty and that makes me a not-so-nice person to be around."

He stared at her for the longest time, the threads of their fragile relationship stretched taut between them. She wondered what was going through his mind. Would he accept her apology, as lame as it was?

"And taking a bath will make you a nice person to be around once again?"

For a second there she thought he might actually be trying to joke with her. But he wasn't smiling. Come to think of it, he hardly ever smiled. Could she blame him? There'd been little to be happy about lately, and she wasn't making matters any better with her smart mouth.

"Yes, as a matter of fact it will."

He glanced out over the lake, then he turned his attention back to her, gracing her with a half bow. "Then by all means, partake of your bath, my lady."

Surprised, she gaped at him. "You're going to let me go? Alone?"

"You are right. If we are to succeed, then we must learn to trust one another. If I have your word you will return quickly, I trust you to do so."

She felt a rush of elation, as if she'd just been given the keys to the car for the first time. She rose on her toes to place a soft kiss on his cheek. "Thank you. I won't disappoint you this time. I promise."

At his stunned expression, she turned and walked toward the lake, wondering if she'd just taken the first tiny step in taming a dragon.

ChApter FifteeN

She had kissed him.

Baelin touched his cheek, still tingling from the caress of Lady Jill's lips. The woman never ceased to confound him. When he'd been loath to touch her, even to wipe her tears away, she'd kissed him without hesitation, without fear, and—most significantly—without disgust.

Could it be possible he did not repulse her? That, dare he hope, she might even grow to care for him?

Just who was this woman from another time? How was it she could see him so differently from all the other maids that had come before her?

She was bold and strong-willed, stubborn and brazen. Aye, infuriating though she may be, it was those very traits that gave him hope. Hope that maybe she was the one after all, the one to break the curse. So far, she'd made it farther than any of the others.

He stood in the shadows of the forest, listening to the sounds coming from the lake as Lady Jill sang an off-key tune while she bathed. Something about washing a man out of her hair. How was that even possible?

What an odd tune. Then she sang a line about sending that man on his way. Was she singing about him? Probably. She was no doubt angry with him. He couldn't blame her. He may have been living in a cave for over two hundred years, but he still recalled how women liked to remain tidy and presentable. He'd behaved like an ass in trying to deny her the small, simple pleasure of a bath.

By the saints, he was at a loss as to how to handle the woman. The other maids had done as he asked, ever fearful of angering the dragon. But not this one. Nay, she seemed to thrive on constantly arguing with him, opposing him at every turn.

She paused in her singing to shout out, "I'm still here."

Her words stabbed through him. He wanted to trust her. He needed to. But he did not dare. His word of honor was everything, and his faith in her word had been shattered.

She began yet another song. This one was about bathing with a rubber duck, whatever this thing rubber was. He didn't even attempt to try to comprehend its meaning.

The woman's very presence tormented his peace of mind, baffling him at every turn. One moment she was a shrieking harpy, ranting about things he often didn't understand, and the next she would gaze at him with a warmth and tenderness he'd not known in centuries.

It was moments like that, when she made her way past the dragon to the man, that he was most vulnerable. The ancient heart within his chest was a desiccated ground, soaking up the smallest drop of her kindness, even at the risk of drowning in the overwhelming flood of those long dormant emotions.

He groaned, the sound of her bathing recalling images he best not think of. But they refused to stay at bay.

He could easily imagine the cool lake water flowing over her soft flesh, caressing her body with liquid fingers—fingers he longed to replace with his own. Another splash brought the vision of her standing by the shallow pool of the cave, drops of water glistening on her pale skin like thousands of tiny diamonds, while streams trickled in a curving trail between her breasts, down her belly, to the enticing thatch of brown curls between her thighs. His mouth grew parched, his throat dry. He was a thirsting man dying for but one sip to drink.

He paced under the trees, wrestling with the need to get away from the temptation of Lady Jill and his wicked thoughts, but needing to stay close in case of danger. The torture of his own imaginings was almost too much to endure, the sound of his own breathing too loud to his ears.

He stopped before a large oak and beat his forehead against it until he thought he might see stars. He had to stop the wicked visions poisoning his thoughts or he would be no better than the leering dragon she'd accused him of being in the cave. He stilled himself and squeezed his eyes shut to calm the beast inside.

When he opened his eyes again, his gaze landed on a small willow tree, its branches supple, always bending to the wind, but never breaking. The willow looked deceptively fragile and delicate, but grew in the rockiest of ground, strong and constant.

That was his Lady Jill. She thought she was weak, unworthy to the task at hand. She said he demanded too much of her. But like the willow, he could see the strength hidden within her. A strength she did not realize she possessed.

But he had to remember she was also alone and afraid, a woman far from her home and family. She'd already been through more for his sake than he had any right to ask. Never, in all the years he'd been taking the maidens, had he imagined the tests would be so physically challenging. He only prayed the tests that yet remained would not cause her more pain and suffering.

Baelin breathed a sigh of relief. At least they seemed to have reached a truce of sorts, after the argument over the bath. If he could remember to allow her small pleasures such as that every now and then, perhaps they would get along better.

He smiled, recalling her chaste kiss on his cheek. Aye, if they could get on like that, they just might survive this quest without killing each other in the process.

It was then he noticed the silence and his smile vanished.

Lady Jill had stopped singing.

Jill stumbled from the icy water before she lost all feeling in her extremities.

The idea of a bath in the lake had sounded good in theory. The reality was bone-chilling, teeth-chattering frigid. Where did the water come from, a glacier?

She'd just pulled the last clean smock over her shivering body when she heard a horse's whinny close by. Her first instinct was to shout for Baelin, but she bit back the sound. What if it brought unwanted attention to where she was, when whoever it was might pass her by if she stayed quiet?

She contemplated diving back into the cold water to swim across the lake to safety, but could she make it? Probably not. With her luck, she'd drown.

Before she could make a move, a lone man rode out of the trees. He wore a white surcoat with a blue gryphon rampant over a suit of mail, complete with a long sword and shiny shield. This was no dirty woodland outlaw. This man was a knight like Baelin.

But that didn't make him any less of a threat.

He pulled his large horse to a halt, surprise at finding her standing before him evident on his handsome face. He surveyed the area, evaluating every tree and boulder in sight. Was he looking for signs of danger? She almost laughed. Like she was a big threat, standing barefoot and shivering in her medieval slip.

Evidently determining it was safe, he left the cover of the forest and urged his horse closer.

Jill glanced around for a weapon and grabbed a branch that had washed up on the rocky shore. She hefted it like a baseball bat and the rough bark bit into her tender palms. She might not be able to do much damage with it, but she hoped it might keep him from coming too close.

"Greetings, my lady."

"Hi there, yourself. That's close enough, if you don't mind."

The knight stopped his horse. "As you wish." He glanced around the shoreline once again. "My lady, how is it you are alone and unprotected?"

Jill looked into the woods behind him, relieved to see no more men materializing out of the shadows. "I was beginning to wonder the same about you."

The knight looked perplexed for a moment and then he laughed. "Ah, you jest with me. Myself, unprotected. 'Tis humorous. But if the truth be known, I am not alone." He called over his shoulder without taking his eyes off her. "Master Owen, come forth and present yourself."

Jill tensed, wondering if a whole army of knights was about to surround her. She breathed a sigh of relief when a lone boy, no older than eleven or twelve, rode out of the forest on a small pony. Guess one knight and a tweener didn't count as an army.

The knight dismounted with ease and tossed the reins to the boy, then walked slowly toward her. Still not sure if he was friend or foe, Jill raised her impromptu bat, prepared to bash him in that handsome head of his if he made one wrong move.

"That's far enough. I think it would be better if you got back on your horse and rode off into the sunset like a good little knight."

He stopped just out of striking distance from her. "Fear not, my lady. I mean you no harm. My only desire is to ensure your safety."

"I'm safe enough, thank you. My friend is waiting just around that bend. He's a knight. A very protective one," she felt compelled to add. "One shout from me and he'll be here before you can get back on that big Clydesdale of yours. And trust me, I don't think you want to be here when he does. He's got a fiery temper." Sometimes quite literally, she thought.

"A fellow knight? Truly?" He glanced around the area once more, as if he didn't believe her. "Then I look forward to making his acquaintance. 'Tis been a long time since I shared the company of a fellow man of the sword."

He took another step toward her but stopped short when she raised the stick higher. Ignoring the possibility she might actually clobber him with it, he bowed to her.

"I am Sir Roderick of Kendal and this young lad behind me is my squire-in-training, Owen." The knight straightened and placed his hand over his heart. "On my honor, my lady, we intend you no harm."

Jill stared at him, trying to gauge whether he was telling the truth or not. If he was anything like Baelin, he would rather eat his mail before tarnishing his honor. Then again, she ventured to guess there was no one else quite like Baelin within a hundred miles. Or a hundred centuries, for that matter.

She glanced at his squire trainee sitting silently on his pony, the lake breeze tousling his blond hair about his young face. Even though he was still more boy than man, Jill felt a bit safer knowing he was around. After all, this Roderick wouldn't try anything funny with an impressionable young kid around, would he?

Cautiously, she lowered the branch but kept a firm grip on it with one hand. Better not to let her defenses completely down.

Sir Roderick nodded, acknowledging her reluctant ease. "I am honored to make your acquaintance, Lady...?"

"Jill."

"Ah, Lady Jill. A beautiful name for a beautiful woman."

Jill had thought the knight handsome when he rode out of the forest, but when he smiled at her, as he did now, he was drop dead gorgeous. Black shoulder-length hair framed a chiseled face and his brilliant blue eyes twinkled with charm and seduction. Now *this* was what the knights in the fairy tales were supposed to look like. They weren't supposed to go around with pterodactyl wings on their back and snorting fireballs.

Distracted by his GQ looks, she hardly noticed when he reached for her free hand and brought it to his lips for a kiss. A frown marked his brow and he turned her hand over.

"My lady, you are injured."

Jill jerked her hand from him, barely resisting the urge to hide it behind her back. "Cooking accident."

"I see." The look he gave her said he suspected she was not telling him the truth, but he had the decency not to question her further about it. "So where, pray tell, is your knight?"

"He's back at our camp, giving me some privacy while I took my bath."

The unspoken inference that he was not as gallant went over his head.

"Then 'tis fortuitous we have stumbled upon you. Allow me to escort you back to him, and then perhaps we can share the warmth of your fire and the company of you and your companion for the night."

"I don't think that's such a good idea. My companion likes his privacy."

"In that case, I shall see you safely into his care, and then Master Owen and I shall be on our way."

Jill ground her teeth. This guy just couldn't take a hint.

"Thanks, but I'm perfectly capable of finding my own way back. Besides, I'm sure you want to get going before it gets too dark. After all, don't you have a castle to defend or a damsel to rescue?"

"Nay. I earn my keep defending not dwellings of stone but the very land you trod upon and the fair skies above your head. And you, my beauteous lady, are the first damsel I have chanced upon in many a fortnight. But if there be more maidens such as you out in the wilds in need of rescuing, I must needs consider changing my calling."

"Your calling? What are you, a priest in shining armor?"

Sir Roderick laughed as he took this horse's reins from the boy. "Aye, in my own way. Like the men of the cloth, I too seek out and destroy evil, wherever it may be."

"I don't understand."

He mounted his horse and smiled as he looked down on her.

"I, my lady, am a dragonslayer."

Chapter Sixteen

Baelin charged toward the lakeshore, slowing when he heard voices.

Instantly alert, he drew his sword, cursing that he'd once again left Lady Jill alone and unprotected. But he heard no screaming. No shouting. Just voices. A man's, low in conversation, followed by Lady Jill's, soft yet aggrieved.

Who was she talking to?

He paused at the edge of the trees and parted the brush hiding the lake from his view. Lady Jill stood on the rocky shore, a small branch clutched in her hand and her spine stiff and straight. He sensed fear from her, a threat of danger on the air, and the presence of another man so near raised the hackles on the back of his neck.

But of the man, he sensed no immediate aggression at all. He sat at ease on a large white steed, his polished mail and fine surcoat proclaiming him to be a fellow knight. Baelin glanced at his own mail, tarnished and decades old. Could he still even call himself a knight?

Disregarding his appearance, he emerged from the cover of the trees onto the rocky shore, ready to defend his lady if need be.

The knight's horse spun on its hind legs and tossed its powerful head in alarm, wide nostrils flaring. A panicked whinny filled the air and a pony reared, tossing its small rider off its back before bolting through the trees. The boy on the ground could do naught but stare after it.

Lady Jill spun around to face him. Was that guilt on her face? What had they been talking about before he arrived? Had she told the knight of her plight? Had she only moments ago been pleading with him to rescue her from the clutches of a dragon?

The knight drew his sword.

"Wait!" Lady Jill moved quickly, putting herself between the mounted knight and Baelin. "It's all right. He's my...friend."

The other knight did not look convinced. The way she hesitated over the word 'friend,' he was not so certain of her meaning either.

Baelin stepped up behind her. "What goes here?"

"I should ask the same of you." The knight lowered his sword but did not sheath it. "How is it you have left such a fair maiden alone and unprotected?"

"I was never far. She had but to call out and I would have been at her side in an instant."

He glowered at Lady Jill, the unspoken question hanging in the air between them. *Why did you not call for me?*

She looked away, tossing aside her pitiful excuse for a weapon. "Um, Bae—Sir Baelin, this is Sir Roderick and his squire Owen. They were just passing through."

"I see," Baelin said. "Then God be with you on your journey."

The other knight's gaze traveled the length of him, taking in the ancient mail and his lack of a shield, trying to determine what sort of man he was. If he only knew that he was not a man at all. At least not a full one anymore.

"As I was saying to your lady, darkness is almost upon us and we were looking for a pleasant spot to pass the night. 'Tis fortuitous we stumbled upon you. We were hoping we could share the warmth of your fire this eve."

Every instinct told him to say no and send Sir Roderick on his way, but his honor would not allow him to be discourteous to a fellow knight.

"Aye, that 'tis fortuitous," Baelin said. Though civility forced him to make the offer, he made no effort to hide the displeasure in his voice. "By all means, come and pass the night with us. We would be honored with your presence."

He heard Lady Jill gasp but did not look at her, even though he knew she was staring at him as if he were mad. Perhaps he was.

"We are grateful for your generosity and look forward to your company. But first, we must chase after young Owen's mount before he gets too far away." The knight looked to the trees where the pony had disappeared. "I wonder what startled him so?" He turned his attention back to Baelin. "Now that I think on it, neither horse became alarmed until your approach."

"Um, wolf. It was probably a wolf," Lady Jill interjected. "We saw one earlier and Sir Baelin had to kill it. The scent is probably still on his clothes and that must've been what spooked the horses."

"A wolf? Truly?" Owen's voice cracked in his excitement as he stood. "I did not know there were any wolves about."

"There are none," the knight informed the boy. "At least naught that I have seen in many a year."

"Really?" Baelin listened as Lady Jill scrambled to cover her mistake. "Well, it sure looked like a wolf to me. Big, mangy thing with wild eyes. Came charging out of the trees snarling and growling, foaming at the mouth. Might have even been rabid."

The knight and young squire stared at her with matching stunned expressions, their brows furrowed, their jaws slack. Baelin shook his head. She was doing it again, rambling on and on, making little sense, and confusing all those around her.

It took a moment to realize what she was doing, and he bit back a smile. In her own odd way, she was attempting to distract Sir Roderick from examining too closely why the horses grew nervous around him. She was trying to protect him. And, as ridiculous as it was, she was succeeding and the gesture touched him deeply.

"In that case, let us be off, Owen. We must find that errant pony before the 'wolves' do." With a helping hand from the knight, the boy pulled himself up on the horse behind Sir Roderick. The knight bowed his head to them. "Lady Jill. Sir Baelin. Until our return."

Spurring his horse, the two cantered off into the trees. When they were safely out of earshot, Lady Jill whirled on him.

"Are you insane? Do you know what he is? He's a dragonslayer. That means he kills dragons for a living. Need I point out the obvious? *You. Are. A. Dragon.*"

"Thank you for reminding me. I had forgotten for a moment."

He was surprised at the tone in his voice and shook his head at the cause. A fortnight spent together and he was beginning to sound like Lady Jill. 'Twas not a good sign.

She fisted her hands on her hips. "You know what I mean."

"Aye. I know what he is. I have seen him hunting in my territory many times." He watched the forest, the darkening shadows swallowing up any sign of Sir Roderick and his young companion. "Hunting for me."

"Then why invite him to stay? Isn't that just asking for trouble?"

"Would that I could turn him away, but for one knight to deny hospitality to another is not done. To do so for no good reason would draw suspicion. He may leave, but he might also remain near to find out why we are so secretive. Better I have him in my sights so he will not surprise us later."

"In other words, 'keep your friends close, but your enemies closer.'"

Baelin was taken aback by her wise assessment of the situation. "I had not thought of it as such, but aye, you are correct. That is a very clever way of putting it."

"Hey, don't look at me. I think it came from *The Godfather*."

"The who?"

"Never mind. You wouldn't understand."

True, he did not comprehend all her words, but he understood the apprehension behind them. "Fear not, 'tis but for one night. Come the morn, we will safely part paths, with the dragonslayer none the wiser."

Lady Jill shook her head. "Well I sure hope you know what you're doing. You do a pretty good job of keeping those dragon wings hidden under that big cape of yours, but heaven help us if you cough up a fireball while they're around."

She stood so close, he could see the green flecks in her brown eyes. Without realizing what he was doing, he found himself leaning toward her. She pulled back and wrinkled her nose.

"Whoa! All that huffing and puffing isn't doing you any favors in the fresh breath department. You better not stand too close because one whiff of that sulfur breath of yours and he's going to know exactly what you are."

Baelin snapped his mouth shut, as if by doing so he could hold back the stench.

Lady Jill clambered about the shore, hanging the gowns she'd washed on tree branches to dry, completely oblivious of the insult she'd dealt him.

"Your advice is appreciated, my lady," he said through clenched teeth. "I will do my best not to belch on him after our evening meal."

The dragonslayer leaned back against a log near the fire, making himself at home.

Baelin was not so at ease. Lady Jill was right. It was dangerous to have a man like Sir Roderick around. At any moment he might slip and reveal his dragon side. But for honor's sake, he had no choice, at least not for this one night.

"Lady Jill, your manner of speech is like none I have ever heard before. I take it you are not from England."

"No," she answered, short and clipped. Was she just as worried about revealing her secrets as he was of revealing his?

"From whence do you come, then?" the knight asked.

"Richmond."

"I have heard of that. 'Tis near Middleham, is it not?"

"No." She choked back an unladylike snort. "Not by a long shot."

"I see." Sir Roderick frowned at her reply as he paused to take another sip of wine from a pewter goblet he'd retrieved from his supplies. The reprieve did not last long. "As I understand it, you and Sir Baelin are not wed nor are you kin. How is it that you have no lady's maid nor escort, save a lone knight, to accompany you?"

"Oh, don't worry. Sir Baelin is more than capable of taking care of me. In fact…" she glanced in his direction and he could have sworn she winked, "I've seen him fight off five men at one time without so much as breaking a sweat."

Baelin stilled, surprised to hear Lady Jill's words of praise. He recalled battling those men and what became of them. He also remembered how she reacted, fleeing from him in fear and revulsion. Had her opinion of him changed? Did she truly see him in such a light now? Or where the words for Sir Roderick's benefit alone? Would that he could see inside her heart and know the truth.

"That is impressive." The knight cleared his throat. "Still, 'tis not proper for a lady to be traveling alone with a man who is not her husband."

Baelin heard the question of her character hidden within the knight's words. He tensed, ready defend his lady's honor. But he didn't have to.

Lady Jill turned her full attention on the knight and cocked a brow at his blatant insinuation she may be more whore than lady. Sir Roderick may not fathom what was coming, but Baelin knew well what that look entailed. He kept silent, waiting for her barbed tongue to set the errant knight in his place.

"Maybe in this archaic, male chauvinistic world you're living in it's not considered proper, but where I come from, women are freethinking, independent individuals. We're educated, we have careers, we own property, we can travel anywhere and be with anyone we so choose. Heck, we can even vote."

Sir Roderick choked on his wine and looked to Baelin for confirmation. "What strange place does she speak of? I have never heard of such things."

Baelin spoke before she could say aught else and reveal that she was more than she appeared to be. "As you can tell, Lady Jill has had an unconventional upbringing."

"So I see."

The knight studied her closely, his gaze sharp, questioning. But Lady Jill did not squirm under his intense scrutiny. Instead, she returned his piercing stare, daring him to say more.

"'Tis late and has been a trying day," Baelin said, uneasy with the silent battle of wills passing between them. "Perhaps 'tis time you sought your pallet, my lady."

"Are you actually sending me to—"

Baelin caught Lady Jill's eye and he silently pleaded with her to not argue with him this one time. Already she'd revealed too much to the other knight. It would be far safer if she spoke no more, and the only way to assure that was if she was asleep, unconscious, or dead.

"Right." She cast him a brittle smile that said she knew exactly what he was doing but she didn't have to like it. "It has been a 'trying' day. Come on, Owen. Let's hit the sack."

The boy stood to follow her, but looked first to Sir Roderick for permission. The knight nodded and sent the boy on his way.

As the pair prepared their pallets, the knight watched in silence, his gaze following Lady Jill's every move. Baelin was not certain if he observed her out of curiosity over her odd behavior, or if he viewed her with a less than honorable interest altogether. Either way, it did not sit well with him.

Once Lady Jill and the boy were settled in for the night, the knight leaned back against the log and turned his attention to Baelin. "Tell me, Sir Baelin, have you lands?"

"I do. I should be returning to them in a fortnight." That is, if the curse was broken. If not, he would be returning to his cold, dark cave instead.

"And what of you?" he asked Sir Roderick, trying to deflect the knight's prying interest away from himself. "Are you landed?"

The knight smiled a bitter smile. "Nay. I am the third son of my father. What fortune I have, I must make for myself. So here you see me, earning my way as a dragonslayer. The gold is not so bad." He cocked his head, his gaze penetrating. "But you would know. You said you were once a dragonslayer yourself, did you not?"

Indeed, he'd told the man that very thing as they ate their evening meal. "I have hunted a few in my time."

"But no longer. Why did you stop?"

Baelin took a large gulp of his wine. What could he tell him? That he couldn't hunt his own kind? "I grew weary of it. You will too. You are young now, but you will soon learn hunting dragons is not all about the riches and the glory."

The knight laughed. "Young? Pray tell, I am not much younger than you."

"I am older than you think," he said. *By over two centuries, at least.*

Sir Roderick poured himself more wine from the sheepskin flask, before moving on to another topic. "How long have you and Lady Jill been traveling together?"

"A fortnight. I am escorting the lady back to her family." It was the truth, in a manner of speaking, if it was as Lady Jill believed and breaking the curse would send her back to her time.

"And where might that be?"

"South."

"We are to the south ourselves. Perhaps we can accompany you and your fair lady on part of your journey. Safety in numbers and all that."

Baelin wanted to shout *no*. Pack your things and leave, but he couldn't.

Did the dragonslayer sense his hesitation, his reluctance to have him along? Was he even now growing suspicious? Better to be rid of him come the morning.

"There is a great deal of England to the south. I doubt we travel the same path."

"But perhaps we are. I am to home myself, to Kendal."

Baelin started. "Kendal?"

"Aye."

His pulse pounded in his ears, the name long unspoken but still dear to his heart. "Then you are a descendent of Amdarch the Black."

Sir Roderick's brow furrowed as he pondered the name. "The Black? Aye. Tales of his valor have been passed down in my family for over five generations. Why? Are you kin to the family of Kendal?"

"Nay. But many, many years ago the families of Kendal and Gosforth were bound together, pledged as allies."

"Aye, that they were, before Gosforth was driven from his lands."

Baelin's grip threatened to crush the cup in his hand. It was true his family had been forced from their home. After he'd returned as the dragon, many who'd once called the Gosforths friend had turned against them, Kendal included.

"I am of Gosforth."

"Are you?" Surprise registered on the knight's face. "I thought there were none of you left."

"I am the last."

Sir Roderick straightened, interest and excitement radiating from him. "So you go to reclaim your lands, then?"

"That I do. But it will have to wait until after Lady Jill and I have completed our quest." *If* they completed it. He couldn't very well take on the mantle of Lord of Gosforth if he was still a dragon.

"A quest? How noble. What is it?"

"That, I am not at liberty to reveal."

"I see." The knight nodded, but would not be swayed. "A secret quest. Tell me, do you both seek the same thing?"

"In a way we do. The same thing, but for different reasons."

"How intriguing." Kendal smiled and toasted Baelin with his goblet of wine. "I always enjoy an adventurous journey. If you will permit it, perhaps I shall join you and Lady Jill on this secret quest of yours, since there seems to be a shortage of dragons about."

Baelin looked down into his goblet of wine. Instead of his own reflection, he saw the dragon staring back at him from its mirrored surface.

"I do not know about that. There may be one closer than you think."

Chapter Seventeen

"What do you mean, they're coming with us?"

Baelin had thought long and hard about allowing the dragonslayer to accompany them as far as the next town. He hadn't told him they'd been avoiding towns ever since Lady Jill's unfortunate experience in the last one.

"After you sought your blankets, Sir Roderick told me more of who he is."

"So?"

Baelin tried to explain, though he knew Lady Jill would never truly understand a knight's code and all it entailed. But after learning of the knight's lineage, his duty to the man's family turned out to be far deeper than a chivalrous pledge made on bended knee. "'Twas his forefather who fostered me, his kinsman who knighted me, men of his blood who died beside me fighting the Dark Witch and her dragons. I cannot turn him away."

Lady Jill shook her head. "That was over two hundred years ago. It doesn't matter who his great, great, great-granddaddy was. The man asking to join this little convoy of ours is a professional dragon hit man."

She was right, and Baelin was just as uneasy about it. But as he'd lain awake last night, contemplating the situation, another possibility had come to him.

"Have you given no thought that this knight may be the next challenge?"

She glanced to where Kendal and the boy were busy packing up their supplies. "Him? Mr. I'm-Too-Sexy-for-Myself? You've got to be kidding."

A prickling akin to jealousy welled within him. Jealousy? Nay, he refused to acknowledge the emotion. But try as he might, he couldn't swallow the bitter taste that formed in his mouth at the notion she found the knight attractive. At least, that's what he thought she meant by her words. With Lady Jill, he never knew for certain.

Nay, it was probably just the dragon's sense of possession rearing its ugly head again. He had to remind the beast within she was not his to possess. She was a means to an end and naught else.

"How are we to know in what form the challenges will present themselves? After all, he found us. Or rather, he found you. We should bide our time and see what this chance meeting brings." He watched her chew on her lower lip, never taking her eyes off the other knight. "Do not worry. I will do all within my power to keep you safe while he is with us."

She finally tore her gaze away from Kendal. "It's not me I'm worried about, it's you. Letting him spend one night with us was risky enough, but traveling all day together is flirting with disaster. What if he finds out who, or rather, what you are? Being the self-proclaimed world champion dragonslayer he thinks he is, he'll try to kill you and where would that leave me?"

"Ah, yes. Where would that leave you?" He regarded her coolly. Alone with 'Mr. I'm-Too-Sexy-for-Myself,' for one thing. "I wonder which you find more disturbing—the possibility I could die at the end of Sir Roderick's sword or that if I am slain, you will be forced to live out the rest of your days in this time?"

"Of course I don't want you to die, you idiot." She punched him in the shoulder with her fist. "I don't anybody to die. But I'm not thrilled about hanging out in the thirteenth century one more minute than I have to, either."

She growled her frustration. Baelin was not certain he'd ever heard a woman make that particular sound before. Another dragon, certainly. But a woman? Nay.

"It's not a one or the other situation and you know it," she continued on. "I want to go home as much as you want to stay alive long enough to break this curse of yours. And to make both of those things happen, we need to make sure Roderick doesn't find out what you are and turn your alligator hide into a new pair of boots. Having him come with us is just asking for trouble. You might as well go ahead and paint a big old bull's-eye on your chest."

Baelin's head spun at her words. He did not know whether to be touched that she worried for his safety or offended she thought he might lose in a fight to the other knight.

"'Tis too late. The offer has been made. I cannot withdraw it now."

"Of course not. I'm sure it would offend some medieval Miss Manners if you did. Personally, it wouldn't bother me one bit to tell him to go find someone else to tag along with." She wagged her finger at him. "Fine. This is your call. But if this blows up in your face, the screw-up goes on your tab this time, not mine."

She turned and stomped away. He stared after her, fascinated by her angry movements as she shoved their supplies back into the satchels.

The brief pang of jealousy he'd felt when she said she thought Kendal attractive was softened by the knowledge she was as displeased as he was to have the other man around. He didn't know why, but foul breath or not, she preferred his company to that of the handsome knight, and the thought stirred a warmth in his chest that had nothing to do with the dragon's fire burning within.

As Baelin moved to pack his own supplies, the wet snort of Kendal's horse announced his presence behind him. The knight made a show of looking around their camp, a frown marring his brow.

"What, have you no mounts?" he asked.

What, have you only now noticed?

Baelin was about to say they'd been stolen, but Lady Jill answered for him before he could put voice to the lie.

"Allergies."

The knight looked at her strangely. "Allergies?"

"Sir Baelin can't be around horses. It's the hair. It makes him sneeze, his nose gets all stuffy. Itchy, watery eyes." She bowed her head and mumbled something about sounding like a Claritin commercial, whatever that was.

"Ah." Kendal nodded in understanding. "That 'tis an unfortunate aliment for a knight to have. How inconvenient."

"Aye, it 'tis. If you will excuse us?" Baelin pulled Lady Jill aside, out of earshot of the knight. "Horses make me ill? Why did you tell him that?"

"Would you rather I told him you ate yours for a midnight snack?"

"I did not eat my horse."

"I stand corrected. You eat other people's horses. But since I couldn't tell him that, it was the only explanation I could think of on such short notice." She shrugged as she slipped the strap of her satchel over her shoulder. "Besides, it's not completely untrue, although it's more the other way around and the horses are allergic to you."

"Why not say 'twas you who has the aversion to the beasts?"

"Yes, I guess that would've been less of a blow to your male ego, but we can't do anything about it now, can we?"

Lady Jill smirked, strolling away from him with a haughty sway to her hips. His frown deepened as he watched her pass by man and steed, the knight also taking note of her enticing form.

"My lady," Kendal called after her. "Since you have no mount, I would be honored if you would accompany me upon mine. I cannot abide to ride when you are forced to walk."

Baelin didn't fail to miss the insult, intentional or not, in the knight's words. Shame lashed at him that he could not provide a mount for Lady Jill, but instead forced her to walk like a common peasant. Little did the dragonslayer realize if his own mount were not so well-trained and accustomed to hunting dragons, he too would be walking, his horse long gone from the fear of the beast.

"Thanks, but I don't want to put too much weight on your horse."

"But you are so light and delicate, I am certain *Flaume Stelan* will not even notice," he patted the horse's neck, all the while smiling that charming smile at Lady Jill.

"*Flaume Stelan?*"

"It means 'flame stealer'."

"Of course it does." She slid her gaze to Baelin, a tight smile painted on her face. "What else would a dragonslayer name his horse?"

As they rode throughout the morning, Kendal held his mount to a slow pace. However, every time Baelin drew near, the horse would suddenly speed up and put more distance between them. Maybe the animal was jittery sensing a dragon on its tail, but he suspected the knight was doing it on purpose.

It did little good. With the dragon's acute hearing, he could not help but overhear every word they spoke, even from a distance. Would that he could close his ears so he wouldn't have to listen to the way the knight flirted shamelessly with Lady Jill.

"Fair lady, your beauty rivals that of any flower of the field and your voice enchants me with its musical lilt from a land far away."

Baelin heard her snort. "Does that cheesy line really work on the women around here?"

Kendal was struck silent for a moment, then he tossed his head back and laughed. Baelin saw him swipe at tears as he struggled to regain his composure.

"Aye, my lady. It usually does. But I venture it is not working with you."

"No, it's not. So you can take your pretty poetry and odes to my eyebrows and shove them back in your pocket, because it's getting pretty deep around here."

The knight sobered and spoke to her with all seriousness. "Ah, but that is where you are wrong. You do enchant me. I have never, in all my travels, met a woman such as you."

"Now that I believe."

He watched on as Kendal rode with his arms wrapped around Lady Jill's waist. He hated that the other knight was able to touch her, to hold her, when he could not. To put his arms about her slender waist and pull her luscious body against his. But he couldn't very well force her to walk when she could ride.

Yet again, Baelin cursed the dragon part of him that prevented him from being like any other man. Prevented him the simple act of riding a horse.

He wished he could take the lead so he wouldn't have to look at them, but every time he attempted to go around, Kendal would nudge his horse and lope ahead, curse the man.

Walking downwind from Lady Jill, the gentle breeze tantalized him, carrying the subtle fragrance that was hers on fleeting wisps to tease him. Only now, her sweet scent was mingled with another's, tainted by horse and man.

It was as if his every dragon sense stood heightened just to taunt him, at least where Lady Jill was concerned. Just then, she laughed at something witty the knight said and the creature within, the one that hoarded treasure of gold and silver and precious gems, roared to life. But Baelin's inner beast coveted a different treasure now—one of flesh and bone, of emerald-flecked eyes and hair of silk. As much as he hated the monster he was, he couldn't deny the nature of the animal within him.

"Mine."

"Did you say something, my lord?"

He turned to find young Owen riding up beside him. The boy struggled to keep his small pony under control as the animal rolled its eyes at Baelin. *Aye, you should be frightened, you mangy beast. With the mood I'm in, I just might eat you.*

"Nay, I was merely speaking to myself." *Just as Lady Jill does.* 'Twas yet another sign how much she'd affected him in the short time they'd been together.

Owen caught Baelin's penetrating stare at the pair riding ahead of them. "Fear not, my lord. Sir Roderick will let no harm befall her."

"I cannot help but wonder if it is not Sir Roderick I should be worried about."

"Why?"

He tried to choose his words carefully. There was no need to insult the boy's master. "He seems to be overly...friendly, does he not?"

Owen's young brow furrowed as he considered the pair riding ahead. "Sir Roderick is that way with all the ladies and they adore him for it. His skill with the fairer sex is quite renowned."

"'Tis what I am worried about."

"You should not worry overmuch. He has never been one to force his attentions. All I have seen in his company have been most willing."

"That certainly eases my mind." *Not in the least.* For in truth, what did he know of Lady Jill and men she fancied? After all, she herself confessed she was no longer a maid, and yet she'd never been wed. Did the women of her time give of themselves so freely? He did not want to think it so, especially not with a man like Kendal about.

Nay, he knew her well enough to know she was not any man's whore. Still, he could not help but wonder that if she had been seduced once before by a man from her future, could she be as easily swayed by a practiced courtier from his time? The very possibility had the dragon snarling to take back what was his.

"Damn it, Roderick," came Lady Jill's annoyed voice from up ahead, "if that hand of yours creeps any higher, you're going to be singing soprano in the next three-point-five seconds."

The knight chuckled, Owen snickered and Baelin growled, his hand on his sword hilt until Kendal raised his arm in a sign of surrender.

"A thousand pardons, my lady. I was merely making sure you do not fall," he said in his defense, but he did not bother to hide the humor in the tone of his voice.

"I'll just bet you were." Lady Jill took the offending hand and placed it on the knight's mail-covered thigh. "Move it again and you're going to have to learn how to wield a sword left-handed for the rest of your life."

Owen couldn't suppress his boyish laughter any longer, even at his master's expense. "Lady Jill, she is not like any other woman I have ever met before."

"Nay, she is not."

He grinned at Baelin. "I like her."

He returned the boy's smile and eased his sword back to rest within its sheath, comforted for the time being that Lady Jill could handle the amorous knight in her own peculiar way.

"So do I, lad. So do I."

At that moment, he caught sight of Lady Jill craning her head around the knight's large form to glance behind them.

"Fear not, my lady," he heard Kendal say. "He is still there, most like staring daggers at my back."

Surprise straightened her spine. "As a matter of fact, he is. So why are you doing it?"

"Paying homage to your beauty?" he shrugged. "'Tis what a knight does when in the company of a lovely lady."

"That's not what I mean. You know I'm with Baelin, but you keep coming on to me. Why?"

Baelin could well imagine the knight's confusion at her strange words. "Coming on?"

"Flirting. Sweet-talking. Trying to get in my pants."

Kendal nodded. "Ah, but as you told me last night, you are a free woman, at liberty to be with whomever you choose. Am I correct?"

"Yes, but—"

"And as I understand it, Gosforth has no claim on you, save as your escort. True?"

"True, but—"

"Then that means I am free to *come on* to you, am I not?"

"No, it does not!" she sputtered.

Kendal laughed, then leaned in to whisper in Lady Jill's ear, but Baelin heard the knight's softly spoken words all the same. "And what of Sir Baelin? Do you hold affection in your heart for him?"

Baelin nearly stumbled. He slowed his steps, his ears pricked to hear her answer.

"It doesn't matter. We won't be together long enough for anything more than friendship."

"Ah, yes. He told me he was returning you to your home. I take it then that you plan to part ways once you reach there?" Kendal asked.

Lady Jill faced forward on the horse once again. "Yes. If everything works out, in two weeks he and I will never see each other again."

Baelin's stomach clenched at her words and his throat tightened to the point he could barely breathe. How could he have forgotten she believed she would return home once the curse was broken, that her hopes for returning to her time rode on the tapestry tucked safely inside his satchel? The burden of carrying it never weighed so much as it did at this moment.

He shifted the satchel to his other shoulder, hating the damn scrap of cloth more than ever.

ChAPTER EIGhTEEN

He hung shackled to the wall, the stones cold and rough against his back, the weight of his body on his arms unbearable. The sharp edge of metal bit into his wrists and warm blood trickled down, falling drop by drop onto the white stone floor.

He didn't know how long he'd been hanging there. Time had lost meaning for him.

But he wouldn't give in. He refused to break.

Because then she would win.

"Come, Baelin. Why do you resist when it would be so much easier to submit to me?"

He kept his eyes closed, his head lowered. Not out of reverence or sub-servience, but out of self-preservation. If he looked at her now, all would be lost.

"I would sooner endure the fiery pits of hell than to serve your dark powers for one beat of your black heart."

She tsked. "Your sense of honor is to be admired, but I do grow weary of it."

Then release me! he wanted to shout. But he didn't. He would never beg for mercy from her. She had none.

He heard her shift one step closer.

"Do you not find me beautiful?" she cooed.

He refused to answer her, refused to pay her the worship her vanity craved.

She gripped his chin, her nails digging into the flesh of his cheeks, and forced his head up. "Do you?" she spat through gritted teeth.

He didn't want to look at her. He didn't want to open himself to the dark power he could not fight. One crack in his will was all it would take. One moment of vulnerability and she would get in.

He resisted the pull as his lids fluttered open with a will of their own, powerless to stop them. He shuddered as he peered into those spell-binding eyes that had no doubt lulled many a man to his doom.

Frozen by those shifting violet orbs, the lie of her stunning beauty faded and her true image took form. The perfect ivory shell of the visage before him cracked, splitting open, to reveal the rotting yolk within. But instead of spilling out on the white floor in a pile of fetid waste as it did each time he relived this horror, the dark core took shape, shifting and solidifying into a familiar form as the outer layer crumbled and fell away.

Dark shifted to light. Thick black sinews coiled, curling into silky brown tresses. Oozing tar softened and smoothed into creamy pale skin, and two dark pits formed into the green-flecked eyes he knew so well.

Jill.

Baelin's eyes flew open, expecting to see the stark white confines of his prison. To hear *her* laughter. But the only sounds were of the wind in the treetops over his head, the hiss of the fire as the ashes died down, and the steady snoring of the knight nearby.

He lay still and tried to calm the rapid beating of his heart, to dispel the hazy tendrils of the dark dream that remained.

The nightmares always returned whenever he was in human form. Even after all these years so far out of her reach, the witch still tormented him. She had no power over him in his waking hours, but at night she crept into his dreams, torturing him over and over again in his memories. This time, the pain had been all too real. He rubbed his wrists out of habit, surprised as always to find there were no deep gashes in his flesh.

But that was not what bothered him. He'd had the same dream many times over the centuries, but this was the first time the witch had changed into the maiden. What did it mean? He rubbed at his throbbing temples, but as the dream faded away on the morning mist, the answer refused to come. A man could go mad pondering the reasoning of it all.

He grabbed his sword belt and strode to the edge of the trees. Though the violence churned within him, as it always did when he dreamed of *her*, he would go no further. He dare not leave Lady Jill unguarded again.

He clenched his fists, itching to wrap them around the witch's neck and strangle her. Drawing his sword, he again heard her laughter and wanted nothing more than to sever her head from her body to stop the pealing sound that had rung in his ears for over two hundred years.

A twig snapped behind him and he whirled, his sword striking out without thought.

Kendal jumped back, the blade whistling through the air, barely missing its mark. The knight raised his hands, his expression wary.

"Hold up there, my man. No need to skewer me for taking a piss."

Baelin lowered his sword but did not sheath it. His hands were too unsteady to accomplish the simple task at the moment. Saints, his nerves were so on edge, he'd nearly gutted the man before he knew what he was about. Without the protection of his mail, the knight's quick reflexes had been the only thing that prevented Baelin from slicing him open from breast to hip.

What if it had been Lady Jill or the boy instead?

"Is aught amiss?" Kendal asked, his keen gaze searching the trees for danger.

"Nay, I thought I heard something, but it was naught."

"Ah, good." Kendal untied his breeches and a yellow stream arched out to douse the dry leaves on the ground. "I do so hate to face battle with a full bladder."

Baelin eyed the puddle of urine as it wound its way slowly past root and grass toward his boot. "Aye, 'tis an uncomfortable feeling." He stepped out of its way.

The knight's horse snorted on its tether near the camp. Kendal glanced at the beast as he retied his breeches before returning his attention back to Baelin.

"I am still amazed you are traveling on foot. To not be able to ride…how is it you compete in tournaments?"

"I do not," Baelin answered. "I find no honor in vying for a nobleman's trinkets and the admiration of those who forget my name as soon as the challenge is over." Not to mention, dragons and hordes of armed knights would not mix well.

"Ah, you must not have won many a joust, then."

Baelin didn't fail to miss yet another couched insult aimed in his direction.

"But I do understand," the knight continued on. "I too grew weary of it myself and sought a more challenging foe than green knights who purchased their spurs with their father's coin."

"And so you choose to battle dragons instead."

"Aye, dragons."

Kendal ran an assessing eye over Baelin from head to toe. "Speaking of spurs, your armor is a bit...antiquated, is it not?"

Unlike the other knight, he'd been forced to sleep in his mail, uncomfortable though it was. But he had no choice. To take it off would be to reveal what hid beneath. He recalled Kendal's shiny armor, more plate than mail, unlike Baelin's *hauberk*, which was at least several decades old. He really needed to have new armor made, the next time he became human.

"I do not pay court to fashion. The mail I wear serves me well enough."

"It would appear, since you are still alive to show for it."

Baelin waited, hearing the pause in the knight's speech. It didn't take long for the next insult to come.

"Of course, if you have not seen battle, mail serves no purpose other than to acquire rust."

Was Kendal deliberately trying to provoke him or was the man so enamored of himself he was unaware of the insult in his words?

"I have already seen more battles than you will ever face in your lifetime," Baelin said through gritted teeth, "which may be shorter than you think if your boasts are not something you can live up to."

"Oh, they are not boasts, Gosforth. I earned my spurs and have continued to do them justice everywhere I go." Kendal smiled, a silent challenge lighting his eyes. "Care to find out just how true those boasts are?"

Jill awoke to the jarring clang of metal against metal.

She turned over, drawing her blanket over her head, and cursed the garbage men who barreled their trucks down the alley behind her apartment at this ungodly hour each week.

Then she remembered she wasn't in her apartment and there were no garbage trucks in the thirteenth century. She bolted upright, her heart racing, expecting to find them under attack by an army of sword-wielding city sanitation workers.

Instead she found Baelin and Roderick trying to kill each other.

"Oh, my God. Stop!" She jumped up and raced toward them, nearly tripping over the blanket wrapped around her feet. She halted just short of the area of trampled grass they'd crushed under foot. "What on earth are they doing?"

"They are sparring, my lady," Owen answered from the spectator spot he'd claimed by the men's other weapons scattered at his feet, completely unconcerned.

She watched as first Baelin, then Roderick waged an attack against the other. The reverberating peal as sword struck shield shot a phantom pain up her arm, and she wasn't even the one getting whaled on.

A flash of white caught Jill's eye. Sweating and grunting with each blow, Baelin was also...smiling. She glanced at Roderick to see the expression mirrored on his face as well.

"They're enjoying this," she murmured in disbelief.

"That they are, my lady."

"Why do men find it entertaining to beat the crap out of each other?"

Owen shrugged a bony shoulder. "Sir Roderick says 'tis in man's nature, to make love or to make war."

She glanced at the boy, still amazed he was traveling around the countryside with a man like Roderick. "You really need to stop hanging around him so much. He's a bad influence on you. What would your mother think?"

"'Twas she who sent me to train under him."

"Give her the Mother of the Year award for that decision."

He grinned, completely missing the sarcasm in her tone. "Aye. Someday when I have earned my spurs, I hope to be just like him."

"Heaven help us all." Jill tilted her head at him. "How long have you been his squire?"

Owen squirmed and she sensed the boy's unease. "In truth, I am not his squire yet. I am still but a page. I must wait until I am five and ten before I can hope to achieve that honor."

"How old are you now?"

"I have passed my twelfth year."

"Twelve?" That surprised her. He seemed very mature for a twelve year old. "How long have you his page?"

"Since I was a lad of seven."

The truth of his statement saddened her. "Sent off to live with strangers at seven, just like Baelin. That doesn't seem right."

Jill watched the men battle each other, dismayed at the barbarism of the world she now lived in.

"Have you never watched knights spar before?" Owen asked.

"No. But then again, I don't get the point of pro-wrestling either."

"Pro what?"

She was saved from having to explain the sport of grown men in shiny spandex body-slamming each other for entertainment by Roderick's loud voice.

"Remove your cloak, Gosforth, so that we might be more evenly matched."

The smile Baelin had been wearing instantly vanished.

Jill was so used to seeing him wearing his cloak, she didn't think it odd that he still had it on during their mock sword fight. No doubt Roderick was right and the bulky garment hindered Baelin's movements.

But she knew why he found it necessary to keep it on.

Jill jogged across the field to Roderick's side as he paused to wipe the sweat from his brow. "A word of advice, I wouldn't ask him to take off the cloak again."

The knight frowned at her. "Why?"

She chewed her lip, her brain scrambling for a reason. "Well, in case you haven't noticed, Baelin has a bit of a hunchback. He's very sensitive about it."

Roderick glanced to where Baelin stood, his gaze taking in the dark, voluminous cloak Baelin wore from broad shoulders to mid-calf, then he gave her a curt nod. "Ah, I see. Poor man. I shall not mention it again, my lady."

"Thanks. I appreciate it." She patted him on his plate-covered shoulder and crossed the impromptu practice field, but she wasn't lucky enough to make a clean getaway. Baelin caught up with her halfway back to Owen, grabbed her by the arm and steered her in the other direction.

"I heard that."

She looked up at him, making her eyes as wide and innocent as she could. "What?"

"Why did you tell him I have a hunchback, of all things?" he growled as he released his hold on her.

"The way I see it, you should be thanking me. I've given you an excuse to keep your cloak on whenever he's around." She paused, crossing her arms. "Unless you want to show off your dragon wings, and wouldn't that be an interesting thing to do while you're play fighting with a very real dragonslayer hacking at you with a very real sword?"

Baelin rolled his eyes. "First, horses make me sneeze and now you have given me a hideous deformity. I shudder to think what 'excuse' you will come up with next."

Jill grinned and wiggled her eyebrows at him. "You never know. I'm always full of interesting ideas."

"By the sword, you are going to drive me mad, woman."

"I do try."

"Come, Gosforth," Roderick called out. "Are we to finish our practice or not? Unless you fear I shall best you in front of Lady Jill and you wish to end it now. She has already requested I go easy on you. I would not want to trounce you overmuch in her presence."

A ring of smoke curled out of one of Balin's nostrils.

"Down smokey." Jill turned him so his back was to the knight. "Don't stoop to his level. You're bigger than that."

"Bigger?" He craned his head to scrutinize the other knight. "I think we are of a size."

"No. I mean you don't need to play his silly games. You're the better person for not resorting to childish taunts and cheap shots."

He returned his intense gaze to her. "Am I?"

"Yes, you are." She glanced at Roderick, who was busy examining the sharp blade of his sword—and probably checking out his reflection in the shiny surface of the steel while he was at it. "Remember, while strength and skill are impressive, restraint is also a very admirable quality. I imagine any other dragon-knight would have singed that man's arrogant eyebrows off by now."

He chuckled. "Aye, I imagine so, my lady."

"Good. Now go kick his cocky ass. Just don't let him mess with your head."

Baelin glared over his shoulder at the other knight. "I am well aware of what he is doing."

"Oh. Then I guess you're also aware it's working?"

His head whipped back around and he scowled at her. "'Tis not."

"Right. So the fact he's got you huffing and puffing has nothing to do with the smoke coming out of your ears."

"I do not have smoke coming out of my ears." But she watched his eyes shift to the left and right, checking the air around his head.

"My mistake. Wrong orifice. Anyway, be careful. You don't want to accidentally give anything away, like a certain pair of bat wings or a flaming hair ball or something."

"I will not reveal myself, especially now that you have so conveniently made it so I can continue to conceal my disfigurement."

"You are not disfigured. You're just...selectively enhanced."

Baelin stared at her for a long moment, his brow furrowed, as if he wasn't sure if he'd been complimented or insulted. Then his mouth crooked until it grew into a full-blown smile, totally transforming his face. The effect was staggering.

"Enhanced, am I now?"

"Yes." Did her voice just come out as a whisper? How could a simple smile affect her so? Jill shook herself mentally, ordering the butterflies in her stomach to stop doing somersaults. What the heck was that all about? This was no time to start harboring some schoolgirl crush over a fairy tale knight in shining armor...with dragon parts.

"Don't let it go to your head," she said. *Are you talking to him or to yourself?* She cleared her throat. "Remember, you're no spring chicken anymore. Roderick's a good 190 years younger than you." At his affronted look, she held up her hand. "No offense intended. Just stating the facts."

"Dragon years," he grumbled, his smile fading. She squelched the disappointment she felt at seeing it go. "In human years, he is not much younger than I."

Jill would wager Roderick was somewhere in his late twenties, which in human chronology would put him about a decade younger than Baelin. But she wasn't going to argue the point and risk insulting him any more than she already had with the Quasimodo comparison.

"All I'm saying is take it easy. You don't need to prove anything to Roderick."

A shadow crossed over his face. "What if 'tis not he I wish to prove something to?"

His admission surprised her. Was he talking about proving something to her, or to himself? She wasn't sure. But she was afraid to examine the meaning behind Baelin's words too closely or those butterflies might start doing abdominal gymnastics again.

So she said nothing. Instead, she stood there like an idiot, silently gazing into his handsome face—until an odd scent drifted by her, one that was at once very familiar but extremely out of place. She'd caught a faint whiff of it a few moments ago, but thought it was her imagination playing tricks on her. She inhaled once again, just to be sure.

"Do you smell gum?" she asked, although she'd wager her last pay check gum hadn't been invented yet.

She sniffed around some more, like a bloodhound on the trail, trying to zero in on the source. Finally, she came back to Baelin. The delicious fragrance seemed to hover around him. She placed her hands on his broad shoulders and pulled herself on her toes, only inches from his face, drawing in his exhaled breath.

"Are you chewing on mint leaves?"

He didn't answer. But the tell-tale bob of his throat muscles as he struggled to swallow whatever he had in his mouth gave him away.

She was right. He was chewing mint leaves. She recalled the callous remark she'd made about his dragon breath the other day and a shiver ran through her body as she wondered, was he doing it because of her...or for her?

Jill became aware of how her entire body conformed to his, chest to breast, stomach to stomach, hip to hip. She looked from his mouth to his eyes and watched in fascination as they changed from a warm chocolate brown to golden amber. They glowed from the dragon fire within him, proving he was just as aware of how close she was—and just as affected.

Darn those butterflies. There they go again.

She let go of his shoulders and stepped back, now more embarrassed at her impulsive actions than he was at getting caught.

"Come, Gosforth," Roderick called out. "My armor will rust upon my body if I must wait much longer for you."

Jill breathed a sigh of relief. Leave it to Roderick and his overblown ego to lighten the mood—and prevent her from doing something stupid, like kiss the daylights out of Baelin in the middle of the field.

They both turned in the knight's direction and the look Roderick sent their way said he'd witnessed every bit of what had just passed between them. She couldn't tell was if he was jealous or amused. That's all she needed—two men driving her crazy on top of everything else.

But she couldn't resist one more look at Baelin. Bad idea. He stood there, tall and silent, watching her with that fire still smoldering in his eyes.

Forget butterflies. She had giant lunar moths break-dancing inside her now.

Jill turned and hurried away before she became a casualty on the battlefield herself.

ChApTER NINETEEN

"Aye, the battle at Termes was a nasty one. Have a scar here where an archer's arrow skewered my arm and came out the other side."

Roderick pulled back the sleeve of his tunic to show there was, indeed, a wicked-looking puncture mark on both sides of his left forearm.

"You call that a scar..." Baelin sneered and proceeded to document the various wounds and gashes he'd received in his lifetime. He had quite a few to boast of, seeing as his lifetime was somewhat longer, and thus more injury-filled, than a normal man's.

Apparently beating the crap out of each other had induced a weird kind of bromance. While Jill wouldn't call them bosom buddies, Roderick and Baelin seemed to have graduated from silently hostile to mutually tolerant of each other since their clash of the tin men this morning.

Tired of listening to battle tales of the maimed and mutilated, she rummaged through her satchel and pulled out a fresh gown. "While you two trade gruesome war stories, I'm going to go take a bath."

All conversation stopped instantly. Roderick's mouth hung open, stalled in mid-sentence. Owen visibly cringed at the thought. Baelin didn't look too happy with the idea either.

Jill shook her head at all of them. "Don't be so shocked. Where I come from, bathing regularly is considered good hygiene." She made an exaggerated show of sniffing the air. "Quite frankly, it's a habit two knights who sweat buckets in their armor and a young squire-in-training who reeks more of horse than boy should consider taking up. A little soap and water never killed anybody."

As she walked away, Baelin bolted up and rushed around the campfire to block her path. "My lady, you bathed but two nights ago."

"Right, and I'm going to do it again. I'm used to having a bath every day and as long as we continue to follow the shore of the-lake-that-never-seems-to-end, I'm going to take advantage of mother nature's bathtub."

"But 'tis not safe."

"Oh, please. Let's not argue over this again. I'm not going to run away and as long as the Loch Ness Monster doesn't nibble on my toes, I'll be fine."

"'Tis not monsters in lakes that concern me," he said in a hushed voice and she saw his glance dart back to the campfire.

"Oh, you mean Owen and Roderick?" she replied back in an exaggerated whisper. "There shouldn't be a problem as long as they stay by the fire and don't come sneaking around to watch me skinny dipping."

She caught him glancing again to see if Roderick had overheard them. He had nothing to worry about. The other knight was too busy sniffing at various parts of his body to notice.

"I'll be quick. I don't have a choice—that lake is like jumping in the Arctic Ocean." The mischievous streak in her couldn't resist torturing him just a little bit. "Unless you could heat it up for me like you did back in the cave?"

Baelin's head whipped back around and he nearly choked on the gulp of air he inhaled. "My lady, there is not enough breath in my dragon lungs to warm the entire lake for you."

She gave a dramatic sigh. "Too bad. You know how I like hot baths."

What are you doing, Donahue? Are you actually flirting with him? Are you out of your twenty-first century mind?

His eyes flashed gold and he groaned, as if the thought gave him physical pain.

Okay, if he was remembering the same thing she was—her naked and wet, him just as gloriously nude, firelight and a certain bearskin rug—it was probably not the best image to put into his male brain. Especially not after that brief zing that had passed between them this morning.

With Baelin thoroughly distracted, she turned and made a beeline for the lake before he could stop her—or act on the heated promise simmering in his eyes.

Bad Jill. She should know better than to tempt a dragon.

"The dragon has left its lair."

Isylte slowly lowered the white swan's quill in her hand, but did not look at the man standing on the other side of the table. Instead, her gaze focused on the paper before her, the words she'd written blurring into black streaks before her eyes.

"Of course he has. He passed one of the challenges. He could not do so otherwise."

"He is traveling with a girl, my queen."

"I am aware of that." She closed her eyes against the image of Baelin with another woman, but it did no good, faceless though the girl was. "'Tis the maiden foretold of in the tapestry. Tell me something I do not know."

She heard the warrior shuffle in place. "They are not alone."

"Really?"

"The dragon and the maid are traveling with another knight." The warrior cleared his throat. "A dragonslayer."

Isylte's gaze pierced the knight, causing him to retreat a step back.

"Baelin is keeping company with a dragonslayer?" Now that was an interesting turn of events. "How unwise of him."

"Aye, we thought so, too. What could it mean, my queen?"

Alarmed, she rose and tore aside the curtain now concealing the ragged tapestry. It remained as it had for the past two days, unraveling no further.

Her anxiety eased, but still the question remained. "What is he up to, that he would risk so much?"

"They appear to be in no hurry, to get wherever it is they are going."

"No, they wouldn't be, for they know not where the next test will take place."

"Tell me where, my queen," the man's voice brimmed with determination, "that we might reach it before them and prevent them from succeeding."

"Would that I knew," she murmured, more to herself than to the knight.

"Do you not know what the next challenge is the maiden must pass to break the spell?"

She whirled about, angered the man would dare question her magic. "Of course I do, you idiot! I am the one who cast the enchantment." She gritted her teeth at his audacity. "However, like the dragon, I do not know in what form the challenges will present themselves. Only the whim of fate determines when and how they shall come to be." She stared at the tapestry, the only thing tying her to him. "And so long as the maiden of the tapestry is with him, that time may come all too soon."

"What would you have us do, my queen?"

She paced in front of the tapestry, a plan playing out in her mind.

"Baelin must have both the maiden and the tapestry if the curse is to be broken. Without one or the other, it cannot be done." She stopped and smiled serenely at the knight.

"Go. Follow them. If you cannot separate the dragon from the tapestry, then separate the maiden from the dragon."

"Will she be safe, do you think?" Kendal asked.

Baelin had returned to the fire, still uncomfortable with Lady Jill going off by herself. But he couldn't deny her the chance to bathe, not if he wanted to avoid another battle of wills like the last time.

"She will be fine as long as another dragonslayer does not happen upon her like the last time."

The knight gazed off in the direction Lady Jill had taken, his face akin to a fox dreaming of a fat, juicy hen.

"Ah, had I but come through the woods only a moment or two sooner that day, what a vision I might have seen." At Baelin's stern look, he laughed and held up his hands. "And then promptly turned about and shielded my eyes, so as not to dishonor the lady."

"Somehow I find that hard to believe."

Kendal casually draped his arm over a bended knee. "I am not the complete knave you think me to be."

"Are you not? Is that why Lady Jill finds herself rebuffing your unwanted attentions at every turn?"

The knight chuckled. "Merely testing the boundaries, just as I was
testing yours this morn."

Baelin found himself momentarily surprised. "The sword practice?"

"Aye. If I am to be in the company of a man, it behooves me to know
if he is skilled enough with the sword should I ever have need of him to
stand at my back."

"And what if that sword should instead turn against you?"

Kendal smiled. "Then I want to know what I shall be up against
should that situation ever come to pass."

Baelin studied the other knight, trying to judge the sincerity in his
words. "You would trust me to fight at your side?"

He shrugged a shoulder. "Trust only comes with the test of time. But
after this morn, I know now we are well matched. Yours would be a
worthy sword arm to have by my side in battle…and at the same time, I
would not be fool enough to underestimate your skill should you turn
out to be my foe instead."

Little did the knight know how close his words were to the truth.
Baelin could easily go from ally to enemy in the span of a heartbeat, if
the dragonslayer ever discovered the truth of what he was.

Still, he couldn't deny how enjoyable it'd been to spar with a flesh and
blood man and not some imaginary opponent. It had been exhilarating,
to practice the skills of battle, and he'd been delighted to know they were
not nearly as rusty as his mail.

'Twas strange, to feel this obscure bond with a man who could inspire
both annoyance and camaraderie in one breath.

He didn't have long to think on the puzzling situation before Lady Jill
stepped out of the twilight, toweling her wet hair with the edge of her
cloak. The tresses hung in dripping waves to her shoulders, dampening
the linen of her saffron kirtle until it was nearly transparent against her
skin. For a long, silent moment, every male eye around the fire stared at
her, even the young lad too green to do naught about it.

She stopped, uneasy with her enthralled audience. "What?"

Kendal jumped to his feet and whisked his cloak from around his
shoulders. "Come, Lady Jill, warm yourself by the fire. We would not

want you to catch a chill."

How chivalrous of you. Baelin cursed the knight's simple act of courtesy, angry that he could not do the same, but was forced to hide within the folds of his cloak to conceal what lay beneath.

He watched Kendal linger overly long as he draped the garment over her slender form and had to suppress the animalistic growl threatening to erupt from him.

Any affinity he'd begun to feel for the man disappeared. He wanted to shout at the other knight to get his hands off of her. But did he have a right? The dragon in him screamed *mine, mine, mine.* But she wasn't his. Or at least only his for the next sennight. After that, he would no longer have any claim on her.

Kendal led Lady Jill to a comfortable spot by the fire, and then sat near her. Though a respectable distance separated them, Baelin still considered him to be far too close to her.

France would be too close at this point.

Lady Jill had been correct. There was no danger lurking in the lake. As he watched the knight wield his charm like a spider weaves its web, he realized there was another sort of danger all too close. Where at first he'd feared only a risk to himself and the discovery of his secret, now he felt a greater threat. The threat was to Lady Jill.

Kendal wanted her. He could smell the lust on the man. If the knight had half the dragon sense Baelin had, he would probably smell a similar scent on him, too.

As he watched them converse with relaxed ease on the other side of the fire, Baelin wanted nothing more than to toss the other knight on his horse and see him on his way. He'd even help him pack up his supplies if he thought it would get rid of him faster.

The knight stood and bowed over Lady Jill's hand. "My lady, now that I see how refreshed you are from your bath, methinks I shall partake of the waters myself. My only regret is I must take leave of your company to do so."

"No, methinks your only regret will be when you get in the water." She pulled her hand away and tugged his cloak tighter about her. "The lake is freezing."

"Worry not for me. A bit of cool water will not harm me."

"Don't say I didn't warn you."

He nodded to her and then turned to the boy. "Come, Owen. Let us be off to our bath."

"Me?" Owen gulped, horrified.

"Especially you," Lady Jill said. "You're the filthiest one of us all."

Muttering under his breath, the boy collected fresh clothing and stomped off for the lake behind the knight.

Once they were gone, Baelin made his way around the fire. He looked down on Lady Jill, wrapped up in the dragonslayer's voluminous cloak, his gaze hot enough to set the garment aflame.

"Are you warm enough, my lady?"

She smiled at him, oblivious to his discontent. "Yes, thank you."

Out of the darkness came two splashes, then a loud yelp, followed by a string of curses.

Lady Jill laughed. "I told them it was cold."

"Perhaps it will cool Sir Roderick's *amour.*"

"You mean his flirting? Oh, I'm sure he doesn't mean anything by it."

"On the contrary, I think he means a great deal by it."

Cocking her head to the side, she batted her lashes at him. "Why, Sir Baelin. Are you jealous?"

"Of course not."

He detected a flicker in her eyes. Was it hurt or disbelief? Probably the latter, for he had a hard time believing the words he uttered himself.

Baelin took Kendal's place beside her and tossed a stick into the fire.

By the saints, how was it one slip of a woman had the power to turn him into knots? After their near embrace this morn and her playful banter this eve, he was more confused than ever. Had he detected some affection for him? Or was it wishful thinking on his part? All those years in the cave left him ill-prepared to deal with the maidens sacrificed to him. But this one... This one he wondered if even a man such as Kendal could handle.

Or could he?

"Should I be?" he asked.

"What?"

"Jealous."

Lady Jill paused in finger combing her damp hair, her penetrating gaze making him uncomfortable. "No."

"Good." And it was. He had no idea what a sense of relief it was to hear her say it until the feeling washed over him.

He plucked at the grass by his foot, unsure what next to say. Even when he'd been human, he'd not been a courtier like Kendal, easy with words to turn a lady's head. So he said the only thing a battle-hardened, dragon-knight could think of to fill the silence between them.

"Aye, 'tis good. Because 'twould not be wise to lose sight of our goal. We need no such distractions in our quest."

She chuckled. "Oh, Roderick is hardly a distrac—"

The knight chose that moment to step out of the shadows, wearing naught but his breeches. Young Owen was quick on his heels, carrying the bulk of their travel-worn clothing which, by any sense of decency, should be covering his master's half-naked body.

Kendal came to stand by the warmth of the fire. Using a cloth Owen handed him, the knight swiped at the remaining droplets of water trickling down his chest and stomach before they disappeared in the turned waist of his breeches. Then he tossed his head back, shaking the damp hair from his face like a wet wolfhound.

Now it was Lady Jill who stared.

"Preening peacock. He might as well be a woman," Baelin grumbled under his breath.

Lady Jill sighed. "Hmm…a strong, chiseled chin with just the right amount of five o'clock stubble. Caribbean blue eyes a girl could drown in. A set of washboard abs an *Abercrombie & Fitch* model would die for. Not a bad looking peacock, if I do say so myself."

Kendal caught her gaze and grinned, revealing even, white teeth. Damn the man. Even his teeth were pretty.

Lady Jill returned his smile, her cheeks flushing pink before she looked away and returned to combing her hair. The smug glance of triumph the knight sent Baelin's way did little to lighten his foul mood.

I would not be so vainglorious, my friend. If I were in my dragon form, I could eat you for dinner and you would be dragon droppings by the morrow. She would not find you so handsome and charming then.

Lady Jill jabbed him in the ribs. "Did you just growl?"

Had he made a noise? He didn't know and didn't care.

Baelin turned his pique on her and glowered.

She had the temerity to laugh at him. "Oh, come on. There's no harm in looking."

Baelin rose and stomped off toward the lake to take his own bath. The cold water would probably do him good.

ChApTER TWENTY

"...and I fell six Turks armed with scimitars with a single log from the fire."

Somewhere behind her, Baelin grunted. It was becoming his go to reply to the multitude of the Roderick's boasts. She started counting the seconds it would take before he came up with a tale of knightly bravery to top this last one the dragonslayer had just gone on and on about.

"Only eight? Why I had not yet earned my spurs when..."

She shook her head. The male egos around here were taking on a life of their own and poor Owen was hanging on every word. First, it started out with tales of valor and bravery, each one exaggerated farther outside the realm of believability from the last. Then it moved onto demonstrations—who could hit the farthest target with an arrow, who could pound the other to a pulp in mace practice, or who could draw their sword from its sheath the fastest.

It was a medieval pissing contest if she ever saw one.

She suppressed the urge to shout at them to grow up, but knew it would do no good because obviously things hadn't changed much in the past eight centuries. Men had an innate competitive streak that wouldn't let them be outdone by another male within fifty miles and no amount of common sense was going to change that.

"This looks a good place to pass the night," Baelin announced.

"Thank God," Jill groaned as she pulled Owen's pony to a halt and slid from its back. She and the boy had started taking turns riding the sturdy animal and today had been her lucky day in the saddle. Her numb rear-end disagreed profusely while her rubbery legs nearly gave out underneath her. Would she ever get used to the non-stop riding? Her beat-up Isuzu never looked so good.

"Are you feeling poorly, my lady?" Roderick's deep voice spoke from right behind her.

She rested her forehead against the pony's sweaty flank. "Just waiting to regain the feeling in the lower half of my body."

"And a most pleasant lower half it is."

"Will you stop?"

He sighed dramatically. "I cannot seem to help myself."

She chuckled. "You are so bad."

"Aye, that I am," he said, his handsome face breaking into a heart-stopping grin. Lordy, his smile could stop traffic on Rodeo Drive. The false scowl she sent his way did little to deter him. He moved a step closer. "Care to find out how bad?" he whispered.

"No!" She shoved him away, failing to hold back her laughter at his antics as she did so.

"Is aught amiss, my lady?"

Like clockwork, Baelin was at her side. Her very own bat-winged watch dog, never allowing Roderick too much time alone with her, as if the man's very proximity was a threat to her maidenly virtue.

"No problems here. Sir Roderick was just leaving to go polish his armor or sharpen his sword or do whatever dragonslayers do when there isn't a dragon around to slay."

"I shall take my leave of you, then." Roderick bowed his head. "My lady. Gosforth."

As the knight sauntered away, Owen's tired pony in tow, Baelin glared at his back. If his eyes could spit fireballs, Roderick would be a walking torch right about now.

"Stop it."

"Stop what?" Baelin turned his attention to her.

"Stop behaving like hormonal teenage boys with testosterone gone wild. You'd think I was the only woman left on Earth."

His brow furrowed as he pondered her words, then he nodded, as if comprehending the truth in them. "Until we happen upon another maid, you are—and a very beautiful one at that."

"Now don't you start. Roderick's too far away to hear us, so you don't have to waste your breath with the false flattery."

"My compliments are not false and I do not consider the words wasted, not when they bring such a becoming blush to your cheeks."

"Stop!" But Jill couldn't stop the flush as it radiating all the way down to her toes. "I'm tired of you two constantly trying to one-up each other. If it's not tales of gruesome battles, it's who has the longest sword or who can spout the most god-awful ode to my big toe. You might as well pee on every tree to stake your territory. It would be just as appealing."

"I would never dare such a thing in front of a lady," he said, affronted.

"I know you wouldn't." She blew a curl out of her face. "It's just that you've been spending so much time with Sir Flirts-a-lot, you're starting to act like him and it's driving me crazy."

"Then how would you have me act?"

"Well, for starters, how about treating me like you did before he came along?"

"Ah." He nodded in understanding, a smile tugging at the corner of his mouth. "Then you would prefer I growl at you and blow fireballs through my nose."

"No, of course not. Since he showed up, you both treat me like a prize to be won. I've seen his type. He's a player. It's all a game to him and I don't take him seriously. But with you, I'm not sure where the competitive knight ends and the real Baelin begins anymore."

"Can they not be one and the same?"

Jill took in the earnest expression on his face. He was no longer joking with her, but very serious about her answer. "No. Just like you can't be a dragon and a man. One is *what* you are on the outside and the other is *who* you are on the inside."

He shifted his gaze from her, frustration evident in the tension of his jaw. "Forgive me. I have been too long a dragon in a cave. I will strive to act more human around you in the future."

Jill took pity on him. He was trying so hard. She supposed if she were isolated from people for decades on end, she would latch onto anyone who was near, bad influence or not.

"You are a fine human being, Baelin. Believe it or not, I like you just the way you are."

At his surprised look, she left him and went to where Owen had started piling wood for their fire. She dropped to her knees and rummaged around in their dwindling supply satchel, pulling out their last loaf of rock-hard bread and some dried meat that looked as if it'd been hacked off Roderick's saddle. Though she was starving after another long day of travel, her stomach recoiled in protest. She'd just as soon never see another piece of beef jerky again as long as she lived.

She glanced up and caught Owen watching her.

"Looks like it's going to be the same old, same old for dinner tonight—unless you've been holding out on me and you have an extra-large pepperoni pizza stashed in your supplies."

Puzzled, the boy scratched his head. "Nay, my lady. Other than a round of cheese, we have naught else but what you have there."

"Happy joy. Hockey puck biscuits and Slim Jims for dinner…again."

"'Twould be my pleasure to bring fresh game to my lady's table." Jill turned to find Roderick hovering over her. He nodded at the pitiful excuse for a picnic she'd laid out on the edge of a blanket. "The ground though that table may be."

"Really?" Her mouth watered at the thought of roast duck or a thick, juicy steak. Wait, did they hunt cows in the thirteenth century?

"Aye. And mushrooms grow aplenty this time of year. Perhaps you could gather what the forest creatures have not yet found while I hunt?"

"Sounds like a plan, although I have no clue what's a good mushroom and what's not." Jill stood and dusted her hands off on her skirt. "With my luck, I might poison us all."

"Fear not. I am certain Sir Baelin is familiar with them. He can help you to gather them."

Jill sensed Baelin standing behind her even before she heard his deep growl.

"That will not be possible for it shall be I who hunts fresh game for my lady. She is mine—my responsibility, and I shall be the one to provide for her."

She turned a raised brow at his inadvertent slip of the tongue. *Mine.* Her stomach did an odd little flip at the possessive tone in his voice. She wondered if Roderick noticed it too.

The knight glanced at the meager offerings on the blanket. "Aye, as I can see you have done so well in the past." He smiled at Baelin, an unspoken challenge reflected in his brilliant blue eyes. "But what does it matter who provides fresh game for my lady, so long as she has it?"

Oh, Roderick had noticed all right. Let another pissing contest begin.

She put her hand to Baelin's chest to stop him as he made to step around her and go nose to nose with Roderick. It was a given if they got that close, one of them would come away with a bloody one. Considering Baelin's dragon blood could do more damage than his fists, that wasn't such a good idea.

"Hold on guys. There's no need to go hunting. I'm sure what we have here will be fine."

Her stomach protested her words with a loud rumble that could probably be heard all the way to London.

Owen stepped up, his wary glance ping-ponging between the two men and their latest game of medieval standoff. "Mayhap I could help Lady Jill with the gathering while both of you hunt. That way, if either of you are successful, we will have fresh meat for tonight."

The boy's young, ruddy face turned crimson under their scrutiny.

Jill looped her arm over his skinny shoulders. "That sounds like a brilliant idea. We'll let the two big he-men go out and stalk defenseless little bunny rabbits while you educate me on the edible fungi in the area."

"Methinks I will find more than rabbit for our supper tonight," Roderick said. "I noticed a fresh deer rub before we stopped to camp."

"Oh, not a deer. Baelin's already killed the Easter Bunny. Don't take out Bambi, too."

"Bambi?" Owen asked.

Jill brushed the shaggy blond mane of hair out of his eyes. "Bambi is the name of a baby deer in a story from when I was a young girl. It would break my heart if they killed one."

"My lady, I vow I would never bring down a fawn that yet suckles at its mother's teat. But to get fresh meat, we must hunt. How is it the thought disturbs you so?" Roderick asked.

Baelin answered for her. "Lady Jill is accustomed to having her game dressed and plucked before it reaches her table."

Roderick nodded. "Ah, that explains many things. So you come from a privileged household, with servants to prepare your meals?"

"Something like that. Only we call them restaurants where I come from."

"My lady is not accustomed to cooking in the field, as you may have noticed."

Jill scowled at Baelin's remark, knowing an insult when she heard it. "I'll have you know I can cook with the best of them. I just need a microwave to do it."

"What is a micro—" Owen started to inquire.

"Do not ask," Baelin interrupted him. "Some things 'tis better not knowing."

He stooped to gather his bow and quiver of arrows. Roderick shook his head, apparently as confused as Owen, then headed toward his horse to get his own weapons.

Jill caught the young boy watching both men as they readied their hunting gear. "I'm guessing you'd rather go with them, huh?"

"Aye," the boy sighed. "Sir Roderick has instructed me with the bow. I am getting quite good at it."

She understood his frustration at being left out and regulated to what amounted to women's work.

"I am sure you are, Master Owen." Baelin's voice said as he clapped the lad on the shoulder. "But someone must stay and protect Lady Jill while we are gone. 'Tis a great thing I ask of you," his eyes shifted briefly to hers before returning to the boy's rapt face, "for she is most precious to me. Should aught happen, I expect you to use that bow of yours to defend her."

Owen stood taller, puffing out his bony chest like the biggest rooster in the barnyard. "Aye, my lord. I will defend Lady Jill with my very life if I must."

Baelin chuckled. "Let us hope it does not come to that, but I shall breathe easier knowing you are prepared to do so."

She wanted to hug Baelin, even though the words were more to ease the boy's wounded pride than the truth. Jill stood a foot taller and had a good fifty pounds on Owen, making her far more intimidating than a twelve year old boy.

Roderick approached and narrowed his eyes as he caught the end of their conversation. Was he jealous that Owen had found another knight to look up to?

Jill sighed. Two competitive men with pointy objects going off in a huff was not a good thing. They were just as likely to shoot each other instead of a deer.

"Perhaps 'tis you who should stay and guard Lady Jill. After all, we are on Westmorland lands. I have leave to hunt his forests. Do you?"

"That I do." Baelin turned as he slung his quiver of arrows over his shoulder. "Or at least I once did from one of his kinsmen," he mumbled under his breath.

Jill wasn't sure if Roderick heard the last part, but she certainly did. She released her hold on Owen and pulled Baelin out of earshot.

"Let me guess," she whispered. "That particular kinsman you knew has been dead and buried for over two hundred years."

He nodded.

"In that case, I'm thinking the statute of limitations on that permission slip has expired."

Ignoring her, he tested the string on his bow. Jill fisted her hands on her hips. Were all knights this pig-headed or was it a dragon thing? "If it's illegal for you to hunt here, don't do it."

"'Tis against the law to hunt anywhere without leave of liege or King. But our only other choice is to venture into a village for supplies." He lowered his bow and looked at her with a twinkle in his eye. "And we both know how dangerous that can be where you are concerned."

At her frown, he pressed his lips together in an attempt to stop them from twitching. "Nay, I prefer to take my chances in the forest."

Baelin was joking but she wasn't finding any humor in the situation. She may be slow to catch on, but she was beginning to learn how serious the consequences could be when it came to breaking the law in this godforsaken time. "They burned me with a hot piker for touching a stupid statue. What will happen to you if you're caught hunting on private property?"

"Oh, naught so terrible as that. They would merely blind me or cut off my bollocks."

"Baelin!"

He lost the battle with subduing his amusement and laughed. "Fear not, my lady. They would have to catch me first." He reached around his broad shoulder and patted the wings hidden beneath his cloak. "And we both know how hard that would be."

"Seriously, Baelin. It's too dangerous. If I'd known the risk you were taking, I'd have never let you go hunting the first time."

"Truth be told, there is little risk to me." He reached out and ran a single finger down her cheek. "But it warms my dragon heart to know you will worry about me whilst I am gone."

ChAPTER TWENTY-ONE

"The tracks are still fresh. The hart cannot be far."

Baelin rolled his eyes. "So it would seem."

He did not require Kendal's help following the deer. He had no need to look for tracks or rubbings or droppings left on the ground. He could follow the stag's trail easily by scent alone, not that he would reveal that to the unwelcome hunting companion at his side.

"Will not Lady Jill be pleased to find more than hard bread and dried figs to fill her belly tonight?"

"She will think it the senseless murder of a harmless woodland creature if I do not miss my guess," Baelin grumbled under his breath. He tended to agree with her this time.

Bring down a deer, indeed. Kendal only boasted of such to impress her.

"A stag is too large. We have no salt to keep the meat. 'Twould be a waste of a fine beast." It was true. The four of them couldn't consume an entire deer before it spoiled if they ate it morning, noon, and night. Now if he were in his dragon form, he could devour it in three bites with naught left but a pair of antlers and a hoof or two.

Kendal slid him a sly smile. "'Twill not be a waste if I am rewarded with a kiss from the lady for my efforts."

"Then you are in for a grave disappointment. Slaughtering animals does not impress her."

"Hmmm. Do I detect the sound of worry in your voice? Are you are threatened by the thought she may eventually come to favor me?"

"You think too highly of yourself to believe I would ever feel threatened by the likes of you." *Truth be known, I could burn you to ash where you stand ere you drew your sword.*

The knight raised his dark brows in mock wonder. "Ah, then could it be that you have not yet received such a boon from the lady?"

Baelin turned his attention to the trees ahead, uncomfortable under Kendal's intense scrutiny. "You are slow-witted indeed if you have not figured out by now she is not so easily swayed by grand boasts or a silver tongue."

"Not easily, aye. But like many a maid before her, she can be swayed by the right man, of that I am certain. 'Twill just take time and skill, of which I have plenty." He had the audacity to wink at him. "And I do so love a challenge."

Baelin fought hard to suppress the growl forming deep in his throat. "As long as she is under my protection, there is no challenge—from you or anyone else."

"Ah, yes, your protection. But the lady is not pledged to you or any other, so it sounds to me as if she is free to be wooed by any man who is of a mind to do so."

"She is not interested in being wooed. All she wants is to return to her home and I have vowed to get her there, safely."

"Aye, true enough. She has told me as much."

Baelin huffed his exasperation, careful not to let a puff of smoke escape in the wave of his irritation. "Then why do you persist in pursuing her?"

Kendal chuckled. "Because it annoys you so when I do."

Taken aback, Baelin could barely form a response. "Why you—"

A crash in the underbrush silenced both knights. They raised their bows in unison, arrows cocked.

Baelin tensed. The scent was wrong. The rustle of undergrowth coming from the wrong direction. It was not the hart.

Before he could shout a warning, a large boar plunged out of the dense scrub and tangled vines, tusks gleaming and black eyes full of predatory rage.

Kendal let fly his arrow, but his aim was too high and it sailed over the charging beast's raised hackles. Baelin let loose his own arrow, the barbed tip slicing through bristles, hide and muscle to strike deep in the boar's shoulder.

It did little to slow the raging animal's attack, to stop its deadly charge as it hurtled by Kendal in a furious blur of territorial instinct and bore down on Baelin.

With no time to ready another arrow, he gripped his bow with both hands and held it out before him. Even if he could draw his sword, it would not help him now, the long blade useless at this close range. He planted his feet and braced for the impact to come. The large beast plowed into him full force, knocking him to the ground.

With the bow wedged in its gaping jaw, the boar's hot breath gusted inches from his face. Baelin's arms shook from the strain of keeping the savage tusks from ripping into his throat.

Kendal slammed into its side, using the force of his weight to plunge his dagger into the animal's broad side, shoving the blade deep between its ribs. Hot blood spurted out, pulsing over the knight's hands and raining down onto Baelin.

The wild hog squealed in pain and outrage. It turned on Kendal, rolling him beneath its heavy body before stumbling to its feet, the dagger still protruding from its heaving side. The wounded boar spun on the dazed knight, intend on using its long tusks to tear him apart.

Baelin quickly regained his feet. Now it was Kendal who waged battle with the enraged beast, struggling to hold off with weakened animal with a powerful grip around its thick neck. He knew he could kill the boar with but one breath of the dragon, but with the beast on top of Kendal, he would incinerate knight and animal alike.

Drawing his sword, he leaped on top of the animal's broad back and brought the blade down, cleaving hide and skull until the boar's head was nearly split in two. The beast shuddered and collapsed, the attack over almost as quickly as it had begun.

He remained atop the boar until he was certain it had breathed its last. The forest surrounding them stood silent, as if every creature held its breath, waiting to see who would emerge the victor.

"Off." The word was so faint, Baelin almost didn't hear it. "Cannot...breathe."

He shoved the lifeless boar to the side. Kendal lay deathly still on the trampled ground, his eyes closed, his white surcoat soaked with blood. Finally, he drew in a rasping breath and his eyes flew open, their brilliant blue vibrant against the crimson blood splattered on his face.

"God's teeth, man. The boar was heavy enough without your sorry carcass added to the pile. I vow submitting to the Inquisitor's press would be easier on my ribs."

Relief swamped Baelin. Apparently, being nearly eviscerated by savage tusks had done naught to ruin Kendal's sense of humor.

"My apologies. Next time I will not be so quick to come to your aid."

Kendal chuckled, then grimaced at the pain it caused. "Pray there will never be a next time. One boar attack is enough for me. Methinks 'tis safer slaying dragons."

Baelin tensed until Kendal smiled and held out his hand. "The least you can do is help me up after squashing the life from me."

Baelin pulled the knight to his feet, but Kendal did not let go. He clasped his other hand on Baelin's shoulder, all trace of humor gone from his usually laughing eyes.

"I thank you, Gosforth. I owe you my life."

"No more than I owe you mine. If you had not drawn the boar's attention away, it would have surely ripped me apart piece by piece."

"Be that as it may, 'tis not a thing I will soon forget, my friend."

Baelin stilled at the sincerity in the other knight's words. It was the first time Kendal had called him friend and he knew without a doubt the man meant it sincerely.

Kendal turned his attention to the boar, tendrils of steam rising from the warm rivers of blood seeping from its wounds. "It did seem to come after you first. 'Tis not the rutting season. Why do you think it would attack us like that?"

Baelin wiped his bloodied sword clean on the boar's bristly hide. "I do not know."

Unless it did not take kindly to a dragon trespassing in its territory.

As the men neared the camp, an arrow flew through the woods to embed with a thunk in a tree just over Baelin's head.

Alarmed, the two knights dropped the gutted boar they carried strapped to a sapling between them and drew their swords. They broke through the trees only to find Lady Jill pulling back on Owen's small bow, a sharp arrow cocked and pointed straight at them.

"Hold!" Baelin shouted, but it was too late. Both knights dodged out of the way as the arrow went flying, missing its intended target of an old stump at the edge of the clearing by at least six paces.

"Oh, you're back. Owen was teaching me to—" Lady Jill's smile vanished and her face paled when she caught sight of them, the boy's weapon slipping from her fingers. "Oh, God. Who tried to kill who?"

He glanced at Kendal. Dried blood covered him from neck to thigh, while leaves and twigs matted his sweat-dampened hair. After dressing the boar in the forest, Baelin knew he probably looked no better.

"Neither of us tried to kill the other. 'Twas a wild boar that tried to kill us."

Her eyes widened in horror as she approached them. "Are you both all right?"

"Fear not," Baelin said. "The boar lost the battle and lies yonder in the forest, awaiting the spit for our supper for tonight."

"A boar!" Owen shouted. "How big?" The boy did not wait for the knights to answer but dashed off through the trees.

Lady Jill looked doubtful. "But there's so much blood. Are you sure neither of you are hurt?"

"'Tis naught but a few cuts and bruises." Kendal made a show of rubbing his shoulder. "I am certain your gentle ministrations will go far in healing them."

"You have a page to tend to your wounds," Baelin grumbled.

"Lady Jill!" Owen called. "You must come see the boar they brought down. 'Tis the biggest I have ever seen."

The three adults made their way toward where Owen stood under the trees, pride showing on his young face as if it was he who'd killed the beast. Baelin noted Lady Jill's frown as she eyed the gutted carcass lying on the ground.

"Let me guess, it reminds you of an animal from one of your childhood stories."

She appeared to study it a bit more, then shook her head. "Lose the tusks and shave the hair and it might pass for Wilbur. But somehow I don't think that kind of makeover is enough to make him cute, pink, and cuddly."

"Wilbur? Who is Wilbur?" Owen asked.

"Owen, Owen, Owen." Jill rested her arm around the boy's shoulders and started leading him back to the camp, leaving the two knights with their bloody prize standing in the trees. "You poor, deprived child. Have I got a story for you."

As she walked slowly away, her head bent slightly toward Owen's upturned face, Baelin strained to hear the softly spoken words she uttered to the boy.

"Once upon a time, there was a little pig who lived on a farm. His name was Wilbur. And his best friend was a spider named Charlotte…"

"…and so, with true love's first kiss, the spell was broken and Snow White awoke in the arms of her prince."

Jill looked away from Owen's spellbound face to find two other listeners hanging on her every word. She fought back a smile. Guess you were never too old—or too macho—to be enchanted by fairy tales.

As they sat around the campfire eating roasted Wilbur, she'd regaled them with an encore presentation of *Charlotte's Web* at Owen's insistence, which led to *Bambi, Cinderella*, and last but not least, *Snow White and the Seven Dwarfs*. Tonight she wasn't surrounded by bold, brave knights, but three little boys enthralled by stories about talking animals, glass slippers, and coal-mining midgets.

She purposefully steered clear of *Sleeping Beauty* because, as she recalled, things didn't end well for the dragon in that one. And while she wouldn't classify herself as a beauty and Baelin wasn't a furry lion-prince, she gave a wide berth to *Beauty and the Beast*, too. That particular tale seemed to hit a little too close to home.

"What happened next?" Owen asked.

"The same thing that happens in all fairy tales—they fell in love and lived happily ever after."

Owen snickered before his grin morphed into a wide yawn that he tried to hide behind his hand. He rallied quickly and pleaded with a child's delight. "Please tell us another, Lady Jill."

"No more for you tonight, young man. It's way past your bedtime."

Owen looked as if he were about to protest when Roderick stood and stretched. "Off with you lad. The sun shall rise early for us all."

As Roderick made his way to the privacy of the trees, Jill walked over to where Owen curled up by the fire and knelt to brush the hair from his brow. "Sleep tight. Don't let the bed bugs bite."

"They would not dare, for I am too full of spit and vinegar even for their tastes."

Jill grinned. The silly exchange of words had become a regular routine for them each night as she tucked him into his blankets. Owen's eyes drifted shut, but they flew back open as she started to stand.

"Thank you, my lady."

"For what?"

"For the stories. Will you tell us some more tomorrow?"

"You betcha."

"I would like that," Owen whispered as his eyes drifted shut once more.

She tucked the frayed blanket around his shoulders, then turned to find Baelin staring at her with those fathomless brown eyes of his. There was no hint of the beast within tonight. But she did see something else— a trace of the boy he once was before he was cursed to be a dragon.

She walked over and sat beside him on a log they'd pulled near the campfire.

"It's sad."

"What is, my lady?"

"Owen. He's so young, still just a little boy in so many ways, and yet he has the worries and responsibilities of an adult." She looked back at Baelin. From what little he'd told her when they first met, his life had probably not been much different than Owen's, and the thought of any child not being able to laugh and play broke her heart. "I guess you never had much of a childhood either. Kids in your time are required to grow up too fast. Where I come from, boys play with plastic toy swords. They don't spend their childhood training with real ones because they'll have to kill someone with it some day."

"My youth 'twas not so bad." Baelin shrugged and stretched his legs out to the fire. "Each morn I went to Mass, then I received schooling from the chaplain with the other boys. When not training, we had duties to perform, from cleaning the stables to serving at table. Once all was done, we were free to seek out our amusement as long as we stayed out of trouble. Is it not so with the children of your time?"

Jill thought about it. "I suppose it is. Kids start going to school when they're five or six and most have chores to do once they get home. But taking out the trash or cleaning their room isn't nearly so hard as polishing a whole suit of armor or mucking stables every day. Plus, they do it in their own homes, with their own families. They're not shipped off to a stranger's house or dragged all over tarnation by a man who isn't their father."

"Owen has had a better childhood than most, I would wager. Kendal is a good man. The lad could have fared much worse."

Jill arched a brow. "My, my. It sounds like you and Roderick kissed and made up out there in the woods."

Baelin bristled. "He is a man. 'Twas no kissing betwixt us."

"Relax." She laughed at his offended expression. "It's just a saying. It means you're not fighting anymore. You're friends now."

He glanced to where Roderick had disappeared into the trees. "Aye, I suppose we are. 'Tis been a long time since I have called another man such."

"Well, I think it's a good thing. Everyone needs friends."

He returned his gaze to her. "Do you miss them, your friends?"

"Of course, I do. I miss my friends, my family. I know they're all worried sick about me. I'm sure I've lost my boring-but-pays-the-bills-job by now. God, I sure hope someone is feeding my cat."

"I did not know you had a cat."

She bumped shoulders with him. "There's a lot of things you don't know about me."

"Tell me then. What else from your time do you miss?"

"Oh, I miss flush toilets. Pizza and cable television. Coffee and chocolate." She winked at him. "And warm baths, of course."

"Of course." Baelin looked over to where Owen slept by the fire. "You are good with the boy. You will make a fine mother some day."

Jill snorted. "I sure hope I make a better mom than I do an aunt.

Speed shopping for my niece's birthday present is what got me into this mess in the first place."

"Then should I ever meet your niece, I shall thank her. For if you had not come, I would still be in my cave with some poor weeping girl hiding in the shadows."

"Zoe would like you. She has a thing for dragons. They're about the only fairy tale characters she's interested in."

"Ah, fairy tales. A talking pig and a pumpkin carriage." She watched as he shook off the last vestiges of the little boy and eyed her with the skeptical gaze of the man. "Can such things truly happen in your world?"

She could tell the adult in him knew the truth, but the boy who'd sat captivated only moments before still wanted to believe in the possibility.

"Only in Walt Disney's world. It's just make-believe." She made a sound half-way between a snort and a laugh. "Then again, I never would've believed in time travel and look how I got here."

"When we first met, you said dragons did not exist, and yet here I am."

"Yes, you certainly are."

He stared at her, taking in every detail of her face, then his gaze rested on her mouth. "Would that, like in the story of the maiden with the apple, a single kiss could break my curse."

The wistfulness in his voice made her catch her breath.

"Maybe it can." Her reply sounded husky to her ears. *Did I really just say that?*

"My lady?" He jerked, startled.

Jill shrugged, attempting to lighten the tension suddenly filling the air. *Are you out of your mind, flirting with a dragon?* "Couldn't hurt to try."

"You would kiss me?" Longing and disbelief ignited in the flame in his eyes.

Too late to go back now. She cupped his cheek, the stubble tingling the sensitive skin of her palm, and she leaned in to touch her lips to his. It was a tender kiss. No tongue. No heavy breathing. No groping. Just a soft brush of the lips and no more—and yet it shook her to her core.

She eased back, surprised at how something so innocent could affect her so. With an single kiss, Baelin had just crossed the line from a ticket back home to something much more.

"Still a dragon?"

He nodded, but she wasn't certain he heard her. Silence stretched between them, his eyes searching her face for a happy ending to his own tale.

Her heart broke for him in that moment, because it was an ending she wasn't sure would come true.

The sound of Roderick trudging out of the woods startled her back to reality and she recognized the mistake for what it was. She didn't want to care about him, and she didn't want him to care about her. After all they had been through, she knew without a doubt that one of them was going to get hurt.

Before Baelin could say another word, she stood and walked away, the pull of his need too intense.

ChApTER TWENTY-TWO

If Jill thought having two knights constantly trying to one up each other in displays of physical prowess and chivalrous deeds was annoying, she was wrong.

Apparently, there was nothing like a little fighting and bloodshed to promote male bonding, even if the enemy in question was a big, hairy, snaggletooth pig. Jill wasn't exactly sure what happened in the woods between the two men, but since then, the knights had done a complete about face and carried on as if they were the best of friends.

Now here they both sat, in a crowded, smoky inn in the middle of nowhere, well on their way to getting drunk.

She shook her head, amazed at how little had changed in eight centuries of male evolution. Put them in t-shirts and baseball caps in a sports bar and they would fit right in. All they lacked was a wide screen TV in every corner and a half dozen well-endowed waitresses in white tank tops and orange shorts two sizes too small.

Speaking of which, at this very moment Roderick was leering in open appreciation as the barmaid leaned over the table to deposit two more tankards of ale, her ample cleavage nearly falling out of the top of her gown. Baelin wasn't much better as he watched the girl saunter away with an exaggerated sway of her hips.

Jill stood corrected. Apparently they did have Hooters in medieval England after all.

She should be glad. At least they weren't at each other's throats anymore. But she wasn't entirely sure being in a public place in the company of the bosom buddies was any better.

They'd stumbled on the busy little inn at a muddy, wagon wheel-rutted crossroads only an hour before. It was the first time since her ill-fated excursion to the village that Jill had seen another building in their travels. Come to think of it, it was first time she'd seen anything resembling a road since then, too.

Delighted, Roderick had suggested they stop for the night. Jill had expected Baelin to say no. After all, the last two times she'd been anywhere near a large group of people, she ended up getting herself sacrificed to a dragon and burned with a hot poker. Not a very good track record, in her opinion. But to her surprise, Baelin had agreed. He'd told her to refuse the obvious comfort of the inn would've been odd and drawn suspicion from Roderick. It was probably not a good idea to have a dragonslayer—even one who now considered Baelin his new favorite drinking buddy—wondering if they had something to hide.

As dangerous as it was, the lone perk in stopping by the inn was waiting up stairs. Jill would have a bed to sleep in tonight. Baelin had procured her a room all to herself and she was looking forward to a peaceful night's sleep in a nice comfortable bed instead of out on the cold, hard ground surrounded by wild animals and snoring knights. She could hardly wait.

Poor Owen was out in the stables. It didn't seem fair to make the boy sleep outside in a smelly old barn like a flea-bitten dog. But Baelin told her it was part of his duties in his training to be a squire, to guard Roderick's horse and weapons throughout the night. Apparently, child labor laws were non-existent in the Middle Ages. At least they'd sent him off with a hot meal before they settled down to their beer guzzling.

Which was another thing that left her uncomfortable. What if Baelin got drunk and slipped up and somehow revealed himself?

Just then, his gaze caught hers and she realized he was nowhere near as buzzed as Roderick. Did being part dragon help him handle his alcohol better than a normal man? Maybe he was a walking flambé and the alcohol burned off the minute it hit his stomach? It didn't matter. She was just relieved at least one of them was sober and they didn't have to worry about driving home tonight.

The barmaid returned with three servings of stew served in hollowed out loaves of bread. It smelled good, although Jill avoided asking exactly what was in it. She probably didn't want to know and she ate it anyway. It was a welcome change from the dried meat and hard bread they'd survived on before killing the boar. And after eating nothing yesterday but roast pig for breakfast, lunch and dinner, she was beginning to hate pork, too. The warm ale was a shock to her American taste buds. She would have killed for an ice cold Bud Light, but beggars couldn't be choosers.

She dug in, not coming up for air until the bread bowl was empty. Blissfully full, her exhaustion and the warm air of the common room threatened to lull her into sleep where she sat, but she was not about to snooze on the hard table when she had a soft, cozy bed to curl up in.

"Well, since you two are no longer in danger of slitting each other's throats without me to play referee, I think I will go to bed."

Roderick stood, steadier on his feet than she thought he'd be. "Allow me to escort you to your chamber, my lady."

Baelin stood, too. His hand already on her elbow, he lifted her from the bench. "Nay, I shall see the lady to her room."

"Ah, and will you be staying there?" Roderick grinned, a knowing gleam in his eye.

Baelin tensed at her side, his fingers biting into her arm. If he wasn't gripping her with his right hand, she was certain he would have drawn his sword on the other knight.

Jill shook her head. "So much for the friendly truce."

Roderick lifted his hands in mock surrender. "I meant no insult. I was merely asking if you intend to seek out your bed also or if you will return for a bit more refreshment."

"I see." Baelin rubbed the side of his face and chuckled. Just as quickly as his anxiety flared, it was gone. Guess having a friend after so long took a little getting used to. "Aye, I shall return. 'Tis obvious it is not safe to leave you to your own devices. The next man may not be so understanding and you might very well lose your head."

"I would appreciate that." Roderick grinned. "Makes it terribly difficult to keep my helm on without it."

She looked back and forth between the two men. "Please don't kill each other after I'm gone."

"We will make every effort not to." The knight laughed as he sat back down and turned his attention to the barmaid.

Baelin guided her through the maze of tables filled with people. There was an interesting mixture of lords and ladies, merchants and peasants alike. So different and yet so similar to what she would expect to see in the lobby of a modern hotel. She smiled as they passed by a family with several small children. The youngest had fallen asleep with his head on the table, his little hand cupping the half eaten bowl of stew as if afraid someone would take it from him while he slept. Too cute.

They made their way to the stairs where a young boy about Owen's age waited with a rushlight to lead customers down the dark hallways to their rooms. What do you know? A medieval bellhop.

She eyed the extreme vertical slant of the steps, more a ladder than a staircase. The boy went first, then Jill, with Baelin following discreetly behind her. About half way up, she glanced back to see he was keeping his eyes on the narrow steps and not attempting to look up her skirt like most men would have done if they were in his position.

Always the chivalrous knight to the very end.

They reached the second floor and made their way down a narrow hallway, the single light the boy carried doing little to dispel the shadows. Entering a dark room at the end of the hall, light flared as the boy lit a candle on the bedside table.

Jill was surprised when Baelin motioned for her to wait and entered the room before her. What happened to ladies first? Wasn't that part of chivalry? Jill followed, the meager flame of the candle casting a pool of light across the floor of the small room.

Whatever she'd been expecting, she was disappointed. The Ritz Carlton it was not. The room was tiny and cramped. The narrow bed, tucked under one of the eaves, looked more like a cot. She doubted even Owen could stand straight without bumping his head on the slanted ceiling.

Baelin tossed the lad a coin and he scurried out the door, leaving them alone in the tiny box of a room. Since the kiss two nights ago, they hadn't had one moment alone without either Roderick or Owen nearby. The awkward we've-shared-a-kiss-now-what-do-we-do situation had been easy to ignore. But without the medieval bellhop to act as pseudo-chaperone, the room felt too close, too confined, too intimate.

A look passed over Baelin's face as if he felt it too, and he busied himself with searching the shadows in the eaves and behind the door.

"What are you looking for?"

"One never knows what dangers lurk in unfamiliar places."

"Oh. Aren't you going to check under the bed for the boogie man, too?"

His brow creased in confusion as yet another modern anachronism flew right over his head. Even so, he knelt to peer under the bed. Apparently satisfied the room was intruder-free, he rose and walked to the door.

"Bolt the door. Open it for no one but me."

"I'm a big girl, Baelin. I'll be fine."

He regarded her for a long, pulse-quickening moment. What was he thinking?

"Aye, you are brave, my lady. But you are no match against a man bent on lascivious intent. More than one has been known to drink too much at an inn and confuse one room for another. Do not make the mistake of opening the door for anyone but me."

Jill couldn't resist. "Not even for Sir Roderick?" she said innocently.

Baelin growled. "Especially not Sir Roderick."

She laughed. Guess their newfound friendship only went so far. "I'm just kidding. I'm going to bed and don't intend to crawl out of it until morning. You go baby-sit Casanova before he gets himself in trouble."

"I will not over long. My room is next to yours. Tap on the wall should you need anything during the night."

"Why, Sir Baelin, is that an invitation?" She made a *tsking* sound. "And here you were warning me about wandering drunken strangers when it sounds like I should be wary of your intentions. Shame on you."

His shocked expression was almost comical, somewhere between insulted and embarrassed at having his words misconstrued.

She shoved him out into the hallway. "Relax. I know my virtue is quite safe in your hands."

Grinning, she closed the door in his bewildered face, shaking her head at his overprotective nature as she bolted the door.

Her smile faded with the sound of Baelin's retreating footsteps down the hall. What had come over her? Had she actually been flirting? And what had she expected in return, a goodnight kiss?

With a jolt in her belly, she realized she had. But she didn't want to care about him. And she didn't want him to care about her. Encouraging whatever had begun between them was not a good idea. No matter how this ended, one of them was going to get hurt.

Deciding not to examine that train of thought too closely, she turned and surveyed her small room. She tossed her cloak and satchel on the lone chair before making a small circle of the space. It didn't take long since it was the size of a closet. She opened the wooden shutter and glanced out the tiny glassless window, but couldn't see much. From the sounds and smells below, she figured her room overlooked the stables where Owen was bedded down for the night.

Jill tugged off her outer gown and kicked off her shoes, eager to sink under the covers. But when she pulled the blanket back off the bed, she recoiled in disgust. The sheets were dirty and stained, and little black dots littered the yellowed pillow.

Looks like maid service has been slacking. I'll have to complain to the manager about this. Had she really expected crisp white sheets and a chocolate on her plump feather pillow? If so, she was out of luck.

Then one of the black dots moved. She grabbed the candle and held it closer. To her horror, all the black dots were moving—and they had legs!

She shuddered. *Oh, my God. Please tell me those aren't lice. Or were they bed bugs?* She didn't know and didn't want to find out. Both gave her the willies.

She flipped the cover back further and found more traveling black dots on the mattress.

Oh, well this is just perfect. I can't win for losing can I? And she'd been so looking forward to sleeping in a soft feather bed. Well, she wouldn't get in this one if her life depended on it.

She grabbed her cloak and balled up her gown to use as a pillow, making a pallet on the floor. Cursing the sick games life seemed to be playing on her, Jill tossed and turned, trying to find a comfortable spot.

Right now she envied Owen, because sleeping in the barn with the horses didn't seem like such a bad idea after all.

The Goose Egg Inn was a large tavern for this remote area. Its location midway between Allerdale and Lancaster made it a popular stopping place on the way to the market fairs in the larger towns. But the inn was not so full that each of them could not have their own room for the night. After leaving Lady Jill, Baelin had almost considered taking to his own.

But he was too restless. So too, it would appear, was Kendal, who had his hands full with the ample charms of the barmaid in his lap.

As Baelin slid onto the bench, the knight whispered in the woman's ear before sending her on her way with a gentle slap to her backside.

"Did I interrupt something?"

"Nay. Merely making arrangements for a wee bit of company later."

Baelin shook his head. The man was a shameless, skirt-chasing dog. If he couldn't sweet-talk Lady Jill into his bed, the closest dalliance at hand apparently would do.

Kendal shoved a fresh mug of ale in his direction. "Drink. The night is still young."

Baelin cupped the mug, but left it on the table.

"I trust the Lady Jill is safely tucked away in her bed?"

"That she is. Quite safe and quite alone."

Kendal eyed him, appearing more sober than he'd been only moments before. "You care for her a great deal, do you not?"

Baelin thought about the all too brief kiss she'd bestowed on him the night before and of the way she'd shamelessly teased him only moments ago. The memory twisted something within him, causing an ache deep down inside. Would she welcome him in if he came knocking at her door?

Nay, he could not dream of such a thing. Not while he was still what he was.

"Aye, that I do."

"I believe she cares for you, too."

Baelin shook his head. "She does not want me."

"Well, 'tis certainly not me she wants. As you have so joyously observed, she has spurned my every effort to win her favor. If I did not have the fair Alice to soothe my wounded pride this lonely night, I would be sore in doubt of my skill with the fairer sex."

Baelin laughed. "If Alice's smile is anything to go by, you are not at risk of losing your touch with the ladies in the near future."

Kendal tipped his ale. "Aye, here's to a good bit of touching soon to come." He set his half-empty mug of ale on the table and wagged his finger at Baelin. "Nay, I see the way Lady Jill watches you, most times when you are unawares. She may not even realize it herself, but I have been around enough women to know when one desires a man."

Baelin chuckled. "I imagine you have." His smile slid from his face. "But you are wrong. Lady Jill may need me, but she does not desire me."

"I beg to differ, my friend. I saw the kiss she gave you the other night."

"'Twas but an innocent peck, nothing more."

Kendal looked doubtful. "If you say so. But then again, you know the lady's heart better than I do."

He could argue with the knight on that point. There were times when he wasn't sure he knew Lady Jill's heart at all. But it didn't matter. Even if she would accept it, he had no human heart to give her.

He gazed out the open window near their table. The moon hung low in the sky, three-quarters full, a mocking reminder of what little time he had left. Six and twenty days come and gone, and only one of the challenges met. Time was running short, and for the first time since he saw Lady Jill's face woven in the tapestry, he feared they would fail in the end.

He looked at the man seated across from him. Kendal was a flirt and a rogue. But he was also a knight, a skilled swordsman who would fight to the death to defend those he was sworn to protect. That, and the pressing sense of time slipping through his fingers, forced Baelin to ask the question he did not want to ask.

"Kendal, I have a request to ask of you."

"Ask, and if it is within my power, 'tis granted."

"Lady Jill, she is adrift in this world. She has no family left to her." By all rights, her family had not yet been born. "If something should happen to me, she will be alone and unprotected. I know we did not get on well in the beginning, but I ask you as one knight to another, would you give Lady Jill your protection if I am no longer able?"

Kendal sat stunned, as if he couldn't believe what Baelin was asking.

Then he reached across the table and clasped Baelin's hand with his own. "I would be honored, my friend. But let us hope it never comes to that."

"Aye, let us hope so."

But as Baelin watched the gibbous moon glide behind silver-edged clouds, he couldn't help but think it was a promise Kendal would have to honor all too soon.

ChAPTER TWENTY-THREE

The inn rested in quiet slumber as traveler and servant alike settled in for the night. It was past midnight, but Baelin was still awake and on edge.

It was so strange, after living for two centuries in a cave, to be spending the night with walls surrounding him and a roof over his head. He ran his hand over the rolled tapestry, a constant reminder of where he came from, and where he would have to return if the curse was not broken.

He glanced out the small window, but he couldn't see anything. Not that he was looking.

He was listening.

Listening for the soft sounds of the woman sleeping in the room next to him.

He strained to perceive the slightest noise. If he pressed his ear against the wall, he could barely hear her breathing. He didn't understand it. He should be able to hear her more clearly, with the bed pressed up against the wall as he remembered. She sounded as if she was farther away. But room wasn't that big. How far could she go?

Baelin cursed. He was so used to having her close, often within arm's reach, that he could barely stand having a wall separating them, thin though it was.

He glanced at the meager furnishings in his room. At least she was comfortable. He'd been able to provide her something she longed for—a bed for the night. It was a small price to pay for her happiness.

So intent on listening for sounds from the next room, he almost didn't notice the smell. But once he did, it grew so acute he could not ignore it.

Smoke.

But not that which crept its way up from cooking fires of the common room below. He sniffed at the air, using his dragon sense to pinpoint what it was. And then he knew.

Straw. Burning thatch.

The inn was on fire.

He flung open his door and found the dark hallway filled with smoke. He shoved the tapestry into his belt and ran to Lady Jill's door, hammering on it with his fist.

"Lady Jill! Awake!"

He prepared to break the door down when he heard shuffling in the room and it swung open. Lady Jill stood in her thin smock, squinting at him from the haze of interrupted sleep.

"What?" She started coughing as the smoke poured in around her.

"The inn is ablaze. We must get out."

"Oh, my God!"

She did not hesitate, but followed him out into the hallway. As they made their way down the smoke-filled corridor, they pounded on every door they passed to rouse the people inside.

Kendal emerged from his room, instantly alert. The knight was strapping on his sword as the barmaid followed him out, the blanket from the bed wrapped loosely around her bare shoulders.

People emerged from their rooms, sleepy and bewildered. But as soon as they saw the smoke, terror set in.

Lady Jill dropped to her hands and knees in the hallway and began to crawl toward the stairs. "Get down! Everybody get down. The air is better down here."

Everyone stared at her as if she was a mad woman.

She grabbed a young girl by the hand and jerked her to the ground. "Keep your heads down low. The smoke will kill you before the fire does if you don't."

The smoke did not bother Baelin. In fact, his dragon lungs relished in it. But he could see the wisdom in what Lady Jill was trying to get the people to do and he aided her by pushing them to their knees. Like lumbering bears, they crawled down the hallway to the stairs leading to the common room below. As they jammed around the opening in the floor, black smoke billowed out of the opening where the steps led down.

There would be no escape this way.

Baelin retreated down the hallway to Lady Jill's chamber, the door still ajar from when she fled the room. He ran to the far end and threw open the shutter. Situated on the second story, they would have to jump if they wanted to live. Baelin knew he could make the leap without injury. But what of the others? What of Lady Jill?

She and Kendal squeezed beside him to look out the tiny window, so narrow only a child could fit through it.

"Can you jump from here?" Baelin asked her.

She looked out. "It's pretty high. I don't know if I can do it without breaking something. But personally, I'll take a broken leg over burning alive any day."

Baelin turned and found himself surrounded by the terrified faces of the people who'd followed them into the room, their frightened eyes begging him to help them. To save them.

"There may be no other way."

"Look there." Kendal pointed to a wagon filled with hay next to the stables. "If we can push it beneath the window, the people may be able to jump into it to cushion their fall."

Baelin glanced at the knight, impressed with the man's quick thinking. "It may just work. But first we must widen this opening, or we may not live long enough to see."

He kicked at the wall by the window, sending shards of wattle and daub flying. Kendal joined him, hammering at the plaster with the hilt of his sword. When the opening was large enough for a man to fit through, Baelin perched the jagged hole. "I will go first and move the wagon under the window. Kendal, you help the others out when I'm ready."

"Aye."

He looked to Lady Jill. "Follow after me, once I am ready below."

She nodded, her wide eyes trying to hold the panic at bay.

Baelin jumped, holding his cloak out wide to shield the wings beneath as he glided to the ground. He could not risk anyone below or above seeing him fly. There were too many lives at stake.

He ran across the inn yard to the barn. There was no time to hitch oxen to the wagon. He grabbed the shaft and pulled with all his strength, his arms and back straining with the effort. At first, it barely moved, the wheels mired in deep, muddy furrows. Then others who'd already made it out joined him and they started rocking it, back and forth. Finally, the wheels edged out of the ruts. They pulled and shoved the wagon beneath the window. He prayed it hadn't taken too long.

Kendal dropped a young girl out of the window first. Squealing and flailing, she landed with a plop in the hay. Baelin grabbed the child by her tiny waist and practically tossed her to the man behind him. There was no time to be gentle. They had to get the people out as quickly as possible or they would all die.

Like ants tumbling out of a disturbed mound, one person after another emerged from the dark hole, hesitating only briefly before they jumped or Kendal shoved them out to land in the hay wagon. Baelin kept an eye on the fire as it consumed the dry thatch of the roof, edging closer and closer to the room.

Where was Lady Jill? Why was she not coming out?

But he knew. She was putting herself in danger, staying behind to help the others out. Fear for her safety ate at his belly, chilling his skin despite the heat of the flames. If she didn't die in the fire, he was going to strangle her for not coming out first as he'd told her to.

One after another jumped from the window, forming a rhythm. As each dropped in the wagon, Baelin pulled them out, and another would take their place.

Finally, Lady Jill's head appeared in the window as dark smoke billowed around her. She hesitated only briefly before falling to the wagon below. Baelin pulled her from the hay and crushed her to him.

Kendal was the last to jump, but Baelin refused to let Lady Jill go to help him out of the wagon. The knight could manage on his own. At this moment, as he held her alive and safe in his arms, Baelin did not think he would ever let her go.

"Ow."

Baelin pulled back, alarmed she might be injured after all. "Are you hurt?"

"No, but you're squeezing me to death."

He eased his grip, but did not completely let her go. "Apologies, my lady."

She smiled, her teeth a brilliant white in her blackened face. "I'm glad to see you, too."

Reluctantly, he eased his arms from around her and they joined the others gathering in the inn yard.

"Did they all get out?" Baelin asked Kendal.

"There were no more in the room. The smoke was too thick to go back into the hall to look for more. I pray there were none left behind."

"I pray you are right."

Behind them, others who'd made good their escape from other ways rushed about the yard, carrying buckets of water to throw on the flames. It was a futile effort to save the inn now. The flames raged, eating at the dried thatch with alarming speed. The roof was almost gone, parts of it already collapsing in on itself.

Through the roar of the flames and the frantic shouts of the people rushing around him, a scream ripped through the night. It was a cry of anguish and despair like no other.

Baelin charged around the side of the inn and found a woman, collapsed on the ground, wailing and clawing at her hair and clothes. As ciders rained down on them, he picked her up and carried her away from the burning wall threatening to collapse on top of them.

Tears streaked ragged trails down the soot covering her face. She coughed and sputtered. She tried to speak. When she was finally able to draw air, she uttered words that chilled Baelin to his bones.

"My children! My children are still in there. Help them!"

Baelin looked at the burning inn, now almost completely engulfed in flames, the fire reaching high up in the air as if to snatch the stars from the sky.

And then he saw them. Two small faces leaning out of a high window the fire had yet to reach, their tiny bodies wedged in the small opening to escape the smoke and heat of the flames. Baelin's gut clenched and he stopped breathing, terrified they would either fall to their deaths or be burned alive before his eyes.

People surrounded him, adding their gasps and wails to those from the distraught mother at his feet. Lady Jill stood at his side, her eyes wide, her hand covering a silent scream.

"Dear God." She clutched at his arm blindly, unable to tear her eyes away from the children. "Baelin, we have to do something."

He could save them. He knew he could. But there was only one way to do it.

As he felt Lady Jill tremble next to him and heard the children's screams on the air, he knew there wasn't any choice. His life for theirs was a small price to pay.

He set Lady Jill away from him and ripped off his cloak, spread his dragon wings and took to the air.

The cries and wails below turned into shrieks and screams, drowned out by the roar of the fire as he rose nearer to the children. Their frightened faces froze when they saw him hovering before them, his wings whipping hot air and cinders about in a frenzied storm. In their terror, they moved back into the room, the smoke swallowing them like a hungry monster.

"Nay!" Baelin shouted. "Do not fear me. I mean you no harm."

He clawed and dug at the window, widening the opening until he could fit his body through. The bright glow of the raging fire at the doorway nearly blinded him, leaving the rest of the smoke-filled room in a choking darkness. More terrified of the beast than the fire, he prayed he hadn't chased the children into the waiting arms of the flames and certain death.

He dropped to his knees, searching with his hands where his eyes could not see. The floorboards snapped and groaned, hot to the touch from the fire burning below. His shoulder hit something large and it shifted along the floor. It was the bed, turned on its side, the straw-filled tick lying nearby. He reached over the frame and touched part of a small body, an arm or leg he could not tell. The child shifted and he grabbed the tiny limb before they could scoot out of reach.

The girl screamed and tried to pull away but he held on tight, not willing to risk her rushing into the hallway. He found the second child near the first. This one did not try to get away, but lay limp and still under his hand. Baelin's heart stopped.

Dear God, let me not be too late.

He gathered them up, ignoring the weak struggles of the girl, and tucked their tiny bodies under each arm. He dove through the window opening, shielding the children from the jagged plaster edges with his body. As soon as he was in the air, he spread his wings. He circled the inn yard once before landing away from the crowd, laying both children gently on the ground.

The people stood frozen, staring at him with wide, terror-filled eyes.

The sobbing mother broke free of the huddled crowd and crawled on her hands and knees, the need to get to her children greater than her fear of him.

The little girl lay on her back, coughing and gagging, drawing in ragged gasps of air. The other child, a boy, lay still. No rise and fall moved within his tiny chest.

The mother cradled the small, lifeless body in her arms. "My son. My son." She glared at Baelin, wild fury replacing the sorrow on her face. "The winged devil killed my son."

"No, he didn't." Lady Jill rushed to the mother and knelt beside her. "He was trying to save them. It still may not be too late. Let me see if I can help."

She reached for the boy and the mother shoved her away, clutching the child's body tightly to her chest. "Begone from me! I saw you, in *his* company." She sneered at Baelin, before turning her tormented gaze back to Lady Jill. "Whore. Devil's maiden. You are consort of the beast. Do not lay your foul hands upon my child."

Lady Jill reared back as if the woman had struck her. "No, you've got it all wrong."

A man stepped out from the crowd and, without taking his eyes off Baelin, shouted to the people around him. "The beast hides behind the face of a man. A beast that breathes fire."

"Dra...dragon!" one old woman wailed.

The mob turned accusing eyes to Baelin.

"He started the fire," someone in the crowd shouted. "He tried to burn us all!"

"No!" Lady Jill stood and faced them. "He won't hurt you. He was only trying to help."

But they weren't listening to her.

Hushed murmurs among the crowd grew louder and louder until the entire mob was chanting, "Dragon. Dragon."

Then one of the men shouted, "Kill the dragon!"

Some of the men rushed Baelin, surrounding him with pitchforks and sickles, any weapon they could find.

"Nooo!"

He heard Lady Jill's scream, but could no longer see her through the crowd.

His hands twitched, the trained knight ready to draw his sword and fight to defend his lady. Inside, the dragon raged, every instinct screaming to kill.

But he couldn't. These were not highway bandits or an enemy army. These were peaceful, innocent people, frightened of what they did not understand.

But maybe he could use their fear, long enough to get Lady Jill safely away. As the crowd closed in, he spread his wings wide.

"Be still and come no closer, or risk the dragon's wrath!" he roared. Then he opened his mouth and shot a fireball into the air over their heads.

The people fell back and he spotted Kendal pulling Lady Jill away from the fray. He knew a moment of relief, thankful she was out of harm's way. But as the knight tossed her onto his horse and mounted behind her, the look Kendal gave him chilled him to his bones. The truth, when it hit, sliced deep.

Kendal was not saving Lady Jill from the frenzied mob.

He was saving her from Baelin.

In rescuing the children, he'd shown his dragon side to the one man who should have never seen it.

A dragonslayer.

Kendal's cold gaze locked with Baelin's across the inn yard, piercing him with white-hot hatred.

"Until we meet again, dragon."

Then he spurred the horse and galloped off into the night, taking Lady Jill with him.

CHAPTER TWENTY-FOUR

"But I don't want to be rescued!"

Roderick didn't even look at her as Owen helped him strap the chausses to his legs. "'Tis too late, my lady. You have already been rescued."

"You didn't exactly give me much of a choice, did you?"

Jill fumed, pacing around the grassy hill where he'd finally decided to stop after hours of riding. She eyed Owen, the young page working with the efficiency and dedication of duty of someone far beyond his years. While Roderick was kidnapping her last night—which is exactly what he'd done—the boy had been busy in the stable, piling all of their weapons and supplies on his sturdy little pony's back, then catching up with them later in the forest.

Jill hadn't been so lucky. All she had now were the clothes on her back, and that was stretching it since she was technically wearing what amounted to a medieval slip. She hadn't even had time to put shoes on.

She watched as Roderick continued to don full battle armor, as calm as a businessman putting a suit on for work. The thing that worried her was he felt the need to put it on now, as if he anticipated a fierce battle soon to come.

"Why didn't you help him? Baelin was outnumbered back there and you knew it. But no, at the first sign of trouble, you turned tail and ran. What kind of knight are you?"

Roderick's head snapped up and he stalked over to her, a half-strapped shoulder plate dangling down his arm. For a second, she thought he might hit her. He stood so close, she was forced to crook her neck to look at him. It wasn't a pleasant sight, with his nostrils flaring like an angry bull and veins bulging at his temples.

"*Do. Not. Ever.* Question my honor," he bit out through clenched teeth. "Did you not notice, my lady, the crowd was about to turn on you, too? Or have you not a care for your life?"

"Of course I do." She took a step back, tired of arching her neck and needing a bit more personal space. "But you left him there, to face that angry mob alone. How could you do that? Where was your precious honor then?"

"There is no honor in saving a dragon. Had I the chance, I would have slain him myself."

The breath rushed from Jill's lungs. He might as well have gone ahead and punched her in the stomach, for that was the impact his words left on her.

"Until a few hours ago, you called him friend."

"That *thing* is no friend of mine. I have spent my whole life destroying creatures such as he."

"How can you talk about him as if he were some monster? You've hunted with him, sparred with him, laughed with him, and never once did he try to hurt you. Or have you forgotten all that?"

"I have not forgotten." His voice sounded distant, tinged with anger and betrayal. "The beast deceived me. 'Tis not unheard of for dragons to be able to bend the minds of men. He bewitched me, as he has bewitched you all along."

"He did no such thing. He has no magical powers. He's a person. A living, breathing, flesh and blood human being, just like you and me. How can you think to kill him?"

His eyes grew hooded as he regarded her. "'Tis simple, my lady. 'Tis what I do."

Jill's breath caught, forming a tight knot in her throat. "Right. You're the mighty dragonslayer."

"And he is a dragon."

"He was once a knight, just like you."

"What he once was matters not. He is an abomination now."

"You don't know the whole story. He didn't choose to be this way. He was cursed, and since then he's been forced to live for centuries being the thing he hates most. I'd like to see you do that and not go completely insane."

Tears pricked like needles in Jill's eyes. Not of sadness or fear, but of anger. Roderick was being such a pig-headed ass. He refused to listen to her, refused to see the truth right in front of him.

"What happened to your knightly code? Isn't loyalty supposed to be a part of that? Until a few hours ago, he was your new best friend. Nothing has changed since then."

"*Everything* has changed since then." His voice was so low and calm, it brought chills to her skin.

"You're wrong. He's the same man he was yesterday. And he's as good a man as you, if not more so, because of what he's had to live through all these years. If you can't see that, you're just as blind as all those other people back there, living in fear and ignorance." Jill wagged her finger in his face and he leaned back as if she were brandishing a sword. "Let me tell you something. I've spent the last three weeks with him and he's shown me nothing but kindness and respect, many times when I didn't deserve it. In the week you've known him, he's been just as civil and courteous to you. And I'll tell you what—that's a hell of a lot more than you've shown him."

Roderick stared at her for a long moment and she saw something pass behind his eyes. A thought. A memory. A doubt.

Just as quickly, it was gone, replaced by a cold determination that frightened her more than any fire-breathing dragon could. This was the look of a cold-blooded killer, a man who could take another's life without fear or regret.

"What are you planning to do?" Jill asked, although she was afraid she already knew.

"Being the possessive creature that he is, the dragon will not let you go so easily. He will come." Roderick glanced up into the violet clouds of the coming dawn, as if expecting Baelin to come swooping down on them at any moment. "And when he does, I shall be waiting."

"And then what?"

"Then I shall slay him."

216

She glanced at the heavy sword strapped to his waist. "How?"

"'Tis not easy. The dragon is a creature of the devil walking this earth, with their breath of fire and their blood the very elixir of hell. The beast's scales are as a thousand shields, hard and impenetrable. It is nigh unbeatable. There is but one way to kill a dragon and I know it well." Roderick pointed to the center of his chest, over his heart. "There is a spot here, where the scales separate. When my blade finds the mark, the dragon will die."

With sudden clarity, she recalled the sunburst scar on Baelin's chest, the place where he said the witch had exchanged his human heart for a dragon one. If he was stabbed there while in human form, would the dragon die...or the man? The very thought chilled her to the bone.

"You talk about killing him as if you'll be fighting him in dragon form. But what if he comes as he is now, as a man?"

"Man or beast, it matters not to me. Either way, the dragon shall die."

Baelin stood in the shadows of the forest, careful to keep hidden from those who continued to hunt.

After hours of chasing him through the night, most of his pursuers had returned to tend to the injured and bury the dead. But others were still out there, searching the forest and the sky above with relentless determination. Only now did he risk returning to the place where Kendal and Lady Jill had disappeared into the trees.

Smoke from the smoldering timbers of the inn drifted among the trees like wandering ghosts dancing about the dark trunks, but there was no trace of the corporeal beings he sought.

They were gone.

Anger and betrayal swirled within him, wrapped in a bone-deep sense of loss. How could Kendal have taken her?

He could not allow this to happen. He would not lose her. Not now.

Before he could scent their trail, the air around him shifted, bringing with it a prickling awareness. He pushed his anger aside, tensing as something darker moved among shadows, slipping in and out of the drifting smoke. The hairs on the back of his neck stood on end as he searched the hidden recesses of the forest. He drew his sword, sensing this time it was not the people from the inn, but something much more dangerous hunting him now.

One dark shadow separated from the rest. He tensed as more followed to join the first, until two dozen surrounded him.

Like their leader, each man wore a black surcoat with a red dragon erect. Baelin knew it all too well. It had been a score of lifetimes since he'd faced one of the Dark Witch's knights. He'd hoped he'd seen the last of them.

"Greetings, Sir Baelin. Queen Isylte sends her regards."

Baelin gripped his sword hilt tighter. He had no desire to exchange pleasantries with the witch's mindless underlings. "Why are you here?"

The man grinned, but the glitter in his eyes held the sharp edge of malice. "She knows, Sir Baelin. She knows about the maid."

His gut clenched. *Nay, she cannot know of Lady Jill.*

But how could he have thought she would not learn of her? After all, the Dark Witch was the one to set this curse upon him, so it stood to reason she would know when the first test was passed. She would now stop at nothing to prevent them from succeeding against the remaining challenges. Baelin sucked in a breath as a horrible possibility entered his mind.

"What has she done?"

The warrior shrugged, his stance calm, unconcerned with the armed dragon-knight standing before him. "She ordered us to remove the tapestry or the maid from your possession, for without one or the other, the curse cannot be broken." The man nodded at the tapestry tucked securely in Baelin's sword belt. "I see you still possess the tapestry, but it appears our little diversion worked, for the maid is no longer with you."

Dear God. Had he unwittingly brought death to those hapless travelers at the inn merely by sheltering with them last eve?

The leader cocked his head to the side, lowering his voice as if to exchange a confidence to a friend. "Tell us, Sir Baelin, for Queen Isylte will surely want to know. Did you watch the girl burn?"

A black vengeance rushed in, filling Baelin with fury and anguish for the innocent lives lost at the Dark Witch's whim. He bellowed with righteous outrage and charged at the knight, his sword raised high.

"Take him alive!" the leader shouted as he drew his sword. The knights rushed in, tightening the circle surrounding him.

Before the first could reach him, Baelin let loose the dragon within and blasted them with its fire, sending several warriors careening across the forest floor, igniting the dry leaves in their path. In the wake of their screams, he hacked and chopped at the others who kept coming, stabbing and slicing in a blur of motion and blood and limbs, until he stood in a circle of the dead, their blood seeping into the mossy ground underfoot.

As quickly as they'd come, those still alive vanished back into the shadows, transformed from men into formless dark clouds a dragon's fire could no longer harm and leaving no trail he could follow. He would never be able to catch them, much less kill them in their present form.

But he knew all too well where they would go. They would return to the Dark Witch and tell of what happened. They would tell her they had not succeeded in killing the maid, for without seeing Lady Jill's death with their own eyes, they couldn't be certain. And to fail the Dark Witch meant a fate worse than death. He knew, for he'd faced her displeasure himself.

Nay, they would be back. And the next time they would make certain the deed was done.

He had to find Lady Jill, for as long as the Dark Witch knew she lived, she would not be safe.

He sheathed his bloody sword and charged through the forest.

Kendal and Lady Jill were on horseback. They would make good time. If he flew, Baelin would be faster, but it would do him no good. The forest offered concealment from the air, so he was forced to follow them on foot, looking for the horse's tracks in the soft ground of the forest floor and broken twigs on the brush as they passed by. It wasn't fast, but it turned out to be deceptively easy. Kendal had left a trail even a child could follow, as if the knight knew Baelin would come after them and he welcomed it.

But even without the obvious signs of their flight through the forest, he would be able to find them. He could still detect the sweet, familiar scent of Lady Jill, faint on the damp forest air where they'd passed. She was so familiar to him now, he would know her scent anywhere, and on that alone he could follow her to the ends of the earth.

As he sped through the forest, questions began to plague him. The Dark Witch had sent her warriors this time. He'd killed several, but more would come. But in what form? More warrior knights? Another dragon? Or something else entirely? And on the edge of those thoughts, other doubts chased Baelin as he slipped through the trees.

Was Kendal truly who he seemed to be? Was he a dragonslayer in truth, or was he one of the Dark Witch's minions, too? Had she first sent a man with a handsome face to turn Lady Jill's head and steal her away? The possibility terrified him.

But nay. He'd been a sennight in Kendal's company. Irritating though the man could be, Baelin would have sensed if the knight was something other than what he appeared to be. Wouldn't he? He prayed for Lady Jill's sake he'd not been wrong.

Then as he leapt over a fallen tree, another thought chilled him even more.

What if she'd gone with Kendal willingly? He recalled with painful clarity how she'd left him the first time after witnessing the dark side of the dragon. Had she left him again? Had she seen in the other knight a means of escape from the beast she felt held her captive?

Baelin didn't want to think it, but he couldn't help but wonder if Lady Jill had chosen to go with the dragonslayer.

And that was the worst possibility of all.

CHAPTER TWENTY-FIVE

Baelin found them just before the sun reached its zenith.

Though plenty of light remained in the day, a large fire blazed out in the open field a stone's throw from the edge of the forest. The smoke billowed up in a thick, black column, entwining with the clouds above, high enough for all the countryside to see.

Or one very angry dragon.

Not that Baelin intended to descend on them from the skies in his dragon form. But from the look of things, Kendal was expecting him to.

He had to credit the dragonslayer's tactics—he'd chosen the site well. Kendal took his stand on high, open ground, able to see for several furlongs, yet he was close enough to the forest edge should the protection of the trees be needed. The knight sat fully armed upon *Flaume Stclan*, the flickering light from the nearby fire glinting off the shiny plates of his armor, waiting.

Just as Baelin knew he would be.

What he didn't know was if he was rescuing Lady Jill or about to take her from the man she'd chosen as her salvation from the beast.

He had no choice. Without her, the curse could not be broken. His life, and very likely any hope Lady Jill had of returning to her time, depended on getting her back.

Baelin left the cover of the trees, walking on human legs as would any other man. He did not draw his sword, but kept his hands at his sides. Though he'd once called Kendal friend, if only briefly, at the moment he wanted nothing more than to run the knight through where he stood. But he had no desire to spill the man's blood in front of Lady Jill if he did not have to. He'd made that mistake once before.

Kendal was not so inclined. Noticing Baelin's approach, he drew his sword, the sudden motion bringing Lady Jill to her feet. She turned wide, frightened eyes his way.

What she was thinking, he could not tell. She made no move either in his direction or toward Kendal, but stood still between them, her face pale beneath smeared soot and ash. Then, as his blood threatened to deafen him with its pounding in his head, she took one small, tentative step toward him.

The knight spurred his mount in front of her and grabbed her by the hair with his free hand, halting her next step, holding her back. The possessive nature of the dragon within bristled at the sight of the man's hand on her.

"I believe you have something that belongs to me."

"Do I?" Kendal asked. "Methinks the lady belongs to herself."

"Then release her and allow her to choose who she wishes to stand with."

"It matters not what she says. You have bewitched her with your serpent's spell. Once you are dead, she will return to her right mind and like as not thank me for freeing her from the dragon's clutches."

"Like as not is right." Lady Jill tried to pry her hair out of Kendal's firm grip, then hissed at him through clenched teeth when she couldn't break free. "And it's none of your damn business if I want to be in the dragon's clutches or not."

Baelin's tension eased a fraction at her words, but not completely. The fact she called him dragon revealed while she may not *want* to be with him, she knew as well as he that she *needed* to be with him.

Perhaps the knight was right after all. Lady Jill had no choice. Not truly.

"This is between you and I, Kendal. Leave the maid out of it."

"Ah, but 'tis just the thing. She is in the thick of it." The knight shoved her away, toward where Owen stood silent, his young eyes darting back and forth between the two men. "If you want her back, you will have to kill me to get her."

"It does not have to be this way."

"Oh, but it does. I have spent my life protecting others from creatures such as you. Before this day is through, only one of us will remain."

"If that is the way it must be, so be it." Baelin drew his sword, the hiss of steel leaving scabbard an answer to Kendal's challenge. "But I will fight you as a knight and no other way."

Kendal laughed, the sound humorless, skeptical. "What, no dragon tricks?"

"On my word."

"What good is the word of a dragon?" he scoffed.

"'Tis the only word you will have from me this day. And be thankful you have it, for if I came before you as a dragon, 'tis a battle you would quickly lose."

"That remains to be seen. I have sent more dragons than you can imagine back to the hell that spawned them. It will be my pleasure to add one more to their number this day."

"We shall see about that."

"Then let us be done with this." Kendal lowered the helm over his face and spurred his horse.

Baelin spared one last glance in Lady Jill's direction to assure himself she was safely out of harm's way. Would that he could blind her to what was about to happen, for surely she would never forgive him for what he must do now. He knew all too well it would be so, for in the end he did not think he would not be able to forgive himself.

He hardened his resolve as Kendal charged, his sword raised high. Baelin consigned the friend the man once was to some small, dark place deep in the pit of his heart. Friendship and regrets had no place in battle. The enemy approached him now. He'd not suffered two hundred years as a dragon to die now when the end of his torment was so near.

They came together in a bone-jarring clash of steel on steel, the re-sounding peal ringing out across the open field. Kendal had the advantage of height astride the horse, but Baelin was quick, darting out of range of animal's powerful hooves.

"To think I shared meals with you." The knight swung his sword in a powerful arc, barely missing Baelin's shoulder. "And hunted with you." He swung again, the steel blade whistling through the air by his head.

"And all this time *you* were what I should have been hunting." He growled as Baelin blocked a hard blow with his sword.

"It appears you are not as good a dragonslayer as you claim to be."

Baelin thrust back, then dove under the horse to come up on the other side.

"Oh, you are good, I will give you that, to have kept your dark nature a secret from me so long." Kendal pulled his mount around and circled, waving his heavy sword before him. "Did you laugh at how easily you deceived me?"

The battle dance trampled the tall grass beneath foot and hoof as their swords came together again and again. The sight of knight and mount fighting as one was a sight to behold. But Baelin was tiring from the effort of keeping up with a mounted warrior. He needed to bring Kendal down or this might very well be a battle he would lose.

At the thought, the fighting instincts of the dragon roared to the forefront, demanding release. He beat the beast down. He'd vowed to fight the knight as a man and would die before he broke it.

But, whispered the creature within, *you never said anything about the horse.*

Before he could stop it, the fire of the beast shot out, barely missing the charger's muzzle. The horse's eyes rolled white and it reared, sending the dragonslayer to the ground.

"You bastard!" The knight shot to his feet. "What of your vow of no dragon tricks?"

"Merely leveling the battlefield. *Now* we fight man to man. Or do you fear you will lose to me without your steed between us?"

Kendal growled with righteous rage. "The people were right. You, with your dragon's fire, started the blaze at the inn, did you not? What evil lives within your devil's heart that you would burn women and children alive?"

Their swords locked and Baelin shoved him away.

"The fire 'twas not my doing."

"Mayhap you did not strike the flame yourself, but as surely as I live and breathe, 'twas you who brought death to those people." The truth of those words struck deep, for Baelin had wondered the same thing himself.

This close, he could see the dragonslayer's hate-filled eyes burning through the narrow slits of his helm. "You are the embodiment of evil, and its like follows you wherever you go. I have sworn before God and my king to wipe your kind from the face of the Earth. Only then will the innocent be safe. Only then will the dead be avenged."

It was in that moment Baelin knew he hadn't misjudged the knight. Kendal wasn't one of the Dark Witch's warriors. His convictions were too strong, his righteous mission too sacred to carry out such a deception for so long. He was a dragonslayer in truth, and just as deadly, if not more so, because of it.

Blow after blow they inflicted on each other, their movements in synch from hours of practice together. But this was no friendly sparring. Today, they fought to kill.

Breathing heavy, Kendal held him off with his sword, circling as Baelin turned in concert with him. He hammered away at the knight, until their swords came together overhead. Then Baelin swung down and under, catching Kendal behind the knees. The knight went down and Baelin stepped on the dragonslayer's sword, preventing any defense. He held the point of his own sword under Kendal's helm, at his throat.

"Finish it, dragon spawn."

Baelin tensed, ready to inflict the final, killing blow.

Lady Jill rushed up and grabbed his arm. "No, Baelin. Don't!"

He froze, every muscle in him straining to do what instinct and training demanded. It would take no effort to break Lady Jill's hold.

But he didn't.

"If I do not end this now, he will never stop hunting us." Was he speaking to her or trying to convince himself?

"No, he won't," Lady Jill said.

"The dragon is right," Kendal hissed through bloodied lips. "As long as I draw breath, I shall hunt you and your kind to the ends of the earth."

"No," she said. "You will give us your word not to come after us, won't you?"

"I will not give my word to a dragon."

"He gave you his word, to fight you as a man, and he did." She paused. "Sort of. Now he has won, as a man. You both live and die by your precious code of honor. Well, let's see some of it now."

The two men remained frozen, Kendal on the ground and Baelin standing over him, his sword poised to strike.

"Roderick, swear on your honor you will not pursue us and Baelin will let you live." She turned her head to look at him, but he refused to take his eyes off the dragonslayer. "Won't you, Baelin?"

He gritted his teeth. The dragon in him wanted nothing more than to kill the hunter, while the knight in him demanded he give quarter to a fallen knight.

But in the end it was the man in him who decided. The man who did not want to kill his only friend, even if that friend now looked on him with hate and loathing.

"Aye, if he gives his word, I will accept it."

"Good." She turned her attention to Kendal. "So, what will it be, Roderick? To die with honor by the sword or to give your word and live to fight another day?"

A battle raged behind Kendal's blue eyes. His voice, when he finally spoke, sounded distant, tinged with anger and betrayal.

"I give you my word I will not pursue you."

Baelin stood back, but he did not sheathe his sword. He knew he would stand by his word, but would Kendal? After all, he'd thought nothing of leaving him behind to face death at the hands of the angry mob.

He backed away, with Lady Jill by his side, never taking his eyes off the knight.

Kendal slowly pulled himself to his feet. Owen rushed to his side, offering the long sword with shaky hands, but the knight waved the weapon away.

"On my oath, I will not hunt you, dragon. But by chance if our paths should ever cross again, I will not hesitate to kill you."

"Then I consider myself forewarned." Baelin bowed his head. "Until we meet again."

Then he and Lady Jill slipped silently into the forest.

"Did you choose to go with him?"

Baelin's voice was so soft, it startled her in the silence of the forest.

Jill glanced at the somber man walking beside her. The first words he'd uttered to her since he'd found her with dragonslayer were not gently spoken. An undercurrent of repressed anger and rage continued to radiate from him, crackling in the air around them as it had ever since leaving Roderick and Owen far behind at the edge of the forest.

"Of course not. He practically kidnapped me."

He grunted in response, and the tension between them rose a notch higher. She grabbed his arm and pulled him to a stop.

"Who are you mad at here, me or Roderick?"

"You. Him. Myself. I know not anymore." He swallowed hard, the thick muscles in his neck constricting with the effort. Then he looked at her, and she'd never seen his eyes so full of pain and doubt. "I cannot help but wonder, did you choose to come with me because you wanted to or because you felt you must?"

"What are you talking about?"

He shook off her grip and started walking again. "You have said yourself you believe breaking my curse will send you back to your time. If that 'tis so, then you had no choice. You had to come with me."

Jill rushed to catch up with him. "Oh, no. You couldn't be more wrong. Maybe that was a big part of it in the beginning, but it's not the only reason. Not anymore."

"Even though I may have started the fire?"

"You didn't start it."

He slanted his gaze to meet hers, his look skeptical. "How can you be certain?"

"Because I know you. You would never do something like that."

The tension on his face eased a fraction before he turned his attention back to the trees ahead of them. "Kendal did not think so."

She heard the underlying regret in his words. The fight with Roderick had been hard on him, more emotionally than physically. She knew what it was like to lose a friend. But witnessing Baelin lose the only man he could claim as one had been almost too hard to watch.

"Roderick is an idiot."

Baelin chuckled, but there was little humor in the sound. "Perhaps, but he was not completely wrong."

"What do you mean?"

"The fire was deliberately set."

"By whom?"

His jaw tensed as his eyes continued to scan the shadows of the forest ahead. "The Dark Witch. She sent her underlings to do her dirty work."

"*What?*" That news flash caused Jill to fall a step or two behind, but she quickly caught up. "How do you know?"

"Because I encountered them. After the fire. After you were gone."

A million questions ran through Jill's mind. Why would anyone do such a thing? Had it been because of them? She strained to see behind every tree and bush nearby. Were they even now being followed by these 'underlings'? So many questions and none of the answers that came to mind were good.

She noted the tension in his shoulders. "Baelin, what aren't you telling me?"

He didn't answer her right away, and that worried her even more.

"The Dark Witch has learned of you. She knows we have succeeded in passing the first test. Now, she will stop at nothing to prevent us from meeting the next two challenges, even at the cost of innocent lives."

The breath rushed from her lungs. "What are we going to do?"

He looked at her, concern etching deep lines around his eyes.

"Keep you alive until the curse is broken or our time runs out, for now that the Dark Witch knows you live, she will do all that is within her power to make it otherwise."

Chapter Twenty-Six

After making their way deeper in the forest, Baelin stopped suddenly.

His gaze sliced toward a high slope ahead of them. She stopped too, instantly in tune to the stiffness in his shoulders, the way his eyes scanned the area around them. Alert. Wary. On guard.

"What is it?" she whispered, instinctively moving her body closer to his. "Is Roderick following us? Oh God, it's not the Dark Witch's thugs, is it?"

"I do not know." He drew his sword and shifted her behind him. "But something comes."

She peeked around Baelin's shoulder as a dozen armed men eased over the rise, moving quietly between the widespread trees like stealthy predators on the hunt. The lead man stopped when he spotted them, surprise evident on his face. He was the same man from the inn, the one who'd urged the mob into a frenzy.

He pointed a sharpened spear at them. "There! There lies the beast."

"Kill the dragon!" the others shouted as they charged down the slope, weapons raised for attack.

Baelin pushed her away from him and she stumbled, falling in the damp leaves of the forest floor. He ran forward to meet the attackers, leaving her behind and out of harm's way.

"Nooo!" she screamed.

As the men surrounded him, she felt defenseless to stop this. Why did everyone want to hurt him? Couldn't they understand Baelin meant them no harm?

Jill stood and watched as Baelin fought off the men, her heart in her throat. But something was different. Something was wrong.

He was using his sword to defend himself, but no more. He deflected their attacks, but he never became the aggressor. He never once drew blood.

Why was he refusing to fight like the mad man he'd been when he fought Roderick? Why didn't he breathe fire to save himself as he'd done when they were attacked by the woodland outlaws?

And then she knew.

He wouldn't do that. These were not trained knights or highway bandits. These were frightened, innocent people. And just as last night at the inn, he would not hurt them now if he didn't have to.

She watched him, every muscle in his body tense, his eyes focused. She could tell every instinct in him wanted to fight, and yet his honor would not allow him to harm them.

Desperate to help him, she rushed into the fray and jumped on one of the men's backs. He shook her off as if she was no more than a pesky fly, and she ended up on her back in the leaves once again.

What was she thinking? She was no match for armed men. But she had to do something, so she did the only thing she could think of.

"Hey! Over here." She jumped up and down, waving her arms. "What about me? I'm a dragon, too."

Some of the men turned startled eyes to look at her. Baelin stood surrounded by the others, horrified. "Nay, my lady. What are you doing?"

With their attention now directed at her, she had no choice but to continue the act. "That's right. There are two of us. What do you think of that?"

As she hoped, some of the men came at her. They wouldn't hurt her if she was unarmed, would they? Then again, wasn't a dragon who breathed fire considered inherently armed and dangerous?

She stiffened, wondering if this was such a bright idea after all. Maybe not, but it might distract the men surrounding Baelin long enough for him to escape.

Bravado gave out to self-preservation, and she turned and ran. She didn't get far before two men grabbed her by each arm with bruising force and dragged her back near the others.

"Unhand her!" Baelin growled. "She does not speak the truth. She is no dragon. She is my prisoner, an unwilling captive, and nothing more."

"We shall see who speaks the truth," said one of the men who held her. A rough hand grabbed the back of her smock and yanked. The sound of fabric rending filled the air as the cloth split down to the middle of her back. The cool forest air touched her bare skin and terror knotted in her belly. Was she going to be raped while Baelin was forced to watch?

The man shoved her away and she clutched at the torn garment to keep it from falling to her waist.

"She lies. She does not bear the wings of the beast. She is no dragon." Then they turned on Baelin again. "But he is. Slay the dragon!"

Just as she'd hoped, those few seconds bought Baelin the diversion he needed and he broke free when the men turned from her with callous disregard.

As they gave chase, he spun on them. Letting out a blood-curdling roar, he shot a ball of flame high into the air over their heads. The men staggered back, even the bravest among them afraid to come near. Some dropped to their knees, while others ran to hide behind the trees.

Baelin spread his dragon wings and took to the sky.

Go, Baelin. Fly. Get away while you can.

He crashed through the forest canopy, sending a shower of leaves down on them like green snow.

With the men distracted, Jill turned and bolted, not willing to give them a chance to remember she was there. Roderick had used her as a lure for Baelin once. She wasn't about to let it happen again.

Sticks and briars stabbed the soles of her bare feet as she hurled herself through the underbrush. Low branches whipped her face and snagged in her hair. She could hear the men shouting, their booted feet pounding on the ground behind her.

She darted to the left, but a man with a long staff blocked her way. She skidded and turned, only to face another man, a scythe pointed at her head. Several men came around her on either side, racing through the trees in an attempt to get ahead of her, to head her off, to surround her.

She dodged around a tree, making a dash through the only opening she could find. The trees thinned and the forest suddenly opened up in front of her. Jill found herself spilling out of the woods and stumbling onto a vast, rolling grassland.

No!

She didn't stop, running until she could go no more, her feet numb, her lungs threatening to burst in her chest. Falling to her knees, she looked over her shoulder to find the men emerging from the forest, slowly closing in. They were in no hurry now. Out in the open as she was, she had no place to hide.

An angry roar split the air and Baelin soared over the top of the trees. He circled far above, then dove toward the men, scattering them in all directions.

Jill struggled to her feet and watched in horrified fascination as he descended with blinding speed. He shot out an arc of fire, igniting a line in the grass until a curtain of fire and smoke separated her from the men.

Baelin punched through the wall of black smoke, heading right at her. Jill stood perfectly still and held her breath, knowing what he planned to do.

"Oh, no. Not again."

He swooped down and grabbed her. One minute her feet were planted firmly on the ground, the next she was in his arms, flying high over the rolling hills. Up, up, up they went.

She clutched her arms around his neck and squeezed her eyes shut. The rush of the wind roared in her ears, drowning out all sound until a strange *whoosh* whizzed by her head, followed by another and another.

She opened her eyes, horrified to see an arrow fly by Baelin's shoulder.

"They're shooting at us!"

A sickening thump lurched Baelin sideways. His arms tightened around her as they rolled in the air, their spinning flight taking them over the edge of the forest.

A second thump, more solid than the first, sent them reeling. Without warning, Baelin released her and was gone.

Without his arms holding her, Jill tumbled through the air, like a skydiver without a parachute. She screamed as the trees below rushed up to meet her. She caught a brief glimpse of Baelin falling too, his graceful flight now awkward and out of control.

Just as quickly, he was gone again, out of sight. The world around her became a dizzy image—sky, trees, sky, trees—until she lost focus, and it all melded into one blur, accompanied by the sound of her own screams.

Was this the end? Were they both to meet their fates splattered on the ground like dead bugs on a windshield?

A sudden impact hit her from the side, knocking the breath from her. Strong arms wrapped around her, holding her tight, but still they tumbled out of control.

Baelin flipped them at the last second and he bore the brunt of the impact as they crashed through the trees. Branches snapped and stabbed, both slowing their descent and at the same time threatening to tear them apart.

With a sudden jolt, they slammed into the ground. Jill's ribs screamed in protest as she attempted to draw air into her lungs, and it was a moment before she could get her bearings. She pushed herself up from where she lay sprawled across Baelin's chest.

His eyes were closed, his face slack. Panic set in. Was he dead? He couldn't be dead.

She cupped his face with her hands and slapped his cheeks lightly.

"Baelin? Can you hear me? Please don't be hurt. Oh, God. Please don't be dead."

His eyes fluttered open and he looked at her, his gaze unfocused. Within seconds, his eyes sharpened, filling with concern.

"My lady, are you injured? Did any of the arrows strike you?"

Jill did a quick inventory of her body. She was in a good deal of pain, but nothing felt punctured. Just bruises and scrapes mingled with the residual terror left over from her freefall from hell.

"I think I'm okay. What about you?"

He closed his eyes and groaned, laying his head back on the ground. "I have had better landings."

She couldn't help but laugh, and he joined her, the soft rumble in his chest vibrating through her entire body, all the way down to her toes. His eyes flew open and they both sobered instantly, noticing at the same time the intimate position they were in with Jill's body straddling his, their faces close together.

She found it hard to breathe again, but for a different reason now. She licked her lips and watched Baelin's eyes flick down to take in the simple action. His eyes returned to hers, heat flaring in them.

He wanted to kiss her. And heaven help her, she wanted to kiss him, too.

His hands went to her waist. But to her surprise, he slid her off his body instead of pulling her closer. He stood and walked away, shaking the leaves and twigs off his surcoat.

Jill's disappointment gave way to concern when she spotted an arrow sticking through his wing.

"Oh God, Baelin. You're hurt."

He glanced over his shoulder at the arrow and shrugged, as if it was no more than a splinter in his finger.

Jill stood and walked toward him. "Let me help you."

"There is no time. 'Twill not be long before those men come looking for us. We must not be here when they do." Concern creased his brow as he searched the trees around them. "I do not think I can fly us away from here. Can you walk?"

"Are you kidding? If you think those guys are still after us, I'll find a way to run."

He held out his hand to her. "Then we had best run, my lady."

Chapter Twenty-Seven

Saying she could run barefoot through a forest was one thing. Doing it was another. Sheena, Queen of the Jungle, she was not.

After stepping on every stick and briar—and trying to bite back each grunt and groan every time she did so—Jill's feet finally gave out. She wasn't sure if they'd traveled five miles or five feet. It didn't matter. She couldn't take another step.

"Stop. I can't—"

Without a word, Baelin swung her up into his arms.

"What are you doing?"

"Carrying you. We must keep moving."

"Baelin, you can't carry me. You're hurt."

"'Tis only my wing that is injured. There is naught wrong with my arms and legs."

True to his word, he pressed on, carrying her through trees and undergrowth as if she weighed no more than a child. But even though he could fly, he was not Superman, and after a while, his steps slowed and his breathing grew labored. Her body sagged low in his arms until she was afraid he was going to drop her.

"Put me down."

"Nay, we must—"

"*Nay*, we must stop. You have to rest. I think we've put enough distance behind us to take a five minute break."

His jaw tensed and she could tell he wanted to argue, but his body disagreed and his shaky arms released her. Pain shot up her legs when her feet touched the ground. She bit back a groan. If Baelin could carry her through the woods with an arrow sticking out of his wing, she could handle a few thorns in her feet.

"Now, let's take a look at that wing."

As she reached for him, he spun away. "Do not touch it. My blood is on the arrow. Remember, it will burn you."

Jill paused. As a matter of fact, she had forgotten. "Well, you can't walk around with an arrow sticking out of your wing for the rest of your life and you certainly can't pull it out yourself, can you?"

He tried to reach around and grasp the arrow shaft, but it was at an awkward angle. As he tugged, he grimaced in pain.

"Stop. You're only going to make it worse. Let me help. I promise I'll be careful."

He glanced at the trees behind them. "We should not tarry here."

"We can tarry long enough to bandage your wing. You know, you don't always have to play the big, tough hero. Every now and then you can let somebody else take care of you."

She could see her words stunned him as he struggled to process their meaning.

"Someone to take care of me, a dragon-knight?" He shook his head in disbelief. "No one has offered to do that in a long, long time."

"Well, I'm offering now, so stop stalling and sit." She pointed at a fallen tree. To her surprise he obeyed, probably more relieved to have an excuse to rest than because she'd told him to do it.

Jill moved behind him and noticed several holes in the webbing of both wings where arrows had gone all the way through.

"It looks like they hit you more than once. Do any of these hurt?"

Baelin fanned his other wing wide and poked a finger through one of the punctures. "Nay, 'tis not much feeling in this part of my wings. These will heal quickly."

"Must be like getting your ears pierced. All skin and few nerves."

She turned her attention to the arrow protruding from his wing. It was sticking out half on one side and half on the other near the shoulder so that he couldn't fold his wing properly. It would have to come out if he ever hoped to fly again.

"I'm no doctor, but it looks like this one went through the muscle. Hopefully it missed any bone. There are bones in your wings, aren't there?"

Baelin shrugged. Guess he wasn't sure either.

"I think I can get it out. Do you still have your dagger?"

He arched a suspicious brow at her. "What are you going to do?"

"Don't look so worried, you big baby. I figure we just need to cut off one end so we can slide the arrow out without tearing a bigger hole."

He nodded, surprised. "Aye, 'tis how it is done. You are very wise, for one unaccustomed to arrow wounds."

"Yeah, well, lately I've gotten very good at medieval improvisation."

She used the knife to carve a groove around the shaft. She tried to do it as gently as possible, without moving his wing. He sat there and did not make a sound.

She gripped the shaft with both hands and snapped the feathered end off. That part done, she looked at the dark blood coating the rest of the arrow where it had come out the other side, wondering how she was going to be able to grab it to pull it out. She lightly tapped the shaft with her fingers, testing to see how bad the blood would burn, each contact lasting a little longer until she felt it was safe to touch.

"What are you doing?" he asked as he twisted his head, trying to look over his shoulder.

"Stop wiggling. I'm seeing just how nasty this blood of yours really is."

She wrapped her hand around the shaft. It was warm to the touch, but it didn't burn.

"Nay, my lady, do not—"

"Take it easy. It's okay. It's not burning me." She cocked her head, pondering why that was. "Either as the blood dries, it loses its toxicity, or after that trial by iron, hot sticks don't faze me anymore."

"Truly?" Baelin sounded surprised himself.

Jill shrugged. "Ours is not to wonder why. Let's just be grateful for the little things and get this over with." She took a deep breath and blew it out. "Okay, brace yourself. I'm going to pull it through now."

His hands gripped his knees and he nodded. She placed one hand on his shoulder, grabbed the arrow shaft with the other and pulled it through with one swift yank.

"There. Almost done." She watched as fresh blood welled up and dripped down his wing. "Although I'm not exactly sure how to bandage this thing."

She dropped the broken arrow on the ground and reached for the hem of her smock. "You know, if we don't stop hurting ourselves, I'm liable to use the last piece of clothing I have left and end up walking around naked."

Baelin spun around and grabbed her wrist, stopping her as she made the first tear. Startled, she looked at him and realized the visual image her words had probably put into his head.

She'd been right. The want, the desire, was there, evident in his golden eyes. She watched the muscles in his throat working as if he was trying to swallow down the emotions. He broke the contact first, releasing her wrist and worked at the ties to his surcoat.

"Nay, use this instead."

Jill didn't argue. She used his dagger to cut the garment into long strips with trembling hands. Holy cow. She didn't have to be a scientist to feel the volatile chemistry brewing on the air, and it wasn't all coming from the man before her. She was giving off a good deal of it herself, and it scared the hell out of her.

She wrapped several strips around his wing, careful not to touch the fresh blood oozing from the puncture wound. Thankfully, the arrow struck at the narrowest part of his wing, where it sprouted out of his back. Otherwise, there wouldn't be enough clothing between the two of them to bandage it, and then they'd both be walking around naked.

A shot of pure lust rocked through Jill's body as she recalled how good Baelin's naked body looked by the firelight in the cave. Okay, so now was not the most convenient time to be having hot and heavy fantasies about the wounded man in front of her. For heaven's sake, he still had on his mail, complete with all the padding that went underneath, yet her mind had stripped him naked in a matter of seconds. What was wrong with her?

"There." She finished the last knot and stepped back, needing a big breath of air to clear her head. "It may not be pretty, but I think it'll do."

Baelin stood and tested the wing, completely oblivious to the lascivious visions torturing Jill's vivid imagination.

"Aye, 'twill do. I do not think any permanent damage has been done. I may be able to fly again in a day or two. Well done, my lady."

Jill made a small curtsy. "Doctor Donahue at your service. Take two aspirin and call me in the morning."

Baelin frowned at her, confused. Great, she was babbling nonsense again. She couldn't be any more awkward if she tried.

His gaze traveled her body and his frown hardened when it stopped at her feet. "My lady! I am not the only one injured. We must see to your feet."

She looked down and sure enough, her feet were a throbbing, bloody mess. Nothing in her modern world had conditioned her for running through the woods barefoot.

"Sit and I will tend them."

She did as he asked, taking his seat on the log, the bark still warm from his body.

He knelt before her and lifted her foot, carefully cleaning the leaves and dirt from the worst of the cuts. Water would've been nice, but there wasn't a stream or brook in sight. He kept his head lowered, intent on his task.

He was being very tender, but he could have taken sandpaper to her toes and she wouldn't have noticed. All the feeling in her body was no longer focused on the pain in her feet, but up higher, where his hand cupped her calf. Tingles radiated out from the spot and she could feel her pulse pounding just under the skin. Could he feel it too? The moan she tried to suppress came out sounding more like a groan.

His eyes flew to her face. "Did I hurt you?"

"No. You have a gentle touch. I hardly felt a thing." *Liar.*

Jill mentally shook herself and tried to shift her mind off this train of thought. "I wish I'd gotten to say goodbye to Owen."

Baelin returned to tending her feet. "It could not be helped."

"I know." She looked at his bowed head, her hand itching to run her fingers through his hair. She gave herself bonus points for controlling the urge. "So, do you think Roderick will keep his word and not come after us?"

"I do not know. Though some men claim themselves knights, they do not always live by the code. Kendal? Perhaps he is honorable enough. In the short time we knew him, I would like to think him to be true to his word. But after taking you, I am no longer so certain." Baelin paused in his task and stared at the ground. "How could I have been so wrong? For a time, I thought him a friend."

"And you were his."

"Then he was a friend I nearly killed. If you had not stopped me…" He shook his head. "I hated him for taking you from me. I could have killed him for it and not thought twice."

"But you didn't."

He didn't respond, but continued in his task, cutting more strips from his surcoat and wrapping her feet.

"For what it's worth, I don't think you were wrong about Roderick. Neither of us were. He's a good man." Jill took a deep breath and pressed on, needing to fill the tense silence surrounding them. "Sometimes, when you're taught all your life that something is one way, it's hard to accept what you thought was right might have been wrong all along. Given time to think about it, I believe Roderick will come to realize he was wrong about you, just like you're wrong about him. You can't blame him for doing what he believed was right any more than he can blame you for being a dragon."

Finished wrapping her feet, Baelin leaned back and surveyed his handiwork. He swore under his breath. "If that is what you believe, then perhaps I should have left you with him. With me, you have known naught but pain."

"But I'm not with him and I don't want to be. You and I, we're in this thing together."

He shook his head. "At least with him, you would be safe. Now that the Dark Witch knows of you, your life will always be in danger."

"Then I can think of no better person to be with."

"I am honored you have such faith in me." Baelin sat taller as his eyes searched her face, serious, intense. "Know this, my lady. As long as you are with me, I will allow no more harm to befall you. I will use all that is within my power to keep you safe and I will gladly lay down my life to protect you."

She looked at his handsome face, illuminated by the sunlight filtering through the treetops, and knew he spoke the truth.

He would die for her.

She didn't think there was another person on this earth—in this time or hers—who would so freely say the same.

She wanted to say something, but the words refused to come. She looked at him, sitting there on his knees in front of her, so big and brave and yet suddenly so vulnerable.

Then his gaze dropped and focused in on her mouth. In an instant, those eyes of his shifted from chocolate brown to a glowing gold, hinting at the fire constantly burning inside of him. She watched his body tense from the force of holding back, his fists gripping his thighs as if he didn't, they might reach out and grab her of their own accord.

He wanted to kiss her. Wanted it so desperately she felt it with every fiber of her being. But he wouldn't, not when he thought she saw him as a monster.

No, with a man like Baelin, it would be up to her to make the first move.

And so she did.

She leaned in and cupped his handsome face in her hands, brushing his mouth with a gentle kiss, showing him with an action better than words that she thought him no beast.

She felt his shock, his initial resistance. When he tried to pull back, she held on, tunneling her fingers into his hair and clasping the nape of his neck. She increased the pressure, crushing his mouth with hers, nipping at his lips with her teeth, probing the crease of his lips with her tongue. She felt the moment of his surrender in the relaxing of his shoulders, in the growl that erupted from deep inside him before he wrapped his arms around her and returned her kiss.

His hands touched the skin of her back where the torn smock gapped open. He pulled away, as if the feel of her exposed skin shocked him. He looked at her, confusion warring with the desire in his eyes.

Before she could stop him, Baelin pushed himself away from her, stood and walked away.

She swayed, feeling suddenly cold and weak without his arms around her.

What just happened? They'd been kissing. A hot, sizzling kiss that had sent tingles zinging all the way down to her toes. She'd been thoroughly enjoying herself. So what did she do wrong? Had she offended him? Had she misread all the signals?

She stared at his stiff back. He couldn't even look at her. Did he not want her?

Embarrassment and shame rushed over her. Well, if this just wasn't the most pitiful thing. Rejected by Puff the Magic Dragon. It looked like her love life sucked in every century.

Jill stood and walked to him, stopping an arm's length away. "Baelin, I'm sorry if—"

He whirled and stared down at her, that smoldering heat still burning in his eyes.

Before she could blink, he crushed her to him as if he could pull her body inside his own. Now it was he who was the aggressor, nipping and teasing her lips before invading her mouth with his tongue.

He tasted of smoke and mint and, strangely enough, just a trace of salt. The sensation of his forked tongue wrapping around hers shocked her. She'd never felt anything like it, and a wave of pure electricity shot through her entire body. Her gut clenched, her legs grew weak, and she thought she might climax on the spot from just that one kiss.

Jill had never felt so consumed by another person in her life, as if the very breath from her lungs gave him life. Holding him in her arms, she marveled that such a strong, brave knight could tremble so.

Without warning, Baelin broke the kiss and dropped to his knees before her. He wrapped his arms around her waist and pressed his cheek against her stomach as his broad shoulders shook and his hands clutched at her.

Then silently, her big, brave dragon-knight wept.

Chapter Twenty-Eight

"Am I to assume by your presence before me that you have succeeded?"

The tall, strong knight squirmed where he stood. "Not quite."

Isylte narrowed her eyes at the man, who seemed to prefer to gaze at his feet rather than look her in the eye.

"*Not quite.*" She mimicked his inflection of the word. "'Tis not an acceptable answer. Tell me, did you kill the maiden or not?"

The warrior glanced at the fellow knights standing with him before he answered. "I am afraid not, my queen. The maid and the dragon are still together, though they were separated for a time after the fire."

Her only reaction was the tightening of her knuckles as she gripped the arms of her throne. "What fire?"

"When we found them, they had stopped at an inn, still in the company of the dragonslayer and the boy. But there were too many others about. We thought to create a distraction, so that we might flush them out."

"And so you set fire to the inn?" she said in disbelief.

"Aye."

"With my dragon inside?" Her disbelief quickly turned to simmering outrage.

The knight finally looked up, alarm mingled with puzzlement in his expression. "Being a dragon and all, we did not think the flames would harm him."

"'Tis where you made your first mistake. You did not *think.*" Isylte glared at the motley crew standing before her who dared to call themselves her guard. "In his human form, he can burn as easily as the rest of you, which may soon become your fate if you do not tell me what I wish to hear."

To a man, the warriors paled at her threat. They might be battle-hardened knights, but they were no match for her powers and they all knew it.

"What happened as a result of this little 'distraction' of yours?"

"During the fire, the dragon revealed himself and the people at the inn attacked." At her alarmed expression, the knight rushed to add, "He flew off before they could catch him. I assure you the dragon was unharmed, my queen."

"I see." She relaxed, if only a little. "And what of the maid who is helping him? What of her?"

"We believed she perished in the fire...at first."

"At first?" Isylte ground her teeth. She contemplated what method of torture would be necessary to get answers out of the man faster.

"It appears a dragonslayer made off with the maid sometime during the tumult. The dragon was none too happy about it."

Reminded once again of how much this faceless girl meant to Baelin, Isylte inwardly seethed. "No, I would imagine not."

The knight continued on, oblivious to his queen's rising ire. "When we found him alone the morn after the fire, we attempted to take him, alive, of course. But he fought fiercely. He used his dragon powers, killing the captain and nearly a dozen of the men before he escaped. The rest of us barely survived with our lives."

"How fortunate for you," she murmured, her tone dry and unsympathetic.

"The dragon gave chase after the maid and we followed. But sometime before we found them, the dragon must have overtaken the dragonslayer and bested him, for when we came upon his camp, the dragonslayer was alone and nursing his wounds."

"So, the maid is under the dragon's protection once again." It wasn't what she would have hoped for, but there was still time to stop them from breaking the curse. "Where are they now?"

"We are not certain."

"And why not?" she growled. By the slumping of the knight's broad shoulders, she could already tell she was not going to like what came next.

"We followed their trail deep into the forest. We were almost upon them when men from the inn found them and attacked. The dragon attempted to fly away with the maid, but they shot at them with arrows. They fell from the sky and landed somewhere in the Grizedale Forest."

"*What?* How dare they try to slay *my* dragon." She breathed in and out in an effort to control her anger. "He is not dead. I would know it if the dragon was dead."

Comforted in the thought, she turned her rage on the men standing before her.

"But you. You have failed miserably. Not once but twice, and in the process endangered my dragon." Her voice was deceptively soft, striking fear in the men before her.

She stood slowly, full of restrained power and coiled rage. She flung a bolt of sizzling magic out into the room, reducing the twelve men standing before her into the puddles of slime they were.

She regretted her action the moment she did it. Now she would have to create more warriors to take their places and that took time. And time was something she no longer had when it came to a certain dragon-knight.

"Grend!" Her voice echoed in the empty hall. There was no one left alive in the vast chamber to obey her order. It did not matter. She pulled the silken cord by the dais, summoning the servants no doubt skulking about somewhere in the maze of corridors of her fortress. She would send one of them to fetch Grend. Her prized pet could always be depended upon to see a task done right.

She eyed the mess the useless knights had left on her pristine floor in disgust.

"You may have won this battle, my dragon. But you have not won the war. I shall see to that."

"I just don't get it. How can being shot at with arrows and plunging in a death spiral from the ozone layer not be the second test?"

Lady Jill sat on a moss-covered rock beside a stream cutting a jagged scar through the forest floor, staring in disbelief at the tapestry in her lap.

Dusk crept through the trees around them, heralding the coming of night. They'd finally stopped after walking for a while longer in near silence. The whole time, neither had spoken of the kiss, or of what had passed between them after.

For now, she seemed more concerned with the tapestry. He did not know whether to be relieved or disappointed.

"Why does this stupid cross stitch project from hell only show what's already happened? Why can't it be like a crystal ball and tell what's to come? At least that way, I could prepare myself for it."

"Are you certain it has not changed?"

"No. See?" She held up the tapestry. It was the same. Nothing had changed since she survived the trial by iron. "Is it because I wasn't the one hurt this time? My sliced up feet didn't bleed enough? Was I the one who should've gotten shot by the arrow?" She gripped the edges of the tapestry and shook it, as if by doing so it would give her the answers she wanted. "Do I have to endure some kind of horrendous bodily torture for these challenges to pass? If that's the way this thing works, it's not fair."

Baelin cleared his throat, uncertain of what to say. "If you have lived as long as I have, you soon learn not all in life is fair."

She looked up at him. Did she know he was speaking of more than the challenges? There she sat, tired and bedraggled and filthy, and yet he'd never seen anyone as beautiful as she was to him right now. Unfair was she could be so close and yet so far beyond his reach.

He glanced away. He didn't dare look at her any longer. And heaven help him if he ever touched her again.

"Rest. I shall see if I can gather us some food."

He left her there, sitting on the mossy rock by the brook, unable to be near her without impossible dreams running through his head.

But as he stalked away through the trees, her kiss was never far from his thoughts. The first one had been chaste and sweet, but this one...

Never, in all his years, did he think something as simple as a kiss would have the power to bring him to his knees. But it did.

Hers did.

Now he wanted nothing more than to take her in his arms and kiss her again. And more.

But he didn't dare. By the saints, he was almost afraid to be near her now. He was a brave knight who'd battled armies and fire-breathing dragons. How could a little slip of a woman turn his world upside down?

He stopped walking and leaned against a tree, feeling the rough bark against his palm.

How long had it been since he'd felt a person's touch? Since a woman had held him without fear? It was nearly impossible to remember. For so long, he'd hardened himself to any such emotions, any such longings. He'd begun to believe the dragon part of him had stolen that part of humanity from him. After being alone for so long, he didn't miss what he could no longer have. But now, with one kiss, those emotions had all come back. And he couldn't think of anything he wanted more than to keep Lady Jill with him. Always.

But he couldn't ask for more from her. Not yet while he was half a man.

That did not stop him from yearning. For with her kiss came hope, and the fragments of a long forgotten dream. If Lady Jill truly was the one, then she held the power to set him free. And when he was once again a man whole, he could live a normal life, with a home that was more than a cave, with a woman he did not have to kidnap and force to stay at his side. A woman who would wed him, give him children, grow old with him.

Love him.

When he pictured that woman—the one he never dared believe he might have—he saw only Lady Jill's face, with her wild untamed hair and saucy grin. If she was the one to finally set him free, dare he hope she would be the one to stay?

Then he recalled her crushed look when she realized the second challenge hadn't been met, and she was no closer to getting home. Baelin pushed away from the tree and continued deeper into the forest.

For the first time, he admitted he didn't want her to go home. That if it were within his power, he wanted this woman to remain by his side once this quest was over. But if she was right, passing the other tests would send her far away from him, to a place where he could never reach her.

His only hope was she was wrong. That perhaps breaking the curse wasn't the key to her going home and she would stay. After all, she was only grasping at the possibility. But did he have the right to wish against the one thing he knew she desired most? Where was the honor in that?

And what if the curse was not broken and she was forced to remain? In three nights he would return to the beast that he was, just as he had year after year for over two centuries. And then where would she be? Alone, with nothing more than a giant lizard—as she so often called him—for company. Would she stay with him then? Could she live in a cave with the dragon, only able to have Baelin the man for one month out of each year?

He did not think so.

Baelin shook himself from his thoughts. After two hundred years of disappointment, he knew it was better not to hope for the impossible, less painful when the dream faded away with the rise of the next full moon.

Jill watched Baelin disappear into the trees. He didn't even bother looking back.

Was he embarrassed, because for one brief moment he'd let down that impenetrable guard of his and allowed her a glimpse of the raw emotions he kept buried deep inside? She didn't have to be an expert on the male ego to figure that one out.

She stared at the spot where the thick forest had swallowed him up, wondering what else was going on inside his head right now. Probably some of the same confusing thoughts scrambling around inside her own brain, like what it would be like to take things beyond a sizzling kiss next time.

Jill ground her teeth. What was wrong with her? She was acting more like a teenaged boy in hormonal overdrive than a twenty-nine year old woman. She needed to get a grip on herself. But it was hard. She'd never felt so sexually frustrated in all her life. And all over a man who was half dragon. It would figure her knight in shining armor would come with wings attached. No one ever said she did things the easy way.

She looked at the tapestry in her lap and ran her finger over the figure of the dragon.

Her dragon.

But he wasn't a dragon. What she'd said to Roderick was true. She'd stopped thinking of Baelin as a dragon a long time ago. He was a man, but unlike any man she'd ever known. He was strong and kind, honest and loyal to a fault. He was a better person than any human being she'd ever known, in this century or her own.

When had she started thinking of him that way?

Had it begun when he saved her from the bandits? Or was it the way he stood beside her throughout the trial, believing in her when no one else would? Perhaps it was something as simple as when he shielded her from the rain with his wing.

Or was it the kiss?

At the memory, Jill's heart tightened in her chest. What had started out as an impulsive gesture had quickly turned into something so much more. And afterwards, when he'd clutched her to him, all thoughts of hot, steamy sex had flown out of her mind, replaced by a feeling of being cherished like none she'd ever known.

Jill was so lost in her thoughts, she almost didn't hear the sound. She glanced up to see if Baelin was returning, but there was no sign of him. She must be hearing things now. She'd probably busted an eardrum, shooting through in the sky like a bottle rocket.

But then she heard it again. It sounded like a small child crying.

She stood and followed the sound, walking along the bank of the stream. She looked around, but could see nothing. Had she only imagined it?

She was about to turn around and go back when she heard it again. She looked back up the stream and there, at the bend on the other side, sat a little girl. What was she doing out her all alone?

Jill approached the child cautiously, not wanting to frighten her. The little girl sat huddled in a ball, hugging her knees to her tiny chest. She had long, black hair and several curly wisps fluttered in the breeze.

"Hi sweetie," Jill called out in her softest, mother-like voice. "Are you okay?"

The little girl's head popped up and she wiped at her runny nose, but she didn't say a word.

"Okay. Stay right where you are. I'm going to come across to you." The child stared at her with wide, frightened eyes. "Don't be scared. I'm not going to hurt you."

Jill tucked the tapestry under her arm and slipped down the bank. She stepped carefully on the exposed rocks and was across the shallow stream in no time. It was a little harder pulling herself up the other bank, but she managed, getting her hands and knees muddy in the process.

As soon as she drew near, the little girl started crying again.

"Aw, honey. What's wrong?" she crooned as she tucked a stray curl behind the girl's ear.

"I'm lost. I want my mother."

"Oh, you poor thing." She took the little girl into her arms, rocking her back and forth to sooth her. She was so much like her own niece, Zoe. Probably about the same age.

"Is she close by? Do you live around here?"

The child shook her head. "Nay. She lives far, far away."

"Then what are you doing out here all by yourself?"

At that, the little girl started crying harder.

"Don't worry. We'll find her. My friend is a knight, and he specializes in things like this. He loves saving damsels in distress and you're the prettiest damsel I've ever seen."

"Truly?" She looked at Jill with the bluest eyes Jill had ever seen.

"Truly. Our camp is just down the stream. We'll make a nice, warm fire and get you something to eat. And as soon as we figure out where you're from, we'll take you home. How does that sound?"

The little girl didn't reply, but merely nodded. Guess that was a yes.

Jill slid down the bank onto the mossy, flat stones and turned back to the girl. "Here, take my hand and I'll help you down."

The little girl's hand felt icy in her own. "My goodness. How long have you been out here? Your hand is freezing."

The little girl shrugged and moved closer to the edge.

"Don't be scared. I won't let you fall."

Jill took one step and then another out onto the rocks to make room for the child. She felt a strong tug on her hand and her left foot slipped on the algae-covered rocks. She wobbled, nearly toppling both her and the child into the cold water. When she regained her balance, she straightened and caught their reflection in the water.

In the mirrored surface, she saw her hand was no longer holding that of an angelic child, but of a horrid looking creature.

Jill jerked around.

The child was gone. In her place squatted a skeletal goblin with glowing yellow eyes. It laughed at her, revealing snaggled, stained teeth.

"You fool!"

The thing reached out and snatched at the tapestry. She made a desperate grab for it, trying to wrestle it away. The creature slashed at Jill's hand with its claws and then shoved her, sending her falling backwards into the shallow water.

"No!" The tapestry ripped through her fingers as she fell. Her butt hit the sandy creek bottom. It was deep enough for her to go under and she came up sputtering, shoving her wet hair out of her eyes.

The thing was gone, and the tapestry with it.

"Damn it!" She struggled to claw her way up the creek bank. She had to find Baelin. He was going to be so pissed.

She stumbled back toward the camp, dripping and cold, shouting his name the whole way.

He came crashing through the woods with his sword drawn. "What is wrong?"

"Baelin, thank God. There was a little girl…who turned into this *thing*."

"Where?"

Jill pointed upstream and tried to calm herself long enough to make sense. "I heard a child crying and there was a little girl, all alone. She said she was lost. I was bringing her back here, but she turned into this horrible little troll baby and before I knew what it was doing, it shoved me into the water. It…" She paused, afraid to tell him the rest. "It took the tapestry."

"*What?*" His angry eyes scanned the forest. "Which way did it go?"

"I don't know." Jill stood there and shivered. "What was that thing?"

"Probably one of the Dark Witch's spawn."

"But it looked just like a little girl. At least at first."

"Some of the witch's creatures have the power to change forms at will. They can appear as an animal, a human, or as a creature we cannot even imagine."

"So you think the Dark Witch sent it?"

"I know she did."

Jill's stomach rolled as the consequences played out in her mind. "What if we don't get the tapestry back? Can we still break the curse?"

When Baelin returned his gaze to hers, the disappointment in his eyes cut her to the core. "I do not know."

"What are we going to do?"

He sheathed his sword and sniffed the air. "I must find the demon and get the tapestry back before it reaches the Dark Witch. If it returns it to Isylte's possession, she will destroy it and all hope of breaking the curse will be lost."

"Do we know that? I mean, it's not as if it's giving us clues to what the tests are. It's just a record of what has already happened. Maybe it doesn't matter who has it. Maybe we don't need it to break the curse."

"Nay, if that were so, the Dark Witch would not be so desperate to have it." His look of despair was almost more than she could stand. "The tapestry is the key to breaking the curse. We must get it back. Stay here. I shall return as soon as I have retrieved it."

"What?"

"You must stay here. I can track the demon faster alone."

"But what if there are more of those things out there? What if it comes back?"

"It will not. It already has what it came for." He started walking away. "But just in case, do not talk to any more children."

"Right. You try to ignore a crying child. I seem to recall you flew into a burning building after one."

He ignored her and continued walking, heading upstream toward where she'd told him she'd last seen the child. Jill hugged herself, suddenly very afraid of being left alone. There had to be another way.

And then she had an idea.

"Baelin, wait." She rushed up and grabbed his arm. "Maybe we don't have to go after the creature after all."

He stopped, his body tense, eager to be on the hunt. "What do you mean?"

She opened her hand, displaying a piece of wet material wadded in her palm.

"That thing didn't get all of it. The tapestry tore when I fell in the water." Her eyes met Baelin's and the unspoken possibility flashed between them. "Something tells me, that little monster will be back when it realizes it doesn't have the whole thing."

CHAPTER TWENTY-NINE

This was such a bad idea.

Which made sense, since she was the one who came up with it.

The night closed in around her as the fire burned low. Jill couldn't see a thing. Not that she was supposed to. She was supposed to be asleep. Or at least look like she was.

She just prayed Baelin's dragon night vision was all he said it was cracked up to be because he was out there, somewhere.

Hiding. Waiting. Watching.

Jill lay by the fire with the torn corner of the tapestry drying on a rock on the other side. But she couldn't sleep. Every sound of the forest, every breath of the wind, made her wonder if the creature had returned. The last time, it hadn't hurt her. What if it did this time?

A crunch in the leaves had her holding her breath. She didn't know what to pray for more—that it was Baelin returning, having decided to give up the ruse or that it was the demon sneaking up to take the bait. She prayed it wasn't something big and hungry coming for a midnight snack. They had enough problems to deal with without throwing vicious wild animals into the mix.

She tried to steady her breathing so it looked like she was sleeping. Through the crack of her lids, she saw it. The little bald, wrinkled troll creature, still dressed in the little girl's clothing, strands of hair sticking out of its bald head where the long dark curls used to be.

The creature crawled out of the shadows towards the fire, its creepy cat's eyes darting every which way as if anticipating a trap. She willed herself not to flinch, not to move so much as an eyelash.

Baelin, where are you? You better not have fallen asleep out there.

The creature stretched out its clawed hand and reached for the tapestry fragment, its piercing eyes trained on her as if it believed Jill might jump up at any moment and snatch it away. But before it could grab it, a sword flashed in the dying embers of the firelight and cut off the creature's hand at the wrist.

All pretense of sleep vanished in an instant.

"Oh my God! Oh my God!"

Jill bolted up and scooted back, horrified at the sight of the hand still wiggling around in the dirt near the fire, grasping and clawing, but no longer attached to a body. The creature screeched and hissed as Baelin swung again, cutting off the demon's head with one forceful slice. She covered her mouth with her hand, trying to smother the scream threatening to erupt from her throat as the headless body crumbled to the ground.

Baelin gave her a passing glance before he knelt and searched for the tapestry. Finding it shoved inside the creature's tattered clothing, he inspected it quickly, then rolled it up and tucked it into his sword belt.

He stood and sheathed his sword, concern wrinkling his brow. "You are unhurt?"

All Jill could do was nod. She was okay. She didn't know if she would ever sleep again, but she was okay. She watched as he gathered up the creature's body and the various parts that were now thankfully lying motionless on the ground.

"Stay by the fire," he said. "I will not be gone long."

She nodded again, suspecting he was going to take the thing out of sight and bury it. While he was gone, she threw more logs on the fire until it blazed. Then she huddled there with her arms wrapped around her knees. No matter how hot the fire got, she couldn't get warm.

It seemed like forever before she heard his footsteps approaching. She pulled out his dagger, just in case, and exhaled the breath she'd been holding when Baelin's tall form stepped into the firelight.

"What did you do with it?"

"'Tis gone."

Visions of every old vampire and *Night of the Living Dead* zombie movie flashed through her head. "Are you sure it's dead? It won't come back to life or anything?"

Baelin shook his head. "I burned it. That particular creature will not be returning to torment us, nor will it reach its Queen with tales of where we are."

Jill breathed a sigh of relief. "Thank God."

She shivered and Baelin sat near her. Close, but not near enough to touch. "My lady, do not tremble so. I regret you had to witness that. If there had been any other way of retrieving the tapestry without causing you such distress, I would have done it."

"Don't worry. Believe it or not, I'm pretty much over it already. I guess because it wasn't really human, it wasn't as bad as the last time." Realizing the truth of her words, she chuckled humorlessly as her body gave one last shutter. "Either that, or I'm starting to get used to the savagery of this place. Now there's a scary thought."

It pained her to watch his broad shoulders sag under the weight of some perceived guilt over what she'd just said.

"Would that I could pluck the bad memories from your mind, so that when you return to your time, you will have only fond ones of your days spent here and not think of me with loathing."

Jill read the concern in his eyes. He was worried she would run from him again, as she'd done the first time she'd seen him kill.

But now she knew the truth—there was no safer place than by his side.

"I could never hate you, Baelin. And I do have a few good memories, thanks to you."

He snorted and a residual smoke ring curled out of his nose. "Now I know you do not speak the truth. In your short time here, you have experienced naught but pain and death while you have been with me."

"If I recall correctly, I sort of volunteered for this job."

Baelin shook his head. "As I recall, you had no choice."

"Yeah, well, I guess neither of us did, thanks to this curse of yours."

She turned the tattered corner over in her hand and ran her finger along the ragged edge. "Do you think with the tapestry damaged, our chances of breaking the curse are ruined now?"

"Only time will tell."

He pulled the larger piece of the tapestry from his belt and unrolled it in his lap. Jill leaned over and lined up the torn section with the larger piece.

"I suppose I could try to sew it together."

"Perhaps, if we had needle and thread, but we do not."

"It's just as well. I couldn't sew a straight stitch if my life depended on it."

He placed the torn corner in the middle of the tapestry and rolled it back up, before tucking it once again into his belt. "I will keep this with me from now on, where I know it will be safe."

"Right. You do a better job of guarding it. Every time I manage to get my hands on it, bad things seem to happen."

"That is not true." His deep voice resonated with heartfelt conviction.

"Oh, yes it is. The first time I touched the thing, it zapped me back to the Middle Ages. The next time I had it, I ended up holding a hot poker in my hands. And the last time, Gollum's ugly little sister tried to steal it and probably ruined our chances of breaking the curse in the process. I'm obviously bad luck when it comes to that tapestry."

"I do not see it as such."

Jill snorted. "How can you not?"

"However it seems, all may not be lost. Though torn, the tapestry is once again safely in our possession, when by all odds it should be gone forever. The second time, you passed the first challenge. As painful and unpleasant as it was, it was meant to happen. And the first time...I do not think bad at all, because it brought you here to me."

A lump formed in Jill's throat. He was talking about fate and destiny and things meant to be. As much as she wanted to disagree with him, she couldn't shake the feeling he spoke the truth and she was right where she was supposed to be.

"If things were different...If I were different..." Baelin stumbled over the words. "Forgive me. I cannot speak the flowery words as Sir Roderick does. But if we succeed and the curse is broken..." He stopped and poked a stick into the fire.

"What?" she prodded.

He shook his head, keeping his gaze glued to the flames. "If the curse is broken, you will return to your time, therefore what I was about to say matters not."

But it did matter. It mattered a lot. And she needed to hear the words he was working so hard to say. "Say it anyway."

"If you stayed...if I were a whole man..."

She put her hand on his arm and stopped him. "But you are a man. More of a man than any I have ever known."

He turned a perplexed gaze her way. "How can you say that? I am a hideous beast. Just look at me." He fanned his wings out, spreading them wide. The impressive effect he sought was lost with her makeshift bandage dangling around one of them.

She brushed the back of her hand across his stubbled cheek, the soft bristles tickling her skin. "I don't find you hideous at all. But it's not because of what you look like on the outside. That doesn't matter to me. Right now, I only see the man on the inside, and he's one of the handsomest men I've ever met."

She watched the muscles in his throat work as he tried to swallow, the look of amazement on his face so unguarded, so innocent. "How is it that you can see me as no one else does?"

"Maybe because I'm meant to?"

Baelin stared at her for the longest time, searching her face as if memorizing every line and detail. Just when she thought he would kiss her, he pulled back, returning his gaze to the fire as he withdrew, but not before she glimpsed the longing in his eyes.

Who said chivalry was dead? It was alive and well in every fiber of his being. But he wore his blasted honor like a shield and was using it now to put a wall between them.

Don't, Baelin. Please don't do this.

He wanted her. Every instinct ingrained in women from the beginning of time stood at attention telling her so. But as long as he saw himself as a monster and unworthy, he was going to deny himself—and her. The weight of it was causing him obvious distress and frustrating the hell out of her.

She cupped his cheek, turning his head back to her with a gentle touch. She gazed deep into those warm, brown eyes of his and was lost in the longing there, drowning in a desire that matched her own.

Let me give this to you. This one thing. It's the only thing I can offer you. I know how long you've been alone, without love or kindness, and it breaks my heart. Let me give you the one thing I can. Let me make you happy, just for a little while.

She wanted to tell him this, but she couldn't. She knew the words would come out wrong. That it would sound more like pity sex than what it really was. And it was so much more, because she wanted it, too. She wanted him, dragon parts and all. And so she told him without words, pulling his head down for a kiss.

He did not resist, and yet he did not give in. He forced her to keep the kiss gentle, not allowing her access when she demanded entry past his soft lips. When she tried to scale his defenses, he pulled away, his breathing labored.

"Do you not understand? If we continue down this path, I may not be able to let you go."

She wrapped her arms around him and pulled him tight.

"Then don't."

Then don't.

Such simple words that had the power to make his warrior's body go weak.

Did she even realize what she asked of him? The tight rein he held on the baser urges of the dragon was so weak at this point, if he were to take her in his arms now, the fragile threads would snap. Then the beast within would be released, while the man he struggled to remain might be lost forever.

Yet, already the dragon was taking over. He damned the creature's acute senses. Why did he have to smell so well? He could detect the scent of her sun-kissed hair, the freshness of her clean skin after her plunge in the stream. But under all that, he scented something different. Something earthy and primal. Something he'd long forgotten the scent of.

The musk of arousal.

Her arousal.

She wanted him—as a woman wants a man—and the knowledge sent his mind reeling.

He tried to master his thoughts, to clear his mind and gather control. Only when the mist cleared did he realize she was indeed in his arms. When had that happened? Had she moved into his embrace or had he wrapped his arms around her and drawn her to him? For the life of him, he could not remember.

Heaven help him, she filled his senses, scattering his hard-won control to the four winds. He was still dressed in full mail, but even that proved not barrier enough. He could feel the warmth of her skin through the chain links and padding, heating his skin, searing his flesh with her body. He steeled himself. He could fight the cravings of the beast.

But then she looked at him from beneath her long lashes, her eyes drawing him in with a call he could not deny. Had her lips ever looked fuller? Her eyes so inviting?

Baelin closed his eyes and tried to think of other things. Bad, horrible things.

Plague. Famine. Being drawn and quartered, then boiled in oil.

But none of it could dispel the power this woman held over him.

He should leave. He should spend the night far, far away—preferably chained to a rock and surrounded by a garrison of pike toting guards. Anywhere far from the temptation of this woman before he dishonored them both.

"Baelin?"

Blessed Mary, the sound of her voice, so soft in the night. But she didn't have to speak to call him to her. Each breath she took sang a siren's song he found impossible to resist.

"Aye?"

"Why are you shaking?"

Baelin cleared his throat, trying to mask the shame at his weakness. "I do not tremble."

"Yes, you do. What's wrong?"

What's wrong? Holding her like this was wrong. Desiring her warm, soft body beneath his was wrong. Wanting her with every beat of his foul dragon's heart was wrong.

Reluctantly, he removed his arm from around her waist. He couldn't touch her any longer without losing what was left of the frail grip he held on his control. "You have had a trying day. Perhaps you should get some sleep."

"I'm not tired."

Damn.

"Baelin? Why won't you look at me?"

Because if I do, I will be lost.

She turned his head to face her. Her fingers tunneled through his hair, tickling his scalp and sending shivers racing across his heated skin. But she didn't stop there. She pulled his head to hers and met his lips with another excruciatingly tender kiss.

He tried to tell himself there was no sin in a chaste touching of the lips. He bargained with his conscience, granting himself this tiny bit of pleasure. He vowed he would ask for nothing more and would leave her untouched for the rest of his days.

He should have pulled away right then. Should have stopped it before it was too late. But she wouldn't let him.

To his shock, she deepened the kiss, her moist tongue probing at his lips until he had no choice but to open for her or go mad. His head swam as her tongue darted inside and began a dance of seduction with his own. His stomach clenched with longing and wanted nothing more than to lie with her, to be inside her in more ways than one.

Baelin finally found the strength to tear himself away. How could a woman so small have the power to hold him so firmly?

"Lady Jill, we must not. 'Tis wrong."

Her eyes were dark, heavy-lidded with passion. "What is?"

"I cannot dishonor you this way."

She pressed her forehead to his, mingling the sound of their heavy breathing. "Let me be the one to decide if I'm dishonored or not."

"But—"

She kissed him again, stealing his words of protest away. He almost surrendered, almost gave in to the dark urges of the beast. But somehow, he found the strength to wrench himself away again and hold her at arms length.

"Nay! I am a monster. I cannot foul you with my touch."

"A monster?" She looked wounded at his words, as if he'd called her a hideous beast instead of himself. "You are not a monster. Sure, you may have a few idiosyncrasies about you, but who doesn't? Inside you are still

Baelin, a true and valiant knight and the most caring, honorable man I've ever met. I've been with you long enough to know the dragon has not taken the person you were away from you. You're still the same man you've always been."

Baelin closed his eyes to the sight of her. Oh, to believe he was worthy of her touch. Of her love.

But he wasn't, no matter what she said. No matter how much he wanted to be. Until this curse was broken, he had no right to even dream of the possibility.

When he opened his eyes again, she was still sitting there. Still looking at him with such longing and desire, he thought he might drown from it.

He noticed at some point her torn smock had slipped down one arm and now the soft curve of her bare shoulder taunted him. The tattered garment was barely hanging on as it was. One nudge and the other sleeve would fall and she would be naked before him. The thought of aiding the cloth in its journey nearly had him doubled over in pain.

"Do you know what you do to me?"

She heaved a heavy sigh. "Probably the same thing you do to me."

"We must stop."

"Why?"

It was sin enough, what they were doing now. If he took it any further, there would be no going back.

"The maiden must be pure."

She smiled a temptress's smile and shook her head. "Remember, I'm not some shrinking virgin from your time. I'm a twenty-first century woman, with the wants and needs of one. And right now, I want and need you, Baelin of Gosforth."

His breath caught at her words. She was right. If she was not a maid, then he could not take from her what had already been given to another.

He tried to tamp down the flame of jealousy that knifed through him at the faceless man who'd lain with her before. But as he drowned in her passion-filled eyes, her lips plump and reddened from his kisses, the possessive urge fled. He couldn't think on that now. All he could think about was the woman sitting before him, offering herself to him as no other had done before.

She took his hand and placed it over her heart. He could feel it beating strong and rapid under his palm, like a tiny, frightened bird. He made one final, valiant attempt to end what had begun by offering up the last defense he could think of.

"I thought…you once told me that you did not…" he paused, trying to recall her exact words, "…that you did not wish to kiss me for fear of being burned by the dragon's fire."

Her breath rushed from her lungs in a tiny huff. "Are you kidding? All you have to do is look at me and I burst into flames."

That slight movement was all it took. As he had feared, the other sleeve of her smock fell. He froze, their joined hands pressed against her chest the only thing holding the cloth on her body. As if she could read his thoughts, she removed her hand covering his, leaving his alone in place to determine what would happen next.

He looked at his hand resting between her breasts, knowing if he took it away, the torn smock would fall, removing the last flimsy barrier separating him from feeling the flesh of the woman beneath. Heaven help him, he wanted to do nothing more.

After two centuries spent in near solitude, with only the fear and loathing of the other maidens to remind him of what he was, he was not prepared to withstand this assault to his senses, to his very soul. The strongest knight in the entire kingdom could not stand against a battle so well fought. With one scrap of cloth, she had disarmed him completely.

He stared at his hand, afraid to look into her eyes. Afraid of what she was asking of him, knowing he no longer had the strength to deny her.

"My lady, are you so eager then, to mate with the dragon?"

"No."

His eyes flew to her face and his heart stopped beating. Was this some kind of cruel jest? Had she been teasing him all along, tempting him with what he wanted, but could never have?

But there was no joking laughter in her eyes, no cruel intent to wound him in the most vicious way imaginable. He saw only desire and affection, emotions he never thought to have bestowed on him from another human being ever again.

"But I want—no, I need to make love to the man."

ChAptER thiRty

With those words, his last defenses crumbled.

Slowly, as if it had a mind of its own, he removed his hand and the smock fell, pooling at her waist. She sat there before him, an angel in the glow of the firelight. He thought he might never draw another breath, she was so beautiful. As it was, he couldn't find the power to move. He could only sit there and gaze upon her.

She wrapped her arms around him, pressing her body to his, bringing her lips closer and closer until they brushed his. She deepened the kiss, probing at his lips with her tongue until he opened to her. She thrust her tongue inside his mouth and he groaned, returning her passion with a fervor that would have brought him to his knees had he not already been there. He wrapped his arms around her, his palms brushing the silky skin of her back, so soft, so smooth.

He felt her hands fumble with the buckle of his sword belt, the straps on his mail. Quicker than any squire could manage, she had the bindings undone and his armor lay in a pile of silver chains by the fire. The thick *aketon* quickly followed, until he sat before her in naught but his breeches.

All the while, she nuzzled at his neck and nipped at the lobe of his ear, sending shivers over his skin. She kissed a slow trail down his naked chest until she reached the starburst scar over his dragon heart, tracing it with her tongue. He closed his eyes and threw his head back as fire shot though his body, radiating out from where her lips brushed the mark of his damnation.

"My lady," he sighed.

"Shush." She put a finger to his lips. "There's no lady here. Tonight I'm just Jill."

He looked in her eyes, the ache swelling within him making it difficult to speak. "Jill."

She leaned back and drew him down on top of her. He covered her body with his own, trying to support his weight on his bent arms rather than give into the desire to crush her beneath him, to drive himself inside her willing body.

He groaned at the feel of her beneath him, so wonderful, so amazing. To think she would allow him to touch her. To *want* him to touch her. He couldn't believe she would offer him this precious gift, and he was powerless to refuse it.

He gazed at her beautiful face. Without inflicting a single blow, this tiny maiden had defeated the mighty dragon, body and soul.

Taking over the part of aggressor, he lowered his head and kissed her, wanting to taste every part of her. He cupped her breast in his hand, thrilled at the wonder of touching her. The way she moved beneath him, moaning, clutching, told him she enjoyed his touch just as much. He bent and took the budding nipple into his mouth, drawing on it deeply, swirling the nub with his forked dragon tongue. She arched beneath him. Jesu, he'd never felt anything like it.

His mouth finally left her breast and found her lips once more while his hand skimmed down her ribcage, over the flat of her belly, before tunneling through the curls between her legs. His fingers parted her, feeling the moist heat pooled there, circling the taut nubbin hidden within before thrusting his fingers inside her.

She gasped against his lips and he captured her cry in his mouth. He ached and strained against his breeches, wanting nothing more than to replace his fingers with his cock inside her, where her muscles could grip him tight and milk the life from him.

He moved from her mouth, along her jaw and down her neck. He nipped at the raised portion of her collarbone before trailing kisses down to her breast where the hard nipple beckoned to be taken into his mouth once again. And he did, suckling her, reveling in the gasps and moans he drew from her.

Warm and pliant, her hands ran up and down his back under his wings, clasping his buttocks, pulling him closer. She writhed under him, her hips undulating, her legs parting so she could rub herself on his thigh. If he had disbelieved before, he knew the truth now. She was no shrinking virgin, but a woman full of passion and experience.

It should have bothered him. It would have, if he could think straight. But right now his head was somewhere below his waist, telling him to stop thinking and just feel. For the first time in over two centuries, to feel.

And he did. By God, he felt every inch of her.

Baelin eased down her body, trailing kisses and flicks of his tongue across her belly. When he reached her hips, he grasped the smock bunched there. She raised her hips so he could push the garment past them, then he eased it down her long legs and tossed it aside.

He pressed his face against her leg, planting kisses along her inner thigh, journeying back up her body from whence he came. He stopped at the juncture of her thighs, where tight, brown curls hid the treasure he sought. So close he could smell her, the scent of her arousal driving him mad. He craved to taste her. But did he dare? She'd already permitted him more than he should take. Would she allow him that great liberty? He journeyed closer to his goal, afraid at any moment she might stop him. Afraid, even more, that she would not.

She didn't. With the barest of nudges, her legs parted easily for him. His dragon tongue flicked out, sweeping the scantest of grazes upon her and she jerked, her hips coming off the ground. Would she stop him now and put an end to it all, when he was so full of need he was near to bursting? His tongue flicked again and she tossed her head back and cried out.

"Oh God, Baelin!"

She didn't stop him. Instead, she lay back, tunneled her fingers through his hair and held him to her. She moaned, twisted and turned, urging him on. The dragon dove in for the feast. He tormented her with darting flicks of his forked tongue, smelling her, tasting her, until her entire body shook as she cried out his name over and over again.

He wanted it to last forever, but his body demanded he seek his own release. He needed to be inside her. Needed to be there now.

He crawled up her body as he fumbled with the ties of his breeches, praying he didn't knot them hopelessly. Jill joined in his efforts, shoving the breeches down his waist and over his buttocks until he could kick them off his feet. He settled between her thighs, aware of the cool night air against his bare skin, a sharp contrast to the warm, soft woman beneath him.

Oh, the feel of flesh against flesh. It was almost too much to bear.

He took himself in hand and guided himself to her entrance. He wanted to take his time, to savor every moment of this, to have it to remember her by if the curse was not broken and he once again became the beast. But he couldn't wait, not after waiting so long.

With the green eagerness of youth he thought lost, he entered her, groaning at the hot warmth surrounding him. She wrapped her legs around his hips, pulling him closer, deeper inside. Unable to restrain himself any longer, he thrust, deep and hard.

And felt something within give way and tear.

He froze, embedded fully inside her, shock washing over him in a cold, harsh wave.

"Ow. Ow! *Ow!*" Jill cried out, pushing at his chest.

He reared back and looked at her, horrified. "You said you were no longer a maid."

"I wasn't." He watched her grimace in pain. "I don't understand—ow!"

Baelin pulled out of her and his cock went slack as shock and disbelief slammed into him. Whether she was a virgin or not was no longer the issue, for she was a maid in truth no more. The fresh smear of blood on her thigh attested to that fact.

He closed his eyes to the irrefutable evidence and shoved himself away from her. In a single act of mindless lust, he had dishonored the maiden and, in doing so, damned them both.

"Dear God, what have I done?"

Jill watched Baelin retreat to the other side of the fire, where he paced like a wild tiger, his expression of betrayal and distrust warring with graceful flex of his nude body.

Damn. Nothing like sharp, unexpected pain to ruin the mood.

She stood and struggled back into her torn smock.

"This is *sooo* unbelievable. I have to be the first woman in existence who's managed to lose her virginity twice." She shook her head, still trying to figure out how that could even be possible. "And let me tell you, it was just as uncomfortable the second time around."

Baelin glared at her as he jerked on his breeches and yanked at the ties. "My lady, you are not the only one who has lost something this night."

"Oh please, don't start in about honor again. We're both consenting adults. We both wanted—"

Baelin's head whipped around and in three strides he was on her side of the fire, towering over her. His bitterness surrounded her and she tried to swallow around the lump in her throat.

"'Tis not honor I speak of." He swept up his *aketon* but did not put it on. He stood there, crumpling the thick padding in his fist. Then he tossed his head back and looked at the moon, a bright spot punching a hole in the night sky. He stared at it for a long time, before turning his piercing gaze back on her.

"For over two hundred years I have had but one goal, one dream that has kept me from going mad. Yet in one moment of weakness, I may have lost any chance I had to break this damned curse the witch has set upon me."

Jill's heart broke at the stricken look in Baelin's eyes, making him look every bit of those 216 years. He was always so strong and brave, so sure of himself and the world around him. She never thought to see such despair weighing him down. That she saw it now scared her to death. What if he was right? What if they had ruined everything?

"Hold on. Let's not jump to conclusions. Maybe this doesn't affect anything."

She reached for him and he shook her off. "Nay, the damage has been done. 'Tis too late. We have failed."

"What are you talking about?"

"The challenges. They are based on the knightly virtues."

"So?"

"Chastity is one of the virtues. The maiden—you—must be untainted. When you said you were not and yet you passed the first test, I began to believe maybe chastity 'twas not one of the virtues required to break the curse. But now...now I know you were virgin in truth. All along, you were pure of body. But no longer. By giving in this night, I have ruined it."

Jill watched those broad shoulders of his sag. He was taking the blame on himself, but she knew the truth. This was all her fault. She'd seduced him. There was no other word for it. He'd fought her tooth and nail the whole way, not because he didn't want her, but because deep down inside he knew he had to.

Ashamed at being so forward and brazen, she looked away from him. She'd won, but at what cost to them both?

His softly spoken words pierced the night and stabbed right through her heart. "I am doomed to forever remain a dragon. And you..."

He didn't have to finish the thought. She knew what the consequences would be for her if the curse was not broken.

"I'm sorry, Baelin. I didn't know."

"How could you not?" Baelin chuckled humorlessly as he slipped his *aketon* over his head. "You strike me as an intelligent woman, one who would know if she had been bedded by a man or not." He turned accusing eyes toward her, hurt softening the edge of his anger. "You deceived me about it, though I cannot begin to fathom why."

"But I didn't lie to you!" Jill huffed, feeling as if the wind of blame was beginning to shift. "I wasn't a virgin. Or at least I wasn't before I landed in this godforsaken place. Believe me, I'm as surprised about that little turn of events as you are."

She couldn't understand it herself, much less try to explain it to Baelin. "Look, I honestly thought that crazy old midwife in the village was lying so they could use me as dragon bait instead of one of their own girls. I had no idea traveling through time would somehow make me a born again virgin."

"'Tis not possible."

She didn't like the way this conversation was going. Usually it was the girl who had second thoughts afterwards while guys couldn't wait to carve another notch on the bedpost, or their sword hilt, or whatever knights did to keep track of their conquests.

"Time travel isn't possible, but here I am. Dragons aren't real, but you are one. I can't begin to understand the how or why of it. For Pete's sake, half the things I've seen and done since I got here don't make any sense, starting with one particularly snippy lizard lover currently having a major case of the morning-after-regrets. For all we know, chastity or a lack thereof has nothing to do with any of this."

"And yet it may have everything to do with this!" he snapped at her. "What we have done here tonight may have ended the quest ere we had a chance to complete it."

Jill growled. If he wanted a fight, he could have one. "Oh, you are such a pig-headed, morally uptight man. Sometimes I think I liked you better as the dragon."

"At the rate we are meeting these challenges, my lady, you may get your wish."

"Fine." Jill crossed her arms and resisted the strong urge to tap her left foot. "Then let's get it over with and find out right now. Check the tapestry."

"What?"

"Let's check the tapestry to see if what we did changed anything. Since it seems to be a living record of everything we've gone through, maybe it will show..."

What? What would it show if they had failed to complete the quest before the time was up? Would the image of the knight be gone and only the dragon remain? Would the maiden still have Jill's face, perhaps branded with a big fat 'S' for slut on her forehead?

There was only one way to find out.

Jill picked the tapestry off the ground where it lay by Baelin's discarded sword belt. He turned his back on her and retrieved his mail, as if he couldn't bear to see that all hope was gone.

She was glad because she couldn't stop her hands from trembling as she unrolled the weaving. She only glanced at it briefly before she let out the breath she'd been holding and closed her eyes, sending up a brief prayer of thanks.

"It hasn't changed. Look, Baelin. The tapestry is the same. Maybe we're okay. Maybe we can still break the curse."

He snatched the tapestry out of her hands, causing the torn section to flutter to the ground. She scooped it up while Baelin moved closer to the fire to examine the larger piece in the light.

Jill moved to stand beside him. "See, it doesn't look like anything has changed one way or the other to me. It's the same as it was before." She waved the torn fragment in his face. "It's even still torn."

The moment she said the words, a tingle shot up her arm and the torn piece flew out of her hand. She heard Baelin's sharp intake of breath and he dropped the tapestry to the ground.

They watched, neither uttering a sound, as the fragment pulled itself across the tapestry to the ragged edge as if a magnet drawn to metal. Before their eyes, the threads rewove themselves, twisting and looping, until the tapestry was once again whole, as if it had never been torn.

"Did you see that?"

"Aye."

"Wha...what just happened?"

Baelin picked up the tapestry with cautious movements, as if he were afraid it might fly away like a frightened bird if he startled it. He stood slowly and held it to the firelight.

"The tapestry has healed itself." His voice was low, soft, awed.

Jill shivered, not quite believing what she'd just seen.

"But how?"

"It must be magic." He couldn't seem to tear his gaze away from the tapestry in his hands. "Can you not feel it all around us?"

Indeed, there was a prickling on her skin, an electricity in the air. But she didn't know if it was from some magical force or coming from the man standing beside her.

"What do you think it means?"

"I think it means we may yet have a chance."

"Thank God." Relief washed over Jill and she learned how to breathe again. "So we're okay. Nothing's changed."

He turned his penetrating gaze to her. Something more than renewed hope now shimmered within those dark brown depths. Something she didn't quite understand, but felt all the way down to her toes.

"That is where you are wrong, my lady. Though the tapestry may be once again whole, *everything* has changed."

CHApCER ChiRCY-ONE

Isylte held the wad of colorful threads in her hands, the thin strands like a nest of wiggling snakes slipping though her fingers.

"No!" she shrieked, the high-pitched sound echoing off the walls of her inner chamber.

Several guards burst through the door, swords drawn, searching the room for the cause of their Queen's distress. When they discovered no visible enemy, they turned cautious gazes her way. The only thing out of the ordinary in the cavernous room was the irate woman standing in a puddle of twisted threads under an unraveling tapestry.

"Get out at once!" she ordered.

The guards stumbled over themselves to do her bidding.

"Hold, Edgar!"

The last guard stopped in his tracks and grimaced, his gaze wistfully following his fellow soldiers' flight before he turned back to face his mistress.

"Where is Grend?"

"It has not returned, my queen."

"And why not? I sent it out at yesterday. How long does it take one demon to kill a girl or steal a scrap of cloth?"

The guard stood silent, his wary gaze darting about the queen's chamber as if the answer floated on the air.

Isylte picked up a small section of the tapestry that had come off in one solid piece, the edge ragged as if it had been torn off instead of unraveling like the rest. She crushed the fragment in her fist.

"Something has happened. Grend has failed and Baelin's tapestry is now stronger than ever, whilst mine weakens with each day's passing as if unseen moths eat away at the very threads." She whirled on the hapless guard, the only other person in the room and thus the unfortunate recipient of her anger. "Must I be surrounded by idiots? My warriors cannot kill one single maid without burning down an entire village."

"'Twas but one inn," the guard mumbled.

"Silence!" Isylte paced before him. "I send one of my wiliest creatures to make certain the task is carried out properly and it not only seems to have vanished into thin air, but it has also somehow managed to weaken my curse in the process. Why must I suffer such incompetence from all who serve me?"

The Dark Witch's pacing brought her face to face with the guard. "Where are they now?"

Edgar cleared his throat nervously. "We think the dragon and the maid are still hiding in the Grizedal Forest."

"You *think*?" she sneered. "I do not want you to think. I want to know where they are. Find them."

"As you wish, my queen." The man bowed his head. "When we find them, shall we kill the maid as you ordered before?"

"Absolutely not. You will only bungle it and Baelin will move further out of my reach than before."

Isylte paused, her eyes resting on the tattered remains of the tapestry. She would not underestimate Baelin again. She had to remember she was dealing with a trained knight, a warrior with a keen mind combined with the cunning of the dragon.

"Nay, find them, follow them, and send word to me of where they go. I will deal with them in my own way." She waved the guard away. "Now go. I want them found before the next sunrise."

Edgar's eyes bulged. "But...but the Grizedale Forest is over four leagues wide. 'Twould take a small army a fortnight to search it all."

She smiled and took a step closer to the large man.

"Then you had best get started." She whispered in his ear, her voice deceptively soft and low. "I do not care if you must cut down every tree and turn over every stone. You will find them or I shall slice you into pieces so small naught a trace of you shall be left to show you ere drew breath in this world."

Jill stared at the broad shoulders leading the way up the mountainside in front of her.

Broad shoulders she'd kissed and caressed in the firelight last night. Shoulders that had flexed with strength and tensed with barely-leashed power under her hands as he'd held his naked body above hers.

Broad shoulders that had been giving her the cold shoulder all morning.

She glared at those same shoulders now, which was a good thing because they stopped so suddenly, she nearly smashed her nose into them.

"We are here."

"What?" Jill stumbled as she tried to avoid trampling over Baelin. Once she regained her balance, she glanced around, but could see nothing but scraggly brush grappling for purchase in the rocks. "And where exactly is here?"

"The cave."

Her gaze traveled up the sheer rock cliff they'd been skirting for the past hour. A sheer rock cliff that looked surprisingly familiar, even from this angle far below.

"How did we get back to your cave so fast?" She narrowed her eyes at him. "What have we been doing, walking around in circles all this time?"

"A dragon lays claim to a territory." Baelin shrugged as if it this tidbit of dragon zoology should be common knowledge to her. "He guards it well and rarely ventures out of its boundaries."

"So what, all this time you've been keeping us in your territory? I thought we'd already been through this. What if the challenges aren't in your territory?"

"Nay, you said the challenges could not be faced by staying in the cave, and you were correct. However, the first test was met within my territory. There is no reason to believe the others will not be also."

"So? There's no reason to believe they will be either. And seeing as we haven't managed to stumble on whatever the second challenge is in the past three weeks, I think there may be a high probably that they aren't."

Her palm itched to smack the stubborn streak out of him. Amazing how quickly almost-had-sex euphoria could morph into the-honeymoon's-already-over irritation. Guess all those pent up emotions that came to an abrupt, screeching halt last night had to come out somehow.

"Damn it, Baelin. The clock is ticking for both of us here. We're wasting time. You need to stop listening to those dragon instincts of yours and start using your man's brain."

His nostrils flared and he clenched his jaw several times before answering her. It looked like she wasn't the only one feeling a wee bit frustrated. "Right now this man's brain tells me we both need more clothing, more weapons, and more supplies."

"Oh." That logical bit of thinking took a good chunk of her pique away. Damn, she hated when he was behaving rationally and she wasn't. "Okay, I suppose you have a point there. So let me guess, you're going to fly up there and get them for us."

"Unless you wish to travel about the countryside in naught but a tattered smock, aye."

Jill looked at the equally tattered bandage wrapped around the base of his wing. "Can you fly? Need I remind you, you were shot with an arrow yesterday?"

"We shall see. Dragons being the immortal creatures that they are, heal quickly."

Jill walked over and sat on a semi-flat rock. "Fine, you fly on up there with your bad pterodactyl self and I'll wait right down here."

"Do you not wish to choose your own clothing?"

"I trust you. Just make sure it's good and sturdy. I don't need to make a medieval fashion statement."

His brow creased in confusion, then she watched his expression change as he mentally shifted gears. "I do not wish to leave you here alone."

"Well, you're going to have to because I'm not about to relive the flying experience any time soon. You dropped me last time, remember?"

"Aye." His pupils dilated a fraction in those fathomless brown eyes of his. "But then I caught you."

Jill's mouth suddenly grew dry. "Yeah, you sure did." *In more ways than one.* She shook off the sex-induced thought. "But I'm still not too keen on the idea of going airborne again without the benefit of a parachute."

"Parachute?"

"It's this thing people wear—oh, never mind. Just get what we need and I'll wait here."

"After all that has happened, are you not afraid to be alone?"

She shook her head. "Not at the moment. You've got the tapestry, so there's no danger of me losing it. Again. And we can see for miles from here. As far as I can tell, there's no place for a troll baby to lie in wait or any nearby towns filled with irate villagers wielding pitchforks. So if it's all right with you, I'm going to sit my tired little fanny on this rock and keep a look out. I promise if I so much as see a chipmunk looking cross-eyed at me, I'll scream the mountain down."

His expression blank, he stared at her for a long moment before he spoke. "If you must scream, try not to cause the mountain to crumble whilst I am still inside of it."

Jill opened her mouth to reply, but he was already airborne. She watched him in flight, struck by the graceful vision he made as his powerful wings bore him upward like some earthbound archangel soaring for the heavens. She looked away only after he'd landed safely on the narrow ledge and entered the dark maw of the cave.

She sat and waited, letting her gaze wonder out over Baelin's 'territory.' There wasn't a tree to be seen, only moss-like grass and occasional scrubby brush finding purchase in the craggy rocks.

Baelin didn't have too much to worry about. Barren and desolate, there wasn't a single living thing in sight, much less a harmless little chipmunk. They were probably all giving the dragon's lair a wide berth to avoid becoming a furry appetizer. There would be no rock slides caused on account of her vocal abilities today.

With nothing to do but watch out for non-existent villains, Jill's mind began to wander. It didn't have far to go. Since the mind-blowing events of last night, she could hardly think of anything else. That, and of what had *not* happened afterward.

By the time she'd opened her eyes this morning, Baelin was already up, dressed and ready to go. What followed had been a one-sided conversation on her part with monosyllabic responses on his, usually tossed over that broad shoulder she'd been staring at for the past few hours. After a while, she stopped trying.

Was he still regretting what had happened between them last night? Or was it something more basic and humiliating, like she didn't turn him on in the harsh light of the morning?

Granted, even on a good day she didn't look so hot when she woke up with a case of major bed head erupting out of her scalp. Without the benefit of a mirror, she could hazard a guess that this morning, she probably looked like something the cat dragged in, gobbled down in three bites and threw back up on the carpet. Still, was a little acknowledgment of the passion they'd shared too much to ask? Apparently it was. Morning-after-awkward couldn't even begin to describe the mood between them.

She was so distracted was she by her thoughts that she nearly fell off the rock when Baelin landed gracefully by her side. Without at word, he dropped a sack of clothing on the ground. Before she could voice so much as a 'thank you' he was on a second run—or rather flight—back up to the cave.

If she didn't know better, she would think he was trying to avoid her—or at least avoiding her as much as he possibly could when they were stuck traveling together twenty-four-seven to break this darn curse of his.

While he was gone, she ducked behind a large boulder to change, all the while mumbling to herself and struggling to fight off the residual memories of last night.

She failed miserably and blamed it on the fact they hadn't finished what they'd started. She didn't understand how he could deny himself—both of them, for that matter—after what they'd shared. How could he ignore the chemistry that had been building between them for weeks now? How could he not want more after that brief blissful taste they'd had of each other last night?

She shivered as a thrilling tingle ricocheted through her body to all the places that had been 'tasted' by that wicked, wicked tongue of his.

Jill almost jumped out of her skin when the mouth containing that magical tongue called her name.

She emerged from behind her rock to find Baelin waiting for her with several more stuffed satchels piled at his feet.

"What did you do, pack up the whole cave?"

"Nay, merely half of it. I wished to leave a few bits of treasure to come back to."

She couldn't help but chuckle at his half-hearted attempt at humor. If he wanted to play ignore-what-happened-between-us-and-it-will-go-away, she could too.

"If we manage to break this curse, I'd think you'd never want to see that hole in a rock again."

His gaze traveled up the cliff face to the dark shadow of the cave. "Where else would I go?"

The melancholy tone of his voice gave her pause. "Anywhere you want to, I guess."

He turned those penetrating eyes on her. "Then perhaps I shall go to your time, with you."

Her stomach sank at the wistful hope in his words. Well, if she'd wanted more attention from him after last night, she sure was getting it now. But the intensity of it made her uncomfortable. And unfortunately, there wasn't a snowball's chance of it happening. Somehow she didn't think when—if—she returned to her time, she'd be able to take him with her.

"Let's not talk about things that might be out of our control."

She'd said it as gently as she could, but the truth of her words caused him pain all the same. She wasn't rejecting him. Their circumstances were. But it came out sounding like a rejection all the same.

Jill cleared her throat, trying to dislodge the knot wedged there, and attempted to focus her attention on the here and now. "Here, let me take a look at your wing."

Baelin stepped back as she reached for him. "Why?"

"It looks like it's bleeding again. You probably shouldn't have tried flying so soon. You haven't given it a chance to heal."

"There was no choice. There was no other way to get to the cave."

"I know. And I appreciate the trouble. Now let me return the favor and check your wing. At the very least, it could use a fresh bandage now that we have more supplies."

"'Tis fine."

"Oh, come on. I won't hurt you. I just want to check it."

"I said 'tis fine." He ripped off the bandage and flapped his wing. "See. Shall I take to the air again and soar about you? Perhaps do a flip or two?"

He stepped back, out of reach, putting yet more distance between them, just as he'd been doing all morning. He wasn't going to let her near him again, no matter how innocent the motive, and it hurt. A lot.

"What is your problem? Are you worried if I come near you, you'll lose that precious control of yours and ravish me on the spot? Or is it me you're worried about? If it makes you feel better, I promise to control my base urges and not jump you in the next five minutes."

He didn't answer, but she could tell by the way he averted his gaze she'd hit close to home.

"Look, I know you regret taking my virginity—which still amazes me to no end that I had it to lose again in the first place—but isn't the fact the tapestry repaired itself afterwards a sign it didn't matter?"

"There is no way to be certain of that."

"No, there isn't. But there has to be some reason behind why I became a born-again virgin, although damned if I know what it is."

"Damned is right."

Jill ground her teeth. And they said women were the ones who wouldn't let things go.

"Stop saying that. We are not damned. All is not lost. It's not the end of the world." She took a deep, calming breath and called on the last bit of rational reserve she had left. "What happened last night, happened for a reason. It had to mean something."

He turned his penetrating gaze to her. "It did. More than you can know."

Jill knew he was talking about more than the tapestry mending itself. "It meant something to me, too, Baelin. So why do you keep pushing me away? What are you so worried about?"

"That we should not tempt fate twice."

"Quite frankly, I don't see what it could hurt," she grumbled. "After all, the damage is done. I don't think I can lose my virginity a third time."

"'Tis a risk I am not willing to take."

As far as rejections went, that one was a real doozy.

"Fine, if that's what you want to believe. But if you really think fate has had a hand in everything that has happened to us so far, then I'm pretty sure us making love was meant to happen all along." She gathered up one of the supply satchels and slung it over her shoulder. "I'm sorry you don't feel the same way."

She made to walk past him, but he stopped her with a gentle hand on her arm. "Nay, you misunderstand me. It is not that I do not want you. 'Tis that I do not dare."

She looked to where his hand rested on her arm, then up into his eyes. "Why?"

He released her and she watched him struggle to find the words. "I do not dare because, what if, in doing so, we undo whatever magic was wrought last night?"

"You still believe what happened between us was because of magic?"

Baelin gazed at her, his eyes full of wonder and vulnerability. "What else could it be when a beautiful maiden gives herself to a dragon?"

His admission surprised her, more so because she knew he believed it.

"Magic had nothing to do with me wanting to be with you last night. At least not the kind of magic you're talking about."

He closed his eyes, as if looking at her was too painful.

"My lady. Jill. I am sorry. I have hurt you and that was never my intent." He tunneled his fingers through his hair. "It is not you I am angry with. I am angry with myself."

"What for?"

"What we did...what I did...I was so stupid. So weak."

He paced away and spoke with his back to her. "Whether you knew or not, you were a maid in truth. And by dishonoring you, it could have ruined everything. My one chance to break the curse nearly lost, because I could not control myself." He shook his head. "What kind of knight am I?" He turned to face her and answered his own question. "One felled all too easily by Cupid's arrow, it would seem."

Jill felt the air rush from her lungs. It was the closest thing to a declaration of love any man had ever said to her.

He looked up at the cave and she could see the strain and exhaustion etching deep shadows in his face.

"For over two centuries I have lived as a dragon. Year after year, with the help of some poor, unfortunate maiden, I have attempted to break this damn curse. Year after year, I have lived with the disappointment of failure when we did not succeed, to return once again to live as the beast in a cave." His gaze shifted back to her, and the forlorn hope she saw in them broke her heart. "But now that I have known you—truly known you—I can never go back to that type of existence again."

"Oh, Baelin." She took one step closer, then stopped. She understood him a little more now, and shared his worry and trepidation. "If there is any kind of justice in this world, then you won't have to."

"I am sorry if I hurt you. For so long, I have not known another's touch. And yet here you are, wanting to take care of me, to touch me, and it does not seem to bother you at all."

"No, it doesn't, Baelin. It never has." She cupped his cheek, relieved he allowed her to. "Is that really so hard to believe?"

He looked at her with such raw need, she ached to throw her arms around him and show him how much she wanted him. But she didn't. She didn't want to risk scaring him off again.

"Aye, it is. Or it was, until last night." Then it was his turn to surprise her. He clasped the hand cupping his cheek and placed a gentle kiss on her palm. "Perhaps you are right. Mayhap it was meant to happen."

He took a deep breath and stepped away, but he didn't release her hand. The warmth was back in his eyes, and with it the promise that a fragment of what they had shared last night was still there.

"Come. We have a great distance to go before nightfall."

They started walking, her hand in his. It was a few moments before she dared to speak, afraid of breaking the fragile bond between them.

"So, now that we're re-supplied and you're so set on not going out of bounds, where to next, oh mighty dragon?"

Baelin's gaze looked out across the valley before them. "Home."

She glanced back at the dark hole punched high in the rocky mountainside. She thought the cave was his home.

But if they weren't already there, then where was it?

Chapter Thirty-two

The drawbridge was gone, not that it was needed.

The deep ditch circling the earthen rampart had run dry long ago, choked now with weeds and tall marsh grass. The climb up the man-made hill proved treacherous and steep, as it was meant to be. When they reached the crest, the massive entrance of the palisade gaped open like some toothless wooden monster perched atop the high, grassy mound.

As Jill and Baelin entered what had once been the bailey, it became clear the barrier was no longer necessary to keep anything out. Only the skeletal remains of the once grand structure within still stood, the thatched roof having long ago rotted away and collapsed onto the dirt floor below.

Jill must have read the misery on his face, seen the desolation that surrounded his soul as surely as the rubble heaped at his feet.

"Oh, Baelin. I'm so sorry."

"'Tis naught more than a useless pile of rotting wood and crumbling stone now."

Jill moved to stand beside him. He watched as her gaze took in the tall wooden palisade that should have enclosed the perimeter of the mound. Built strong, meant to protect and defend the buildings within, now it was a pitiful fragment of what had once been a mighty fortress. Two of the four main walls were gone, the large timbers having toppled down the rampart at least a century before. He knew, for he had watched it happen, year by year, post by post.

"I thought castles were made of stone and could stand for centuries."

"Nay. I am aware of only a handful of keeps made entirely of stone. When my family ruled these lands, our manors were built of timber on high earthen mounds like the one we now stand upon. As you can see, though strong, they do not last forever." Baelin took in a deep breath, biting back the bitter memory of what had brought about his family's fall. "But time 'twas not the only thing that brought this fortress down."

Jill looked around at the ruin that had once been a grand manor house. "What did?"

"The people did this."

"Your people?"

"Aye. They blamed my family for the dragon's presence in the land and the villagers drove away the last of them long ago. Once they were gone, I watched from the skies as those who had once pledged fealty to my father tore down his house timber by timber, stone by stone, until all you see now was left."

"Why?"

"A few carted off timber and stones to use for their own crofts and outbuildings, but most considered the house evil and destroyed what they could so that my family would not return and bring the dragon back with them."

"I don't understand."

Baelin stood amid the ruins of his home, a place so familiar yet so changed from his distant memories of it.

"After the Dark Witch cursed me and I escaped into the world as a dragon, I returned here, to the land of my birth, to my family."

"Did they know what had happened to you?"

"Nay. They only knew that a dragon had laid claim to the nearest mountain and the surrounding land as its territory. My own family—my father, my kin—came after me, hunted me, in an effort to protect their people—my people—from the dragon. From me."

"But didn't they know the dragon was you?"

He shook his head, recalling the fear and heartbreak of being hunted by his own. Fearing even more that he would not be able to control the dragon, and would harm those he loved most, should they corner him.

"Not until after the first year, when I could take human form for the first time. Only then could I come to them and tell them of my fate."

"How did they take the news?"

"My mother cried. My sisters fled in horror. My brothers vowed to destroy the Dark Witch as she had surely destroyed me, though none of them were yet old enough to wield a sword, much less go to war against the likes of her."

"And your father? What did he do?"

Baelin tasted the bittersweet memory on the back of his throat. "He cursed. He raged. Then, for the first time in my life, my father wept before he turned me away and told me never to return."

Jill gasped. "Your own father kicked you out? How could he?"

"How could he not? He was the lord. His first duty was to his people. He could not protect them while he harbored a dragon in their midst, even one that had once been his son. He did what he had to do and I never faulted him for it."

"But you were his own son, his flesh and blood!"

"In his eyes, and those of his people, I was not. Not any longer."

Jill stood there, silent for a long moment, her gaze roaming over his face, reading the raw emotions he did not even try to conceal.

"So what did you do?"

"I retreated to my cave in the mountains and hid. From there, I was able to watch over my family…" He paused, trying to speak around the lump that had formed in his throat. "But to never be a part of them again."

"Oh, Baelin. That must have been so hard for you."

"Leaving my family 'twas not nearly so hard as watching year after year as each of them slowly grew old and died before my eyes. Always waiting, always watching from my dark hole, I remained the same while generation after generation was born and died in this house, until none were left who remembered me as more than a legend, an ancient family secret to be feared and appeased."

Jill waved her hand, indicating the destruction surrounding them. "So when did all this happen?"

"After a half century or so of living under the dragon's shadow, the villagers decided the family itself was cursed by the beast and they drove what was left of them from this place in shame and disgrace. They left these lands, left England, forever." He chuckled without humor. "But as you know, it did not work, for to this day the dragon has remained."

"I'm so sorry. I can't imagine what losing your whole family must've been like."

He looked into her sad, green-flecked eyes and knew the lie for what it was. She did know, only too well. Time was running out for both of them and with it, any hope that she might see her own family ever again.

"Do not grieve for my loss. Though they turned me away, my family did not turn their backs on me completely. True, I left to spare their honor, but not before I told them of the curse and what was required to break it. From that moment on, the tradition of offering up the maiden to the dragon began. My father asked his people to make this sacrifice each year in the hope that one day I would be set free and return to them as their son once more."

"But you never did."

"Nay, I never did. And now, though my family is gone, the dragon still remains."

"And the annual sacrifice of the maiden continues on."

Baelin gently brushed his fingers across her smooth cheek. "And so it does."

He strode through the rubble of the once great timber hall while Jill followed behind him. They passed the massive fire pit in the center of the packed dirt floor. It sat cold and empty, now more a ditch for catching the rain falling through the skeleton of the rafters than the warmth of a roaring fire. He ducked through a narrow doorway in the remaining far wall, stepping over the wooden door that now lay flat on the floor and into the small antechamber.

"This was my parents' private sleeping quarters." Baelin spoke without turning, sensing Jill's presence in the doorway behind him. "Some of the fondest memories of my life before took place in this very room."

He glanced around at what had once been a small but grand chamber, imagining a warm fire blazing in the brazier, rich hangings adorning the walls to keep the winter chill at bay, and fresh rushes scented with heather and herbs scattered across the dirt floor.

But all of that was gone now.

He listened for the remembered sound of his parents' laughter that once filled this room. He strained to catch even one faint echo that might somehow have remained trapped within these crumbling walls. But he heard only the restless breeze as it wafted across the top of the roofless chamber and the scurrying of tiny creatures making their nests in the cracks and crevices of the rotting timbers.

The enormity of all he had lost at the whim of the Dark Witch had never been more acute.

He looked at the wall where his parents' bed had once been, now a gaping hole open to the rear bailey. Only one post remained standing in silent refusal of defeat. Baelin walked over to it and shoved the massive timber, toppling it onto its kindred where it splintered at his feet.

"I am lost. Even if I break the curse and become the man I once was, what good does it do me? I have no home to return to, no lands to claim as my own. My family is gone, long ago turned to naught but bones and dust in the ground." He closed his eyes against a truth he did not want to acknowledge, but could no longer deny. "All this time I have been trying to return to what I was, and it can never be. The man I was died the day the dragon came to life within me."

"Oh, Baelin." He heard Jill walk up behind him, felt the warmth of her presence at his back. "I'm so sorry."

He felt her hands brush over his shoulders. Her small, delicate hands that could set his warrior's body to tremble with the slightest touch.

"In different ways, we have both lost our homes and families, and neither of us knows quite where we belong anymore." Her hands glided down his arms, her palms resting over his clenched fists until he relaxed enough for her to entwine their fingers. She brought their clasped hands around in front of him and wrapped both their arms around his waist before resting her head gently against his shoulder.

An embrace had never felt so dear, nor been so needed.

"If it's any consolation, you still have me."

She spoke the words softly, as if she was unsure he would value their worth.

Baelin turned in her arms and gazed down at her. "You are no mere consolation, my lady. You are a prize, a treasure beyond my wildest dreams."

"Then don't shut me out anymore."

He gazed down at her. "For over two hundred years, I have been the one shunned. And yet here you stand before me, asking me not to spurn you. What a strange pair we make."

God help him, now that she was in his arms, he never wanted to let her go. He kissed her, the soft touch of lips growing more forceful as their tongues danced, their breaths merged, and each fed the hunger of the other. Finally, he broke the kiss, resting his forehead against hers, his eyes closed.

"Ah, Jill, you tempt me beyond bearing."

"I certainly hope so."

His eyes flew open and he pulled back to look at her. "But I cannot offer you a bed, nor even a roof over your head."

She smiled and ran a finger along his jaw. "It didn't matter to me the first time. I don't think a little thing like the lack of a mattress will bother me now."

Jill drew her hands down his mail-covered chest, then held her breath as her nervous fingers unbuckled the belt holding his sword. When it started to slip down his hips, his hands covered hers. She froze. Was he going to stop her? Was he going to deny them what she knew they both wanted?

She dared to look up and found herself gazing into eyes dancing with golden flames. He took the belt from her and tossed it to the ground before spinning her around.

"Baelin?"

"Hush." He brushed her hair aside, placing a whisper-soft kiss on her neck. "Since that first night in the cave, I have dreamt of doing this."

She felt a pull at the back of her gown as he untied the laces, tugging them loose. He kissed her neck, her shoulder, the ridge of her shoulder blade, as inch by inch, her skin was revealed.

Slowly, ever so slowly, he peeled the gown down her arms as that wicked dragon tongue of his licked circles down her spine to the small of her back. His touch was so tender for a battle-scarred warrior dragon, his attention to her so gentle. Jill trembled, her legs nearly buckling with need as she stood naked in the ruins of his parents' chamber.

Behind her, she heard the clink of mail, the rasp of cloth. Then his arms came around her waist, pulling her back against the naked, hard length of him before he trailed his hands up her stomach to cup her breasts.

"Know you what you are about, my lady?"

"Yes."

"Then, before we go any further, I must know one thing—do you trust me?"

She only paused a heartbeat to answer.

"With my life."

He spun her back around. Pure pleasure lit his face before a cocky grin crossed his features. His eyes hinted at some deep secret he held just out of her reach. "Then I need you to trust me now, and know that I will never let you come to harm."

Jill shivered. They were about to make love. At least she hoped so. He was making it sound like they were about to do something life-threatening. All she could do was nod.

"Then my lady, prepare yourself to mate with the dragon."

Before she knew what was happening, Baelin wrapped his arms around her waist. He spread his mighty dragon wings and took them up through the opening in the roof, soaring into the darkening sky.

Jill squealed and held onto his neck for dear life.

Higher and higher they soared, until she wondered if they were going to touch the clouds.

All the while, he kissed her, his wicked tongue distracting her from their rapid ascent. He held her tightly to him, one arm firm around her waist, the other cupping her buttocks, his rigid cock pressed between their bellies. Terrified at first, passion gave over to the sensation. Lost in the heat of his kiss, Jill almost forgot that her feet weren't touching the ground.

And then they stopped and hovered in the air, broad sweeps of his wings keeping them aloft as if they were treading water. The cool temperature of the high altitude licked at the skin of her back, making her front where she pressed against his bare skin feel as if it were on fire.

"What are you doing?"

"'Tis the way dragons mate," he whispered in her ear as his hands lifted her ever so slightly, urging her legs around his waist. Jill obeyed, locking her ankles at the small of his back. "Trust me, Jill. I will not let you go this time."

"I do trust you."

"Then hold on to me. Now!"

With one smooth thrust, he was inside her. Then they were falling, tumbling, spinning. In what she would have once thought was an out of control plummet, she knew now by the grip he held on her that he was in total command of what was happening. In the waning light, she could barely make out the ground below them. But it didn't matter any longer. The movement of his body inside hers distracted her until she thought she would pass out into oblivion.

Baelin spun and tumbled them, her stomach turning flips, and all the while he thrust inside her, over and over. As they plunged toward the earth, the building pressure inside rose to a peak she'd never reached before. What should've been utterly terrifying became the most erotic experience of her life.

They plummeted toward the ground, coming closer and closer as they tumbled in the air, two joined bodies falling like a shooting star in the twilit sky. Jill cried out as a burst of sensation shot through her entire body from where Baelin filled her. He roared in triumph as his hot seed shot inside her, pulsing and throbbing, once, twice, a third time. Just when they were only seconds from crashing into the ground, he spread his wings wide and they soared back up into the sky again.

Jill clutched him, wondering how he could still hold onto her when her whole body felt weak and drained of all strength. She hardly noticed as he flew them over what had once been his village, to land softly on the grassy plateau of the fortress mound.

He walked, still carrying her, through the opening in the ruined wall and gently laid her on the ground in the remains of the place he once called home.

The Dark Witch was in her courtyard when the hunting party returned.

If the knight thought it odd that she would sit in a garden of stone in the dead of night, he made no comment.

"What news do you bring of my dragon, Edgar?"

"We have found him, my queen."

"Good. Now that was not so hard, was it?" If the man thought otherwise, he kept it to himself. Isylte smiled. At least this one was learning. "Where is he?"

"The dragon and the maid are passing the night in the ruins of his family stronghold."

"Is he now? How touching. Could it be after all these years, he's grown sentimental, longing for that which he has lost?" She looked up at the moon, hanging high in a starless sky, only the last crescent left in shadow. "Or does he feel his chance slipping away and already mourns the loss of his humanity?"

"Perhaps…"

"Perhaps what?" Isylte shifted to regard Edgar, unease creeping up her spine at the faltering tone in the man's voice. The knight stood there, worry etching deep lines in his brow. "*Perhaps what?*"

"Perhaps the dragon took the maiden there for another reason."

"And what, pray tell, would that reason be?" Isylte's anger escalated when the knight would not answer. "Tell me."

"The maid is…no longer a maid."

She stood, her fists clenched at her sides, her nails digging into her palms, but she ignored the pain. "*What?*"

"The dragon has mated with the girl."

She did not want to believe the words he spoke. "How do you know?"

"I saw it with my own eyes." His gaze darted to the sky and then returned to the ground at his feet. "'Twas hard to miss."

Isylte paced the flagstone path of the stone garden, the air about her crackling with violent energy.

"How could he? How *dare* he?" She whirled on the knight. "Since you were so close, were you able to deprive Baelin of the tapestry or his whore?"

"Nay, my queen. We did exactly as you ordered and did not approach them. But even if we did, we could not remove either without a battle. The dragon guards his treasure well."

"What did you call her?"

The knight swallowed, a fine sheen of sweat erupting on his brow. "His treasure?"

"Well, in that case, take Lorcan and bring his treasure to me. If he values it so highly, the dragon will come here to get it back."

Isylte seethed. All this time, Baelin had refused her, yet he'd taken the maiden. For over two hundred years she had called to him, yet he had not set foot in her realm. He'd never come back to her.

But Baelin would come for the girl. She knew he would.

And for that reason alone, the maiden would die.

CHAPTER THIRTY-THREE

"Well, that just gave a whole new meaning to being a member of the Mile High Club."

"My lady?" Baelin sighed, his warm breath tickling the back of her neck.

"Never mind. It's a twenty-first century joke."

Jill stretched, her body limp and satiated in some places, sore and tender in others. Then she resumed her spooning position with him under the blanket they'd hastily tossed over their naked bodies. His arm snaked around her waist, drawing her against him.

"You know, for someone who's been living as a dragon in a cave, you sure have some amazing sex tricks up that chain mail sleeve of yours." As soon as she said it, an odd, creepy thought popped into her head. "Please, please tell me you don't have some cute little she-dragon out there on the side."

He chuckled, his broad chest rumbling against her back. "Nay, my lady. You are my only lover, both of the flesh and of the scale."

"Good to know."

But her relief only went so far. What she'd just done—sleeping with a man who was part dragon—probably technically bordered on bestiality in most states. As kinky as that seemed, she wouldn't be able to handle it if she found out Baelin had been getting his rocks off with some little dragonette all along.

"But if you've never done it dragon-style, how did you know how to do...," she waved her hand in circles in the air, "...that?"

She felt him shrug against her, apparently unconcerned with her probing and totally inappropriate questions. "Instinct, I suppose."

"Instinct?"

"Aye. In human form I should not know how to fly or breathe fire, yet I do. The same obsession that compels a dragon to hoard treasure drives the man in me to amass gold and silver too, though I try to fight the urge. As you recall from the bounty in the cave, I have not always been successful at denying that particular impulse." He shifted, rolling her on her back to lean over her. "And when the lust is upon me, as it always seems to be with you..." He gave her a shameless look that said he was more than ready to prove his point all over again. "I feel I must take you in the air. I almost did that first time in the forest, but did not dare with the wound still fresh to my wing."

At her shocked gasp, he frowned. "I am sorry if you did not find pleasure in the experience. It seemed the most natural thing in the world to me."

Jill laughed. "The most orgasmic experience of my life, yes. Natural, no."

"Orgasmic? I do not know this word."

His hand traveled down her belly to tangle in her curls, still damp from their recent aerial escapade. The look in his eyes and the smile on his face said he had a pretty good idea of its meaning all the same.

Jill shoved him over on his back and sprawled her body on top of his. "Hmmm, as thrilling as it was, I'd just as soon have the next orgasmic experience safely on the ground, if you don't mind."

She began a slow, tortuous exploration of the tender flesh behind his ear. Baelin's entire body tensed and he sucked in air as she nibbled her way down his neck to his collarbone.

"I will do my best to restrain the urges of my inner beast."

"Oh, your inner beast can 'urge' all it wants." She rubbed herself slowly up and down the hard length of his erection. "Just try to keep it under twenty thousand feet."

He rolled, pinning her beneath him. "As my lady wishes."

Then, true to his word, he kept her body physically on the ground, but still managed to take her soaring to the stars once again.

When they finally drifted back down to earth, Baelin built a roaring fire with the worm-eaten timbers that had once been part of his ancestral home. Content in the afterglow, he was reluctant to venture out for real firewood, and Jill was as reluctant to let him. Too soon they would have to leave the sanctuary of this place, but for now, both were content to stay in the illusion of the two lovers they'd become.

"I am sorry I cannot offer you more, my lady."

"Are you kidding? I have a castle with the biggest skylight in the world. I get to lay here, watching the stars twinkle in the sky. A girl can't ask for more than that—except maybe that it doesn't rain any time soon." Jill rested her head on his shoulder. "You know, where I come from, little girls dream about knights in shining armor coming to their rescue. Who'd have thought one day I'd be living out the real thing." She ran her hand over his body, her fingers caressing each ridge and muscle within reach. "A knight, I might add, who looks even better without all that clanking metal hiding this deliciously naked body of his. Why, I'd be the envy of all my friends back home."

To emphasize her point, she ran her tongue down his chest, raising gooseflesh in its wake. But instead of eliciting the groan of returning passion she expected, the taut stomach under her hand growled loudly in response.

"Hmm, sounds like the dragon is hungry." She rose up and playfully called out into the night, even though there was no one to hear her. "Attention. All juicy maidens in the vicinity please report immediately to Gosforth Castle to be eaten by the resident dragon."

Baelin chuckled and pulled her back down to him. "There is only one maiden this dragon has any desire to eat." His stomach growled once more, not appreciating the teasing talk of food. "Yet it does appear all this mating has made me quite ravenous."

"There you go, using that 'mating' word again. You make it sound like we're two jungle animals having wild monkey sex. I prefer the term 'making love', if you don't mind. It's much more refined."

"Forgive me. 'Tis the beast rearing its ugly head once again. The dragon mates…" With a wicked grin, he nipped at her breast.

"Ow!"

"…while the man makes love." He placed a gentle kiss over the spot where he'd just bitten her.

"Hmm." Jill stretched beneath him, relishing the pleasurable torment his wicked dragon tongue was inflicting on her taut nipple. "Mating with a dragon and making love with a man…since it appears I've done both at once and we haven't exactly been practicing safe sex, if I get pregnant, am I going to have a baby or lay eggs?"

Baelin stilled and his eyes flew to hers, alarm erasing the jovial look they held only seconds ago. What she'd meant as a joke he had obviously taken all too seriously.

"We should wed as soon as possible."

Way too seriously.

"Hold on. Let's not jump the gun here. We don't know if I am pregnant. Besides, it's the wrong time of the month."

A quick calculation in her head to verify that detail threw Jill into a major panic. How stupid could she be? It was actually the prime time of the month, or pretty darn close to it. She just prayed she wouldn't be taking any little souvenirs back when she returned to her time.

"That is beside the point. I have lain with you three times as only a husband should."

"Well, technically, the second time we weren't lying, we were flying," she said, making her tone deliberately glib to hide her unease.

Baelin wasn't about to be swayed by any attempt at humor. "We shall marry as soon as we can find a priest to do the deed."

"Slow down, Baelin. That's really not necessary."

"But it is. I will not dishonor you that way." He paused, staring deep into her eyes. "Besides, once a dragon mates, he mates for life."

"Stop referring to yourself as a goddamn dragon. You're not. You're a man. And in my experience, most men are not innately monogamous."

"This one is."

She looked into his eyes and knew he was deadly serious. Where the idea of a man like him loving her, being faithful to her for the rest of her life should have thrilled her, instead it felt like a weight around her neck. Boy, did their timing suck.

"Look, I know what you're offering and I'm truly honored. In another time, another place, I'd…Oh Baelin, I'm afraid marriage just isn't in the stars for us."

His jaw tensed and he rolled off her onto his back, turning his gaze up toward the real stars hanging overhead in the dark, black sky.

"Why? Because I am part dragon? You do not wish to tie yourself to someone who is only a man for one month out of each year?"

"There you go, bringing up the dragon thing again. Of course it's not that." Jill sat up and cupped his check in her palm, willing him to understand. "But think about it. When we break this curse, I will probably go back to my time. I don't want you to feel tied to me if I'm not going to be here. You need to be free to live a normal life, get married to a woman of your own time, and live the happily ever after you deserve."

He turned his blazing eyes to her, hurt and denial glistening within them.

"I do not want another woman. I want you."

Jill lay back down, resting her head against the starburst scar on his chest. "Baelin, let's not make promises neither of us may be able to keep, because no matter how much both of us want it, I may not be here to keep my promise to you."

The truth of her words broke her heart as surely as it was breaking the one beating strong and steady beneath her cheek.

He lay naked on the hard stone floor, no longer shackled upright to the wall. But he was chained, nonetheless.

A metal collar encircled his neck and heavy iron links bound him to the wall, kept like a hound in the kennel.

He heard her enter the cell, but he did not open his eyes. He did not have the strength to do so. He knew she stood just out of reach, the chain allowing him to move a foot or so, no more. Not that he could hurt her now. He was too weak, his body broken.

"Baelin. I tire of this game you play. It is time to decide."

He refused to answer her, for it was always the same.

"Do not force me to take the choice from you."

What did it matter? She'd taken everything else. Osmund. His men. His dignity. The only thing she could not take from him was his honor, and that he would die to protect.

She hissed, and he imagined her violet eyes flashing with indignation. "Very well. Uhtred, come."

In the beginning, she'd had her guards accompany her, and watched as they did her dirty work. Once he was too weak to fight, she came alone to taunt and torture him. This was the first time she'd brought another with her in weeks. But he did not care. Not anymore.

A heavy scrape whispered across the floor, so different from the footfall he was expecting. But he did not look up.

The void of the chamber diminished as a large presence filled the room. Still, he did not look up.

A deep growl rumbled off the walls, the eerily familiar sound vibrating through his bones. He opened his eyes then, and gasped at the sight.

The Dark Witch had summoned a dragon into the chamber.

Was this to be his end, then? Since he would not give in to her, she would feed him to one of her dragons? Somehow, he was not surprised.

"If you will not bend your will to mine, I have no choice but to make you that which I can control."

She reached out and plunged her hand into his chest, the searing pain tearing through his body. He wanted to scream from the agony, but no sound would come. She ripped his heart from his chest and he stared, disbelieving, at the bloody mass still pulsing within her grasp.

Baelin bolted up, his breathing shallow and rapid, his muscles tense and quaking. He clutched at his chest. There was no blood, no gaping hole in his flesh. But the pain was there, still slashing through him, crushing in its intensity.

Once his vision adjusted to the dim light of his surroundings, he remembered where he was. His parents' antechamber.

And who he was with. Jill.

He looked down at the woman sleeping peaceful at his side, oblivious to the war raging within him. He rested his elbows on his raised knees and tunneled his fingers through his hair.

How was it he could resist the Dark Witch for so long and not Jill for little more than a score of days?

But he knew the answer.

He loved her.

And that had proved his undoing.

He eased back down on his side and looked at her beautiful face, reaching out his hand to trace the delicate line of her cheek, his callused fingers not quite touching her skin so as not to wake her.

Each time he recalled how she felt in his arms, and remembered that sweet glimpse of heaven, his body hummed with the memory. Now that he knew her completely, how would he ever be able to let her go?

But as she'd so bluntly put it last night, he might have to.

He rose, careful not to disturb her slumber, and went to stand in the open break in the back wall. He watched the sun rise over the barren fields that had once been his domain, the day dawning anew before them. What had seemed so fresh and promising only hours before now heralded what little time they had left.

Two days. Two days to pass the last two challenges and find a way to do it without sending Jill back to her time.

In all his years of solitude, he'd never felt so alone as he did right now, even though the woman he loved slept not an arm's length away from him. Never had he been so close to another and yet been farther away. It was as if the centuries threatening to separate them already stood between them, vast and untraversable. Would that he could bind her to him with more than a vow. But if she was right, it would take more than words to hold her in this world.

Baelin wanted to howl in frustration, to call down the power of the dragon and the battle skills of the knight to keep her here. Time was his enemy, an invisible foe with no form, no mass, yet waging war on him just the same. But he could not fight what he could not see, or even begin to understand.

But there was one thing he did understand. Jill was his heart. And wherever she was, here or in her time, it would be so from now on.

He dared a glance at the beautiful woman sleeping behind him before returning his gaze to the brilliant sunrise. For the first time in over two centuries, he did not want to break the curse. Not if it meant losing her.

She was wrong. She had to be wrong. Fate would not be so cruel to bring her eight hundred years across time only to tear her away from him in the end.

But the truth of her words hung over him as the day dawned anew.

For if the curse was broken, he would be a man whole but alone once more, because the woman he loved would go where even a dragon could not follow.

CHAPTER THIRTY-FOUR

Baelin stopped so suddenly, Jill walked several steps passed him before she stopped herself.

"What is it?"

She watched him breathe in the air, his nostrils flaring like a hound on the scent. "We have entered another dragon's territory."

Jill sniffed at the air herself, not that she'd be able to detect anything unless it registered on the ammonia or gasoline scale. But that didn't matter. If Baelin said he scented another dragon, she believed him.

"Is it a dragon dragon or a human dragon?"

"That, I do not know."

"So what do we do?"

"We should not tarry here. Dragons are very territorial. Human though I may appear, he will scent my presence as I scented his and come looking to defend it."

"But I thought we were still in your territory."

"Not any longer. I listened to what you said, that the challenges may not be within my domain. Now I may regret having left it."

"Then what are we waiting for? Let's go. No offense, but one dragon in a lifetime is enough for me."

He pointed to a forest in the distance. "We had best seek the cover of the trees. 'Twould not be wise to be caught out in the open."

Baelin started walking and Jill had to do double-time to keep up with him. "Do you really think another dragon would come after us?"

"I would if it were me."

She stumbled and fell behind a few steps, the words driving home the knowledge that if the curse were not broken in two days he would return to being one.

Though it appeared close, it took them another hour or two of walking before they neared the safety of the trees. They stopped right at its edge, where the trees stood straight and tall, silent guardians of the creatures within. Could a rogue dragon be one of them?

Jill couldn't help but notice that Baelin had yet to let down his guard. "Are we out of the other dragon's territory yet?"

"Nay. If anything, we are deeper into it."

"*What?* Then why are we going this way?"

"A dragon's territory can span hundreds of leagues. The wind shifts, the dragon takes flight, the scent is lost." She watched his eyes sweep the landscape around them. "Now, 'tis stronger than before."

He did not have to bother telling her this was not a good thing.

The crunch of leaves and rustle of underbrush broke through the shadows of the forest. Baelin dropped his satchel to the ground, his sword hissing from his scabbard at the same time he shoved Jill behind him.

But it was no fire breathing dragon that bore down on them. Instead, a familiar white horse with a black-haired rider charged out of the trees.

"What are you doing here?" Baelin growled in warning without lowering his sword.

The steed reared, but Roderick managed to keep the animal under control. "I could ask the same of you, dragon." Then he acknowledged Jill's presence with a slight nod of his head. "And I see the fair Lady Jill is still in your company."

"And there she shall stay. Be on your way, slayer. I want no quarrel with you."

"But now that our paths have crossed again, my quarrel is again with you, dragon."

"Can't you just go away and leave us alone?" Jill said, hating the whine that crept into her voice. "Why don't you go find some other dragon to torment?"

"As a matter of fact, 'tis what I was about." Roderick's lip curled, the sneer marring his handsome face. "For two days, I believed I was hunting a different dragon. Imagine my surprise to find all this time it has been you."

"'Twas not I. We only entered these lands this morn."

Roderick shrugged and dismounted his horse, drawing his sword before his feet hit the ground. "Just the same. One dragon is as good as another, as long as it is a dead one."

"You gave us your word you would not come after us," Jill said.

"So I did. And I have kept it, my lady." Roderick kept his eyes trained on Baelin. "But I also warned you if our paths ever crossed again, I would see the dragon dead. I just did not expect to accomplish the feat so soon."

Jill couldn't believe the ease with which Roderick thought to kill Baelin. She didn't understand how he couldn't see the living, breathing human being standing before him. All he saw was a dragon, masquerading as a man.

"Are you ready to meet your fate, dragon?"

Baelin shoved Jill to the side and out of the way. "As ready as I hope you are to meet yours."

Jill couldn't stand by and watch this happen. Not again. She'd throw her body between them if it would keep them from killing each other.

She was just about to do just that when a small hand on her arm stopped her.

"Nay, my lady," young Owen said.

She hadn't even noticed him come out of the forest behind Roderick. "When the battle lust is upon them, 'tis best to stay out of the way."

"But we can't let them do this. One of them is going to get killed."

"Probably."

The clang of sword against sword rang across the open hills, hammering in her head and causing her heart to beat in frantic rhythm with each clash of steel.

"Stop it!" Jill shouted, but neither man paid her any attention.

She watched in dismay as the two knights battled to the death. She screamed at them, calling both of them every kind of stubborn fool, until her throat grew raw. Owen wrapped his skinny arms around her waist, half holding her back, half clinging to her as he watched the two men he admired most try to kill each other.

Jill opened her mouth to plead again for them to stop and an ear piercing shriek rent the air—but it wasn't hers.

Owen's pony reared, its eyes rolling back in a state of panic before it bolted into the trees. What had caused him to spook like that?

Then she noticed, beyond the clanging of steel and the grunting breaths of the battling knights, silence had descended around them. Not a bird sang in the trees, nor a creature stirred in the forest. The skin on her arms prickled and she listened, like every other creature in the forest, waiting. And then she heard it.

The *whoosh-whoosh* of giant wings beating on the wind.

She turned as the creature dove out of the clouds at them and found her voice once more.

"Dragon!"

Baelin and Roderick broke apart and dove on the ground as the creature plunged toward them, breathing fire and leaving a wave of scorched wind in its wake. As it landed nearby, Jill decided the pony had the right idea and she ran for the trees with Owen fast on her heels.

Roderick and Baelin had no such inclination. Abandoning the fight with each other, they turned as one on the greater foe. Baelin took the head, waving his sword before the elongated snout and blazing yellow eyes.

"Take Lady Jill to safety!" Baelin shouted at Roderick. "'Tis me the dragon wants."

"What, and let you have all the fun?" Roderick laughed. "I think not. 'Tis not often I have the chance to slay two dragons in one day."

"Methinks we need to slay this one first afore you attempt to take me on again."

"Methinks you are right."

Roderick lifted his shield and advanced on the dragon, moving behind the creature so it couldn't keep both knights in its sight at once.

The dragon twisted and turned, lashing out with dagger-sharp teeth at one, a ball of flame at the other as each knight took turns drawing the beast's attention away from the other.

She shook her head. "Nothing like combining forces against a bigger bully to make two boys play nice again."

"It appears so, my lady," Owen replied. "If they succeed in defeating the dragon without one of them getting killed first, we shall see if the feeling lasts."

As she watched the dragon lunge at Baelin, its powerful jaws snapping, the muscles beneath the glistening scales bunching, she worried it was a pretty big 'if'.

In a flash, the dragon spun on its hind legs, its thick tail whipping out and catching Roderick in the side. The impact sent him flying through the air without the benefit of wings. He landed with a sickening thud thirty yards away in the tall field grass.

Baelin continued to battle the beast, dodging the fireballs tossed his way, using his wings to shield himself from the flames.

Roderick rose slowly on one arm, the other clutching at his side. Owen bolted from the cover of the trees before she could stop him, running to help his master. The flash of movement caught the dragon's eye and it turned, stalking after the fallen knight and the boy, now frozen in terror.

"Nay!" shouted Baelin. He spread his wings and took to the air, landing on the dragon's back. The beast craned its neck, turning to gnash its sharp teeth at its unwanted rider. Unable to hold on with only one hand, Baelin lost his sword. Jill watched as it tumbled end over end to stab into the ground at the dragon's feet.

With the dragon distracted, Roderick struggled to his feet and Owen helped him to the relative safety of the tress, leaving Baelin alone to battle the beast. The dragon twisted and turned, trying to dislodge him, an unholy sound erupting from its long, reptilian throat. Baelin released his hold and took to the sky before the raging beast could throw him. The dragon sprang into the air and gave chase, following him out over the rolling hills and up into the clouds.

Jill emerged from the cover of the trees and watched as Baelin led the dragon away from them. Would it catch him? Was Baelin fast enough in his human form to out-fly a full-blooded dragon?

She shielded her eyes with her hands, watching helplessly as Baelin became little more than a dark speck against the brilliant blue sky, the dragon a larger, more powerful form racing behind him.

Just as she thought she might lose them in the sun, the dragon banked, veering away from Baelin and abandoned the chase. Slicing through the air on crimson wings, the dragon focused deadly aim on a new target.

The dragon was coming for her now.

She turned and sprinted for the trees. Roderick emerged as she bolted past him, still clutching his side, his sword gripped firmly in his other hand.

"Run, my lady. Go deep into the forest where the dragon cannot easily follow."

But Jill didn't. She went only as far as the first stand of trees where Owen hid, wide-eyed and trembling.

Roderick did not follow. He stood in the open, injured and without a shield to protect him from the dragon's flame, a brazen challenge to the oncoming demon.

She couldn't leave him like that. She left the cover of the trees and ran back out on the field, searching desperately for the shield, but it was lost somewhere in the tall, concealing grass.

The dragon hissed fire, igniting a scorching path toward Roderick. He twisted sharply, dodging the flames, but it cost him dearly. He stumbled and fell. He tried to regain his feet, but groaned and collapsed back down on one knee.

Smoke curling from the beast's gaping maw, the dragon landed and crept toward him with single-minded intent, zeroing in for the kill.

Jill looked to the sky. Baelin was coming back, but he was still too far away. He'd never make it in time to save him.

"No!" she cried.

She spied Baelin's fallen sword sticking out of the ground, a lone silver cross standing tall in a waving sea of green. She ran and yanked it out of the soft ground with both hands and charged at the dragon.

"Don't you hurt him, you overgrown Gila monster."

She brought the sword down on the dragon's flank with all her strength, the shock of the impact reverberating up her arms to her shoulders. She might as well have been a fly pestering a rhinoceros for all the notice it took of her.

She felt panic swell in her as the creature continued to stalk Roderick. She swatted repeatedly at the dragon, trying to draw its attention away from the injured knight.

"Nay, my lady. Stay away. Save yourself," Roderick called to her as he struggled to regain his feet.

Jill ignored him and continued her attack. "Come on, you Everglade reject. I've seen tougher lizards in my backyard."

The dragon finally turned on her, its golden eyes glowing with predatory intent.

Jill held the sword with both hands in front of her as the dragon advanced. She backed up slowly, hoping to draw it into the woods where it would have trouble maneuvering. Praying, too, that Baelin would get here soon to finish what he started before the thing thought about incinerating her on the spot in a great ball of fire.

But it didn't spit fire at her. It stalked her like a cat corning a mouse. She knew if she dropped the sword and ran, it would catch her within seconds. But she couldn't fight it either. Baelin and Roderick had tried and barely scratched it.

Then she remembered something Roderick had told her. The heart. The weakest spot in the scales was over the dragon's heart.

And she remembered something else. The tale Baelin had told her of how he'd slain his first dragon.

Jill stopped retreating and stood still, willing the dragon to come closer. She gripped the sword with both hands, her palms sweating on the carved hilt, her heart pounding in her ears.

When the beast was almost upon her, she tucked and rolled, coming up on her back under the dragon's belly with the sword pointed upwards. The dragon hovered over her, its neck craning to see her, its teeth bared and nostrils flared.

Jill searched the dragon's underbelly, wondering where its heart would be. Then she saw it—a starburst shape of scales, slightly lighter than all the others.

Praying she had the strength to do it, she gripped the sword and shoved the blade hard into the dragon's chest.

Its yellow eyes widened in surprise and she heard a whimper, though she couldn't be sure if it came from her or the dragon.

Jill held tight to the sword as the great beast's weight slumped over her. She braced the hilt against the ground at her side, afraid if she let go or moved the beast would impale itself completely and come crashing down on top of her.

Her arms shook from the dragon's massive weight above her. She watched, transfixed, as a trickle of blood seeped from between the speared scales to slide down the blade, a crimson streak against shining silver inching its deadly way toward her.

The instant it touched her hand, searing pain shot up her arm and she screamed.

"Jill!" Baelin shouted from somewhere nearby.

He slammed into the dragon's side, shoving it over to crash on the ground. Then she found herself yanked up and pulled away from the creature's grasping claws.

His panicked eyes swept her from head to toe. "The dragon's blood, did it touch you?"

"Yes." She cradled her hand to her chest. "Oh God, it's burning."

Baelin dragged her over to where their satchels lay discarded in the grass. He tore through them, retrieving one of the calfskin flasks. Biting off the stopper, he poured the cool wine over her hand, washing the burning blood away.

He held her hand between his own as he examined the injury. A vivid red streak ran in an angry trail from the juncture of her thumb and forefinger across the back of her hand.

"Is it still burning?" he asked.

"A little. I think I'll survive." She winced as her hand began to throb. "I'm not sure what is worse, a red hot poker or acidic dragon's blood. I tell you what, the Middle Ages is wreaking havoc on my hands."

He crushed her in his embrace. She closed her eyes, amazed she was still alive to feel his arms around her.

Over Baelin's half-hearted scoldings mingled with whispered murmurs of endearment, she heard a gurgling noise. She pressed her face deeper into Baelin's chest, trying to shut out the sound of the death rasp of the creature as it thrashed nearby. But try as she might, she couldn't ignore it as the desperate guttural noise began to take on the muffled sound of pleading words. It was as if the dragon struggled to call to her with its last breath.

She looked at the beast that had tried to kill her, had tried to kill them all. She wanted to hate it, to rejoice in their victory over the dragon. But all she saw now was a magnificent, magical creature lying there, suffering in its final moments of life. It was almost too much to bear.

The dragon raised its head and pinned her with those damning golden eyes.

Then, as she watched, its form wavered. Scales blended to become flesh, horns softened into hair. What had once been a horrifying beast was now a naked man lying in the crushed grass with a sword sticking out of his chest.

A sword she'd put there.

Jill broke away from Baelin and knelt by the dying man. He opened his eyes and looked at her, the golden glow within fading, shifting to the clear blue of the sky over their heads. He spoke, his voice too soft to be heard.

She leaned closer, startled when he clutched at her hand. He strained up, gasping out two painfully uttered words before he closed those beautiful blue eyes and died in her arms.

ChApTER ThIRTY-FIVE

His satchel lay on the ground beside him, the tapestry tucked safely inside.

He didn't want to look at it. He didn't need to. Baelin knew in his heart this had been the second challenge. Surely no more could be asked of her than what she endured this day.

But he loosened the straps anyway, lifted the flap and reached inside. He pulled out the tapestry. Already it felt thicker, heavier in his hand. He unrolled it and there, depicted in vibrant threads, in an area that had not been there yesterday, was the image of the maid slaying a dragon.

He should be elated. Overjoyed. The second test had been passed.

But at what price? What cost, to the woman he loved?

"It changed, didn't it?"

He heard her words spoken softly from across the campfire.

"Aye."

Jill nodded and turned her attention back to the fire, tucking her knees up under her chin.

"What has changed?" Kendal asked without looking up as he plucked at the bandage wrapped tightly around his bruised ribs.

He eyed the dragonslayer. His friend, turned enemy, turned friend once more.

Earlier, as they buried the man in a shallow grave, Baelin had explained to him how he'd come to be a dragon. As each stone was placed on the fresh mound of earth, Kendal had gone from disbelief, to horror, to calm understanding.

"There is a tapestry attached to my curse. It tells the tale of a maid who must pass three tests of knightly valor to free the dragon-knight from the witch's spell."

Kendal looked up, his eyes alight with interest as his gaze darted between Baelin and Jill. "And Lady Jill is this maid?"

"She is. On our quest, we have discovered as she passes each test, the tapestry weaves a new part of itself, showing the feat she has accomplished. The first challenge occurred right before we met you. She proved her honor by enduring a trial by iron."

"Saints! The burns on her hands..." Kendal's gaze settled on Jill where she sat. "And after the ordeal?"

"A new part of the tapestry appeared showing what she endured for my sake."

Kendal's gaze flicked to the tapestry in Baelin's hands and he answered the unspoken question that crossed the knight's face.

"And now, with the slaying of the dragon, the tapestry has changed once again."

"May I see it?"

Baelin handed the knight the tapestry, then shifted his attention to Jill as she sat captivated by the fire. What visions did she see dancing within the flames? What thoughts troubled her so? He asked the questions, though he already knew the answers.

"Incredible," Owen's voice broke through the silence of the night as he too examined the tapestry from over Roderick's shoulder. "It does show a lady slaying a man who is part dragon."

"Forsooth, I would not believe it had I not seen her accomplish the deed myself." He held up the tapestry to examine it closely in the firelight and pointed to a particular section. "Is that supposed to be me?"

Baelin did not reply, for the truth was in the weaving. In addition to the knight, the maid and the dragon-man, two more figures had magically appeared that had not been there before—a second knight with a young boy standing by his side.

"And this is connected to your curse? The same one that poor wretch was likely under?"

Jill flinched at Kendal's carelessly spoken words. She held out her hand, palm up, her jaw clenched tight. "Let me see it."

Baelin watched Kendal give it to her, not certain how she would react when faced with her image driving a sword through the dragon's breast and into a man's heart.

Her breathing quickened and her hands shook as she clutched at the tapestry.

"I can't do this, Baelin. I can't go through with this." She looked over at him. "What if the next time it's you?"

She stood abruptly and walked away from the fire.

"My lady." Baelin surged to his feet and followed her. "Jill."

The whisper of her name stopped her where the last vestiges of fire-light fought back the darkness. She held herself erect, her back stiff, and stared out into the shadows beyond, to one shadow darker than all the others—that of a freshly dug grave.

"Who was he?" she asked softly, but with her back to him he was not certain if she spoke to him or to the ghosts on the wind. "Was he a man, cursed like you, existing year to year in the hope of breaking the witch's spell?"

She appeared so brittle in that moment, staring out into the night-cloaked field, the tapestry clutched to her breast. He stood not an arm's length behind her, but was afraid to reach for her for fear she might fracture and crumble at the lightest touch.

"Perhaps. I do not know."

"Well, I do." She whirled on him, turning her back on the grave. The sorrow wracking her slight frame hardened before his eyes, her expression turning cold, angry. "Every time I think about the dragon I killed and the man who died in my arms, I see your face instead. I can still hear the last words he spoke echoing over and over in my head, but they're whispered in your voice, not his."

She looked at him with eyes swimming in pain and remorse. "Do you know what he said to me just before he died? Do you?"

Baelin shook his head. Even with his keen dragon hearing, he had not been able to perceive the words.

"He said 'Thank you.' That man I stabbed through the heart with a sword thanked me for setting him free. So tell me, is that how the curse is broken? Do you have to die to be released from the Dark Witch's spell?"

"We cannot be certain what the final challenge will be."

"No, we can't. But you know as well as I do each challenge has gotten harder. The first required my blood and suffering. The second, the life of that poor man now lying cold and dead in the field. What if the next challenge demands an even higher price? What if it demands your blood? Your death?" She brushed a trembling hand down his surcoat, stopping to press it over the dragon heart beating deep within his chest. "I can't bear to lose you like that."

He placed his hand over hers, willing her to feel that he was still very much alive. "You will not."

She jerked her hand away and stiffened her shoulders, resolute. "You're right, because I'm not going through with the last test. I can't do it. I won't." She shoved the crumpled tapestry into his hands. "I'm sorry, Baelin, but I'd rather have you one month out of each year for the rest of my life than to not have you at all."

His dragon heart skipped a beat at her words. Did she truly mean them? He had to be certain. "But if the curse is not broken, what will become of you? You will never be able to return to your time."

Just as quickly as it came, her anger left, leaving her weary and forlorn before him. "Maybe that's a sacrifice I'm willing to make, because if my going home means you have to die, then the price is too high."

She turned and walked into the field, leaving him to stand alone and watch as the shadows of the night swallowed her up.

In all his life, as both knight and dragon, he'd killed many a man in battle. He knew without asking that she had never spilled another's blood. Until tonight. And it was taking a toll on her conscience, perhaps on her very soul, and he was powerless to help her through it.

He'd only taken one step to go after her when a hand on his shoulder stopped him.

"Leave her be. She needs time."

Baelin turned to find Kendal standing behind him.

"Owen," the knight summoned the boy. "Go. Watch after Lady Jill and make certain she stays safe."

"Aye, my lord." The boy grabbed a burning branch from the fire and darted off into the dark meadow.

He silently thanked Kendal for sending Owen after her. He knew she would not venture far, but after all that had happened, he did not like her out of his sight, even for one moment. Knowing the boy would cry alarm if there was any sign of danger eased his anxiety somewhat.

The knights watched in shared silence as Jill began gathering wild-flowers from the tall grass while Owen held the torch aloft to light her way.

"What is it she is about?" Kendal asked.

"Honoring the life that has been lost, in her way."

They stood side by side, their gaze following her as she went about her somber task, the silver light of the moon gilding the edges of her form with an ethereal glow.

"She is a remarkable woman," Kendal finally commented.

"That she is." He stood silent for a time, then he put voice to the thoughts plaguing his conscience. "Never, in all the years I have been under the dragon's spell, did I imagine how hard it would be on the one chosen to break the curse. I always thought it would be my burden to bear. My pain and blood and sweat that would be required." He turned his back on the sight of Jill kneeling by the grave, placing the flowers she'd gathered one by one on the stone-covered mound. "Not hers."

By God, he loved her too much to put her through this. It wasn't worth it.

If he could spare her...

"Damn this curse! Damn this piece of cloth that holds our fate in the secrets of its threads."

He flung the tapestry at the fire, not caring if it condemned him to live as a fire-breathing beast for all eternity if it would spare her one more moment of pain.

But the flames were denied their sacrifice.

Kendal snatched it from the air before it could land in the fire.

He held the crumpled mass up to Baelin's face. "Have you gone mad?"

"I cannot do this to her. I cannot ask her to suffer any more for me." Baelin waved his hand in the direction of the grave, for he couldn't bring himself to look at Jill and watch her in her torment. "Did you see her? Did you see the look in her eyes? Lady Jill, who has always been so full of life and fire. 'Tis gone now, extinguished, washed away with the blood of that man. Each test grows harder. What if she is right? What if the next time she has to—"

"What if she is wrong?" Kendal interrupted. "What if you both are? You cannot know the morrow until it becomes the day." The knight began rolling up the tapestry. "If what you say is true, and she is from another time, another place, by not breaking the curse, you condemn her to stay here. What of *her* family? What of *her* home? If you do not break the curse for yourself, you must break it for her."

Baelin clenched his jaw, the effort of holding back the honesty of his reply nearly cracking his back teeth. He needn't have bothered. All too quickly he watched the realization wash over Kendal's face as the knight comprehended thoughts and desires Baelin could not put into words.

"You do not want her to go back. You want her to stay here with you."

He closed his eyes against the truth in Kendal's words.

"Aye, more than anything." He wondered how a man could feel cleaved in two without a drop of blood shed. "But not because she feels she must. I wish her to remain with me because 'tis what she wants to do."

"Baelin, for whatever purpose, this task has been put forth to both of you. You must see it through to the end. Any future you may have together depends upon it." Kendal handed the tapestry back to him, then placed his hand on Baelin's shoulder. "Take heart, my friend. She loves you. Of that, I am certain. Perhaps, once the curse is broken, she will decide to stay."

Feeling the weight of the rolled weaving in his hands, Baelin wondered yet again what fate it held for them within its twisted threads.

"The choice may not be hers to make. I am beginning to fear even if we do succeed in breaking the curse before the full moon rises, that the fates will not be kind. That Lady Jill will be torn from me as quickly as she came, and returned to her time where I will not be able to reach her."

"Time will only tell, my friend. Do not lose hope. We cannot know what the future holds. We can only trust God to guide us down the right path to get there."

"I pray with all my dragon heart it is so. That there is a way to break the curse and keep her with me."

"Perhaps there is. After all, if a witch's spell can turn a knight into a dragon, surely there exists some magic in the heavens that can keep a man with the woman he loves."

It seemed so simple for Kendal. And perhaps it was.

"Ah, but whatever magic it is will cost dearly. In the end, I may have to give the Dark Witch what she has wanted all along."

"And what is that?"

"Me."

Baelin stilled as a heavy silence descended upon them. All was not right.

He searched the dark night, to where Jill and Owen had only moments ago stood near the grave.

But they were no longer there.

"Jill!"

He charged toward the grave, Kendal quick on his heels, a scattering of wildflowers on the freshly-laid stones and a smoldering torch the only sign of where they'd been.

"Where did they go?" Kendal asked, his gaze darting to the dark tree line beyond the meadow. "Surely they did not venture into the forest?"

"Nay, they were here but a moment ago. They could not have gone far without notice."

"Then where are they?"

Chills pricked the back of Baelin's neck. A low moan drew his attention to the tall grass nearby. Owen lay on his side, curled as if asleep. When they rolled him over, his eyes flickered open, dazed and unfocused.

"What happened, lad? Where is Lady Jill?" Kendal asked, kneeling by the boy's side.

Owen looked back and forth between the knights, confusion puckering his brow. Slowly, his eyes cleared and he focused on Baelin, panic taking the place of his disorientation. He clutched Baelin's surcoat in a frantic grasp.

"My lady. She has been taken."

Baelin's dragon heart stopped beating.

"I tried, my lord. Truly I did. But they came upon us without a sound.

'Twas as if they formed out of the very darkness itself and disappeared back into the night before I could do aught. They took Lady Jill with them."

His stomach clenched in a tight knot at the boy's words. "Who?"

"They had the look of knights, but like none I have ever seen before. They wore black surcoats with a red dragon." Owen broke down in soul-racking sobs. "I am sorry, my lord. I was unable to speak nor move, as if a spell was cast upon me. I would have fought with my last breath to stop them if I could."

"I know," Baelin said softly, aware the boy's anguish mirrored his own. "You did well. 'Twas a foe even a knight grown could not stand against alone."

"Before they disappeared, they bade me to tell you…" Owen gasped then hiccuped, trying to catch his breath.

"What, lad?"

"They said to tell you Lady Jill would live only until the rise of the next full moon."

Kendal stood, his angry gaze scouring the shadows beyond the meadow for an enemy Baelin knew was no longer there. "By all that is holy, these men, when we find them, will pay dearly with their lives if they harm Lady Jill."

"They told me to tell you something else, my lord."

"What?" Kendal asked, as he pulled the boy to his feet, although Baelin already suspected the answer.

"That you would know where to find her."

Cold resolve spilled over Baelin. "Aye, I know where they have taken her, only too well."

"Where?" Kendal asked.

"'Twas the Dark Witch's warriors who spirited her away, of that I have no doubt. Already Lady Jill will be deep within the walls of the witch's realm. Dawn comes soon. I must hurry, before 'tis too late."

"Then there is no time to waste," Kendal said as he strode back to the fire. "Owen, ready my armor."

He grabbed the knight's shoulder and spun him around. "You wish to fight by my side?"

"Of course. Think you I would leave you to battle this foe alone?"

316

"But only hours ago you tried to kill me."

Kendal shrugged. "I am a dragonslayer. 'Tis what I do."

"Then we are enemies no more?" Baelin asked as he tucked the rolled tapestry in his belt.

"I think not." Kendal chuckled, appearing more concerned with donning his armor than with the beast standing at his side.

Baelin watched Owen arm his master for battle, surprised a dragonslayer could dismiss the creature he was so easily.

"But I am still part dragon."

Kendal looked him in the eye, all joviality gone. "And part knight. A very honorable one, I might add. Lady Jill tried to tell me that when I took her from you, but I would not listen. Now I have seen with my own eyes that all is not what it seems. I will not soon forget you saved my life, perhaps when 'twould have been easier for you to let the dragon have me."

"You are giving up slaying dragons, then?"

"Perhaps. I may take up witch hunting instead. It appears you could use some help with this one."

"I shall help, too," Owen said as his handed Kendal his sword belt.

"Nay!" Baelin immediately regretted the harsh tone of his voice. "I am sorry, Owen. 'Tis not possible."

The boy glanced back and forth between the two men, then looked to his master for an answer. "But I have always accompanied you into battle, my lord. Who will ready your armor? Who will tend *Flaume Stelan?*"

Baelin placed a gentle hand on the boy's bony shoulder. "The horse will have to stay behind, as will you, I am afraid."

Kendal arched a dark brow and Baelin answered his questioning look. "To go where they have taken Lady Jill, we must fly. And since neither you nor your horse has wings, I will have to carry you. You are heavy enough, with the added weight of your armor. Strong though I may be, I can only manage to carry a horse while in my dragon form."

Kendal's brave façade slipped a notch. While he had no qualms about facing witches and dragons, the prospect of taking flight left him looking a bit green.

"You do not have to go."

"Of course I do," Kendal said as he cinched his belt tighter. "There is a battle to fight and a damsel to save. What kind of knight would I be if I ignored such a challenge?"

"One that would live to see another day."

Baelin turned to Owen, his young face pale with the dawning realization of the danger the men were about to face.

"If we do not return before the full moon rises, you must leave here at once and never return, for it will be too late for the rest of us."

"With God's help and my sword at your back, perhaps it will not be." Kendal pulled his helm over his head. "Come, the time for talk is done. Let us be off to rescue your lady."

Chapter Thirty-Six

Jill sat on the cold stone floor of her latest prison, any hope of escape fading with each passing moment.

While it was clean, not fetid or disgusting like the one in the village, it was no less frightening. Maybe because this time she didn't have Baelin's comforting presence on the other side of the wall to help her through whatever was to come.

Was he looking for her? Did he even know where to look?

Probably. But that didn't mean he would come.

He'd been avoiding this place all along, not wanting to come here, not wanting to face whatever nightmares the witch had put him through.

As Jill looked at the stark room, she could hardly blame him. The brilliant white walls of her cell glistened in the torchlight as if carved of crystal. A cool chill permeated the air, drawing the warmth from her body. Was this what Baelin feared, knowing the Dark Witch had the power to slowly suck the life out of anyone near her? She could only imagine what would befall her when the witch decided to make her presence known.

Jill didn't know how long she'd been here. The last thing she remembered, she'd been standing with Owen in the field by the grave and then she woke up here. She didn't have to ask where 'here' was. But with no windows in her crystal cell, there was no way to measure the passage of time. It could've been hours. Or days. Or—having witnessed only a fraction of the Dark Witch's powers so far—years.

Was it already too late? Had the full moon come and gone and Baelin returned to his dragon form for another year?

Already she felt his loss, so great she could hardly draw breath around the painful ache it left deep in her chest. Everything she'd been through, everything Baelin had been through for over two hundred years, all for nothing.

She never heard the click of a lock or the creak of an opening door. In fact, since the room appeared to be carved out of a block of solid stone, she hadn't been able to even find the door, though she'd spent what seemed like hours searching for it. All she knew was one moment she was alone and the next there were two guards in the room with her, their faces covered by dark helms, completely dressed in black.

"The Queen summons you."

And your fate awaits, echoed a voice off the walls inside her head.

Jill rose unsteadily to her feet. The guards led her down a long arched corridor to a cavernous hall. The walls, ceiling, and floors of the chamber were made out of the same glistening white crystal as her cell. Led to an empty stone throne at the end of the great hall, the guards left her to stand alone before its imposing presence.

Still dressed in her dark, travel-worn gown, Jill felt like a messy stain on a crisp white table cloth. Everywhere she looked was white, so bright it hurt to keep her eyes open. It was as if the entire fortress had been carved out of a mountain of colorless crystal. The entire chamber was stunning in its brilliance, captivating in its achromatism.

But there was no sound. No birds singing or insects chirping through the arched openings framing either side of the chamber. No hurried bustle of servants or happy laughter of children from other rooms within the fortress.

No music. No voices. No life.

How could a place so pristine and beautiful feel so dead?

Into the stillness, a gust of wind blew from outside the archways, a cold breeze dancing in the gossamer curtains like ethereal ghosts.

And then Jill saw her.

A woman dressed in a white satin gown encrusted with sparkling diamonds sat on the throne that moments before had been empty. Or rather, a girl. She looked no older than seventeen or eighteen. Long, cascading curls so light a shade of blonde they were almost white, framed a heart-shaped face. A flawless pale complexion complemented plump, pouty lips and enormous crystal clear violet eyes.

A white angel holding court in a palace of sparkling crystal. She was the most beautiful creature Jill had ever seen.

"Oh, my God. He turned you down?"

The witch, who until then had showed no expression on her beautiful face, cocked a brow at Jill. Then she laughed, a musical sound that filled the chamber, bouncing off the crystal walls and back again.

"Ah, Lady Jill. I had heard you were different, but I had no idea how so."

"Was that supposed to be a compliment?"

"No. I do not pay compliments to anyone, least of all a mere mortal such as you."

The Dark Witch rose from her throne and moved down the steps toward her. She glided with such fluid motion, Jill had to glance down to see if her feet touched the ground.

"I am Queen Isylte."

"I gathered as much."

This close, the witch's lavender eyes sparkled in a kaleidoscope of violets and purples, the colors moving and changing in a mesmerizing dance. Jill looked away before she fell under their powerful pull. The witch might look the part of the innocent, but she radiated malice from the inside out.

"You slew one of my dragons."

"Not on purpose."

"But you did, none the less. I should kill you for that."

The fact she hadn't been turned into a toad yet made Jill bold. "So why haven't you?"

"Because I am not done with you, yet." Isylte smiled, the catty grin never reaching her eyes. "Come, Lady Jill. I have something I wish to show you."

The witch turned and walked away, her confidence and regal bearing at odds with her youthful appearance. A doorway materialized in the wall behind the throne and Isylte disappeared into the next room without looking back.

Jill supposed she could refuse to follow, but that would get her no-where. She wanted answers. She needed to find a way to save Baelin, if it wasn't already too late. The key to his curse was hidden somewhere within these cavernous walls, perhaps lying just beyond that door.

She really didn't have any choice. She followed.

Baelin looked down on a place he hoped never to see again.

A place of pain. A place of degradation. A pit of hell.

"It does not look so bad."

He glanced at the knight standing beside him among the ragged crags of the mountainside. He knew what Kendal saw before him. A beautiful fortress, its towering walls of gleaming crystals cloaked in shifting clouds of mist.

"Do not let its beauty deceive you. The Dark Witch's magic is power-ful. She can make the day seem as night or the sun be the moon and you will believe it, until she has your soul."

Now that he'd recovered from their flight, Kendal would not be swayed. "How then do we scale walls of ice built on a mountain of mist?"

"We do not. Already she knows I am here. The gates will be open, and she will be waiting." Baelin turned to his friend. "'Tis not too late. This is not your battle. You have seen what the Dark Witch has done to me. I cannot promise once we enter the walls, we will ever leave again."

Kendal smiled and checked his sword. "But if we could be assured of the victory, what fun would there be in that?"

"Ah, victory. Would that we could be guaranteed it just this once. But I fear no matter what the outcome, I am going to lose Jill. Time has run out for me. Already the sun begins to set. In a matter of hours the full moon will rise and I shall become the dragon once more."

"Do not concede what has yet come to pass. Hours may be all that we need. Mayhap the last challenge you seek lies within those walls of ice."

"Perhaps it does." Maybe all he'd been through, all the long years of fighting against his fate, had finally brought him to this point.

Back to *her*.

Baelin readied his weapon, knowing it had little power against the witch's magic.

"Be warned, the closer I get to the Dark Witch's realm, the more power she has over the beast within me. 'Tis why I have never returned before. If we still remain within her walls once the sun sets, I will return to my dragon form and then she will have complete control over the creature I become. I will not know you for the friend you are, nor Lady Jill for the woman I love. If that should happen…"

He could not finish the request.

"I give you my word. " Kendal placed one hand on Baelin's shoulder and squeezed. "But I pray it will not come to pass."

Baelin hoped he was right. For if he was not, Kendal would be Jill's only hope.

He would be the only one left to save her—and he would have to slay the dragon Baelin would become to do it.

The door led to another chamber. A bedroom, to be exact.

Though the room was large, like the great hall before, the furnishings within were sparse. A lady's dressing table carved out of pale wood occupied one corner, its edges gilded in silver. Two high-backed chairs with white pillowed cushions faced a roaring fire that did little to dispel the chill in the air. A large bed big enough to sleep the entire Brady Bunch family at one time sat on a raised dais. Covered in white furs, its massive frame dominated the entire room.

With such an obvious fondness for white, Jill wondered where the queen got the nickname of the Dark Witch.

"I like what you've done with the place. Very impressive. But the whole white monochrome thing must be a bear to keep clean."

Isylte frowned, as if the concept that dirt would dare mar the pristine perfection of her domain was inconceivable.

"I am pleased you approve. There are not many mortals who have ever gained entrance into my private chambers."

"So what makes me so special?"

"'Tis what I would like to know." The Dark Witch paced a circle around her, her amethyst gaze examining her from head to toe and back again, analyzing, studying, judging. "What makes you different from all the others? How is it you have succeeded where the others have failed?"

"Just lucky, I guess."

"Nay, there is something more. Something different. Over the centuries I have watched the other maidens come and go. You are not as beautiful as some, but you have a knowledge and experience the others did not have."

Without warning, Isylte put her hands on Jill's shoulders, sending an electric current rushing through her body. The Dark Witch's eyes widened in surprise at the static shock that passed between them. She released Jill and stepped back.

"Ah, I see. How interesting. When I created the curse, I knew there was no maid alive with the courage and honor to break it. But I did not foresee a woman from the future coming through time to face the challenges. Yet here you are."

"Yes, here I am. Guess the devil is in the details, isn't it?"

Isylte cocked her head. "Hmm, I like that. 'The devil is in the details.' I shall have to remember it." Her smile vanished as quickly as it came. "And you are one minor detail I did not plan on."

She sauntered away, turning her back on Jill, dismissing her significance with that one single gesture. "But no matter. All I must do is wait until the moon rises and it will be too late for Baelin." She whipped around, her pale hair fanning about her shoulders, the lines of her face cruel and vindictive. "And for you."

Now she knew why they called her the Dark Witch. She may look like an angel on the outside, but inside she was nothing but selfishness and cruelty.

Isylte walked over to the wall by the bed and pulled aside a white curtain. The sudden splash of vibrant color against the white stone shocked Jill's eyes, but it was the image depicted in the weaving hanging there that broke her heart.

It was Baelin. Or at least what was left of him. From the chest down, the rest of the tapestry was missing, the lower edge fringed with dangling threads.

"A remarkable likeness, is it not?"

Jill found it hard to speak around the painful knot in her throat. "Yes, it is."

"It was once magnificent, but you have managed to ruin it."

"Me? How? I never touched the thing."

"Do not be naive. You did not have to. The challenges. With each one you have passed, you have managed to unravel my magic."

A puzzle piece finally fell into place in Jill's mind. "Just like Baelin's tapestry has been reweaving itself each time."

"Yes, but so long as a portion of this tapestry remains intact, the curse still holds its power."

Jill looked at the ragged tapestry. There was so little left of Baelin. So little time left for both of them. That their lives had been turned upside down by this woman's caprice enraged her. She wanted to strike out, to hurt the witch as she'd hurt Baelin.

"Looks like your little curse is hanging on by a very thin thread there, lady."

"Do not taunt me!" Isylte shrieked. She made a motion with her hand and Jill braced herself to be turned into some slimy, reptilian creature. It didn't happen. The witch lowered her arm and breathed deeply, her nostrils flaring in her bid to regain control. "No, not yet. But when this is over, you will regret your ill-chosen words."

"I usually do," Jill mumbled to herself. "But it's not over yet."

"No, it is not. I will admit you surprised me when you made it this far. I underestimated you. But there is still the final challenge. One I am confident you will fail."

"How can you be so sure?"

"For one thing, Baelin must be with you to complete it."

"Then I guess you've already won, because he won't come." The words tasted bitter on her tongue.

"You think not?"

"I don't know what you did to him while he was here, but he's been avoiding this place like the plague." Jill's heart twisted at the grim truth. "He won't come. In all this time, if he wouldn't do it to end the curse for himself, what makes you think he'll come for me now?"

"Does he love you so little, then?"

Jill didn't want to believe it, but the possibility was there just the same. Did he love her enough? She honestly didn't know.

"We shall have to see, will we not?"

She began to understand the witch a little more. She might be older than Moses, but emotionally she was little more than a vain, spoiled child. A child who lashed out and broke her toys if she didn't get her way.

"You can't make somebody love you, you know. It doesn't work that way."

"Who said I wanted him to love me?"

Jill opened her mouth to respond, but the witch was no longer paying attention to her. Instead, she'd turned to look at the tapestry once again. As Isylte gazed upon Baelin's image, a shadow crossed her face, a whisper of longing Jill recognized all too well.

The Dark Witch was lying. She was a desolate creature, much like Baelin had been, living alone in her palace of ice. She did want someone to love her.

Jill almost felt sorry for her. Almost. But she refused to feel pity for the spiteful woman-child after all she'd done to Baelin.

"Everyone wants to be loved, even those who don't deserve it."

Isylte chuckled, but there was no humor in the sound. "And what do you know of love?"

"Enough to know it has to be freely given, not forced. Have you ever heard the saying, 'If you love something, set it free. If it comes back to you, it's yours. If it doesn't, it never was?'"

The Dark Witch looked at her, perplexed, before laughing.

Jill rolled her eyes. "Yeah, it's a pretty hokey saying in my time too, but it's still true."

"But I did set him free. Yet he has never returned."

"Because you set him free as a monster, so he would be forced to come back to you. But it didn't work, did it?"

"We shall see about that."

Jill opened her mouth to respond, but the witch was no longer paying attention to her. Instead, she'd turned to gaze at the tapestry once again.

A brittle smile formed on the woman's pouty lips. "Well, well. It appears we both underestimated Baelin's affection for you, after all."

"What do you mean?"

The witch did not answer, but continued to stare at what remained of the tapestry.

Jill followed her gaze. The ragged cloth hanging on the wall began to wave and flutter, yet there was no longer any breeze coming from the arched doorways, no draft in the vast chamber that she could detect. She looked closer and realized it wasn't the tapestry that was moving, but the image within the threads itself, as if the rendering of Baelin was trying to unravel itself and break free of the weaving. She blinked her eyes, trying to clear her vision, but the image continued to undulate and sway before her eyes.

"Your gallant dragon-knight seems to have had a change of heart. He has come." Her beautiful face grew tight and pinched, her violet eyes cold. "Let us go greet him, shall we?"

Isylte sailed past her and back into the great hall, leaving Jill behind.

She turned to follow the witch, her heart pounding in her ears, drowning out any other sound in the room.

Baelin was here?

She wanted to shout with joy at the same time she felt like crying out, *No, you should never have come for me. I'm not worth it.*

As she left the chamber, Jill cast one last glance back at the tapestry, still wavering under a power all its own, and wondered what it meant.

In the great hall, Isylte was back on her ivory throne, every fold of her flowing white gown in place.

Jill found herself flanked by two guards, their black-clad forms a stark contrast to the white walls around her. She turned her attention to the immense doors at the back of the chamber. The same doors the Dark Witch stared at, her gaze so intense Jill was surprised it didn't burn twin holes in the thick carved panels.

Footsteps echoed down the long hallway on the other side and she could picture Baelin in her mind's eye, his long purposeful strides leading him to this long-postponed confrontation.

Or to his death.

CHAPTER THIRTY-SEVEN

Baelin shoved the massive doors open, entering the Dark Witch's inner sanctum for the first time in over two centuries.

Jill's eyes drank in the sight of him, so tall and sure. He showed no fear, only a determined resignation to end the Dark Witch's hold over him, one way or another.

"Baelin," the queen practically purred. She sounded so cool and serene. But Jill watched as the witch's long fingers clutched the arms of her throne, the nail beds turning white from the force of her grip. She was not nearly as calm as she seemed. She was as surprised as Jill that he had actually come. "My love. It has been too long."

"You are right about that, Queen Isylte. It has been 216 years too long. 'Tis time to put this to an end."

He strode through the hall, ignoring the black knights lining the way with their weapons at the ready. Jill was not surprised to see Roderick close by his side, equally prepared for battle.

"Oh, Baelin. Must you be so rude in front of our guests?"

He stopped before the dais. "There is no civility between us. There never has been."

"And whose fault is that?" Isylte looked down her nose at him. "I offered you everything a man could want, yet you repudiated me time and again."

"Your offerings were gilded with unacceptable conditions, their price too high for any honorable man to pay." He shook his head, his hand resting on the hilt of his sword. "Nay, Isylte. You forced and you took, but you never offered a choice. Not truly."

Her plump lips thinned into a tight, harsh line. "Do not test my benevolence this day. There are worse things than being turned into a dragon."

"Aye, there are. As you shall soon discover when I send your black soul to hell where it belongs."

The Dark Witch's eyes flared, amethyst crystals shimmering with cold heat. "Try and I shall destroy all that you hold dear before your very eyes. I did it once before. Do not think I shall not do so again."

For the first time since he entered, Baelin's gaze strayed to Jill and she read the first hint of fear on his face. But it wasn't for himself. It was for her.

Don't, Baelin. Don't let her use me to get to you.

Not now, when they were so close. So close, she could feel it. She knew with a soul-deep certainty the last test was somewhere within the witch's fortress, the final challenge to be met here where it all began. It had to be. But where?

Behind Baelin, something caught Jill's eye. Through one of the arched openings a dark object appeared in the sky, its form silhouetted against the flame-colored sunset.

She knew what it was instantly.

The great beating wings. The long, reptilian tail. It reminded her so much of the first time she'd seen the terrifying beast side of Baelin as he soared down out of the clouds to claim her as his own.

But this dragon was not Baelin. And as the winged beast loomed closer, she realized the thing clasped in its claws was not a sacrificial maiden.

"Owen!"

All eyes turned as the dragon dove through the archway, its massive wings tucked to avoid clipping the stone columns. It skidded to a stop on the floor of the great hall, the thunderous crash shaking the fortress to its very foundation. Steadying itself, the great beast sat back on its haunches, its fore-claws still clutching its prize.

"Ah, look." Isylte sat straighter, a look of feigned surprise artfully painted on her beautiful face. "Uhtred has come to see you. Surely you remember him, Baelin. After all, you two share so much."

Jill looked closely at the dragon. A starburst mark blazed the scales of its broad chest. Was this another dragon like the man she'd slain while he was in his dragon form? Could it be another dragon-knight like Baelin?

No. Somehow, she knew this one was different. Maybe it was the smug tone of the Dark Witch's voice as she greeted its arrival. Or maybe it was the horrified look on Baelin's face as the dragon pierced him with its predatory golden eyes.

This wasn't just any dragon. This was the one whose heart beat within Baelin's chest. And if that were so, did Baelin's human heart even now beat within this dragon's breast in return?

"And look what Uhtred has brought me. A gift. A pet. A new plaything." Isylte clucked her tongue. "But he does seem a bit young yet, even for my tastes. Perhaps I'll turn him into a baby dragon." She slid her violet eyes to Baelin. "Just. Like. You."

"Never!" he growled.

"Never?" She laughed, the throaty sound at odds with her angelic façade. "You once told me you would never set foot in my realm again and yet here you are. Never does not seem to be as long as it once was."

"You have no interest in the boy. Let him go. Let them all go. They mean naught to you," he spoke through clenched teeth. "'Tis me you want."

Isylte descended the dais and approached Baelin, circling him. He stood tall, his fists clenched, following her movements with only his eyes.

"But you have brought these mortals to my door, so they very much concern me now." She strolled past Roderick, her walk fluid, sensual. "Your dragonslaying friend here, while quite tempting to look upon, has destroyed more of my pets than any other, even you. He has cost me greatly and for that he shall pay." She gave the knight a seductive smile. "One way or another."

The witch's stroll took her by the dragon, still holding Owen, pale and trembling, in its sharp claws. She ran her hand down its glistening scales in an affectionate caress, startling Jill when it enticed an otherworldly purr from deep within the massive beast.

"As for the boy, his worth remains to be seen. If he means as much to you as I think, he may turn out to be quite valuable indeed."

Isylte turned cold eyes Jill's way. "Which leaves her."

She glided into the center of the chamber, her pet dragon watching her every step of the way. "To you, she is the dearest of all, therefore she is the one who concerns me the most. The others, I may set free eventually, if we can come to an agreement of sorts. Or not." She glanced back at Baelin from over her shoulder. "'Tis up to you."

Isylte glided up the stairs to sit primly upon her throne.

"What do you want, Isylte?"

"Why, Baelin, you know what I want. In all this time, it has not changed." She smoothed the folds of her gown with the ease of someone who didn't have a worry in the world. "I already have your heart, in the physical sense." She looked up, piercing him with her gaze, all girlish pretense gone. "Now I demand all of you. Your warrior's skill on the battlefield and your body in my bed. I will take naught less than your total and complete submission, body and soul."

Baelin's eyes closed and his nostrils flared. "And if I give you what you want, you will release them, unharmed? Unchanged?"

"Baelin, no!" Jill shouted, but neither he nor Isylte took notice of her.

"Perhaps." The Dark Witch smiled without humor. "But I may have to keep them close at hand to make certain you keep your promises."

"I would never break my word."

"I am aware of that, only too well. But still..." Isylte glanced out over the courtyard to the horizon beyond and the sinking sun hovering above the mountains in the distance. "The decision is yours. But do not take too long. Already the sun is setting. You have but moments to stay the half-man you are before the dragon returns." Her gaze came back to Baelin. "Stay with me and I will lift the curse and you shall be a man whole once more. Choose the maiden and you will remain the dragon forever."

"Don't do it, Baelin." Jill tried to go to him, but the guards on either side of her barred her way, holding her back. "You've held out this long. Don't give into her now. The sun hasn't set yet. We still have time. We can still break the curse."

Isylte laughed. "My, what a poor, simple creature you have chosen, Baelin. She will not be able to finish it. You and I both know it, so why did you even try?" She cocked a finely arched brow at Jill. "You gave over your dragon's armor so she could survive the first test, did you not? And the second? An unfortunate accident. An accident that cost Lorcan his life and one she will pay dearly for once I am done with this nonsense."

"I will never allow you to harm her." Baelin stalked toward the witch.

Isylte's hand shot up and a wave of power blasted through the air. "Stand down, dragon."

Baelin stopped instantly, as if his feet were glued to the flagstones.

"Have no fear. I will not harm her. But I know as long as the maiden lives and breathes, you can never be completely mine. 'Tis an obstacle I shall not tolerate. " Isylte smiled as she leaned back on her throne, the cold violet of her eyes cruel and calculating. "Nay, my love. I will not harm the girl. You will."

Raw fear drained all color from his face. "Isylte, do not…"

"Slay the maiden, dragon-knight."

No! his mind screamed even as he took a stilted step toward Jill, fighting the motion with all the strength in him.

Though he railed against it, the dark power welled up from within, forcing his limbs to move, following a command his body could not disobey. He fought against it nonetheless, nearly tearing muscle from bone in the effort to regain control over his body. And yet he couldn't stop himself from taking another step, and yet another, drawing closer and closer to the woman he loved.

To the woman he'd been commanded to kill.

"Nay, Gosforth!" Kendal reached out, grabbing Baelin's arm. "What in God's name are you doing?"

"Guards, remove that man from my hall."

Kendal's fierce grip was wrenched away. An uproar commenced at Baelin's back, but the dark power commanding him would not allow him to turn around. He heard swords drawn, curses shouted, blade striking blade and knew Kendal fought against the knights with the same skill he'd used so many times against him. One man against many. But there was naught he could do to aid his friend. He had another battle to wage.

The one within.

"Do not kill the dragonslayer...yet," the witch ordered her men. "I have something much more entertaining in mind for him later."

Isylte's veiled threat did little to deter Kendal as he continued to battle against the witch's warriors, no doubt in an effort to break free and stop Baelin from doing the unthinkable.

As he approached Jill, Baelin could read the fear in her eyes, the comprehension of what was happening. Isylte held rein over the dragon within him and though he'd fought the beast for over two hundred years, now, when it mattered most, the beast was winning.

The two guards on either side of Jill grabbed her arms, stretching her out between them, holding her in place. She stood there, unable to move, more the sacrificial maiden now than she ever had been bound to the stake on that windswept field.

And at this moment, he was more the beast in coming for her.

"Fight her," Jill pleaded. "She can't make you do this. Not if you fight her."

He did fight. With everything he had within him, he waged war against the dragon's pull as never before, but it was a foe neither honed skill nor sharp steel could defeat. Sweat broke out on his forehead from the strain of his inner battle and yet he couldn't stop himself from taking another step closer, drawing ever nearer to the kill.

"Don't, Baelin. Please don't do this." Jill's lower lip trembled as she struggled against her human bonds. "I love you."

His dragon heart swelled with joy at her words, even as he drew his sword slowly from its sheath, the warm sting of a single tear trailing down his cheek.

"Yes, my love. That's right," Isylte crooned. "Finish it."

His sword arm tensed and shook, even as his fingers refused to release their grip. Nay, he could not let this happen. He had to end the witch's control over the beast inside of him. He had to stop the dragon. He must. He could not harm Jill.

God in Heaven, *he would not kill her.*

"For the love of God, my lord, do not hurt Lady Jill!" Owen cried out.

Baelin heard the deep rumbling growl of the dragon holding the whimpering boy captive. He forced his gaze away from Jill to face the beast. Its jaws were half open, revealing razor-sharp teeth. It was as if the creature was laughing at him, knowing it had a hand in this wicked game the witch played. As its golden eyes pierced him with their evil glow, its massive claws closed in reflexively, slowing crushing the small boy within its grasp.

"Owen!" Kendal shouted. Baelin watched from the corner of his eye as the knight rallied, breaking free of the warriors surrounding him and charged to the boy's aid. The witch's warriors gave chase but slowed, more afraid of the fire breathing beast than the witch's wrath.

Kendal's sword sliced down on the dragon's claw, the sharp blade skittering across the impenetrable scales without leaving a mark.

The beast swung its horned head, its massive jaws snapping closed on naught but air as the knight jumped out of harm's way. He edged down the dragon's side, stabbing the tip of his sword at the edges of the scales, trying to find space between the tight plates to thrust the blade inside and into the vulnerable flesh beneath. It did the beast no injury, but only served to anger it, forcing it to turn to keep the dragonslayer in its sights.

Enraged, the dragon opened its maw wide, spitting fire at the pest plaguing him. With no shield of hardened metal to protect him from the hot flames, Kendal dove into the midst of the witch's guard, availing himself of a human barrier instead.

Shrieks of agony rang through the great hall as several of the unfortunate men tasted the kiss of the dragon's fire.

"Uhtred!" The Dark Witch stood, her violet eyes wide with anger and just a trace of alarm. "Do not wipe out my entire garrison in one breath!"

As the remaining knights attempted to aid their comrades, Kendal rushed the dragon once again.

Baelin's soul felt torn in two, one part desperate to join the battle and help his friend to save the boy. The other, darker side, still wrenched against his will, urging him on to the kill.

The witch laughed at his plight. "Ah, poor Baelin. Why do you struggle so? The dragon is a part of you. You cannot fight yourself."

Baelin stilled, cold sweat chilling his skin, and he knew at once the truth in the Dark Witch's words. The beast was indeed a part of him. Not the flesh and blood dragon Kendal battled nearby, but the one inside. And if he couldn't slay the creature within, then he must destroy the vessel that shielded it before he lost control over what little humanity still remained of him.

With calm resolve, he raised his sword and looked into the eyes of the woman he loved.

"You are wrong, Isylte. I can."

Jill's face paled as she read the intent in his eyes.

"No, Baelin. Don't!"

The dragon twisted and reared, its large form reaching the arched ceiling of the great hall. In its single-minded pursuit of the dragonslayer, the beast had forgotten Baelin's presence. It was all he needed.

He looked one last time at Jill. "I love you."

He said the words calmly, softly, not certain if she even heard them. Then he pivoted and threw the blade with all his might, impaling the dragon through the starburst scales on its chest and deep into his human heart.

He heard mingled screams. The furious shriek of the witch. The anguished shout of Kendal. The pain-filled roar of the dragon as it stumbled and crashed to the ground. But Jill's mournful wale overrode them all, breaking his heart as surely as the sword's blade had cleaved it in two.

"*No!*"

But he couldn't see her. He dropped to his knees, unable to stand any longer as his world closed in. Blackness encroached all around him as pain from the phantom blade piercing his chest shot out, racing down his arms and legs, exploding in his head until there was nothing else.

"Jill." Her name came out in a whisper, and then the floor rushed up to meet him.

Suddenly, she was there at his side, turning him over. Tears streamed down her pale cheeks, her beautiful image blurring as his vision grew hazy.

"No, Baelin. No. Why did you do that? There had to be another way."

"There was not, my lady." He struggled, the effort to draw air into his charred lungs growing harder with each breath. "I could not allow harm to come to you. Not by my hand. Ever."

"Oh, God." Her hand pressed against his chest, the heart within struggling to beat. She raised her hand, her palm covered with his blood. "Blood. There's so much blood."

He could feel the warm wetness seeping out, soaking through *aketon*, mail and surcoat. How was it that his blood did not burn her?

And then Kendal was there, on his other side.

"We have to stop the bleeding," Jill cried. "Give me something to stop the bleeding."

There was a tug at his waist as one of them pulled the tapestry free from his sword belt. Then pressure, as both of them pressed the weaving against a wound that was not there, to stop blood that would not cease to flow.

He heard the frantic thrashing of the dragon nearby, the pain-filled groan of the beast an agonizing sound echoing his own.

"Owen. The boy. Is he safe?"

"Aye. He is unharmed." Kendal glanced over to where the dragon lay. "The beast is breathing its last."

"As am I."

"*No!*" Jill cried. "Don't leave me, Baelin. Please don't leave me." She glared at the witch standing nearby. "You bitch! You did this to him. You put this curse on him. You forced him to do this. Do something! Save him!"

"I cannot," Isylte said, her voice soft and tinged with remorse, as if she already mourned his loss. "Death is beyond my power to overcome."

Baelin felt the cool tile of the floor beneath him as his wings withered and shriveled away.

"Stay with me, Baelin." Jill squeezed his hand, pressing it hard to her chest. "If I could give you my heart, I would. Take it, and it's yours."

The blood in his veins ceased to burn and the fire in his lungs cooled and died down, his breath easing out on a sigh.

"Oh, God, no. I can't lose you," she sobbed, her tears falling, warm drops on his cold skin. "I love you."

As I love you.

He tried to speak the words. He needed to. But he no longer had the strength. So he looked at her, willing her to see all the love he had for her in his eyes.

Then, slowly, the dragon heart within his chest beat once, twice.

And then no more.

Chapter Thirty-Eight

Jill opened her eyes to find her own startled image staring back at her. She had to blink several times before she realized where—and when—she was.

She stood on a sidewalk, facing the plate glass window of a storefront, staring at a reflection of herself, tearful and pale, in its mirrored surface.

She didn't understand. She spun around and looked at all the people passing by on the street. There was no mistaking it. She was back where she started. Back in Carytown, with its eclectic shops and cozy cafés.

Back in the twenty-first century.

How had this happened? How did she get back to her time? And if she was here, where was everybody else? Where was Roderick? Owen?

Where was Baelin?

She turned around and examined the store in front of her. "World of Mirth" was printed in colorful letters across the large display window. Life-sized stuffed animals and elaborately painted marionettes, magic kits and erector sets stood on display behind the glass. It was the toy store she'd been looking for before everything went crazy and her life had changed forever.

Or had it?

Had any time passed at all? Had everything been a wild figment of her imagination? A vivid hallucination experienced all within a few seconds of hitting her head on the window? But she'd never had a dream seem so real, or experienced such devastation, such loss, upon awakening.

Then she examined her reflection for the second time. Clutched in her hands was a piece of fabric. A piece of fabric she would know anywhere.

The tapestry.

And she wasn't wearing the blouse and slacks she'd had on when she went shopping for Zoe's present. She was wearing a torn and tattered medieval gown. A gown with dried bloodstains marring the faded saffron wool.

Baelin's blood.

Jill closed her eyes to the sight of it, fighting back tears, but feeling them stream down her cheeks all the same.

She hadn't imagined it all. She had gone back in time. Baelin was real.

And he had given his life to save her.

She wanted to curl in on herself and give into the misery drowning her from the inside out.

Then raw determination gave her new-found strength. No, she would not let it end this way. She had to find the vintage clothing store. She had to find that crazy sales lady who'd given her the tapestry fragment and figure out how to get back to Baelin, to a time before he sacrificed everything for her so she could stop him from doing it again.

She ran up and down the sidewalk on both sides, searching for the shop with the moth-eaten clothes and creepy mannequin sitting at the front window drinking tea, but she couldn't find it anywhere.

Confused, she ended up back where she started, standing in front of the toy store.

But that couldn't be right. This was where the vintage clothing shop had been. She was sure of it. She looked around once more. Yes, there on each side was yarn store and the cosmetics boutique, just as she remembered. So where was the vintage clothing shop and that mysterious little saleslady?

She barged into the toy store and went straight up to a young woman with a short, choppy haircut and heavy black-rimmed eyes standing behind the counter.

"Can I help you?" the clerk asked, eying her blood-spattered gown.

"Didn't there used to be a vintage clothing store here?"

The girl shook her head, sunlight glinting off the silver stud in her nose. "I don't think so."

"No, I'm sure of it. Bygone Treasures or something like that. A tiny old lady with coke bottle glasses ran it." Jill tapped the glass counter with her index finger. "It was right here. I was in it just a month ago."

Goth girl arched her black brows, taking in Jill's medieval gown and disheveled hair, and gave her a great-I've-got-another-crazy-customer look. "Sorry, but this store has been here for twenty years. As far as I know, there's never been a vintage clothing store at this location. Ever."

No! That wasn't true.

Jill stumbled out of the store into the bright afternoon sun. She turned around on the sidewalk and looked at the toy-filled display window in disbelief. It didn't make sense. How could it not be here? It was as if the entire store had vanished off the face of the earth. Or that it had never existed at all.

She knew it had been real, just as she knew with all of her heart Baelin had been real, too.

But if she couldn't find the shop, she would not be able to find the saleslady and the strange little woman was her only hope of finding Baelin again, if he was still alive.

Jill found herself standing at a street corner, not completely certain how she got there. She didn't have the will to walk one more step. She didn't want to take one more breath. She leaned against the lamp post, needing its firm support before she collapsed in a puddle on the sidewalk among the torn flyers and discarded cigarette butts.

A flapping sound pricked her ears and a passing shadow crossed her face. Her heart leapt in her throat. Could it be a dragon knight—her dragon knight—soaring through the sky?

She looked up, hope giving her wild imagination wings. But that hope came crashing to the ground when she saw the real cause. A banner decorating the lamp post flapped in the warm afternoon breeze, the vivid red watermelon on a bright yellow background mocking her with its whimsical display.

But the watermelon banners were for the big Watermelon Festival held every year in mid-August. When she'd gone shopping, the Fourth of July banners were still up. Proof yet again that she had lost an entire month out of her life.

Jill shuffled over to an empty bench and sat down, clutching the tapestry to her chest, hugging it to her like a child seeking comfort from a stuffed animal. She held it for the longest time, afraid to look at it. Afraid of what she might find woven within its magical threads.

But she knew she had to look, because it was the only way she would know for sure.

With trembling fingers, she unrolled it on her lap and just as she knew she would find, the tapestry had changed. The knight in the tapestry now wore no helm and his face was clear to see. A face so dear to her heart, she sobbed at the sight of it.

Baelin.

The dragon was still in the tapestry too, only now it lay dead at Baelin's feet, the knight's sword piercing its heart.

Overwhelming joy drew the breath from her lungs. He was alive! Sweet Jesus, he was alive.

But one thing was missing. There was no sign of Jill in the tapestry anymore. A ragged edge ran from top to bottom, separating the knight from where the maiden's figure should be. Her throat grew tight, constricted by the pain of losing him all over again.

"No!" she cried. "It's not fair!"

She wanted to damn whatever unseen force had torn them apart as surely as it had rent the threads of the weaving.

Her tears fell on the tapestry, dampening the ancient threads. She felt a sense of loss so acute she wanted to scream from the agony of it all. She knew in her heart Baelin was alive and free from the curse that had held him for so long. The tapestry told her so.

But he was living eight hundred years in the past without her.

How could she have gone through everything she had only to lose him in the end? She would gladly go back and endure it all again if she could just hold him in her arms one more time.

Lost in her misery, she paid little attention to the blare of car horns and people shouting around her until the commotion became too loud to ignore. When she looked up through bleary eyes, she could barely make out a tall form coming down the middle of the street, causing a major traffic jam. When the moving object came into focus, Jill's heart soared.

A knight, dressed in full chain mail, strode down the middle of Cary Street, brandishing his sword at the veering cars attempting to swerve around him.

Baelin.

She stood and clutched the tapestry to her chest.

"Hey, nut case. Get out of the damn street!" someone shouted behind her.

Baelin turned his head her way and their eyes locked. She was afraid to move, afraid if she so much as blinked he would disappear again before her eyes.

But he didn't. He sheathed his sword and charged toward her, one car nearly hitting him before he vaulted over its hood, the links of his mail carving deep scratches in the shiny red paint.

Before she could draw breath, he snatched her up and crushed her in his arms. When she finally pulled back, her fingers caressed his handsome face as tears streamed down her cheeks.

"You're here. I can't believe you're here."

"Aye, wherever here 'tis." He touched his forehead to hers and drew in a shaky breath. "When you faded away before my eyes, I knew I was dying. I never thought to see you again. Then I awoke to find myself surrounded by these strange metal beasts and angry people shouting at me."

Jill chuckled. "Welcome to my world."

Then she sobered, taking in every angle of his face, every inch of his tall, strong form. "Your dragon wings are gone."

"Aye. The curse is broken. I am a man whole now." He wiped away her tears before crushing her to him again, and commencing a kiss that was probably against the law to display in public in at least twenty states.

"A-hem."

At the soft clearing of a throat next to her, Jill reluctantly broke the kiss. She looked down and gasped, surprised to find the strange munchkin lady from the vintage clothing store standing next to them, grinning with a self-satisfied smile.

"I hope you enjoyed your trip, Jill." She grinned wider, deepening the wrinkles creasing her weathered face, and turned her attention to Baelin.

"And Sir Baelin, it's so good to see you looking more yourself these days."

Jill and Baelin exchanged confused glances.

Clo held out her hand. "I'll need that tapestry back now, if you don't mind."

Jill gripped the tapestry tighter. Strange, it'd been such a burden to carry for the past four weeks, but now it seemed so much a part of her she was reluctant to let it go.

As if reading her mind, the tiny woman shook her head. "Don't worry, you won't be needing it anymore."

She eased the tapestry from Jill's hand and held it up, the weaving now almost as large as the munchkin lady herself.

Jill's breath caught. Since the last time she'd looked at it, only moments before Baelin had appeared on the street, it had changed. Now the maid was back in the weaving, standing next to her knight.

"I don't understand. We never passed the final test. How can the curse be broken?"

"Oh, but you did, my dear. By giving his life for the woman he loves, Baelin ended the witch's power over him. And when you offered your heart for his, well… Suffice it to say, there's more than one way to slay a dragon. In the end you both displayed bravery, honor, sacrifice, and unconditional love—virtues no curse could ever withstand."

Clo heaved a heavy sigh, a smile of pride on her cherubic face.

"The tapestry is finished, this part of the story now complete." She started rolling up the weaving with more ease than it should take for someone who looked so small and frail. "Now, a new tapestry has begun for you both. Mind you, there will still be plenty of tests and challenges to pass, as there are for each and every one of us who draw breath in this world. But like all who have come before you and all who will come after, you must face them as they present themselves, on your own. You won't need to see them woven in threads to guide you through the rest of your lives."

"But what about Roderick and Owen? What happened to them?" Jill asked.

"Oh, they're where they should be." She tucked the tapestry under her arm and gave it a little pat. "Besides, they have tapestries of their own to weave and there is yet plenty of thread left to tell their stories."

The strange old woman smiled once more before she turned and walked away, leaving the knight and his lady standing on the crowded sidewalk to stare after her.

"I'm not sure I understand what just happened."

"Nor I, my lady."

She turned to Baelin, searching his eyes. "But one thing I do know is that you died in my arms."

"But I did not." He brushed her hair away from her face with gentle fingers and tucked it behind her ears. "For the first time in over two centuries, I am truly alive."

"But how? You killed the other dragon. You stabbed it through your human heart."

"I do not know. Mayhap my heart was never in the dragon's breast at all, but captured within the magical threads of the tapestry all along." He shook his head. "We will probably never know."

He gazed into her eyes and she saw herself reflected in their warm chocolate depths. The dragon's fire that once danced within them was gone, replaced by the warmth and love of the man with her now.

"All I do know is that I have my own heart back."

Baelin placed her hand on his chest, where she felt his human heart beating within, strong and sure.

"And now I give it to you."

Coming Soon

Roderick's story

TREASURE

OF THE

GRYPHON

BOOK TWO OF THE BESTIARY SERIES

OUT OF THE ASHES

EPIC eBook Award Winner
Award of Excellence Winner
Aspen Gold Readers' Choice Award Winner
and
Heart of Excellence Readers' Choice
Award Winner
for Best Paranormal Romance

Theirs was a love destined to be — torn apart by the wrath of Vesuvius

Pompeii, AD 79

David and Sera are soul mates meant to be together, if only their bumbling guardian angels could do their job right...

First united in Pompeii as a privileged merchant's daughter and a slave gladiator, their young love is cut short when Vesuvius unexpectedly erupts. After several botched attempts, their angels get one final chance to bring the couple together and personally escort them back to war-torn Italy, nearly two thousand years later.

WWII, 1943

Sera is now an archaeologist excavating the ruins of Pompeii. David is an American soldier masquerading as an Italian, sent to spy on the Germans camped near the ruins. With the help of their earth-bound angels, they soon find each other again as they excavate the ruins.

But will deception, the horrors of war, and the forgotten tragedy of their past lives, prevent them from unearthing the love of a lifetime?

Available in Print and E-Book

ABOUT THE AUTHOR

In a previous life, Lori was a graphic designer for fourteen years. In her current existence, she lives in Virginia with her engineering geek/hero husband, two kids who test her sanity on a daily basis, a dog named Hokie (named after the Virginia Tech Hokies, of course), and various other critters of the furred and finned variety.

If you enjoyed Baelin and Jill's story, please consider posting a review on Amazon, Barnes and Noble, Goodreads, or any other book review site. Good word of mouth from readers is the life blood for an independent author.

Lori loves to hear from her readers.
You can contact her at lori@loridillon.com
or visit her at www.loridillon.com

www.ingramcontent.com/pod-product-compliance
Lightning Source LLC
Chambersburg PA
CBHW030403180626
46812CB00005B/1915